PRAISE FOR

Soulmates

"Warning: this book will demolish your heart as it has
demolished mine."
CJ Skuse, author of *Rockoholic*

"A fantastic contemporary YA romance with a dark edge."
Melissa Cox, Waterstones

"This novel is one epic love story."
Dark Readers

"I had butterflies in my stomach, clammy hands and a
dry mouth. My diagnosis? I've fallen head over heels in love
with *Soulmates*!"
Jess Hearts Books

"Forget Romeo and Juliet, and meet Poppy and Noah."
Pam Norfolk, *Lancashire Evening Post*

"An ending too beautiful for words!"
Once Upon a Bookcase

"Wonderfully original...as British as Bridget Jones."
Narratively Speaking

"Exciting, smoulder̶ing͙ ̶ ̶ ̶ ̶ ̶ ̶ ̶ ̶ ̶ ̶ ̶ ̶ ̶eally does

To my parents, Larz and Olivia
For everything

First published in the UK in 2013 by Usborne Publishing Ltd., Usborne House, 83-85 Saffron Hill, London EC1N 8RT, England. www.usborne.com

Text © Holly Bourne, 2013

The right of Holly Bourne to be identified as the author of this work has been asserted by her in accordance with the Copyright, Designs and Patents Act, 1988.

Cover photograph of heart © David Paek / PM Breakfast / Getty Images

Photograph of Holly Bourne © Jonny Donovan

The name Usborne and the devices ♀ ⊕ are Trade Marks of Usborne Publishing Ltd.

A CIP catalogue record for this book is available from the British Library.

JFMA JJASOND/16

ISBN 9781409557500 02904/10

Printed in the UK by CPI Group (UK) Ltd, Croydon, CR0 4YY

Soulmates

HOLLY BOURNE

USBORNE

"Soulmates" wasn't something I had ever believed in. It was a Hollywood word – a notion created to sell romantic literature and movie rights.

Love, as I saw it, was a worldwide obsession born out of desperate fantasy. People could call it love, romance, finding their soulmate, and all that other nonsense. But in my mind? It was just hormones, biology, chemistry – dressed up in some happily-ever-after, self-created delusion born out of a fear of being alone.

Of course, you're always a cynic before you fall in love yourself…

The problem is, Hollywood, Stephenie Meyer, Mills and Boon – they got it right. Soulmates *do* exist.

But what they fail to understand is that finding them isn't always a good thing.

1

It started just like any other day, with the sun rising.

I suppose whenever anything extraordinary happens to anyone, they've always started that day with the humdrum of waking up in bed. Whether it's a near-death experience or meeting the person you want to spend the rest of your life with – it all starts with the sun rising, alarm clocks ringing and getting out from under the covers. So dull. So ordinary.

The day my life changed was no different.

I lay in my single bed, under my duvet, looking at the beam of light sneaking between my curtains and casting itself upon my legs. And as I did, I practised my breathing exercises. I kept my hands on the base of my stomach, focusing on how it expanded and contracted with each breath. I repeated this for ten minutes.

It was Saturday and I had nothing to get up for. I drew the curtains back, letting the rest of the light invade every corner of my room. I then pulled myself onto the window sill, curled my legs under me and looked outside.

My name is Poppy Lawson, and I don't like where I live. Though it's overtly clichéd to be seventeen and hate where you live, it's the truth. In fact, there is nothing about my life that isn't typical. I live in a small town, a perfect commuting distance from London. Every morning at 6.30 a.m. the men leave, trickling in a line towards the train station, all wearing suits. The wives remain at home, getting their children ready for private school and shovelling down bowls of organic muesli, before climbing into their four-by-fours for the school run. It's a town where everyone has a front garden, a place where everyone knows you and you know everyone, and extra-curricular activities are thrust down teenagers' throats as if the success of the family depends solely on how good the children are at lacrosse. It's all a giant cliché and I hate it. But I figure that's pretty damn predictable too.

My contemplations were interrupted by my mobile phone ringing. I looked at the screen and smiled. It was Lizzie.

"It's early, you cow. I could still be asleep you know," I said.

"Shut up. It's past ten thirty, and I have news."

"Well, spill then." I uncurled my legs and stretched them out on the window sill.

"It's about tonight. It's going to be amazing."

Lizzie had a way of making everything a drama. Her ambition was to be a journalist and she spent most of her time practising. She traded titbits of gossip between friendship groups, "sexed-up" even the dreariest house party the morning after and, of course, she had an encyclopaedic knowledge of everyone's business. I had learned she was physically incapable of keeping a secret, but loved her anyway. She made this place – our lives – seem dramatic. She brought colour to the monochrome.

I sighed. "Lizzie, it's another Band Night, what can possibly happen?" I replied. "Oh no, don't tell me. One of our friends' going-nowhere bands has actually signed a record deal?" I squealed to ring home my sarcasm. "I don't believe it. It's a miracle!"

She laughed. "No, of course not." Then she paused, pre-empting my reaction. "But there *is* a new band playing tonight and they're supposed to be incredible. They're called Growing Pains. I've heard the lead guitarist is gorgeous, and apparently a record label *is* interested in them."

I sighed again.

"Seriously."

"Lizzie, we've been going to Band Night for how long? Two years? We know how many boys in bands who *apparently* have record labels interested in them? And pray tell me, how many of them have actually ever made it? I bet you ten million pounds that they all grow up, go to uni and do Business Studies, spend a gap year pretending they're not going to get a job in Daddy's company and then take one on a starting salary of £32,000." I re-curled my feet under myself and took a quick breath. "AND then when they're middle-aged they'll entertain their posh friends at dinner

9

parties with stories of their 'troubled' youth being a 'rock star'."

It was Lizzie's turn to sigh. "Christ, you're miserable."

I shrugged over the phone. "Just speaking the truth."

"Okay. Well forget the band-bashing, Miss I'm-So-Much-Better-Than-Everyone, and let me at least tell you about the fit guitarist."

I laughed. "That I will allow."

We spoke for a few more minutes and when I hung up I felt happier. Okay, it wasn't going to be the social highlight of my life, but at least Band Night was something to do on a Saturday night that didn't involve ordering pizza, watching a trashy film, and wallowing in my own uncoolness. With a sudden burst of energy I flung my legs off the window sill and went down for breakfast.

Mum was making tea as I entered the kitchen. She stood in her dressing gown, frowning at the cupboard doors. She'd been trying to talk Dad into refitting the kitchen for about two years, but he refused to "waste money on something as boring as cupboard doors".

"Morning," she said, tearing her eyes away. "Fancy a cuppa?"

I opened a cupboard and pulled out a box of cereal. "Please."

As I poured out muesli, she brought a mug over and ruffled my hair.

"Mum!"

"Sorry, love."

She sat next to me, warming her hands on her tea while I started eating.

"So what's the big plan for today then?"

I swallowed. "Just going to Band Night. Some new band is playing, supposed to be good. Apparently they have a fit guitarist."

Mum perked up. "Ooo, really? That's exciting. Wow, a fit man in Middletown. It must be a miracle."

"I know." I rolled my eyes. "But stranger things have happened."

Mum laughed. My constant disregard for every potential suitor was something she teased me about. She ribbed me that no one would ever be good enough, but I swore I wasn't picky. It was just that all seventeen-year-old boys were disgusting. And the few that weren't had over-inflated egos from the constant attention. My theory was that boys stopped being gross aged nineteen, and as I wasn't pretty enough to attract an older guy, I was quite happy to wait for two years until every boy my age didn't nauseate me.

Mum, however, didn't agree with my thinking and worried about me. In fact, worrying about me was her favourite pastime.

As if on cue, her face turned serious over the steam of her tea.

"So, how did your appointment with Dr. Ashley go the other day?" she asked quietly.

Oh God, so it was going to be one of *those* mornings.

"It was fine," I replied non-committally and carried on eating.

"Just fine?" What was it with parents and *that* phrase? "What did you talk about?"

"You know, the usual."

She nodded. "Okay."

I focused on chewing muesli, waiting for her to start up again.

It took less than thirty seconds.

"So what is the usual?"

I swallowed.

"Jesus, Mum, I don't know. I whinged about my coursework, he made me practise that stupid breathing thing again, we talked about how to cope when…you know…it happens."

She looked concerned and I held my breath, waiting for her to say it.

"So he still doesn't know what causes it?" Her eyes filled with tears. Bloody hell. How many times can you have the same conversation?

"Mum." I spoke slowly and carefully. "This isn't your fault. You didn't screw up my child-raising or drop me on my head as a baby. You brought up Louise exactly the same and this didn't happen to her. It's bad luck. That's all. You've got to believe me."

She looked up at me like a child. "Really?" she whispered. "Dr. Ashley didn't say it was anyone's fault?"

"Of course he didn't. Because it's not. It's just my biology, my hormones. Whatever. No doubt it's something I'll outgrow and we'll look back and laugh at it. Okay?"

She looked relieved. For now. No doubt I would have this conversation again at some point the next week. And the next. And the next.

"Okay." She grabbed both of our empty cups and took them to the sink.

"You can borrow my handbag for tonight if you want," she said, smiling.

"Can I? Brilliant. Thanks, Mum."

Then she walked out of the kitchen.

Here's the thing. Much as I try to fight it, I'm the biggest cliché around. I've got "mental health" problems. I know. Original, right? I detest myself for my lack of creativity, but unfortunately it's out of my control. It's like, because I'm middle class, my mind isn't preoccupied with worrying about money and stuff, so it's busying itself with this instead.

About two years ago, I was in school, just listening to my Geography teacher banging away about fair trade coffee, when it became quite obvious I was about to die. The walls closed in on me. Everything went black, and I couldn't breathe.

Blind panic rushed through my body like an adrenalin shot as I realized that these were my last moments. I remember thinking, as my body frantically fought for air, how dreadfully awful it was that I was going to die in Geography. And I had never swum with dolphins, or seen the Grand Canyon, or ridden a motorbike, or done any of the things you're supposed to do before dying. I wouldn't see my parents again. Or Louise. It would wreck their lives if I died.

And then I realized I was going to die without ever having a boyfriend. Though the world was hazy, all I could think about was love. And how I'd never had it. How I would never understand what it felt like to fall asleep knowing another person was thinking of you. I would never have someone touch the small of my back as they steered me through a crowd. I would never know every contour of someone's face off-by-heart, and yet not be bored with it. And, as I sank to the grey, chewing-gum stained carpet, all I could think was how sad that was.

Of course, I woke up. Surrounded by concerned faces, my palms bleeding from digging my fingernails into them. I got to go home for the day. And all my romantic revelations were forgotten. I put them down to concussion or whatever, and I got a lot of attention for about a week until everyone forgot about it.

My life continued without consequence until it happened again.

I was shopping for tampons with my mum – probably the most embarrassing items you could be carrying in a public near-death experience. Like the first time, the walls squashed me in and I felt I was being suffocated by nothing. That was all I could remember. I came round screaming on the cold marble floor, while dozens of terrified shoppers stared at me. My mum was clutching my hand desperately, her eyes wide with fear.

There were doctor's appointments after doctor's appointments. My mum argued with our GP so, of course, we "went private". After hundreds of blood tests, two more "incidents", and dozens of referrals, I was taken to a large white house and forced to talk to some smiling man with perfectly straight but yellowing teeth. He eventually gave me a term for the incidents. Panic attacks. Very common, apparently. Stresses of modern life and all that.

And so began my weekly appointments with Dr. Ashley. Or the Shrink, or Head Doctor, or whatever you'd like to call him. And for two years I've been forced to endure the guilt in my mum's face every morning. Searching for an answer, a reason, and only finding her innocent self to blame.

I ran my cereal bowl under the tap, washing off all the leftover muesli so it wouldn't stick like cement to the sides. Then I waited for the evening, where hopefully, something original would happen in this stupid, stupid town.

I spent the day busying myself with being a girl. I ran a huge bubble bath with some of Mum's posh stuff and shaved my legs. I then tried on about six million different outfits. After much speculation, I decided on my dark denim miniskirt and the faded Smiths T-shirt I'd begged Dad to buy me from a vintage store. After applying lashings of mascara, eyeliner and lip gloss, I checked my phone and realized I was meeting everyone in five minutes. I took one last look in the mirror – not bad. Not brilliant either. My brown eyes stared back at me, covered slightly by some of my mousey hair, which I had tried and failed to backcomb into a rock-y look. I slipped my feet into my battered ballerina pumps, grabbed my jacket and ran out the door.

It was still light as I half-ran, half-walked to meet my friends. The sun was low in the sky, casting everything with a golden light. I momentarily revelled in how pretty everything looked, before reminding myself that I hated it here. My friends were waiting for me at the corner – Elizabeth, Ruth, and Amanda.

"You're late!" Lizzie said. "I swear I spend half my life waiting for you." She looked nice. New jeans and a black top. She'd twisted her hair into some complicated-looking knot and was wearing loads of eyeliner.

I jogged the last couple of steps to meet them. "Sorry," I panted. "Wardrobe crisis."

"Yeah yeah. If we've missed the fit guitarist, I'll give you a real crisis to worry about."

At the words "fit guitarist", Ruth's eyes lit up. I gave her a quick hug to say hello.

"Have you seen this mysterious fitty?" she asked.

Ruth was always interested in a conquest. Once she set her sights on someone, she was pretty much unstoppable.

She also had a DD chest to bounce off any competition. I was always relieved I didn't fancy anyone, as I wouldn't stand much chance with Ruth around.

"I only just heard about him. But I saw a pig fly past my window this morning, so I'm quite sure a hot man has moved to town."

"Poppy," she said. "It makes me so sad to hear you speak like this. There are so many hot men around. If only you opened your eyes to the countless possibilities."

"There are hot *boys*," I corrected. "I don't think we know any hot men."

"Oh, they're men by the time I'm finished with them." And she winked.

I linked arms with Amanda, who hadn't spoken yet. Bless her. She'd spent so long hanging around Ruth, she'd learned not to bother trying.

"How are things going with Johnno?"

Johnno was Amanda's sort-of boyfriend. She'd surpassed herself by finding someone even shyer than she was. They spent most of their time apologizing to each other or awkwardly holding hands like children put together for a wedding photograph.

She blushed deeply. "Things with Johnno are going fine," she stammered slightly. "We managed to kiss yesterday without bumping noses."

I couldn't help laughing. "Well, baby steps, eh?"

Lizzie linked her arms through mine and Ruth's so we were all in a line.

"Right, ladies," she said. "I have a feeling tonight is going to be incredible."

"Yeah right," I muttered.

"Shut it. Seriously, I feel a burning in my loins that something is going to happen tonight."

"You can get a cream for that. You know, for the burning?"

Ruth's eyes brightened in recognition. "Oh yes, she's right. I can recommend you one. Clears it up straight away."

"Silence," Lizzie said and we dissolved into laughter. "Things are going to happen tonight. I can just feel it." She paused. "It's my *news sense*."

We all rolled our eyes.

"Let's just get this over with," I said.

And we started walking towards the club.

2

Band Night sounds much more exciting than it is. It's basically a dilapidated club in the town centre that invites local bands to play every other weekend or so. The owner turns a blind eye to the fact that everyone is underage in return for bands bringing all their fans/friends along to fill the otherwise empty dance floor. We'd been going ever since Ruth grew her boobs and learned how to distract bouncers with them.

It was getting dark as we reached the club entrance.

"Oh no," Lizzie said. "There's a line. Everyone else must've heard about the fit guitarist too."

True enough, there was a queue stretching out around the club's corner. Groups of girls gathered in shivering clumps, silently grading each other. The four of us shuffled to the end, watching other girls scowl at us and at Ruth's blatant cleavage as we passed. Ruth smirked and stuck her chest out more.

"I think we should have queue-jumped," she said.

"There's no point," Amanda said. "It's moving quick enough."

Ruth stamped her foot in a mock tantrum. "But all these girls in front are getting to know fit-guitarist-man before I am."

I smiled. "Come on. He's probably not even that fit. I'm sure he's perfectly ordinary, but girls just think he's fit because he plays the guitar onstage."

Lizzie let out a deep sigh. "Can you just imagine," she asked, "how beautiful it would be to date a musician?"

The other two sighed with her.

"Imagine standing in a huge crowd, watching your boyfriend being worshipped by everyone around you, knowing you are the one to take him home," Ruth said.

"Or imagine him getting out his acoustic guitar to sing a love song and you know it's written about you," Lizzie added.

"Or imagine getting to read his interviews in glossy mags about how much he adores you," Amanda said.

I raised an eyebrow as we moved forward in the queue.

"Or…imagine feeling sick with paranoia whenever he's on tour because it's certain he's cheating on you. Imagine only being known as so-and-so's girlfriend and not for your own merits. Or imagine being stuck at home with his kids while he's still off pretending to be a 'rock star' despite having a flabby old-man belly and a receding hairline. Or—" I broke off my rant when I realized they were all glaring at me.

Lizzie let out a low whistle. "Bloody hell, Poppy, why do we bother bringing you?"

"Yeah, killjoy," Ruth said. "There's nothing wrong with a bit of fantasy."

We stepped forward again. We were getting near the front.

"There's nothing wrong with fantasies," I said, defending myself. "But dating a musician? Come on, guys. It's such a cliché."

They all groaned simultaneously.

"You're obsessed, woman!"

"I'm not obsessed. I just don't know why you're all excited about potentially pulling some melancholic prick who writes songs about his 'growing pains'."

Lizzie smirked. "Who knows? He might be amazingly talented but self-aware and fall madly in love with one of us."

"Lizzie. We don't live in a romantic comedy."

"And by being friends with you, don't I bloody well know it?" She linked arms with me as we entered the club.

The influx of wannabe groupies made the place more crowded than normal. The usually half-empty wooden dance floor was jammed full of mascaraed girls with their elbows out. I checked my watch – it had just gone nine thirty. The band wouldn't start for another half-hour but females were already fighting for prime front-row spots. Their desperation was so pungent you could almost bottle it and sell it as perfume.

Despite myself, I quite liked this place. The walls were bright purple and decorated with old black-and-white photos of famous musicians. The once-white ceiling was now off-yellow, stained by years of spent cigarettes. But what I loved most was the bar. The owner, in true rock-and-roll spirit, insisted everything that could be sold in optics must be sold in optics – even wine. He had even had optics specially made that delivered rosé in 250 ml quantities. It was a bit gross but the club had character – which was rarer than blue steak in this cookie-cutter town.

The girls and I picked our way through the throngs of people to get to the bar. I elbowed my way to the front and leaned forward to attract the barman's attention.

"What do you want?" he yelled over the loud heavy metal pumping out of the speakers.

I held up my fingers. "Four double dark rum and Diet Cokes please." It was getting hot and I started fanning my face. "With ice," I added.

As I waited, I watched Lizzie mingle. The girl knew everyone. She was darting from one group to the next, like a hummingbird addicted to secrets instead of nectar. I guessed she was asking about the new band and their mysterious new guitarist. Lizzie liked to be in the know. She said it was her way of preparing for her future.

The barman handed me the drinks and I chucked him a ten and a five before carefully scooping up the glasses. I pushed my way towards my friends, who had now grabbed a spot closer to the stage.

"So what did I miss?" I shouted over the music, handing them each a drink.

"Thanks," Lizzie shouted back, taking a glass. "Guess what? I've got the best gossip about Noah."

"Who's Noah?" I asked, taking a long gulp of my drink.

She shouted something back but I couldn't hear her.

"What?!" I leaned in further.

"I SAID NOAH IS THE FIT GUITARIST."

I nodded. So his name was Noah.

Lizzie beckoned to us all to come in closer.

"I heard..." Lizzie tried to whisper in a dramatic fashion but had to half-shout to be heard. "Rachel was telling me he lives alone after his parents chucked him out."

"Really?" Amanda asked, wide-eyed, as if Lizzie had revealed he was a merman or something.

Lizzie nodded seriously. "Apparently he gave them a really rough time – he's really screwed up. He moved here about two years ago and got diagnosed with depression," she said. "But he refused to go to therapy and apparently turned to drink and girls. He's a complete man-whore by the sounds of it. Proper bad boy."

The other two looked wistful as I sneered. Typical.

"Anyway, apparently joining the band has really sorted him out. Music helps him...feel better apparently."

"Wow," Amanda said. "He sounds so...tortured."

Ruth agreed. "I know. What a hard time he's had. I bet all he wants is a proper girlfriend to ground him. A shoulder to cry on. Someone he can trust and depend on."

We stood in silence as the other three contemplated being this wonder girl to mend all his problems. Groan.

We finished our drinks and Ruth went to get another round as we saved our viewing spot. It was getting really crowded now, and really hot. I could feel a thin film of sweat begin to collect under my fringe. Lovely. Despite being at the back of the entrance queue, we'd actually got a pretty good view of the stage – a couple of lines from the front, dead centre. We defended our territory as more people began to squash in. Ruth arrived back with our drinks and I checked my watch again. Two minutes to ten. The band would start any moment. More spectators were jostling to get a better view and a few idiots started throwing their beer into the crowd. There was a Mexican wave of shrieks as girls' carefully crafted hairdos were obliterated.

The lights turned off and everyone began to whoop and scream. I could see the shadows of the band walk on and a huge surge came through the crowd from behind. My feet were swept off the floor and I was carried by my ribs half a metre forward. I clenched my feet in my ballet pumps to keep them on, and panicked slightly as I realized I'd been separated from the others. I twisted my head round to see Lizzie some way behind me. She smiled, excitedly waiting for the music to begin. I smiled back and then suddenly the stage lights came on, catapulting the band into a bright white light. Music erupted from the speakers…

And then I couldn't breathe.

The loud music became tinny and my head filled with fug. I tried to inhale but no oxygen entered my lungs. My legs buckled and I felt the crowd push me forward. I could hardly stand. I relied completely on other bodies to keep me upright as I tried to practise my techniques from therapy.

You are not dying, I told myself. *You're just having a panic attack. You're not going to die.*

But I didn't believe myself. This was worse than anything I'd experienced before. My lungs burned and the edges of my vision went hazy.

"Help," I rasped pathetically, hoping someone would hear. But no help came.

I tried to breathe again. Nothing. Panic rippled through my body like a tsunami.

I have to get out. I'm going to die.

With my remaining strength, I tried to stumble out of the crowd, vaguely aware that people were yelling at me. I couldn't see my friends. I couldn't see anything. It was all going dark.

JUST BREATHE, I instructed myself. But I couldn't. I kept taking empty gasps. My lungs felt like they were going to explode.

I'm drowning, I thought. *I'm drowning in no water.*

I felt my feet slipping on the beer-covered floor and the burning in my lungs began scorching through my insides. I let my body buckle. I could vaguely hear the dim sounds of loud chords echoing from the speakers. And then everything went black and it was finally quiet.

3

Pain.

Burning.

It was still black but the serene silence had gone.

"Her eyes are flickering," I heard. It sounded far away, like I was underwater.

The scorching filled my lungs again. It hurt so much. I had to get rid of it. My eyes blinked open. I was on my back. That wouldn't do. Using all my strength, I flung myself over onto my side as vomit bucketed out of me. I retched. I gagged. The sour taste of regurgitated rum and Coke burned up my throat. I lay on my side, being generally disgusting, for a few minutes. I kept spitting, wiping my mouth, retching again. I didn't care who was watching. I needed to get whatever poison there was out of me. When I finally finished, I rolled onto my back and wiped my hair. It was slick with sweat.

"Well look who's bringing sexy back," someone said sarcastically.

It was Lizzie's voice. I concentrated on focusing and her face became clear beside me. We were outside the club, on a small piece of grubby grass round the side. Lizzie and Amanda looked concerned. Well, Lizzie looked a bit more disgusted than concerned.

I took a deep breath. "What the hell happened?" I tried to lift my head but Lizzie firmly pushed it onto her lap.

"Not so soon. You're staying put for a few minutes." She looked at me in a motherly way. "You had one of your attacks. Scared the crap out of me and Amanda."

Amanda was sitting cross-legged on the grass, a respectful distance away from my puddle. She looked terrified. I remembered she'd never seen me have a panic attack before.

"How long have I been out?" I always lost track of time when this happened.

"Just a few minutes. You've not missed anything, don't worry."

"Where's Ruth?" I asked.

A look of irritation crossed Lizzie's face before she composed a smile.

"She's saving our spaces for us. I told her it wasn't worth bothering as you're obviously going straight home, but she stayed inside anyway."

"Home? I'm not going home."

"Yes you are. Poppy, I've never seen anything like it. I mean, I've seen you collapse before, but not like this. I thought you were dead."

I could see that she was genuinely concerned behind her forced grin. "Was I that bad?" I asked. "It felt worse than the others."

"You were terrifying. I was trying to keep an eye on you because I know crowds can sometimes set you off. You seemed fine, even though it's absolutely mental inside. My fringe is completely ruined..." She stopped herself and started again. "Anyway, as soon as the band came on you started twitching. I tried to get to you but the crowd was too solid. You were staggering around like your feet weren't working. And then you just went down. I managed to reach you, and you were unconscious but shuddering, like an electric current was surging through you. It was seriously messed up. If I didn't know better, I would have thought you were having an epileptic fit or something."

I lay silent for a moment, taking in everything she'd told me.

"So I made a complete idiot out of myself then?"

Lizzie let out a low whistle. "Jeeeee-sus. Why would you even care about that, Poppy? You're safe, that's all that matters."

I ignored her and looked up at Amanda. "Amanda?" I asked.

She looked nervous, probably because Lizzie had put her death-glare on.

"No one really noticed," Amanda reassured me. "Everyone was too involved with the band. They're actually surprisingly good."

I lifted myself so I was sitting. The evening summer breeze felt good on my clammy face.

"Well if that's the case," I said, slowly standing up, "then we'd better go in and see them."

Lizzie was shocked. "Poppy, no. Come on. We need to take you home."

"I'm fine. Please, just let me be normal."

"But you might have another attack."

"I won't. It's passed now. Come on, let's go find Ruth."

Lizzie looked desperately at Amanda. "We can't let her go back in."

Amanda shrugged. "Do you really want to try and stop her?"

"Ha ha, victory." I punched my fist in the air, immediately felt woozy and stumbled. Lizzie steadied me just in time and glared.

"Okay," I sighed. "I'll stay right at the back like a saddo. Just in case it happens again. Which it won't."

We walked slowly to the doors of the club, showing our stamped hands to the bouncers as we passed. They clocked Lizzie and Amanda supporting the majority of my body weight and one of them raised an eyebrow.

"Your mate alright?" he said, eyeing me suspiciously.

"She's fine," Lizzie answered, before turning to me. "Aren't you, Poppy?"

"Me? I'm high on life."

They laughed as we entered the club, where we were immediately blasted by loud music. We stood at the back and within ten seconds I decided I liked the band. They were amazing. Different. My heart thudded madly to the music and I clutched at my chest to steady myself. Steam was rising off the crowd in giant clouds.

"THEY'RE INCREDIBLE," I shouted over to Lizzie and Amanda, who both smiled in return.

"DIDN'T I SAY SO?" Lizzie screamed back. "AND CHECK OUT THE GUITARIST."

My eye followed Lizzie's finger through the crammed room as she pointed out Noah.

I've never run smack bang into a brick wall before but I imagine it would feel a bit like how I felt then. Time slowed down – like in a really cheesy movie. I felt my breath catching as I studied him. Lizzie was right – he was beautiful.

He stood at the left of the stage, his guitar resting lazily on his lower hip. His face was focused, concentrating on his chords. Sweaty dark hair fell into his black eyes, framing his perfectly angular face. A green T-shirt was sticking to his thin but muscular frame and his jeans were slung low across his waist. I quickly scanned his legs and sighed in relief – his jeans weren't skinny. It was a miracle! I licked my lips involuntarily. I wanted to turn and discuss his fitness in detail but couldn't tear my eyes from his face.

Bloody hell, what was happening to me? I forced my gaze off him. Lizzie was smiling.

"Fit much?" she said.

"Very fit." I nodded furiously. "You were right."

She put her arms around Amanda and me, pulling us into her.

"One day, my little munchkins, you will realize I'm always right. Fancy him then?"

That stopped me in my tracks. "What?" I spluttered. "No!"

Lizzie nudged me in the ribs. "Only winding you up, don't worry. Anyway…" She pointed to the crowd. "Looks like you'd have competition on your hands and I, for one, wouldn't fancy taking on Ruth."

I followed her finger again. It led me to Ruth, who had somehow managed to wiggle her way to the front row. She was standing directly below Noah, staring at him intently, a determined look on her face. My stomach sank and I tried to gauge why. This was standard Ruth behaviour, but tonight it bothered me.

"What's she playing at?" I hissed at Lizzie. "She looks well desperate."

"Never put anyone off before."

It was true.

I turned back and watched Ruth at work. She was right under Noah's eyeline, eye-flirting the hell outta him. For some inexplicable reason her hair hadn't succumbed to the heat like everyone else's, and she'd probably employed her fail-safe method of undoing another button on her top.

It all seemed incredibly unsubtle but, as Lizzie said, Ruth's determined charm had never failed her before.

The only solace I could generate to ease my random anger was that Noah didn't seem to have noticed her. His eyes were on his guitar and his blurring fingers. In fact, he hardly looked at the crowd at all.

The band was playing an upbeat song now and everyone was dancing and flicking sweat over each other. The lead singer – a solidly built lad, attractive, but no Noah –

obviously loved the crowd's response. He was clapping his hands over his head, trying to encourage the audience to sing along.

As the song reached its climax, Noah finally dragged his eyes away from his guitar and took in the swarming mass of people worshipping him. His face contorted into a breathtaking smile as he raised one hand in the air. The crowd went wild and all the girls started screaming. I could almost make out Ruth's individual scream over the others. As I studied Noah's face, I realized suddenly that he was staring back at me. My vision began to blur and the all-too-familiar feeling of faintness hit me. Bloody hell. Not again.

It happened for less than a second. For a tiny moment we just stared at each other, and my belly flip-flopped and my heart pounded. Then, as quickly as it started, it stopped.

There was a massive *bang* and the band came to a sudden halt. Confused silence replaced the upbeat song and the crowd searched for an explanation. They found one in the smoke pouring from Noah's guitar amp, filling the stage with a foul-smelling fug. He ran to his amp like a mother running in front of a car to save her child. The rest of the band leaped across the stage and fought their way through the smoke to try and help.

I turned to Lizzie and Amanda and gave them a questioning look. They shrugged their shoulders.

"Drink?" I asked.

They both nodded.

I took a quick look behind me as I walked to the bar.

Smoke was still rising from the amp. I had a feeling the gig was over.

"Two dark rum and Diet Cokes, and a large glass of tap water," I asked, leaning over the bar. The water was for me. I knew drinking after a panic attack wasn't the smartest of plans.

As I waited, the stocky singer approached the mike.

"Umm, hi, guys," he said to the crowd. He'd lost his onstage cockiness and looked a bit nervous. "I think we're going to have to cut the gig short. This amp is well and truly annihilated."

The crowd groaned and booed.

"Sorry, people, but there's nothing we can do. Thanks for coming. We'll be back here next month. Check out our website in the meantime."

Most of the crowd were exiting at this point and I felt sorry for him. Noah was at the side of the stage being comforted by a huge horde of girls. Ruth was at the front, touching his arm, and whispering in his ear. Again, I felt a surge of rage. I beckoned the bartender over.

"Make that three rum and Cokes."

I grabbed the drinks off him aggressively and then tipped my drink down my throat in what I hoped was a melodramatic manner. Much as I knew jealousy was a pointless and destructive emotion, I couldn't help but seethe with envy when it came to Ruth and her ability to talk to boys. She was like some sort of magical lust fairy, able to bewitch all mankind with a flirtatious wink or subtle innuendo. Men disintegrated into stumbling wrecks. Even the strongest-minded man couldn't resist her charms – either of them. It didn't bother me often, but then again, I'd never been interested in anyone before. I looked at the other two drinks, contemplating whether to drink Lizzie's or Amanda's. I decided against it, and turned back towards Ruth and Noah, who were now deep in conversation. I saw her whisper in his ear again before throwing her head back laughing. For just a second, I could have *sworn* I saw them look in my direction.

Just paranoid, Poppy, just paranoid.

It was easier to navigate my way back to my friends as the club emptied. Both Lizzie and Amanda were staring at Ruth too.

"Lucky bitch," Lizzie said, taking her drink and draining it in an equally melodramatic fashion. I raised an eyebrow. Obviously I wasn't the only one who suffered from occasional Ruth-envy.

Amanda nodded. "She does have a way, doesn't she? I'll never understand how—"

"Look," Lizzie interrupted, "they're coming over."

Ruth was holding Noah's hand, guiding him through the remaining dregs of the crowd. She had a self-satisfied grin plastered across her face. The three of us pretended not to notice them approaching. I rubbed the toe of my ballet pump across the floor and peeked out from behind my still-sweaty fringe. I couldn't tell if it was just my wishful thinking, but Noah didn't seem particularly happy to have his hand in Ruth's. As they drew nearer, I became aware of my heart pounding against my ribs like a sledgehammer. Was this what really fancying someone felt like? The thought alone made me blush. As the two of them arrived, I decided it was best to keep my eyes on the floor.

"Noah," Ruth said, in a loud obnoxious voice, "meet my best friends in the whole wide world." She gestured to each of us individually. "This is Lizzie, Amanda, and Poppy." My head nodded instinctively as she mentioned my name. I was still fixating on the floorboards. Nodding was friendly enough, wasn't it?

"Hey, great to meet you," Lizzie said. "Great gig. Well, it was before the amp exploded."

I heard him laugh. A gorgeous gravelly sound. The sledgehammer in my ribcage smashed harder. I played with my foot, hoping like mad no one would notice my mini nervous breakdown.

"Yeah, that was weird." His voice was deep, slightly husky. I tried to control my body's strange reaction to it. "I would like to think it was my immense guitar shredding that destroyed it – you know, like the amp couldn't keep up with my insane guitar solo abilities?" He paused for effect. "But it looks like it was just a technical fault."

The others laughed at his mock egotism. Well, I think it was only mock egotism. I, in the meantime, stayed rigid, like a socially-challenged idiot.

"Well, I loved the show," Ruth simpered. "But I didn't have a *physical* reaction to it…like Poppy here."

At the mention of my name, my head snapped up and I looked at her in confusion.

"Poppy's the one I was telling you about," she continued, her voice still sickly sweet. "She enjoyed your little performance so much she passed out." Then she tossed back her hair and laughed as I stared at her in disbelief.

A speedball mixture of humiliation, confusion, hurt, and rage surged through me. I started shaking, my cheeks blazing red, tears welling in my eyes.

"Is that right, Poppy?" Noah asked. His voice sounded controlled, like he was trying not to laugh. "Did you pass out? Was I that good? Am I that gorgeous?"

I took a deep breath, counting like I had been taught to, and slowly forced myself to look at him.

Looking at him, it appears, was a mistake. He was just outstandingly…yum – like someone you would see on television. His eyes burned into mine and my lungs deserted me. I could feel the walls closing again and forced myself to breathe. I gulped for air as he eyed me curiously. I knew I was supposed to reply but I couldn't. The world had turned hazy again. My heart was still thumping; a fresh wave of sweat broke out across my body. I couldn't take my eyes off his. Oh my God, he was going to think I was a total freak. Why did Ruth do this to me? What was her problem? Then the anger arrived, like a late dinner party guest, and it pushed away any other emotion I was feeling.

I opened my mouth to speak.

"Actually," I said, spitting the words out, full of aggression, "I didn't pass out." I fixed my eyes on his. "I suppose you're used to girls losing consciousness whenever you even look at them, and therefore assume you're responsible for my little...episode. But you're wrong. And, to be honest, it's weirdly cocky of you to even *imagine* you could be to blame. I suffer from panic attacks. It's a common physiological problem I have no control over, keep very secret, and is, quite frankly, nobody's business." I turned to face Ruth, who was staring at me all agog. "It's not something I like to share with the world...just my dearest friends," I said, imitating her sickly sweet voice.

"Ruth, of course, knows about this. And when I was collapsing at the beginning of your set, she used it as an opportunity to take my place nearer the front row so she could hit on you. And, as my *real* friends held my hair back outside while I was sick," I said, pointing towards an equally surprised Lizzie and Amanda, "she was elbowing her way to your side."

I took more breath, refusing to let my courage subside until I'd finished.

"Anyway, I'm sure this is all very amusing to you both. Why don't you just go off and enjoy how *hilarious* it is that Ruth's stupid friend had a panic attack."

I was quite certain I sounded mad, but the anger kept the words tumbling out of my mouth like sick.

"Anyway, on that note, I'm going to go home now. Ruth,

in the future, can you please refrain from using my illness as a pulling method?"

I turned on my heels and made for the door, forcing myself not to break into a run. In one last moment of courage or madness – whatever you want to call it – I turned back and examined the stunned looks on their faces.

"Oh, and watch out," I added. "She's had chlamydia twice."

And I flicked my head round and walked out into the night.

Dr. Anita Beaumont listened to her heels clacking on the polished floor as she made her way down the corridor to the laboratory. She was in a bad mood, a really bad mood. She'd already planned to take it out on her assistants. How dare they beep her on a Saturday? Didn't they know how important she was? She'd given those idiots her beeper number for emergencies only. What could possibly be an emergency on a Saturday afternoon while she was having a manicure?

The click of her shoes echoed loudly, bouncing off the clinical white walls. They only had a skeleton crew at weekends and most of the building was empty. She held her swipe card to a wall and a door appeared from nowhere. She turned left through it, looking down at her half-finished nails and cursing herself for hiring that new assistant. He was much too eager to impress, too earnest. He was straight out of college and excited to be working somewhere so secret, so important – a place where he could make his childhood superhero fantasies a reality. He would soon realize how hard it was. He'd probably only beeped her to show off some minor accomplishment so she could pat him on the head and praise him like a schoolkid. What was his name again? It was something ridiculous. River? No, that wasn't it. Storm? Nope. Oh yes, she remembered with a wry grin. Rain. His name was Rain, poor guy. His parents used to be hippies apparently.

Dr. Beaumont reached the end of the corridor and faced another security door. She held her card up again and a computer keyboard slid out from another hidden compartment. She quickly keyed in the password – smiling to herself as she tapped out the letters. S…O…U…L…M…A…T…E.

A blue laser took a retina scan before the security door glided open. She walked briskly into the lab.

"I hope this isn't a huge waste of my time," she called. "Now who the hell is going to get me a coffee?"

Rain and another assistant appeared before her.

"Hi, Anita." Rain could barely contain the excitement in his voice.

She glared at him. "My name's Dr. Beaumont. Where's the coffee?"

The other assistant ran towards the kitchen while Anita approached the computer bank, with Rain trailing after her.

"So what did you drag me here for?" She bent over the largest computer and typed another password in. "It'd better be good."

Rain grabbed a stool and sat next to her, encroaching too far into her personal space for her liking.

"Oh, it's good." His smile stretched right from one side of his face to the other. "The reading came in less than an hour ago."

The other assistant arrived with coffee. Anita grabbed it out of her hands before batting her away.

"What reading? On which machine?"

"The matchmaker. What else?" Rain always delighted in calling it that. Although now was no time to enjoy a good pun.

Anita was shocked. "You mean there's been a…?"

"A connection between two matches." Rain nodded. "Quite a big one."

Her manicure was instantly forgotten. "Show me."

Rain started jabbing coordinates into the keyboard and brought up a graph on the monitor. To the uninformed eye it looked like a seismogram, showing the impact of an earthquake. A green line travelled steadily across the screen before exploding into a flurry of ups and downs, like a toddler's scribble.

Anita felt a slight stab of guilt for doubting Rain's ability. He was right to have beeped her.

"Wow." She stared at the screen. "It's huge."

Rain looked delighted at her response.

"Have you been able to pinpoint the location?"

"Not exactly. Looking at the coordinates, I think it's definitely in Europe. At a guess I would say France, maybe Germany or the UK."

Anita traced the green line on the screen with her finger.

"It starts and stops so violently. Whoever they were, they obviously didn't stay in the same place for long…thank God," she added, almost as an afterthought.

"I thought that too. I don't think they met each other. They might've just ridden the same bus or something."

Anita thought about it. "How…romantic." Her lip curled slightly.

"So what do we do?"

She stood up and drained her cup of coffee.

"You were right to beep me. I think we've narrowly avoided something potentially catastrophic. What's important though, is that we avoided it. I'm quite sure it's a one-off. Fate just messing with us."

Rain nodded. "That's what I thought."

He was annoying her again. Smug jerk.

"Just keep an eye on all possible locations for the next week or so. Let me know if another reading comes up. I doubt it will." She tried to ignore the instinctive shiver rippling down her spine. "Well, let's hope it doesn't."

Then she turned on her heels and walked out of the lab.

4

It didn't take long for the tears to come. As I stormed home I could feel them streaming down my cheeks. I couldn't tell if they were tears of rage or humiliation. What had I been thinking? Normal people don't have emotional outbursts like that. It wasn't like I lived in a movie where the hero makes evil people recognize their wrongs just by delivering a dramatic monologue. This was real life. Reality. Mean people never worry about their misgivings and generally flourish. Whereas people like me keep their mouths shut, take the abuse, and waste their lives waiting for karma to arrive before sorrowfully realizing that it doesn't exist.

What a night. I started to shiver, ignoring the looks I was getting from passers-by. I guess a sobbing teenager running alone in the dark isn't something you see often. My phone was beeping manically in my bag but I chose to ignore it. I would deal with tonight's fallout tomorrow, when I had the strength. I couldn't stop thinking about the look on Ruth's face when I mentioned her chlamydia. And I had promised her so reverently I would never tell anyone. Oops.

As I got closer to home the streets got quieter and darker. The houses got further apart until, eventually, they all had their own moat of perfectly manicured lawn. My tears were beginning to subside, and the crying had calmed me.

You can't change the past, I told myself. Another little lesson from therapy. *So there's no point in obsessing over it.*

I tried not to think about Noah, but it proved difficult. I'd not reacted like that to a boy before. I wrapped my arms tightly around myself, and my mind flashed to the first moment our eyes met. Maybe I was delusional but I was sure his eyes had found mine through the crowd. Like he was searching for me. Okay, definitely delusional, but it had felt that way. My heart began thumping like a nightclub bass beat just from thinking about it. So I did have a crush then. Well, that wouldn't do. Especially as it had taken less than five minutes for him to reveal himself as a complete asshole. Imagine laughing at someone's mental illness. Especially as Lizzie said he'd suffered from depression himself.

I turned the familiar corner into my road and dug in my bag for my keys. As I walked up the drive, I forbade myself to think about any of it until I was a tad more sober, less sweaty, and less emotional.

Dad was waiting for me in his usual spot. I dumped my bag on the living room coffee table, and he peered at me through his half-moon spectacles, lowering his newspaper.

"Good night, hon?"

"It was…" I paused for a moment. "…Okay."

He coughed and folded his newspaper up neatly. Then

he tapped the arm of his chair in invitation. "That bad, eh? Come on, tell me all about it."

I kicked off my smelly ballet pumps and curled up next to him.

"Well," I began, "I had another panic attack. That was pretty embarrassing."

He raised his eyebrows but didn't say anything. If my news upset him, he kept it to himself.

"And then Ruth told this guy I had passed out because I thought he was so good-looking. I think she was trying to impress him by making fun of me."

Dad's face didn't register surprise. "Sounds like Ruth."

"Yep, that's her alright."

He picked up the paper again. I squinted to see his page.

"So what's going on in the world?" I asked, more out of habit than real curiosity.

Dad shook out the pages. "Oh, you know, the world is ending, etc., etc."

I rested my head on his shoulder. "Just another normal day then? Complete misery?"

He smiled. "Indeed."

I watched him read, snuggling into the maroon woolly jumper Mum kept trying to put in the charity shop but he kept buying back because apparently Paul McCartney once wore the exact same one. Is it weird to say I loved the way my dad smelled? It was so comforting. So well known.

The thing is, I was a complete Daddy's girl. His little princess. I was a "happy accident", as my mum so adoringly put it. They weren't expecting to have another child after my sister Louise, especially as late afterwards. And when she got married and moved away, I think it freaked them. My dad especially. So I was lavished with a lot of attention. And sometimes I wished I wasn't, because I couldn't imagine meeting anyone else who treated me as well as my dad did.

I started to get sleepy, but stayed nestled.

"I yelled at Ruth," I said. "I told her off for using my panic attacks as a pulling mechanism." I paused, wondering whether to continue. "And then I told the bloke she was trying to pull she had an STI."

Dad was definitely surprised by that. He put his paper down again and stared at me.

"It's such a mess," I continued. "I don't know what came over me. I was just so angry. She's never going to talk to me again. And now this random bloke knows all about me. I'm so humiliated."

I came to a stop and waited for his response, his wisdom to make it all better.

"So…" he said. "Just another normal day then? Complete misery?"

And despite myself, I laughed.

Waking up on a Sunday morning is supposed to be a pleasant experience. And for about the first five minutes, it was. The light streamed through my curtains and I happily savoured being warm and snugly in bed. Then, of course, I remembered what had happened. I jerked up and dived for my phone, which I had left buried in a discarded pile of last night's clothes. Flicking open my screen, I saw I had nine missed calls: four from Lizzie, four from Amanda, and one from an unknown number.

I shouldn't have run off like that. At the time it had seemed dramatic and important, but now I saw it was selfish and silly. They must've been worried. Angry as hell but still worried. I ran my fingers through my hair and sensed it was going to be a day for apologies.

The doorbell rang and I heard my mum answer it. Probably one of the neighbours asking to borrow some milk – it was that type of road. We had a neighbourhood watch scheme and street parties.

I was surprised when Lizzie stormed through my bedroom door, her face livid.

"So," she said, "you're alive then."

I picked up a hoodie from my floor and quickly pulled it over my head. "Lizzie, I'm so s—"

She interrupted me. "If you're going to apologize for your hysterical outburst last night, then don't."

My stomach relaxed in relief.

"It was the funniest thing I've ever seen in my life. The look on Ruth's face. And Noah's. Priceless. Okay, the whole thing was a tad overdramatic, but you bloody well had a right to do it. Although I think you're absolutely mental. Taking on Ruth? You're braver than I gave you credit for."

"So Ruth is…?"

"Absolutely furious, of course. Do you blame her?"

"No," I squeaked. "And you?"

"Let's just say you're not my favourite person this morning. Why the hell did you run off like that? And not even bother answering your phone? You could've been hit round the head with a hammer for all we knew."

"I'm sorry, Lizzie."

She smiled. "Yeah well, by the time it got to midnight and we hadn't had a frantic call from your neurotic mother, I assumed you'd made it home unscathed."

I patted the empty space next to me and she sat down.

Good. I was forgiven.

"So what happened after my dramatic exit then?"

Lizzie shuffled herself back on the bed so she was leaning against the wall. "Oh, it was brilliant. Amanda and I were trying to contain our hysterics while Ruth went schizo. Of course we had to nod furiously when she told us what a conniving bitch you were."

"Great, thanks."

"Ha ha. She'll get over it…eventually."

"Is this whole thing going to make things awkward…you know…between the group?"

She waved her hand vaguely. "Nah, it'll be fine. I figure you're even stevens. What she did was pretty low and you trumped her. I think even she realizes she took her seduction technique a bit far this time. Poor Noah."

My body spasmed at the sound of his name but luckily

Lizzie didn't notice. As casually as I could, I said, "So what did he make of it all?"

She paused.

"Bless him," she said. "He looked like he'd been smacked in the face. Don't think the poor bloke is used to being spoken to like that. God, he was fit, wasn't he? Didn't I tell you?"

I nodded, frustrated we had gone off track. "Yes, very gorgeous. Well done, Mystic Meg. So…what did he do next?"

"Ooooo," she cooed. "You're keen, aren't you?"

I flushed red. "Shut up."

"Ha ha. Poppy's got an uber-crush," she said, elbowing me in the side.

"Yeah yeah, very funny. Okay, so there's a man in Middletown whose face doesn't resemble hell. It doesn't mean I'm in love with the guy."

I wasn't, was I? I couldn't be. Shut up, thoughts.

"I believe you, thousands wouldn't. He's a nice guy actually…"

My mouth fell open. "Lizzie! How can you say that? After he laughed at me and my panic attacks?"

"No he didn't. He just thought you'd fainted. He was mortified when he found out the real reason, kept asking me for your number so he could apologize."

I swear my heart stopped beating. "He did?"

"Yeah. He kept insisting until I gave it to him."

The unknown number on my phone. It must have been him. I blushed again but crossed my arms stubbornly.

"Yeah, well, why would I want to talk to him?" I said in a sulky voice.

"Jesus bloody Christ, Poppy. I swear you're crazy. God, if he was calling me I would lick the phone." She leaned back against the wall and fanned her face with her hands.

"And you're calling me crazy? You're the one who wants to dribble on a piece of technology."

"Yeah well, I think he wants to make it up to you."

The words triggered a warm gooey feeling. I quickly summoned the rational side of my brain. He wasn't interested in me, just wanted to make peace. I supposed I could let him. But what if he *was* interested? I entertained the thought for a second – it made me quiver just thinking about it. His hand on the small of my back, those dark eyes locked on mine, the touch of his lips brushing mine…

Lizzie interrupted my fantasizing by standing up.

"Where you going?"

"I'm off to Middletown Lakes," she said, swinging her bag over her shoulder.

"Umm…why?"

"I heard the council has drained one of the ponds too shallow by accident and some fish died. Mum saw it this morning when she was walking the dog. I thought I would go down and get some pictures and quotes and then try and flog the story to the *Middletown Observer*."

Her ambition never failed to stun me. "Lizzie. It's a Sunday. The day of rest."

"The news never rests, my dear," she said, acting like my mother and patting me on the head like a child. "You know that."

"You're mad," I yelled as she strode out of the room.

"You smell," her voice called back.

As I heard her footsteps descend the stairs, I leaned back into my pillows. I closed my eyes and Noah's face appeared instantly. This had to stop. I was turning into an obsessive – I was beginning to scare myself.

"One more thing."

I jumped and my eyes snapped open. Lizzie was peering round the door.

"Ring Ruth and make it up, will you?" she said. Then she disappeared before I even had the chance to protest.

I eventually got up, showered and pottered about – the usual mild hungover Sunday activities. Every so often I examined my phone, but the blank screen stared back at me. I couldn't decide whether I wanted Ruth to call. Or Noah. Or both. Or neither.

After nearly a day of driving myself insane I decided to get out and pulled on my trainers.

As I stepped outside I knew I'd made the right decision. Much as I despaired of where I lived, I couldn't deny its luscious lawns and green-belt land were beautiful. My phone felt lighter in my pocket as I walked to the common. I passed several middle-aged neighbours, squatting in their front gardens, bums out, eagerly tending to their immaculate flower beds or topiary hedges. Some children were playing on their bikes in the road, which was always clear of traffic at the weekend. Massive cars sat hibernating in everyone's double driveways, resting before the perilous school run on Monday morning.

I turned a sharp left into a slightly overgrown alleyway, the trees on either side forming a green tunnel. I'd walked this path so many times I knew exactly when to raise my legs to avoid stinging nettles. The path got steeper and I pulled off my jumper and tied it round my waist – hoping like mad that no one would see my fashion crime. Eventually I emerged into startling daylight. I was here. My favourite place.

To anyone but me, it wasn't anything special. Just a clearing where dog walkers exercised their pedigrees and a meeting place for fourteen-year-olds to drink a bottle of cider together and dry hump. But I loved it here for several reasons. Firstly, the view. The clearing overlooked the whole town, making everything look tiny, like Toytown. Any silly problem my brain manufactured would relinquish its hold the moment I sat down on the lone bench and looked out. I could see the local airport's landing strip in the distance, miniature planes stuffed full of people landing and taking off.

I also loved how undiscovered this place was. Middletown was full of parks and green spaces, tarted up with lottery money we didn't need or deserve. At the slightest hint of sunshine, a stampede of mothers with prams, dads with footballs, and teenagers with disposable barbecues would descend onto those spaces. But up here it was usually mostly empty. I felt I had ownership of it. I only had to share with the odd rambler or dog walker. It was my own little space where I could sit and think, away from my turbo-charged mother and my cramped bedroom, and try and make sense of whatever problem was distracting me at that moment in time.

Today it was two problems: Ruth and Noah. Up here I felt I had the strength to evaluate last night's events. Solving the Ruth crisis was easy enough. I would have to beg for forgiveness and suck up for a couple of days. I was certain I would never receive an apology in return, but that was the way the world worked, wasn't it? My friendship with Ruth was largely successful as long as I suspended hope of her ever growing a conscience.

I sighed, flipped my mobile phone open and dialled her number.

She let it ring before answering. "I'm not talking to you."

I stared out over the view below me. I could handle this…up here anyway. "Come on, Ruth, I'm sorry."

"And so you bloody well should be. I've never been so humiliated in my life."

She'd never been so humiliated? SHE'D never been so humiliated? My cheeks burned with fury but I kept my voice even. Getting angry wasn't going to resolve this. "I said I'm sorry and I mean it."

She was quiet for a moment, thinking. "Yeah, well, I suppose you were just jealous Noah and I were getting along so well," she said finally.

I swallowed. "Maybe…yes. That must be why." I tried to keep sarcasm out of my voice and just about managed it.

She jumped on my admission like a defence lawyer. "So you admit you like him then?"

Oh God. Why did I make this phone call?

"I'm not saying that," I said. "I mean, he's okay-looking and everything, but I didn't really get to know him."

"Well, I don't think you're his type."

My hand holding my phone was shaking. "And why is that?" I asked quietly.

"Well I don't think he goes for the brooding, sarcastic thing. I think someone like Noah likes girls with a bit more sass."

Of course you do. "Someone like you, Ruth?"

"Yes, well, probably," she snapped. "Although he's not going to be interested now, is he? Not after you told him I was an STI-ridden TRAMP."

I switched my phone from one ear to another. It would be over soon.

"Ruth, as I said, I'm truly sorry. I was just jealous at how easy you find it to talk to boys and I acted out. I hope we can be friends again."

Another pregnant pause.

"Yeah well, don't do it again, right."

Relief.

"Anyway," she continued, "I don't actually like that Noah guy. Much too pose-y for my liking."

I stifled a laugh. Honestly, you couldn't make people like Ruth up. No one would believe you. Her own self-belief was extraordinary.

"Of course. Much too pose-y. So what time you starting college tomorrow?"

We talked for another few minutes, getting things back to normal, before I hung up. I tilted my head back in relief, inhaling the fresh summer air. I'd thought she would make me suffer much more than that. Maybe there was a tiny shred of her that felt bad. And then I laughed aloud at my own naivety and startled a passing dog walker.

With the Ruth fiasco sorted, I let my mind drift to Noah. My memory was drowned immediately – the curve of his jaw, the intense look in his eyes when they met mine. I firmly pushed this to one side, determined to compartmentalize whatever these emotions were and deal with them practically.

I supposed it had to happen at some point. There had to be at least one boy out there who got attractive before the age of nineteen. But the strength of my attraction concerned me. I'd only just met him and I couldn't get him out of my head. As I saw it, there were only two possible outcomes. One – the much more realistic option: he'd barely remember me, let alone feel anything, and I'd feel rejected and awful. Or two: he'd fall for me, soon realize I was way below his league, dump me for someone beautiful and I'd feel rejected and awful. So there was only one solution: to remove him from my brain entirely. I didn't have the mental strength to be hurt by a guy, not now. My head was already too preoccupied trying to stop me from passing out.

So no. I wouldn't let myself fall for him. For anyone. I wasn't ready.

With my decision made I felt lighter. I watched another plane disappear through the thin cloud layer. The sun was going in so I slowly made my way across the clearing, savouring every last moment of the view. And then, checking first that no one could see, I skipped down the alleyway towards home.

5

When I woke up the next morning, I groaned. It was Monday.

I hit the snooze button, pushing my head under the pillow to block out the light shining optimistically through my window. Lying on my front, I practised my breathing exercises again. I breathed in and out slowly, but it was difficult not to doze off. For a moment I slipped back into sleep and my thoughts floated elsewhere.

Noah's eyes appeared before me the moment I closed my own. In a dozy haze I let myself imagine how it would feel to have his arms wrapped around me – those same strong arms I'd seen playing the guitar...

The frantic trill of my alarm jogged me awake properly. I took my time getting ready for college, as I had a free period first thing on Mondays. I'd washed my hair the night before and plaited it into four sections. I slowly unravelled them so my hair was wavy and dabbed on some make-up. I pulled on some light blue jeans, a white vest, and twisted my long turquoise-stone necklace around myself. After breakfast, brushing my teeth and checking I had all the right books, I set off. It was a gorgeous day, the sort that rarely bestows itself upon England. I wondered if anyone would bother with lessons or just sit in a beer garden instead. I put my iPod headphones on and turned the music up loud. It was definitely a morning for The Beatles and I picked "Here Comes the Sun". Dad had once said this was the only song that really summed up a British summer, and he was right. Everything looked beautiful. The roads were quiet, green leaves burst from trees, birds sang out like ambitious reality-show auditionees, and everyone was wearing summer clothes and had a grin across their face.

I played my favourite walking-alone game where, in my head, I pretend I'm in a music video. Imagining myself leaning into a wind machine and practising my dramatic-singing face made the journey go quickly and soon I was walking up the college path. I was enjoying myself so much that I didn't really notice somebody tapping my shoulder. I was singing under my breath, oblivious to everything, when I felt it again.

I turned round, music still blasting in my ears, and there he was. Right in front of me. Noah. Wearing a rolled-up pair of jeans and a blue T-shirt. Looking perfect. My heart started thudding and I felt out of breath. I stared at him gormlessly, music still roaring. I couldn't hear what he was saying; I was too busy concentrating on staying upright. So, so perfect. His so-dark-brown-they-were-almost-black eyes were wide and questioning. My breathing was getting faster and I was scared I was panting. Noah motioned to me but I just stared back like a fool. Then he was reaching towards me. The pace of my heart picked up as his arm approached – the arm I'd fantasized about only this morning. He reached for my face. Was this happening? Was he going to cup it? Was this morning's daydream actually a premonition?

And then the reassuring sound of The Beatles disappeared and I realized he was just taking my earphones out.

"Sorry. I didn't mean to shock you. Can you hear me now? Poppy, isn't it?" He was smiling but it was strained. I think he was nervous. Probably scared I would yell at him or pass out again.

I gulped and nodded idiotically. Memories of the other night whirred back. The humiliation, the hurt. I felt my face turn tomato.

"Hey," he continued. "I tried to call you Saturday night but you didn't pick up."

I didn't know the correct response so I stayed silent. My heartbeat was so loud it was stopping my mind from thinking of anything coherent to say. It felt like a warning drum and all the hairs on my arms stood on end, like when I'm home alone and I hear an inexplicable bang – a primal fear reaction. But Noah was just a boy. He wasn't dangerous, was he?

"I feel really bad about what happened." His smile had gone. My silence was obviously bothering him. "I didn't really understand what was going on. Your friend Ruth just dragged me over. I only laughed out of nervousness."

His speech sounded rehearsed, like he'd been practising alone. That made me feel good. He had been thinking about me. I glowed and then focused on being normal.

"It's okay, don't worry about it." I'd just about held it together enough to get those six words out. But if I hung around much longer I would completely give myself away. "Bye then," I stammered, then turned and walked off.

"Wait," he called.

And then my hand was burning like it was on fire. Noah had grabbed it. His touch scorched my skin. I looked up in confusion and his eyes met mine. They looked tortured, burning with intensity, and my insides turned to blancmange. He kept hold of me and the fire coursed up my arm. We stared at each other for a few seconds, both silenced. My breathing got quicker, matching my panicked heartbeat, and the familiar feeling of sickness drew in. Wrong wrong wrong. Something was wrong. My whole arm was screaming. Just as I was about to pull my hand away, he withdrew his and shook his head as if to restore clarity.

"Sorry," he said again.

"S'okay." My heart rate slowed the moment the physical contact ended. I looked down at my arm and it was normal again, like nothing had happened. Had it?

He stared at his shoes and scratched his head, looking embarrassed.

I cleared my throat and tried to break the atmosphere. "Umm, I didn't know you went to Middletown College."

He looked straight into my eyes and my heart went into

overdrive again. But, as if he knew what he did to me, he quickly lowered his gaze. "I don't go here."

"Oh. Then why are you here?" It was a direct question and it came out nastily.

He flinched and I felt guilty.

"Erm," he said, "I was hoping to see you actually."

I hadn't expected that reply. I blushed and tried to hide my face with my hair. "Oh," was the only reply I could muster.

"Look…" he said. Again I got the feeling he'd rehearsed this. "I couldn't stop thinking about you and what happened. No one's spoken to me like that before. I've never known anyone to speak their mind so bluntly."

I kept my face down, not trusting myself to look at him. "It was stupid," I muttered. "I'm sorry I was rude. I just lost my temper."

My chin began to burn and he was touching me again. Pushing my face up, forcing me to stare into his dark eyes.

"You don't understand," he said, his pupils blazing into mine. "I liked it."

All I could do was stare back. He still had his hand on me. It felt like a thousand watts were sprinting through my body, like when you touched that static machine in primary school science lessons. I felt a little sick again.

He spoke again. "Will you come out for a drink with me tonight?"

My brain was foggy. All I wanted to do was say yes. But something stopped me – the deal I'd made with myself yesterday, up on the common, when Noah wasn't there to distract me.

I analysed what he'd said. He *liked* that I was rude to him. Scepticism began to replace the adrenalin. I'd become a challenge. I hadn't fawned on him like he was used to and that intrigued him. My self-preservation superpowers kicked in. Once Noah had won me over, he would lose interest and piss off. It was textbook stuff. Well, if your textbook was *Cosmo* magazine.

Ignoring every physical impulse in my body that wanted him, I opened my mouth to speak.

"I don't think that's a good idea." And for a moment, that actually felt like the truth – because suddenly an instinctive part of me was telling me to leave. Get away. Now.

Noah looked shocked. More than shocked. His eyebrows stretched up across his forehead in disbelief. This was probably the first time he'd ever been refused.

"Not a good idea?" He tried to smile, laughing it off. "Why not? I'm not going to drug you or anything. I just want to take you out for a drink."

I forced myself to look directly into his eyes, ignoring the feelings it stirred. "I've got class in a minute."

His face wavered with anger but he controlled it and pushed out another forced smile. He removed his hand, and shook it, like the movement would dislodge his embarrassment at even touching me in the first place. My skin still tingled from where it had been.

"Yeah, of course, sorry," he murmured. "I should let you go."

I stepped past him towards college. A few groups of students were milling around, wasting time before the bell went. I made about three metres' progress before he called after me.

"Oh, Poppy?"

I hated myself for smiling when I heard him call my name. I quickly arranged my mouth into a more neutral expression before I spun round.

"What is it, Noah?" I tried to sound nonchalant.

He jogged over. "Hey," he said, running his hands through his hair. "Maybe I was too...forward. Sorry about that, I'm not used to being turned down."

I scowled and he noticed.

"Okay. That sounded really big-headed, didn't it?"

I giggled. "Just a bit. Okay, a lot. Just because you're in a band doesn't make you an irresistible Adonis, you know." I thought of Ruth, and smiled, wrinkling my nose. "Well, not to everyone."

I was bluffing, of course. He *was* an irresistible Adonis. Anyone with a pair of working eyeballs could see that. But the bluff appeared to be believable. Noah didn't look happy.

"Yeah well, I realize that now."

I paused, waiting for his next move. The bell had just gone and all the other students had disappeared, but it didn't seem important.

"Well, if the thought of going on a date with me is so

repugnant, how about a drink with friends then?" He attempted another grin.

I shifted my bag from one shoulder to another. "I don't understand."

"After college," he said. "I'm meeting the band in the Lock and Key for a few drinks. You could come along? Bring a few of your mates as well?"

I thought about it. The girls would kill me if I said no. Yet I was nervous. Seeing more of Noah wasn't exactly going to help me exorcize this crush.

"I don't understand *why*," I asked.

"God – to be friendly?" he snapped. Then he shook his head. "Sorry, this is going all wrong. I shouldn't have just sprung out on you like this. It seemed like a much cooler idea in my head. I just feel bad about what happened and I want to make it up to you and get to know you…" He saw me raising my eyebrows. "…And your friends much better. It's a lovely day, it will be a lovely evening. The lads are really friendly and it will be fun."

I found myself nodding.

"Is that a yes?"

"Erm…okay then."

"Brilliant. See you at the Lock and Key at five-ish."

Then he smiled a huge genuine smile, turned and jogged off, leaving me standing there open-mouthed like a fish.

6

I was late for my English lesson. I burst through the door to a class full of unimpressed and stony faces. I apologized to my teacher, who waved me away and continued teaching.

Frank had left a space for me and I scuttled over to him.

"What have I missed?" I whispered, getting my A4 notebook and biro out.

He handed me a copy of a book. I grimaced at the front cover. Ergh. *Romeo and Juliet*.

"It's our Shakespeare play for this term," he said. "Aren't you supposed to simper and gush on about how romantic it is?"

I raised an eyebrow ironically at him in reply. He raised one back and we both laughed. He knew "simpering" wasn't part of my vocabulary.

Frank Dayton was one of those friends you make out of convenience when you don't know anyone in your class. None of my friends took English, so luckily I'd sat next to Frank in my first lesson, who didn't know anyone either. We quickly discovered we shared a mutual love of sarcasm, passing judgement on everyone, and weird sci-fi loner novels. I sometimes spent time trying to decide if I fancied him. He was technically good-looking. Blond hair, green eyes, worked out, all the usual box-tickers. But he just wasn't my type. And he played rugby. Ergh. It was one of the things we argued about, as I usually couldn't bear rugby players and their massive egos.

If I was really bored I would wonder if he fancied me, but was mostly certain we only mutually used each other to get through English A Level. We didn't really speak outside of class and he never went to Band Night. He was into trance music. Double ergh. I regularly teased him on his musical choice. Why bother liking clubbing music when you live in Middletown? Where are you going to rave? In your Renault Clio?

My teacher, Ms. Gretching (very important you remember the Ms., she goes nuts otherwise) was still talking. She was droning on about how Romeo and Juliet were meant for each other but "true love" always self-destructs. I had an inkling this academic point wasn't actually on the syllabus, and had rather more to do with the white strip of skin on her finger where her wedding ring used to be.

I groaned and lay my head on the table.

"Do you really hate *Romeo and Juliet* that much?" Frank asked, finding amusement in my dismay.

"Yes," I whispered back. "The whole story is ridiculous. It's just about a pair of melodramatic teenagers high on dopamine ruining their lives because of some adolescent crush. I wish we could have done *Macbeth* instead."

Frank looked at me for a moment. "You're really not like other girls, are you?"

I looked at the row of girls sitting opposite us. They were four identikit blondes Frank and I regularly took the piss out of because they obviously spent about two hours getting ready for college – full face of make-up, GHD ringlets, fake eyelashes EVERY day. They were hanging on Ms. Gretching's every word, simpering whenever she used the words "soulmate" or "true love".

I gestured towards them. "Thank God," I replied.

We were instructed to start reading the first scene. Frank and I flipped our books open and read for a few minutes.

"So why were you late anyway?" he whispered, turning over a page. I saw he was two pages ahead and it bothered me. "You looked a bit flustered when you came in."

I had a quick flashback to my Noah encounter and felt my breathing speed up. "If you must know," I said. "I was being asked on a date."

I studied Frank's face for a reaction. He didn't look upset. More surprised. So he didn't fancy me then. Oh well, it figured, I supposed.

"Who would want to go out with a grunger like you?"

"Grunger? Seriously, Frank? It's not the nineties. Just because I listen to real people making real music instead of a computer beeping repeatedly doesn't mean I'm Kurt Cobain." I was a little hurt by his remark. I knew he was joking, but he had just validated one of my biggest insecurities. Why *would* anyone want to go out with me?

Frank realized he'd picked a topic of conversation I wasn't prepared to be sarcastic about and waved his hands like he was surrendering.

"Okay, firecracker. I didn't mean it. I'm sure you're lovely to go out with."

"I'm delightful."

"Of course."

"Everyone's dream woman."

"Definitely."

"I'm just jealous," he said, eyes mischievous. "You see, I've been dying to take you out myself. There's this great trance night I know about. Just your sort of thing. About time you started listening to proper music...oww."

I had elbowed him in the ribs.

Ms. Gretching heard his yelp of pain and glared at us.

"Well," she said. "Poppy and Frank have obviously finished the first scene. As you are both so *enthusiastic*, why don't you read the parts of Romeo and Juliet in the next one?"

We both groaned.

"I blame you entirely," I whispered as I forced myself to stand and read the part of wet, stupid Juliet.

English was a double lesson so, by the time I'd finished pretending to hurl myself around a balcony, it was lunchtime.

"You made a lovely Juliet," Frank said as I pulled my chair back. "Very convincing."

"Shut up, you," I said, chucking my pen at him. Annoyingly, he caught it. "Anyway I noticed you doing loads of dramatic pauses in your Romeo monologue. Who do you think you are, Leonardo DiCaprio or something?"

"You're just jealous." Frank chucked the biro back at me.

I lunged for it but whacked it with my hand and it rolled under the table. I ducked to retrieve it, slightly conscious that my arse was poking out right in front of him.

"Of you? You've got to be kidding me," I said, finally grabbing my pen, wiggling up, and turning to leave. "Anyway, lovely as it was and all, I'm off."

"Bye bye...Juliet."

"Shut up."

My friends were all in the canteen already, sitting at our usual table. Lizzie was sitting cross-legged, writing something in that bloody notebook she incessantly carried around. Ruth was, funnily enough, admiring herself in a compact mirror – ever the stereotype. And Amanda had Johnno with her. They were holding hands but both looked constipated with fear.

"Poppy!" Lizzie yelped when she saw me. "Guess what? The paper is interested in my dead fish story."

"That's brilliant," I said, dumping my bag on the table

and pulling out a chair. Amanda and Johnno smiled hello, while Ruth just nodded.

So she was going to be like that, was she?

"I'm a superstar," Lizzie said, beaming.

"Lizzie, you're not supposed to say that about yourself."

"Screw that. Who else is going to pump me up? Journalism is a cut-throat world, you know. You have to believe in yourself."

I rolled my eyes and pulled out my peanut butter sandwich. Lizzie's determination was disconcerting. I was seventeen and didn't have a clue what to do with my life. I didn't particularly enjoy any of my A level subjects. I wasn't particularly good at any of them either. I liked reading books, but only as a leisure activity. I hated studying narrative technique and all that drivel in my English lessons. I bit into my sandwich and let Lizzie's excitable chatter wash over me, pondering the evening ahead. I didn't want to admit it to myself, but I was flattered Noah had picked me out, even if he was bad news. Admittedly, I didn't know for certain he was bad news. Was I being unfair? Assuming he was a player just because he was good-looking and in a band?

No. It was more than that. He did something to me that I didn't understand. I'd lost myself in just one weekend because of him. A sixth sense inside of me was flashing a warning light. Half of me wanted to ignore it and run straight to our date. But the other, sensible half had me on reins.

Lizzie eventually stopped droning on about newspapers and asked, "So what are we up to tonight? I'm not staying in on a Monday, it's too depressing. Plus its ultra-gorgeous outside. We have to make the most of it."

I cleared my throat and tried to keep my voice casual.

"Actually," I said, screwing up the foil from my sandwich, "I bumped into that Noah guy this morning on the way to college and he invited us to go to the Lock and Key with his band."

Everyone's eyes were on me.

"What? When did you see him?" Ruth asked. She looked suspicious.

"We just bumped into each other and he asked if we wanted to come out." I thought it best not to tell her he'd been waiting for me, hoping he would bump into me.

Lizzie looked like she was going to explode with excitement. "Tell me everything that happened," she said. "Every last detail."

I shrugged and tried to ignore Ruth's dark look. "There's no more detail. The whole band is going. It should be fun. Plus, if we get to know them better, we might be able to get free entry to Band Night." I opened my bottle of water and took a much-needed gulp. "So, are you up for it?"

I surveyed their faces. Ruth was still glowering. Lizzie wiggled in her seat like a hyperactive five-year-old on Christmas morning, and Amanda just looked overwhelmed. She was clutching Johnno's hand, who wasn't paying the situation any attention at all and was staring absent-mindedly out the window to where his mates were playing football.

"Of course we're up for it," Lizzie said. "Sounds like a laugh."

I looked to Ruth. She glared for a few moments, and then her face softened.

"Yeah, I'm in. I quite fancied the bassist anyway. I might make him my new conquest." She puffed up her chest theatrically and made us all laugh. I nervously reminded myself that, until yesterday, Noah had been her intended conquest.

We turned to Amanda in unison, waiting to hear her inevitable excuse.

Blinking at us desperately, she said, "Tonight? I think I'm supposed to be having dinner with my family tonight."

We groaned. Nobody could lie worse than Amanda. She was incapable of pulling the wool over even a sheep's eyes.

"Come on," I said, poking her in the ribs, which I knew she hated. "It will be fun. New people. New conversation…"

"New totty…" Ruth chipped in and she smiled at me genuinely. So we had made up then. Phew.

Amanda looked to Johnno for backup but he was still watching the football. "I…I…did say I would have dinner with them…"

Lizzie took over. "For God's sake, Amanda," she said. "Even a nun could lie better than you. Isn't that right, Johnno?"

Johnno pulled his attention back and looked at Amanda adoringly. "Yes," he said to her. "You're the most honest person I know. That's why I like you so much."

Amanda flushed the colour of a radioactive beetroot, and, as a result, Johnno turned mauve as well. They dropped each other's hands and both looked at the floor.

Lizzie, Ruth and I all smirked.

Johnno got to his feet ungracefully and pulled his rucksack onto his shoulders. "Anyway...I'd better go join the guys outside for...er...the...rest of the match."

Amanda could barely look at him. She shrugged her shoulders in a vain attempt at a breezy and non-committal manner. "Sure," she said, her face still bright red. "See you later."

Johnno stood there awkwardly for a moment more, like he was trying to build up the courage to say something, but then bottled it and practically ran out of the canteen.

The moment he'd gone, the rest of us dissolved into hysteria.

"Oh my God," Lizzie said, tears in her eyes. "You two are so funny."

Amanda looked at her in dismay.

"You really are," Ruth added. "You're like the two shyest people I've ever come across in my whole seventeen years. How you even got together is a miracle of science."

Amanda looked like she was going to cry. I could see the angry comebacks forming in her mind, never to be expelled. Then she shook her head and grinned.

"Shut up," she said. "Okay, I know we're both a little... repressed..."

Her choice of word made us lose control again.

"But we'll get there. Anyway..." She struggled to build the courage to say the next sentence. "...At least I've got a boyfriend."

Ruth, Lizzie and I looked at each other, still laughing and raised our eyebrows.

"Now that is true," I said, moving into Johnno's seat and putting my arm around her. "We shouldn't mock you. You are, after all, the only one who's found somebody."

"I find somebody about once a week," Ruth said and the hysterics began again.

The girls at the table next to us looked at us like we were mad, which only made us laugh harder.

When we had finally regained our self-control, I turned to Amanda again. "So, are you coming?"

She gulped but I knew she was going to give in. "Okay," she said. "I'll go to the pub."

"Brilliant." I stood and looked at the clock. I had less than five minutes to get across campus to my next lesson. "Meet you all outside the gates after college."

They nodded, and I turned and made my way towards class.

7

The rest of the afternoon passed pretty quickly.

I feigned concentration during Psychology, and double Photography took me through to the end of the day. I hid myself away in the calming red light of the darkroom and listened to my iPod while I processed some David Bailey-style photos I'd taken of Ruth. The mixture of music and darkness soothed me as images came to life in the developer liquid. But my calmness evaporated the moment the final bell went. I ran to the girls' toilets, poured out the contents of my make-up bag into the sink and got to work making myself semi-presentable. Five minutes later and I was... improved. On the outside at least. My insides still felt like unset jelly.

I worked on my game plan as I made my way to the gates. It consisted of two words: "stay cool". So easy in theory, without Noah there to distract me. Ruth, Amanda and Lizzie were waiting for me at the entrance. They all looked slightly more made-up than at lunchtime, so I obviously wasn't the only one who'd made a last-minute dash to the ladies'.

"You ready?" I said, linking arms with Lizzie.

"Of course, of course," she replied.

I grabbed Amanda's arm, who was already linking with Ruth, and wondered if girls ever grew out of the arm-link. I hoped we wouldn't.

"I can't wait to get my hands on that bassist," Ruth said. "I decided to seduce him while I was bored in Travel and Tourism."

"Honestly, woman. You are such a perv," Lizzie said, mock-outraged.

Ruth shrugged her shoulders. "Just treating men like they've been treating us since the dawn of time. It's role reversal. It's empowerment. It's feminism."

I laughed. "All valid points, Ruth, but I'm with Lizzie. You're just a perv – using half-baked ideals about equality to cover up your bad habit."

Ruth looked proud of herself. "Maybe."

We flip-flopped our way towards the pub, the sun still shining high in the sky. When we arrived, the band wasn't there yet. We shuffled in nervously, using Ruth as our confidence. The Lock and Key was an overly trendy pub, very typical of Middletown. It had supposedly groovy purple lighting and high bar stools with red velvet covers. The place attracted up-themselves young professionals – the sort who liked to roll their shirtsleeves up and laugh loudly while necking a four pound bottle of beer with an "edgy" label. We usually avoided the place. The female manager had a nasty habit of ID-ing young girls more attractive than her, but luckily she wasn't on duty today. We pushed Ruth to the front and, without hesitation, she confidently ordered four bottles of Corona and lime. The barman, a skinny guy with hair that must've taken at least half an hour to craft, took her money without question and pulled the tops off for us. Ruth expertly handed them over before leading us into the beer garden.

I looked down at my drink, bemusedly, as we followed her outside.

"Since when do we drink beer?" I whispered to Lizzie.

"Since we've been invited out by a cool band." She took a short swig. "Hmmm, not entirely awful," she said, wiping her mouth with her hand.

The saving grace of the Lock and Key was the beer garden, especially on such a sunny day. The owners had presumably spent huge amounts of money hiring a landscape architect, who'd sculpted the space into something almost magical. Hedges and trees hid tucked-away tables, while twinkling lights and electronic heaters gave the place a fairy-tale glow after sunset. Right then though, it was still blisteringly hot and many tables had already been taken by groups of slightly sweaty businessmen, who were trying to look cool by rolling up their trouser legs and wandering around barefoot.

Ruth steered us towards the last large table and sat on the central seat with the best view of the pub's back door. She pulled out a pair of massive red sunglasses, wrapped them round her face, then took a long drink of her beer.

"Ahhhh," she said. "This is the life."

I looked down at my drink and tentatively took a small sip. It actually wasn't bad. I took another, larger sip, and tried to forget Noah would be arriving imminently.

We spent a while pretending to be interested in making conversation, but the atmosphere was tense. We were all nervous. Well, Amanda and I were for sure. Ruth's eyes snapped towards the door whenever it opened, surveying everyone who walked through, and sizing up any girl who dared intrude. Meanwhile I replayed the words *play it cool play it cool play it cool* over and over.

I felt him arrive before I saw him.

My throat closed up, my heart attack started and the faintness hit me full force. I gulped on my beer to try and calm myself. Big mistake. The liquid gushed down the wrong tube. My eyes bulged and I started choking. Then there was a sudden feeling of burning on my back. I was being thumped. I couldn't see who it was but feared the worst – every time the hand made contact with my back, it fire-blasted my skin through my thin vest top. It had to be Noah. After four giant whacks, I could breathe again. Tears were running down my face as I gasped in precious air and pulled myself together.

I slowly looked up to survey the damage.

Lots of confused faces stared back at me. I noticed the singer from the band, and two other boys who had to be the bassist and the drummer. Lizzie and Amanda were giving me *What the hell?* looks. Ruth was stifling laughter, obviously ecstatic I'd made such a show of myself again. And there was Noah, crouching in front of me, a massive smirk on his face.

"Wow, Poppy," he said dryly. "You really know how to turn a guy on, don't you?"

He reached into his pocket and pulled out a hanky. "Here." He handed it over. "You've got mascara running down your face."

Blushing, I snatched the hanky off him and dabbed it around my eyes. "Thanks," I said. "But seriously, Noah – what sort of guy carries a HANKY round with them? What are you? A character from an Enid Blyton story or something?"

Everyone laughed, except him.

"You're making it worse," he said. "You're just smudging your make-up round your face. Aww bless, did you get all made-up just for me?"

I scowled in return. "You wish."

He looked hurt for a second, then stood up and threw a hand out to his bandmates.

"Boys, this gorgeous choking girl is Poppy Lawson." I waved, still mortified. "And this," he continued, "is Ruth, Lizzie and Amanda."

Lizzie waved back maniacally, Amanda squeaked hello, and Ruth coolly acknowledged them with an aloof wiggle of her fingers. God, life is unfair.

The boys sat down. I got wedged next to the singer guy, who told me his name was Ryan.

"So, singing…" I said, taking a small neck of my beer and not choking this time. "What happened? Can you not play an instrument?"

"Oi," he said, but laughed. "My voice is the instrument."

I furrowed my eyebrows.

"Actually that sounded really pretentious, didn't it?" He looked worried, his blue eyes searched my face with genuine concern. Ryan, bless him, seemed to have that surprisingly common lead-singer problem of actually being shy and insecure in real life.

"I'm just trying to cover the fact I'm musically dyslexic," I said, hoping my own self-deprecation would calm his anxiety.

"So you can't play anything?"

"Just the recorder when I was little. So what are your band's influences then?"

I let his enthusiastic babble wash over me and nodded whenever I heard key words like "The Smiths", "The Libertines", "The Clash".

As I smiled and nodded, I took in the scene around me. Ruth had, unsurprisingly, found herself in a Noah and Bassist sandwich. She was in full seduction mode again, batting her eyelashes at the bassist, who I think was called Will. Her back was deliberately turned to Noah, trying to prove what a catch she was and how uninterested she was in him simultaneously. Lizzie was talking to the drummer, Jack, about some political biography they'd both read. She was firing questions at him and arguing with every statement he made, but they seemed to be getting along. Amanda was listening intently to Ruth's flirty banter and playing "best friend" by laughing hysterically at every slightly witty comment. And Noah...well, I hadn't let myself look at Noah. Until now...

I regretted it immediately.

The moment I stole a glance, his eyes met mine instinctively, and I felt my chest tighten. He held my gaze steadily, the smile wiped from his face. I didn't allow myself to breathe and I let whatever was passing between us pass. Every part of me yearned for him in a way completely new to me. I wanted to jump over the table, grab his face and taste him. Like an animal. It was terrifyingly overpowering and I could tell he felt the same. His hands were gripping the dry wood of the table. He looked...almost hungry. I realized then that all those bonkbuster chick-lit books I sneered at actually had it right; those tired old clichés were true. I wanted to devour him, rip his clothes off, consume him – all those melodramatic things I used to read aloud and laugh at. A tiny part of my brain was reminding myself to get a grip, but that flicker of logic was powerless against my body's sensory overload.

"Poppy?" I heard someone say. Was it him? It wasn't. His eyes had lowered. The moment was over.

"Poppy?"

"Huh?" I snapped back to reality. It was Ryan talking.

He had finished speaking and I obviously hadn't noticed. He looked upset again, like he knew he wasn't interesting enough to hold my attention, and I felt guilty.

"I was just saying…" he went on, clasping and unclasping his hands. "…I was wondering who your favourite band is?"

"Oh," I said, frantically scanning my brain for a suitable answer. But it was oxygen-starved. I grasped for words. "The Beatles," I heard myself say. Stock answer. No one can argue with The Beatles.

"Really?" Ryan said. "Yeah well, I suppose you can't argue with The Beatles."

Exactly.

I could still feel Noah's attention on me and began to feel a little sick. I needed to get away from him. He was like kryptonite or something. I couldn't stand it.

I stood up and felt my legs buckle slightly beneath me.

"Hey, would you excuse me a sec?" I asked Ryan, grabbing his hand for support, not caring what he might think of the physical contact.

"Of course."

"I just need to…er…get another drink…"

And then everything went black.

I regained consciousness before I opened my eyes.

"Is she okay?" I heard a worried voice say. Maybe it was the drummer.

"She's fine." That was Lizzie's voice. "I think she just got too hot."

The realization of what had happened dawned on me. Humiliation seeped through my face and I felt my cheeks flush.

"She's still not awake. Should we call 999 or something?"

I kept my eyes closed. That way I could pretend it wasn't real.

"Let's tickle her," I heard Noah say.

He wouldn't, would he?

"Noah, are you really going to tickle her?"

"Yep."

I knew if he touched me again I wouldn't be able to handle it, so, cursing him silently, I reluctantly opened my eyes and let the scene come into focus.

"See. She's awake."

I was on my back. Squinting up against the sun, I could see everyone's expressions. Ryan, Will and Jack looked absolutely terrified but were trying to hide it, pretending girls randomly passed out in beer gardens all the time. The girls, Ruth included, looked suitably concerned. It was just Noah laughing. I glared at him.

"Wakey wakey," he said. "Nice of you to join us."

I tried to sit up. Bad move. Everything lost focus again and I fought to stay conscious.

"Careful now," Lizzie said, kneeling down and letting me put my weight on her. "Let's go to the ladies' and get you sorted out."

My face burned. I hated my stupid body and its bad

habits. "Sorry," I said, stumbling to my feet. "I think I just got too hot. Didn't drink enough water…"

I leaned on Lizzie for support and she guided me expertly to the loos, Ruth and Amanda in tow.

"Maybe you guys want to get another round in," Lizzie called behind her. "We won't be long."

I staggered into the toilets and Ruth put a loo seat down so I could sit. I fell onto it and put my face in my hands, willing myself to wake up from the nightmare. I practised my breathing exercises, counting in and out again, and gradually felt myself getting stronger.

The toilets were insanely plush and over the top. Instead of a sink there was a stand-alone basin which spurted out water like a fountain. The walls were painted deep purple and adorned with giant gold-framed mirrors. I could see at least six images of myself reflected around the room.

I looked a mess.

When I got my breath back, I looked up at my friends.

"Well, where the hell did that come from?" Lizzie said.

I looked down at my flip-flops. "Sorry," I said. "Twice in a week."

"What happened?" Ruth asked gently. I found it vaguely amusing that she was here playing the "caring friend" role. She obviously wanted to impress Will with her (fake) generous nature.

"I don't know," I replied honestly.

"Was it another panic attack?" Amanda said. "It wasn't like at the gig. You just passed out like a normal person."

I winced at the word "normal". "No," I said. "I don't think it was another panic attack."

"Well, what was it then?"

I had an idea but the words seemed stupid. I tried them anyway.

"I dunno… It's Noah…it's like I'm allergic to him or something… Whenever I'm around him I feel like I'm in danger… No, that's silly…I don't know."

My friends looked confused.

"You're allergic to Noah?" Lizzie was sceptical.

I half-smiled. "No. I'm just being stupid."

"Well, this has happened both times you've seen him," Amanda said. "Maybe it's his aftershave? Did your doctor say you had any allergies that brought these things on?"

I shook my head. "No. It's just a coincidence. Forget it."

It didn't *feel* like a coincidence, but I knew I sounded like a madman and I didn't like them all looking at me. I just wanted to go back to normal.

"I'm fine," I said. "You guys go back. I'll sort my face out and meet you in five."

Lizzie put her hand on my shoulder. "Sure you're okay?"

"Positive."

"Well, if you're not out in five minutes I'm coming in to check on you."

"I'm fine. I just need a moment…you know…alone."

The girls filed out of the loos, leaving me alone in the ornate toilets.

I got to my feet and wandered over to a mirror – my face falling when I saw my reflection. I didn't look great. Mascara was smeared under my eyes and my forehead was covered in sweat.

I pulled my hair back into a messy bun. Using some toilet paper, I carefully erased the black mess under my eyes and then reapplied some lip balm.

I studied my reflection again. Okay. Slightly improved. It was going to be embarrassing to go back out there. I knew I must have put Noah off – there was no way he'd still fancy me after such a performance. But it was probably for the best. That was the plan, right? Don't fall for him, don't let him break your heart... Looking at the facts, two times I'd seen him, two times I'd lost consciousness. Coincidence or not, that wasn't good.

I took a deep breath and pushed my way through the toilet door, rehearsing the story in my head about being dehydrated.

Noah was waiting outside. I jumped when I saw him.

"Sorry," he said. "I didn't mean to startle you."

He looked gorgeous leaning against the wall, his eyes worried, mouth downturned. This was going to be hard, but I knew what I needed to do. I was already going crazy and I'd only met him a few days before.

"S'okay," I said, playing with a strand of my hair.

"I was worried about you."

I didn't look at his face. I didn't trust myself not to pass out again. "You shouldn't be. I'm fine."

"Poppy, can we talk?" He grabbed my hand, intertwining his fingers with mine. His touch burned, but I couldn't bring myself to pull my hand away.

"What about?" I shrugged my shoulders, trying to look casual.

"It's quite obvious, isn't it?" he said, temper flaring in his voice. "Can we talk about us?"

I mumbled something.

"What?"

"I said, there isn't an us. I only just met you."

He squeezed my hand tighter. "Don't be stupid. You must have sensed there's something between us. It's driving me mental. I can't stop thinking about you and I don't even know you. It's crazy. Just now, out there, when you looked at me, I thought I was going to explode. I know you felt it too." He searched my face for a reaction. "It's why you fainted, isn't it? You couldn't handle it."

I let his words sink in, trying to analyse logically what he'd just said to me. I was shaking. I felt so happy I wanted to dance down the road. He couldn't stop thinking about me! Me? Plain, sceptical little me. But the rational part of my head was screaming at me to ignore these emotions: *He will hurt you. He'll get bored. And most importantly…something is wrong here. This guy makes you sick.*

I forced my voice to go cold. "Nice line," I said. "Bet you use it on all the girls."

His face screwed up in what could only be described as pain. "You've got to be kidding me!"

"Did you honestly think I was stupid enough to fall for that?" I made my voice harder. "I'm not one of your groupies, you know."

The pain on his beautiful face turned immediately into rage. "Of course I know," he almost growled. "You know this isn't a line. I know you feel it too. You're just scared. Scared of whatever this is."

I laughed nastily, hating the sound of my own voice. "God, can you just listen to yourself? You sound like someone out of my mum's Mills and Boon books."

It was his turn to be humiliated. He blushed, hurt bleeding across his face. I felt awful. Hollow. But something was telling me this was the right thing to do. I had to protect myself. From whatever this – he – was.

"I completely overestimated you," he said. "You're not the person I thought you were at all." The words stabbed me. He withdrew his hand, and mine felt freezing without his touch.

I couldn't stand it – the way his face had changed from admiration to hatred so quickly. I wanted him back already. I ached for his affection.

"Look," I said, almost pleadingly, wishing I could undo what I'd just said, "I know I'm being a bitch and I'm sorry."

He glared back at me.

"It's just…I don't think you and me are very good for each other. We've only just met and we're already fighting."

"You're lying to yourself."

"I'm not."

"Yes you are. And you know you are."

I had to end this. Everything he said was true but I couldn't let myself fall for him. I would get hurt – badly hurt. I made my voice cold again.

"Noah, you just need to get over the fact that I DON'T FANCY YOU!" I shouted for effect. "I know that's probably never happened before, but deal with it."

He stepped back from me, disgust on his face.

"You're right," he said. "You are a bitch."

Then he skulked out of the corridor towards the exit, leaving me standing alone.

Dr. Beaumont stared at her computer screen, not daring to blink. She wasn't sure how long she'd been sitting there. Six hours? Maybe seven? A cup of cold coffee lay abandoned next to her keyboard, along with empty pretzel packets. This was no week to worry about dieting.

The laboratory was buzzing but she was concentrating too hard to notice the bustle of people around her. If she'd been able to drag her eyes from the screen, she might have noticed that most of them were staring at her, concerned looks on their faces.

Her focus was broken by that stupid assistant.

"Alright, Anita?" Rain's voice was remarkably chirpy considering the circumstances. And he'd called her "Anita" again, the idiot.

He placed a freshly made cup of coffee on her desk. "I thought you might need a refill."

She looked up at him, annoyed that she'd been distracted but grateful for the drink. "Thanks, Rain," she replied curtly, before turning back to the screen.

The monitor was full of green code. Complete nonsense to an outsider, but to Dr. Beaumont it was easier to read than an airport novel.

Rain pulled up a chair and sat astride it.

Again, she was forced to turn away from her monitor. "Yes?"

Rain looked nervous for once. "We were just wondering…"

Anita was really annoyed now. "You were just wondering what?"

"Well…er…people, I mean, myself and others… We were just interested to know if, you know, another reading had come up?"

Anita sighed. Of course they wanted to know. Everyone did. The Defence Secretary wanted a twenty-page report by midnight.

She leaned back and shook out her harshly scraped-back bun. It felt good. She ran her fingers through her hair and sighed again. "Not since last night."

Rain pulled his stool closer. His voice went down to a whisper. "And last night?" he asked, the whites of his eyes shining with fear. "This reading was…high up on the scale?"

Anita nodded. "It's a true match. Worst-case scenario. The shit-hitting-the-fan scenario you wrote essays about in training."

Rain gulped involuntarily. "And you think they've made…?"

She finished his sentence for him. "Physical contact? No doubt about it. You don't get these from chance encounters."

She pressed a button on her keyboard and a graph slid silently out of the printer. She passed it over to him, noticing her fingernails were still unfinished from that disrupted manicure the other day. "Here, look for yourself."

Rain held the paper away from himself and squinted, trying to read the pattern. He blinked a few times and held it further away. It fell into place. "Jesus H Christ."

Anita took the paper off him. "I know." She sipped her coffee and turned back to the monitor.

"But there's not been another reading since last night?"

"I've been staring at this for God-knows-how-long and got nothing."

"I can help if you want…?"

She considered it for a moment. If she were honest, she would be glad of the company. "Alright."

Rain pulled the stool even closer and peered at the coding. He couldn't believe she'd said yes. The others would never believe him. Right. Concentrate. Save the world, remember? He focused on the screen and let his eyes blur slightly like he'd been taught.

Anita sat silent next to him, hardly breathing.

He wasn't sure how long he'd been there but, out of nowhere, Rain saw a momentary flash on the screen.

He looked at Anita. Her eyes were wide.

"Did you…?"

"I saw."

Anita jumped off her chair and hit a large red button at the end of her desk. She began frantically typing indecipherable things into her keyboard, her fingers blurring with the speed of her work.

"Try and get some coordinates," she instructed, still typing.

Rain pushed his chair over to the next computer, logged on as quickly as possible and he too started bashing his keyboard in earnest.

"It's too late for an exact location."

"What? You're telling me we've lost them three times now?"

"I'm sorry. We just weren't there quick enough."

Dr. Beaumont fired directions over her shoulder. "Check the news. Anything that's happened in the north of Europe in the past twelve hours, I want to know about. Any flood, any fire, any odd death, no matter how unrelated, I want to know about it FIVE minutes ago."

Rain logged onto their newsfeed, stabbing in keywords before pressing return.

Headlines flashed up onto his screen and he quickly devoured each one before springing on the next. "Nothing's come up."

"That can't be possible."

"I'm telling you, no disasters… Not yet anyway."

Anita stopped typing. She lay her head down on the desk – suddenly vulnerable, everything stripped away. "We got lucky," she whispered, counting her breaths.

The latest reading slithered out of the printer. Rain snatched it and could see the pattern immediately.

"We definitely got lucky."

8

When I got home I cried harder than I'd ever cried before. I lay face down on my bed as my body emitted hollow wretched sobs. I closed my eyes to try and stem the tears but, whenever I did, I saw Noah's disgusted face, which created a fresh wave of hysteria.

At one point I became vaguely aware of my mother gawping at me – transfixed with anxiety over yet another development in my ever-dwindling mental health. I couldn't look at her and turned to face the wall to continue blubbing and gasping for air. And all because of a boy. Mum wouldn't believe it anyway. Last week I wasn't remotely interested in any male in a fifty-mile radius, yet now I was hysterically bawling over some silly guitarist I hadn't even kissed. There was no way she would understand. *I* didn't even understand.

There comes a point though, when you physically can't cry any more. The sobs slowly began to subside and turn into hiccups. I hugged my legs and practised my breathing until I was eventually calm enough to walk over to my dressing table. I sat down and dared myself to look into the mirror.

My dressing table has always been one of my favourite things – 1970s-style with a huge gilt mirror and tacky gold leaf. Right then, sinking down on the mini-stool, I wished I'd never got it. My reflection horrified me. My face was puffed up like I'd been through ten rounds of boxing, my eyes barely visible under the swelling. My hair was slicked back with tears and my general complexion resembled a blotched painting by a kid who likes using the colour red. A lot.

"Looking good, Poppy," I mumbled to myself.

I stared at myself for a long time, exhaustedly running through the past few days and trying to identify what the hell had happened. No wonder they called it a "crush" – I was a car wreck. I'd neglected all my carefully honed anti-men beliefs just because I'd met someone with floppy hair.

No, Noah had been right – it *was* more than that. What the hell was going on? I tried to convince myself that it didn't matter, that these feelings would pass. Without bothering to brush my teeth or wash my face, I clambered into my single bed and fell into an uneasy sleep.

I spent most of Tuesday at college in relative hiding without bumping into anyone. When the final bell went, I hurried out to meet Mum in the car park. Following the previous day's crying extravaganza, she'd booked me an emergency appointment with Dr. Ashley and at the time I'd been sobbing too hard to protest.

I spotted her, looking out worriedly from behind the steering wheel of her car. I felt a sudden surge of love for her. And then the inevitable surge of guilt. I hated that I made her worry more. Another reason why purging Noah from my life was a good idea, I told myself.

I slumped into the front seat, a strained smile across my face.

"Hello, Poppy dear. Good day at college?"

I stretched my smile wider. "Oh yes, brilliant day, thanks."

My response only drew a worried sigh. She knew I was lying. Parents' psychic abilities never failed to surprise me.

"Yes, well did you learn anything? I suppose that's the most important thing."

I nodded my head enthusiastically. "Yeah, loads," I said. "In Psychology we learned about this guy who showed violent videos to children and then gave them a doll afterwards to see if they beat the doll up."

Mum raised her eyebrows. "I see."

I turned the radio up to avoid any more of the third degree and we both stared out the windscreen in silence, pretending to enjoy the cheesy dance track pumping tirelessly out of Radio One. It was called something stupid like "Short Attention Span" by a "band" called ADHD. I'm not even kidding. Frank had been trying to make me listen to it for weeks.

When we arrived at the doctor's office, or mental health clinic, if I'm being honest, I opened the car door.

"Hang on," Mum said, tugging my shoulder.

"What is it?"

She dug in her handbag to retrieve Dr. Ashley's cheque. I looked down at the amount scribbled in my mum's neat cursive writing and felt a fresh surge of guilt. Not only was I making her feel awful, I was bankrupting her. Maybe I should have been paying more attention to what Dr. Ashley was saying instead of trying to outsmart him all the time.

"Thanks," I said, ashamed.

"I'll pick you up later."

"Cheers."

She leaned over and kissed my forehead gently before putting the car into gear. I clambered out awkwardly and made my way towards the imposing doors of the surgery.

The clinic tried very hard to be "normal" – if there was any real meaning to that word. The receptionist was always chirpy as you tried to ignore the high-security entrance process. As I hadn't completely lost it, I only ever went in for day sessions, but the place had lots of residential patients. The walls were painted a chipper yellow and there were fresh flowers everywhere to combat the distinct hospital smell. The waiting room even had current magazines – good ones as well, like *Vogue*, rather than the tattered ten-year-old issues of *Good Housekeeping* so commonplace in GP surgeries. It paid to go private, I supposed. They had to justify charging such huge amounts of money somehow. There was always this fake and very British let's-pretend-this-isn't-a-mental-hospital attitude here – you would smile and nod at each other in the waiting room, trying to ignore the bandaged wrists and scratched faces, while really thinking, *So what's wrong with their brain then?*

After about five minutes my name was called and I tentatively knocked on the door of Dr. Ashley's office, even though he was expecting me. Another weird and totally unnecessary social norm for going to the doctor's.

"Come in," I heard and I pulled open the door.

He was sitting in his normal chair, an old antique thing – the sort that fetches a lot of money on *Antiques Roadshow*. The rest of the room was pretty sparse. A few nondescript paintings hung on the magnolia walls, a PC sat on the corner of the desk. A square glass coffee table sat between Dr. Ashley and "my" chair. The telltale box of tissues was displayed neatly in the middle. I cringed when I remembered how many I'd got through when I'd been here in the past.

"Good afternoon, Poppy."

I sat down awkwardly and started scrunching my hands together, pretending I wasn't there. *This isn't happening. This isn't my life. I'm not really one of those people who need therapy.* "Afternoon."

We sat in silence for a good thirty seconds before he asked his next inevitable question. "And how are you today, Poppy?"

I gave the same stock answer. "Fine."

Another silence.

"But how are you really?"

I sighed. It was all so predictable. So forced. Although there wasn't a leather couch in the office, I could still picture myself lying on it, hand over my head, talking about some terrible childhood memory.

My thoughts turned to the hefty cheque folded in my jeans pocket and I forced myself to play along. "Well, I've had two fainting attacks in the past week."

Dr. Ashley nodded, almost unimpressed, like I'd just listed everything I'd had to eat that day or something. The only sign of his interest was his pen, frantically scribbling across his notepad.

"I see," he said, still scribbling. "And that's not…usual, is it?"

"Nope."

He finished writing and studied me over his notepad. I wished I could read it.

"And why do you think that is?"

Honestly. Maybe I should do a psychology degree. All you have to do is ask questions in a nice calm voice and you get a hundred and fifty quid an hour.

I shrugged my shoulders, playing the nonchalant teenager role. "Dunno."

This prompted another burst of notepad scrawling and I fidgeted as I waited for him to finish. I crossed my legs and uncrossed them.

"Your mother," he began, finally taking the initiative. "When she rang this morning she said you had your first of these attacks at a gig. Is that right?"

How did Mum know that? Dad must have told her. I cursed him under my breath.

"That's right," I said. "It was horrible. I puked and everything."

I didn't like the way the word "puked" sounded. It was crass. But it made Dr. Ashley flinch and I enjoyed that. I wasn't sure why.

"You were sick?" he asked, his hand picking up pace again across the secret notepad. "Hmmm, that's not happened before has it?"

"Nope."

"And the other attack? What was that like?"

"No puking. The usual. I think I'm going to die. It's horrible. Then I don't die."

Dr. Ashley was deep in thought, chewing the top of his pencil. This obviously wasn't part of his plan. I'd been getting better. I was a "success".

"And when the panic attacks happened…you did all the techniques I've taught you?"

I nodded.

"And you've been practising your mindfulness of breath?"

I nodded again. "Every morning."

He looked stumped. Maybe it didn't pay to go private after all.

We fell silent again. I shook my foot about and let him think things through. I was a little unimpressed. Usually he was so…sorted. He usually had all the answers.

"Has anything changed in the past week? Have you done anything differently that might have brought this on?"

My mind immediately went to Noah and I welled up again. But it was stupid. Noah couldn't be causing this. It didn't make sense. Anyway, even if he was, I couldn't tell Dr. Ashley about a *boy*. It would be too embarrassing.

He had caught the change in my face though. Dammit. I was going to need a cover story.

"Poppy, you know you can tell me anything. It's a safe environment here. I'm not here to judge you."

I knew he was right. I wanted to tell him. I wanted to make Mum's money worthwhile. But how could I? How could I honestly tell him *I think I'm going crazy because I fancy a boy*. It was laughable. Stupid.

So I took a deep breath and let the lie fall out of my mouth effortlessly.

"...Well..." I stammered, thinking of Noah and letting the tears come. "It's my mum...I just worry about her so much. I think we're in an emotionally exploitative relationship..."

He handed me the box of tissues and the session went on as normal.

9

The days passed, as they have a habit of doing. Weeks passed without anything of real note happening. Summer became autumn. It got cold. Only the most determined show-offs (Ruth) were still parading around in a skirt, showing off their blue legs. We finished *Romeo and Juliet* in English and moved onto World War I poetry. My panic attacks stopped. Whether they were Noah-related or not, I had no idea. All in all, life returned to normal. Whatever that was, anyway.

I still thought about him. Far more than was appropriate. During the daytime I was okay. I filled my days with seeing friends, doing coursework, helping Mum cook dinner – normal boring teenage stuff. But at night-time my body physically ached for him. I would climb into bed, determinedly telling myself I wouldn't think about him, and yet the moment I turned out the light, he was there. I replayed every moment I'd spent with him, analysed every word he'd said. I trembled with humiliation when I remembered my behaviour.

I knew it was just a crush. I knew it would pass. Well, I hoped it was just a crush. I hoped it would pass.

On one not particularly special day, Ruth dropped the bombshell.

The four of us were sitting round our favourite table in the canteen. It was next to the windows and radiators so we could keep toasty while perving on the footballers outside. Prime college real estate. It was pretty dismal outside, the usual English crappy day. The drizzle was constant, mixed with the sort of wind that immediately blows your hair onto your lip gloss. I was snuggled in my favourite hoodie and we were playing Cheat.

I was doing quite well, with only five cards left, when I heard Ruth speak.

"Growing Pains are playing Band Night tonight," she said, putting two cards face down on the table. "Two sixes," she added.

Noah's band was playing tonight. I was too stunned to call Cheat. "What?" I said.

The other two looked up in vague interest.

"They're on at nine." Ruth ruffled her hair with her hands. "They've made it a Friday because someone's renting out the place tomorrow for a Super Sweet Sixteenth. Will told me you should all come along."

Ruth and Will had been "seeing each other" since the infamous night at the Lock and Key. God knows exactly what that meant in Ruth terms, but we knew she had slept with him numerous times as she had bored us with all the disgusting details afterwards. She didn't seem to realize, a), how uninterested we were in her sex life, and b), how intimidating it was to hear about when the rest of us hadn't slept with anyone yet.

I'd been using their developing relationship to spy third-hand on Noah, but it seemed Ruth spent most of her time "alone" with Will rather than hanging out with the band.

"I'm up for going," Amanda said, surprising us all. We looked at her, shocked. "Well, Johnno is going," she muttered, before retreating back behind her cards.

I turned, open-mouthed, to Lizzie. I didn't want to go. Surely Lizzie wouldn't want to go?

Well, okay, of course she would want to go.

"I'm in," Lizzie said, confirming my fears. She put down a card rather sheepishly. "One six."

I looked at my hand and saw I had two sixes, meaning either Ruth or Lizzie was cheating. But I was still too shell-shocked to call it. I couldn't go. I couldn't see Noah.

"Well, I'm going," Ruth said. "Will's always on such a sexual high after playing a gig. It's amazing."

She didn't say it with the slightest bit of irony, and I wondered for the millionth time why we were friends.

They were all now looking at me, so I returned my eyes to my hand.

"Poppy?" Lizzie asked.

"Mmm?" I peeled off two random cards and slapped them down. "Two sevens. Amanda, your turn."

But she didn't play. I could feel all their eyes on me.

"Poppy, are you coming?"

Quick, brain. Think of an excuse. Anything.

"I can't, guys," I said. "Tonight I'm making a cherry pie from scratch."

What the hell? That was the worst lie I'd ever heard.

"You're what?" Ruth looked mildly entertained. She leaned forward over the table. "I didn't know you baked, Poppy."

I nodded manically. Well, I might as well run with the lie now I'd started it. Anything to get me out of going. "Yeah, I love baking, you know that. I'm really excited about trying out this new recipe I got in a newspaper supplement."

"You're lying," Lizzie declared.

I switched from furious nodding to furious head shaking. "No I'm not, honest," I said, wide-eyed. "I just really enjoy baking. You guys don't know every little thing about me. There's loads you don't know." I thought of Noah and all the feelings I'd carefully secreted from them. I wasn't lying there. Not entirely.

"Poppy, I've seen you burn a frozen pizza," Lizzie said. "You hate cooking! Why don't you want to come to Band Night? You're usually really up for it."

I needed more lies. "I just don't feel like it, that's all."

"But it's Friday night. It's live music. It's the only half decent thing to do in this stupid town."

"Yeah but..." I was out.

Ruth was watching me critically. "Are you sure it's not because you're scared to see a certain someone?" she asked, flicking her cards out one by one.

I felt myself flush. "What?" I said, feigning ignorance. "What are you talking about?"

"Noah," Ruth replied. "It's obvious you had a little thing for him a while back."

God, I hated her. "Huh?"

"You don't want to go because he didn't fancy you and it broke your heart."

I pushed my chair back to give myself enough personal space for a rant.

"What. The. Hell?" I said. "I never fancied bloody Noah. He's a complete loser and if you don't believe me I'll go to this crappy Band Night. You're COMPLETELY wrong about me fancying him—"

"CHEAT," Lizzie yelled triumphantly.

Seriously? There was no fooling that girl.

"I'm not lying, Lizzie. I don't fancy Noah."

She shook her head. "No, cheat as in Cheat," she said, pointing at the cards. "You don't have two sevens." She flicked over my fraudster pair. "Ha ha. Now you have to pick up the whole pile."

I sighed and scooped them up.

10

I agonized over my appearance that evening. I tried on outfit after outfit, discarding them one after the other. I really didn't want to go and wished I'd thought of a legitimate excuse. After a painstaking hour, I finally decided on dark blue skinny jeans, a black strappy top and lashings of silver jewellery. I spent another half-hour attempting to create something exotic with my hair, before giving up and wearing it down around my shoulders.

Dad was at the bottom of the stairs when I left my bedroom.

"You look nice, dear," he said, shuffling past with the newspaper. "You going anywhere special?"

I shrugged. "Only Band Night…again."

"Well, you're very dressed up. Are you trying to impress a certain someone?" He looked at me with genuine intrigue.

"Eww," I said, making my way down the stairs. "No way. You know all the boys here are uber-losers. They're either posh grammar-school rugby snobs or whingey immature acne-ridden idiots."

"Of course, of course, how could I forget?" He began to shuffle towards the living room to scout out his favourite armchair. "Well, you look lovely."

I chewed a piece of hair. "Thanks, Dad."

"Be back by twelve or your mother will worry."

"Yeah yeah."

I grabbed my bag and let myself out.

I wrapped my leather jacket tightly around myself as I walked to meet Lizzie at the corner. It was darkish already and the wind was cold. Summer was definitely over. It was that twilight time when it's dark enough to see inside people's houses, but they haven't thought to close the curtains yet. The road I met Lizzie on was called Park Drive – a private road where only the wealthiest could afford to live. I walked slowly, dawdling outside the particularly massive houses, trying to get a look at the people living inside them.

Lizzie was waiting for me impatiently, tapping her toe with annoyance. It was just us two walking tonight. Ruth was "going with the band"– she'd been boasting about it the whole afternoon. And Amanda had stunned us all by saying her and Johnno were walking there together.

"You're late, fellow spinster," Lizzie yelled, her arms tightly crossed against her chest to keep the cold out.

I jogged up to her. "I think we're a bit too young to be calling ourselves spinsters." I gave her a quick hello hug. "Sorry for being late. I was rich-people perving again."

Lizzie shook her head. "Again? We need a new meeting spot so you might be on time for once."

I hooked my arm through Lizzie's. She looked pretty. She'd kinked her blonde hair and was wearing electric blue eyeliner, the sort I couldn't pull off in a million years. "You look nice."

"Cheers, m'dears. I nicked the eyeliner off my sister."

As we walked, I thought about Lizzie calling us spinsters. She'd never really showed any interest in boys, though she got plenty of attention.

I wondered. "Lizzie?"

We stopped to cross a road.

"Yes?"

"Why don't you have a boyfriend?"

I wasn't sure why I'd asked. We didn't often have in-depth talks about guys. Weird, I know, but Lizzie seemed to be as picky as me, so neither of us had ever really had a boyfriend. Boys were a topic we laughed about, discussing who was and who wasn't fit, but we'd never really deeply discussed our shared single-status.

Lizzie watched the road, which was jam-packed with traffic. She looked a little shocked at my directness and I regretted asking her.

"That's a question and a half," she answered, looking left and right.

"I was just wondering. Well, you never seem particularly interested in guys but they *like* you. And it occurred to me you've never done anything about it."

The sun had almost completely set. All the cars' headlights were on, creating two hazy lanes of red and white lights blurring past. It was too busy to cross and we were going to have to walk to the pedestrian crossing. But I waited for Lizzie to answer first. She was switching her weight from one foot to another, contemplating her response.

"I dunno," she said finally. "It's not like I don't want a boyfriend. It's just…and don't you dare bloody laugh at me…I haven't felt that thing…"

Now I was really shocked. Lizzie? A romantic?

"What exactly is that *thing*?" I asked.

She looked bewildered. "I dunno. I'm not some sappy romcom-loving girl, but I believe in…*it*…you know? The One. And I really believe that one day I'll just be going about my day-to-day life, probably looking like a turd, and then I'll just meet this guy – completely by coincidence. And I'll know straight away he's it, and we're going to live happily ever after and grow old and wrinkly together."

I opened my mouth in astonishment.

"And it may sound stupid, but I honestly don't see the point in going out with someone if you don't feel like that about them. And I know we're only seventeen, and we're supposed to be kissing the frogs before we get to the prince and all that bollocks, but boys are just such…hard work that I really don't see the point unless it's *it*, you know?"

I was silenced by her words. She certainly had a way with them. I remembered the night I met Noah and found myself agreeing with her.

The cars were still rushing past us, blindly ignoring the

30 mph speed limit. I decided humour was the best way out of this situation.

"So who would have thought?" I said, nudging her in the ribs. "You? A hard-nosed, cynical, wannabe journo with such a...romantic side?"

She hit me. "Shut up, you. I know you've also got some stupid little princess trapped inside, dying to be rescued by some fit bloke with floppy hair who tells you he wants to marry you."

I did shut up. She didn't realize how close I was to becoming that soppy.

We were late so didn't have to queue and the bouncers ushered us past the red rope immediately. The moment we pushed our way through the double doors, we were greeted by steam rolling off the packed dance floor. The place was heaving. Word had obviously got out that Growing Pains were good – despite having one of the most stupid names in teen band history.

Lizzie and I scanned the crowd for friendly faces. Most people were already milling round the stage, staking out a front row spot.

With last time's panic attack still a raw memory, I leaned over to shout in Lizzie's ear. "Is it okay if we stay near the back?"

"Are you kidding? Of course! I don't want a repeat performance of your joyful fainting fits."

I realized then that Lizzie was my best friend in the world. "Thanks."

It was impossible to find anyone, so Lizzie and I gave up and fought our way to the bar.

As she ordered, I tried to mentally prep myself for seeing Noah again. I really didn't want to be near him. But at the same time I wanted time to hurry up so I could look at his perfect face once more.

Lizzie handed me a rum and Coke and we drank them while looking for our friends. Some of the gothy people from college were dancing to the background music, casting their elaborately decorated bodies into interesting shapes. Some guy was pointing and laughing at them. He was clutching two beers and wearing a polo shirt with the collar deliberately pulled up – looking completely out of place for Band Night. The bloke was now imitating the goths' dancing while miming slitting his wrists. His two accompanying mates shrieked with laughter.

"What an arse," Lizzie commented, spotting them.

"I know." I nodded. "I mean, why bother coming if it's not your sort of thing?"

The main piss-taker bloke had, thankfully, gone unnoticed by the goth group, who were mainly dancing with their eyes closed and waving their hands in the air. Okay, they did look a little ridiculous. But they were goths. That was the point!

The guy turned round, imitating someone who was spinning repeatedly to the soundtrack of Megadeth.

My mouth fell open. I grabbed Lizzie's hand. "Oh my God, it's Frank."

Lizzie looked at him, confused. "Who the hell is Frank?"

"My friend from English."

She looked over and wrinkled her nose. "You're *friends* with that guy?"

Frank saw me. I raised my hand in a half wave. He raised his bottle, then whispered to his friends. The three of them began making their way over, Frank half-jogging, a smile on his face.

"Oh great," Lizzie said. "They're coming over."

"Sorry."

"You should be."

Frank was the first to reach us. "So, Poppy Lawson – this is your world?" He raised one unimpressed eyebrow.

"What are you doing here, Frank?"

He gestured towards the group of goths with his beer-holding hand. "Just checking out the local…talent. Seriously, this place is better than a circus freak show."

He really could be an arse sometimes.

His friends caught up and put their arms around Frank's shoulders in that cheery we're-all-blokes-us way that I hated.

"Alright, mate? Who have we got here then?" They quickly did a blatant full body scan of us both. Lizzie shuddered.

"This is Poppy. I do English with her." I didn't offer my hand to shake. "And this is…" He gestured towards Lizzie.

I finished his sentence. "This is my friend Elizabeth."

She didn't offer her hand either. The boys just nodded.

Frank took a sip of his beer. "This is Simon and Jedd," he said, clapping them on the back.

"Let me guess," I said dryly. "You all play rugby together?"

Frank looked surprised. "How did you know?"

"Seriously. Why are you here?"

Simon and Jedd had already turned their backs on us. Obviously Lizzie and I didn't have enough cleavage out to pass the full-body-scan test.

"Well," Frank said. "You're always going on about how I should experience *real music*. So I thought I may as well come along and prove to myself how crap it really is."

I crossed my arms. "You honestly didn't have anything better to do?"

"I'm thinking of it as an educational experience. Who knows? I might like it."

I shook my head.

"Anyway," he continued, "as I've made the effort, you should educate yourself too. Come to this rave Jedd is having, it's going to be awesome. His parents are super-loaded and we're setting up decks in his garden."

I pushed him friendlily, spilling a bit of his beer. "Frank. I can honestly say I would rather die than go to a rave."

"You don't know what you're missing."

"I don't need to know."

"But how do you know you won't like it?"

"I just know."

"You're stubborn."

"You're an idiot."

"Shh," Lizzie interrupted, as the club was plunged into darkness. "The band's starting."

The stage was cast into a vibrant white light as the band walked on. Everyone in the room started cheering and immediately I felt my stomach flip and my vision go hazy.

Not here. Not again. Please.

I staggered a little and bumped into Frank.

"Woah, Poppy, you okay?" he asked, putting his hands on my shoulders to steady me. I embarrassingly found myself clutching at his shirt in an attempt to keep balanced.

"I'm fine. Just a bit dizzy."

I felt a different, firmer grip on my shoulders. Lizzie was steering me towards her.

"She's fine," she barked at Frank. She turned and gave me a subtle but sharp slap across the face. "Snap out of it."

I was about to get in a mood and slap Lizzie back, when I realized I could breathe again. Her tough love had worked. I was okay. I took another gulp of air to check. Still fine. Thank God.

Disaster narrowly averted, we turned our attention back to the band. Ryan, the lead singer I'd talked to in the Lock and Key, was yelling into the microphone and stirring up the crowd as the band tuned up. His offstage shyness had vanished. I took another deep breath and let myself look at Noah. And there he was, looking as ludicrously good as I'd remembered. He was ignoring the baying crowd and concentrating on tuning his electric guitar. His dark hair flopped into his eyes. He wore dark jeans and a light-green checked shirt with the sleeves rolled up. Yeah, okay, he looked amazing.

Lizzie interrupted my illicit thoughts. "I can't see the others anywhere."

"I think we're going to have to wait until afterwards before we find them," I replied, my eyes still on Noah.

"Well at least we've got *him* for company." She pointed towards Frank, who was standing with us instead of his jock friends. Frank's attitude had changed. His green eyes were narrowed. He was alternately staring at Noah, and then studying the hordes of screaming girls flinging themselves against the stage in a desperate bid to get his attention. Frank's chest puffed out involuntarily and I saw him flex his large rugby biceps. I giggled. Frank obviously wasn't used to such competition.

Without any introduction, the band launched into their first song and everyone went crazy. The crowd started jumping and yelling along. They were even better than last time, more polished and tight. And their sound was infectious. I'm usually one of those girls who refuse to dance. I much prefer standing at the side, nodding my head in a hopefully nonchalant cool-looking way. But tonight my body was moving to the beat of its own accord. I looked at Lizzie. She was the same.

I finally managed to spot Ruth over everyone's heads. She was right near the stage, in front of Will, dancing seductively and far too slowly to the music. It was practically a striptease. She shimmied down to the floor, gyrating her crotch upwards and exposing almost all of her flesh. Will's eyes were wide as he tried to concentrate on his bass playing. I nudged Lizzie and pointed out the spectacle. Her eyes went from Ruth to Will and she dissolved into laughter.

As the band went straight into their second song, I turned to Frank, who, to my surprise, was also dancing along.

"Do my eyes deceive me?" I asked him, bringing my face close so he could hear me. "Or are you actually enjoying yourself?"

"They're not bad," he shouted back. "Though that guitarist looks like a right idiot. How full of it is he?"

We both looked at Noah. His eyes were half-closed as his fingers trembled up and down the neck of his guitar. A group of girls were screaming at him, Beatlemania-style, but he remained aloof. A resolute-looking blonde girl wasn't screaming however. She stood right beneath him, her hands clutching the sides of the stage. She was one of those girls that made you feel sick she was so unnervingly beautiful. I caught a glimpse of the side of her through a gap in the crowd as she peered up at Noah through her butter-blonde hair and slowly nodded her gorgeous head to the music, looking how I always tried and failed to look. For one brief moment she caught Noah's eye and his face broke into a broad grin, displaying his beautiful white teeth. My stomach flip-flopped and I turned away, not wanting to see any more.

"See, he's a right idiot," Frank continued. "Why is he doing that eyes half-closed thing? Who does he think he is? You're not in Kasabian, mate."

To my surprise I found myself laughing. "You're just jealous because you haven't got any groupies."

Frank puffed out his chest again. "What the hell? Yes I do. You should see the girls who come and watch me play rugby."

"No thank you."

"There's loads of them. They all cheer for me from the sidelines."

I grimaced. "Let me guess. None of them wear coats even though it's freezing. They all wear a face-load of make-up even though they're only standing in a field. And afterwards they corner you in the pub, wearing oversized rugby shirts as minidresses, and try and impress you with their knowledge of the game."

Frank looked confused. "How did you know?"

I rolled my eyes. "What happened to you, Frank? I thought we bonded over our mutual hatred of people like that?"

"Hey. I know they're silly, Poppy. I don't actually like them."

"You don't?"

"No. But come on! It makes me feel pretty good about myself. Even if they do have a combined IQ of about minus 208."

"That's better."

He finished the last of his beer and threw the cup on the ground before grabbing both my hands. "Come on, let's dance."

I don't normally dance in public but, with Frank, I didn't feel embarrassed. He twirled me around and kept turning me upside down. Even Lizzie began to thaw to him. At one moment he grabbed her and spun her round like a dad trying to make his daughter dizzy in the park. She screamed but you could tell she was loving it. Then Frank started ballroom-dancing me round the back of the club.

"You know, don't say 'I told you so' but I think I actually like this music," he said, twirling me under his arm.

"I told you so."

"Shut up. Maybe it's just the beer."

He dipped me, and I threw my head back, laughing.

"People are going to think we're crazy," I protested. "We must look nuts."

He shook his head. "Nah. We just look like we're having fun."

And he was right. I couldn't help but notice I was getting quite a few jealous looks from other girls. That was the thing with Frank. His looks and cheeky charm allowed him to get away with the most cringey of activities – even stupid dancing.

Frank spun and dipped me again. As I looked back, I could see the stage upside down. And I saw Noah's face. Our eyes met instantly and Noah hit a bum note on his guitar.

He looked furious. Frank pulled me back upright and I strained my neck to look at Noah once more. Our eyes met again and I could see hatred burning in his. He continued to play but gave me the most disgusted look before returning his attention towards his groupies.

I immediately stopped having fun.

"Let's stop dancing. I feel stupid," I told Frank.

He shrugged his shoulders. "Fair enough. I should probably go and find my mates anyway."

Shamefaced, I returned to Lizzie.

"Your mate Frank is actually pretty funny."

"He's alright."

"I think he likes you."

I shook my head. "Nah. It's not like that."

And we watched the rest of the set in silence.

Amanda found us just as the band was finishing. She excitedly made her way through the crowd, clutching Johnno's hand.

"There you are," she squealed, her black hair damp with sweat. "We've been looking for you for ages."

We both gave her a hug and nodded at Johnno.

"It's Poppy's fault," Lizzie said. "She made us late."

"Again?"

"Hey. I'm not always late."

Amanda pushed her hair back from her forehead and turned towards the band, who were raking in the applause.

"They were amazing, weren't they? I reckon they could really go places."

Lizzie and I nodded in unison.

"Really good," I agreed.

"Ruth's around here somewhere. We were chatting to her before the set started."

We turned and saw Ruth still in her spot at the front. Will was sitting at the side of the stage with Ruth clamped between his legs. They were kissing, their hands all over each other.

Lizzie wrinkled her nose. "Eww."

I nodded. "Double eww."

As the crowd continued to clap and cheer, I watched Noah. He was smiling again, surveying the crowd contentedly. My heart started to thump but I took a deep breath and managed to regain control.

Then, for the tiniest second, so quickly I could easily have missed it, I saw him look at me. He grimaced slightly. Then he held out his hand to the beautiful blonde girl in the front row.

Time went into slow motion as Noah plucked her from the crowd. Everyone stared as she took his hand and clambered gracefully onto the stage to join him. Then my heart sank as Noah wrapped his arms around her waist, pulled her gently to him, and kissed her.

My eyes stung as I watched, unable to tear them away. The crowd, re-energized by the grand gesture, cheered them on and they kissed for about thirty seconds before breaking apart. Noah then took her hand and raised it into the air. Everyone screamed and clapped.

I felt sick.

"Who's that girl with Noah?" Lizzie asked, her gossip-hungry eyes on the new couple.

"Her name's Portia," Amanda said. "The band introduced us earlier. I think she's been seeing Noah the past week or so."

People had begun to leave. They were trickling past, bumping into us every few seconds as they exited into the cold night air.

Noah and Portia sat onstage next to Ruth and Will and started kissing again. The burning behind my eyes intensified and I focused on the sticky wooden floor.

"Is she nice?" Lizzie asked.

Johnno answered. "She went to my primary school," he said. "She was alright. Her family are minted though. She lives on Park Drive and goes to the grammar school. I think her dad invented Listerine mouthwash or something."

Park Drive? I could have been looking into her house earlier tonight.

"Listerine? Wow. I use that," said Lizzie.

I listened to my friends discussing what they would spend all their money on if they were a mouthwash heiress, while I focused on breathing and holding in tears.

By the time they'd finished, all agreeing a swimming pool would be the first purchase, the club was mostly empty.

I made myself look up again and saw that Ruth and

Will had managed to disentangle themselves and were coming over.

"You came," she said, nodding towards me and Lizzie. "We thought you hadn't bothered."

"We just got here late," Lizzie said. "Couldn't find you before the gig started." She turned to Will. "Great set by the way."

Will looked like he'd won the lottery. He had his arm around Ruth proudly, like she was the top prize in a raffle. "Cheers," he said. "Well, I had Ruth to spur me on."

I remembered Ruth's stripper dancing and it lightened me a little. I tried not to smirk.

Lizzie was obviously remembering the same thing. "Yep, you definitely did."

"So what are you guys up to?" Ruth asked. "I think the band are heading to a late bar if you fancy joining?" She turned back to Noah and Portia, who were STILL kissing. "Well," she said. "If we can yank those two apart."

Ryan bounded over to join in the conversation. "Alright?" he said. "How did we do then?"

I tried to gulp down the enormous lump in my throat and act normal. "You did good." I said. "Very good."

His eyes lit up. "You think so?"

I nodded.

"Wow, thanks."

"Where you heading now?" I asked him. I figured distracting myself from Noah's new conquest was the only way I'd be able to get through the next ten minutes.

"Going for a few celebratory pints if you fancy joining?"

I shook my head. "I've got to get home," I lied.

His face dropped. "That's a shame. A whole load of us are going after we pack up."

"Who's that then?" Lizzie asked.

"Erm. Just me and the rest of the band. I think Noah's bringing that Portia girl he's with."

Well, I definitely wasn't going to go now, was I?

Lizzie looked at me. "Sounds fun. You in?"

I fake-yawned. "Sorry. I'm knackered. Ruth's going though, isn't she?"

Lizzie wanted to stay out with the others but Amanda and Johnno wanted to get home, so I decided to go with them. Any excuse to get out of the place. We said our goodbyes and started towards the door. For some stupid reason I made myself look back at the stage and saw Noah and Portia had stopped kissing. She was leaning towards his ear, whispering something suggestive, no doubt. But he was staring at me. He caught my eye and I saw him smirk, in an annoying self-satisfied way. It was too much. The tears I'd been holding back began to spill down my face.

I cried silently on the way home next to an oblivious Amanda and Johnno, grateful the dark was hiding my embarrassment.

The next day I felt different.

Maybe it was the healing power of crying-induced sleep. Maybe the logical part of my brain was finally winning over. Or maybe enough was enough and I just wanted to be Poppy again. Either way, when I woke up, I had only one thought. Get over it.

I'd cried too much over Noah. It was suddenly clear. I'd wasted tears and hours of anxiety on what? A boy. A stupid boy. That wasn't who I was. I remembered that day on the common when I'd promised myself not to get involved and was annoyed at my lack of resolve. I hadn't shut him out. And now, as predicted, I felt terrible. It served me right really.

When I remembered him kissing Portia my body responded unfavourably to the memory. My chest tightened and tears welled up. But I took a deep breath, exhaled and let the emotion leave my body.

"I will not let that boy make me feel crap ever again," I said aloud. And I believed myself. Finally, after all these weeks, I had gained some perspective and felt strong. I was sure if I were to see him again, my body wouldn't respond as it had before. It had only taken weeks of torment and constant crying. Not great. But I'd got there in the end.

Feeling better than I'd done in ages, I skipped downstairs to greet Mum and Dad for breakfast. Mum was stirring something on the hob and Dad was already buried in the weekend paper.

"Mmm, something smells good," I said, announcing my arrival.

"Eggs in five minutes," Mum replied.

"Yum. Thank you."

I got out some of the posh orange juice we're only allowed on weekends and poured myself a generous glass, before sitting next to Dad.

"So what's going on in the world?" I asked, taking a large gulp.

"You know. The usual. Complete misery." His stock answer.

"Wars and bombs?"

"Nope, not today. More politicians ruining everything."

"Same old then."

"What are you up to today?" He turned over a page of his paper.

I thought about it. "I might go for a walk. It looks pretty nice outside. Then I've got some Psychology coursework." I made a face.

"Learning anything interesting?"

"Not really. Psychology sounds a lot more interesting than it actually is."

Dad looked at me over the paper. "I'm afraid that's the same with most things in life."

Mum arrived at our sides, brandishing plates piled high with luscious yellow scrambled eggs.

"Oi," she said, putting a plate down in front of my father. "It's far too early in the morning to be so pessimistic."

"But it's true!" I said, taking a bite of toast.

"That's no excuse. You're supposed to be happy and positive when you're young, then learn from our mistakes and not make them again."

"That's not how it works. We just relive your mistakes, try and ensure our children don't do the same, but they end up like us anyway."

Mum turned to Dad, frowning. "It's your fault she's so cynical," she snapped. "Where else would she get this from?"

He just took a mouthful of egg and retreated back inside the paper.

It was a nice breakfast. Not just the food, but the vibe. I felt good after my Noah epiphany and Mum seemed to sense I'd come out of whatever "phase" I'd been going through. She didn't even mention Dr. Ashley and, for once, things were how they were supposed to be. After I'd helped clear the dishes, I ran upstairs to chuck some clothes on.

The house phone rang and I picked it up on my way out.

"Hello?"

"Poppy, how are you? I've not seen you in ages."

It was my sister, Louise. Just hearing her voice made me smile.

"I'm good. Same old exciting Middletown."

"Ahh, it's not that bad."

"It's alright for you, you've escaped."

She laughed. Louise met her husband at uni and they got married straight after graduation. Maybe that's romantic. I wasn't sure. Sometimes I wondered about what would have happened if she went to a different uni, would she have met and married someone else? Or would she have bumped into Dave, her husband, another way?

"Is Mum in? I need to discuss Christmas with her."

"Already?"

"Already. Dave's mum is getting itchy about what sized turkey to buy and wants to know if we're going to hers or ours."

"Ergh, come here! Anyway, I'll just go get her."

"Call me soon for a proper chat."

"Will do."

I yelled for Mum, waited for her to pick up the other phone, and then called out I was leaving.

You could tell autumn had arrived by the air. I sat on my favourite bench, at the top of the common, and felt the slight chill in the breeze. I had the place to myself again. I stretched out on my back, closed my eyes, and let calmness overtake me. The sun was just about warm enough and I listened to the birdsong as I lay with my eyes shut. I smiled as I felt my body delve into half-awake-half-asleep mode.

I'm not sure how long I'd been lying there when I felt cold on my face. It had been plunged into shadow. I opened my eyes and squinted to see who was responsible for blocking my sun. And I almost fell off the bench in surprise.

It was Noah.

"Poppy?"

I struggled to get upright as I tried to imagine why on earth he was there. He watched me, amused, none of the nastiness of the previous night in his expression.

"How come whenever I see you you're never vertical?"

I analysed my body's reactions to him as I sat up like a normal person. My heart was beating slightly faster but he had shocked me. Other than that…no…everything seemed normal. That was good. My epiphany had obviously worked.

"What the hell are you doing here?" I hadn't forgotten his horrid smirking and wasn't prepared to be overly friendly.

"I was about to ask you the same thing." He gestured to the space next to me. "Do you mind if I sit down?"

I shook my head and he sat. Not close though. In fact, if he'd sat any further away he'd have fallen onto the muddy ground.

"I always come here," I answered, still shell-shocked at his sudden appearance. "It's my favourite place in the world." I turned to look at him, holding my breath to ensure my body behaved itself. He stared back at me.

"That's so weird," he said. "I'm up here all the time too."

We both contemplated the coincidence silently.

"Where do you live?" I asked.

"On Green Acre Drive."

"So just round the corner then?"

"How about you?"

"Ash Road." I thought about it. "I suppose the common is just one of those places you only know about if you live nearby."

Noah nodded. I risked another quick look at him, trusting my new-found strength. He was still gorgeous, even though he'd obviously dressed not expecting to bump into anyone. He was wearing a baggy pair of jeans with a hole in the knee and a grey woolly jumper, and his hair was dishevelled and standing on end. Anyone else would have looked a bit ropey, but he managed to pull off the scruffy look. Then I realized I also hadn't been expecting to see anyone and panic set in. I wasn't wearing a scrap of make-up, my hair hadn't been washed and I was wearing a giant hoodie emblazoned with the logo for a now-embarrassing band I used to worship back when I was fifteen. I tried to rake my hair back with my fingers and we sat together in silence. Enough had been said already. It was awkward. Horribly awkward.

Noah eventually broke the silence.

"I can't believe you're here," he said, looking at me. "This is just too weird."

I couldn't believe he was speaking to me after what I'd last said to him. Maybe now he was with Portia he wasn't upset any more. The thought made me feel a little ill.

The words came out of my mouth before I even knew I was going to say them. "Noah, I'm really sorry."

He raised an eyebrow. "For what?"

The words continued to gush out. "I was a bitch. I'm not usually like that. Ever. Okay, well sometimes. But, anyway, I've not been able to stop thinking about what happened and I feel awful about it. I've not said sorry. But I am. So... sorry, I guess."

I held my breath as I waited for his reply.

He looked out over the view and I felt stupid – and also very aware of how greasy my hair was.

"This really is too weird," he said, still focused on the distance.

"Why?"

When he turned back I got the full force of those dark eyes. He stared at me searchingly and I stared right back. My heart was quickening a little, but no fainting spell yet.

"It's weird because I come up here when I need to think. And for the past couple of weeks all I could think about was you."

I gulped, not quite believing my innocent walk had brought this boy back into my life. So intensely. So quickly.

"In fact I came up here to clear my head after last night. I'd been getting better at *not* thinking about you until I saw you yesterday. And then to find you here is very strange."

I still didn't say anything.

"Why were you lying on the bench by the way?" he asked. "It's not a bed, you know."

I smiled. "It was comfortable."

"I could see that."

"I wasn't expecting to see anyone. Which is why I look like crap, by the way."

He stared at me again, and then, very slowly, he tucked a loose strand of my hair behind my ear. "You don't look like crap."

I blushed.

Not able to handle the intensity, I turned back to the view, trying to collect my thoughts. More silence fell. And it was still awkward.

"So that guy you were dancing with last night..." His voice had an edge of anger to it now. "...Is he your boyfriend?"

That's when I burst out laughing.

"What?"

I was unable to answer for a moment, still laughing. "Are you being serious?"

Noah looked baffled. "Umm. Yes. Why? What's so funny?"

"That wasn't my boyfriend." I shook my head, trying to compose myself. "That was Frank. Honestly, if you met him you would know immediately he wasn't my boyfriend."

Noah's face remained confused. "Why?"

I threw my head back. "God! Frank is like my anti-type. I only know him from English and our whole relationship is based on torturing each other."

He didn't look convinced. "It didn't look like you were torturing each other last night," he said, through slightly gritted teeth.

I remembered the dancing and Noah seeing us. I suppose it had looked suspect, if you hadn't known we were just mucking about.

I shrugged. "We were just dancing. In fact he usually hates that kind of music. You should take it as a compliment…" Then I remembered Portia and got indignant. "ANYWAY, what's it to you who I dance with? Surely you were too busy sucking the face off that rich cow to even notice? By the way, public displays of affection are not cool."

The anger in Noah's face had gone and his devastating playful grin returned.

I, however, remained angry. "What?"

"Are you jealous, Poppy?"

I was rumbled. "Shut up. No I'm not. I just don't like people snogging in public. It's disgusting." I fixed him with a glare. "*You're* disgusting."

Instead of getting cross, he shuffled up closer to me on the bench. I stared at the disappearing space between us.

"I think you're jealous."

"I think you're a man-whore."

It was his turn to burst out laughing. "What on earth is a man-whore?"

"It's what people say about you," I explained, not sure why I was telling him this. "They say you go through women like incontinent people get through loo roll."

Why did I have to bring up incontinence? Noah didn't seem the slightest bit angry at the personal attack I was launching though. In fact, he was still grinning infuriatingly. "So is Portia your latest conquest then?" I waited for his answer with bated breath.

Noah leaned closer so our faces were almost touching. I melted a little.

"Would you be upset if she was?" he whispered.

Of course I would be bloody upset. I kept my face close but looked down.

"I don't care what you do," I lied. "It's your business."

Noah sat back, looking out at the view again. "So you wouldn't feel anything if I told you I was just using her to make you feel jealous," he asked casually.

I replied equally casually. "Nope," I lied again. "Although any feminist might want to have a few harsh words with you for being a complete arse wipe. Poor girl." Another lie.

Noah rolled his eyes. "Poor girl indeed. She's just using me too. She doesn't care the slightest bit about who I am. She just likes the image of having a rock god on her arm."

"Noah. I hate to be the one to tell you this but you're not a rock god. You're just a guitarist in one of the worst-named bands I've ever heard of."

At that, he grabbed my hand and clutched it hard. I looked down at our entwined fingers and felt an insane pulse of energy rush through me. It almost hurt but it was also amazing. I looked into his black eyes and got lost.

"Poppy," he whispered, still clasping my hand.

"Something is happening here and I would really appreciate it if you would stop pretending it isn't." My breath shortened. He continued. "I'm not saying you have to marry me, or even go on a date with me. But could you just go for a coffee with me or something and we can try and work out what is going on?"

I paused for a moment, and then sighed. "Okay." Another brilliant smile and dolphins started diving through my belly. "I don't think I could say 'no' any more if I tried."

He stood up and offered me his hand. I took it, feeling another surge of energy pass through us.

"Thank God for that," he said.

And we walked back down the stinging-nettle-fringed path together, holding hands.

12

I insisted we stop at my house so I could make myself more presentable.

"But you look fine," Noah complained.

"Fine is the polite word for crappy," I replied, wondering if he would mind waiting while I washed my hair.

"Girls are so weird."

"It's what keeps us mysterious."

"Mysterious is an understatement."

I hesitated when we got to my house and dropped his hand. "Umm. Do you mind waiting out here?" I asked, looking down at the ground.

Noah took in my little detached house and smiled. "So this is where you live?"

"You're not going to stalk me now, are you?"

"You would love it if I did."

"I don't think people enjoy getting stalked. It's not up there on the list of great things to happen to you."

Another stomach-flipping grin. "Yes, well, they've not been stalked by me, have they? I'm wonderful. Very polite.

Why can't I come in?"

I struggled for the right words. "Well…if you came in you would meet my mother…and that's just not a good idea."

He looked puzzled.

"She gets worried about me, you see. And, well, if she sees you I'm going to have to explain you, and I'm not sure I can, and…it's just easier if you stay outside."

He nodded. "Fair enough."

"I'll be five minutes."

I knew it would be more like ten minutes and I felt mildly guilty about leaving him standing in the street, but Mum would be UNBEARABLE if she saw him. I dashed inside and, as if she knew I was thinking about her, Mum appeared on the stairs just as I was about to run up them.

"Hello, dear," she said, cradling a pile of laundry. "Did you have a nice walk?"

I shimmied past her to make the interrogation as short as possible. "Yes thanks."

"Where are you off to?" she called after me.

"Just into town."

"Where into town?"

"To get some coffee."

"Who are you going with?"

She should have been an MI5 interrogator. I closed my eyes and lied yet again. "Just meeting Lizzie to go through some coursework."

That seemed to satisfy her. I buried the guilt. There were

much more pressing things happening. Like, Noah was outside my house. MY house. And we were going for coffee. Together. Less than six hours after promising myself I wouldn't let him into my life. Well, promises were made to be broken, weren't they? Or was that rules? Either way, I felt happy. Hallelujah happy. Happier than I'd been in for ever. And, much as I was aware how awful it was to attribute such happiness to a boy, I was fed up with denying myself him. Right, now where was my mascara?

The five minutes became fifteen as I frantically overhauled my face, hair and clothes until I resembled someone worthy of having such an attractive man by their side. When I emerged back onto the street, Noah was leaning against a tree.

He scanned me and I forced my heart to behave itself.

He whistled. "Well, I was just about to moan about you leaving me so long, but as you look so beautiful I might have to forgive you."

I felt my face go red. "Sorry. I got sidelined by my mother, who was very interested in where I was going."

We started walking towards town.

"And what did you tell her?"

I thought about whether to lie again and decided against it. I wanted him to hold my hand again and the need made me feel slightly pathetic. "I told her I was meeting Lizzie."

"Poppy, I hate to be the one to tell you this, but I'm not Lizzie. My name's Noah. You know? That guy from the kick-ass band?"

We were still walking without hand-holding.

I wrinkled my nose. "You don't do low self-esteem very well, do you?"

Noah shrugged. "That's just as well considering you're so ashamed of me you're lying to your parents."

Deep breath.

I turned to him, hoping I wouldn't stumble on the pavement. "Look," I said. "I don't know you. You don't know me. But, as you know because Ruth blurted it out, I have… *stuff* in my life. It's all very boring and clichéd, but my mum's part of it, and if you can be bothered to stay around long enough I might tell you, but I really don't feel like it right now. Okay?"

A sudden scorch shot through my arm. Noah had taken my hand.

He looked at me intently. "I plan on staying around long enough."

And then he fixed me with such an incredible smile I'm surprised I didn't keel over right in the middle of the road.

Middletown town centre wasn't an attractive place. Okay, so it wasn't ugly – far too uppity for that. But it lacked any character. The pedestrianized area was clogged full of bland chain stores – the upmarket ones, of course. I didn't go into town very often. Whenever I needed clothes I much preferred to hop on a train to London so I could scour the vintage shops.

But, despite the distinct lack of choice, I was still surprised when Noah led me to a Caffè Nero.

I hesitated at the door.

"What is it?"

"You're taking me to a Caffè Nero?"

He looked confused. "So?"

I couldn't resist the urge to take the piss. "Isn't it a bit 'commercial' for an anti-establishment rock star like yourself?"

He dropped my hand and dug into his pocket. "But I've got a loyalty card," he protested. "And I've got enough stamps to get you a free coffee."

This was too much fun.

"So you're not only a sell-out but a cheapskate as well?"

He looked slightly pissed off but still smiled. "Are you ever nice to *anybody*?" He opened the door for me.

"Only people who earn it," I replied, walking in.

"I can't believe you don't like coffee. I feel like I'm taking my five-year-old niece out for the day."

We had found a comfy sofa to share and Noah was getting revenge for my ribbing him earlier.

I took a big sip of my banana-flavoured milk unashamedly. "Oi," I said. "This is a very grown-up sophisticated drink."

"It's not embarrassing to order grown-up sophisticated drinks. Did you see the look the shop assistant gave me when I ordered *banana milk*." Noah shook his head.

I refused to get upset. "Nobody really likes coffee. They just pretend to because drinking coffee makes them feel like a proper adult."

"Is that right, Einstein?"

The place was packed. We'd been lucky to get the last sofa. Other couples and groups were dispersed around us, slurping and gossiping, enjoying Saturday.

Noah and I were almost touching. He was leaning back, relaxed against the arm of the sofa. It was still strange to be here. I could feel the energy build between our bodies, but again, felt able to contain the reaction he usually brought out in me.

I nodded. "Everyone who orders coffee secretly wants a banana milk. I just have the courage to order what I really want." I held out my straw. "Come on, taste it."

He batted my glass away. "I don't want your banana milk."

I pushed it at him again. "Go on. Just a little taste."

"No."

"You're scared."

"Of banana milk?"

"Yep. You're not comfortable enough with your masculinity to try some."

I shoved it under his nose and he hit it away again, spilling some over me. I squealed and got up off the sofa to dry myself off, but Noah grabbed my waist and pulled me onto him. I squealed again and my body automatically nuzzled into his shoulder while he rested his face against mine. My breathing became short. I was getting incredibly hot.

We stayed like that a moment, both trying to ignore the distinct smell of banana emanating from my top.

"You're not exactly what I thought you would be like," Noah said without warning.

My stomach dropped. Dread quickly filled my body. I'd felt so relaxed around him, I'd let my guard down almost immediately. "Is that bad?" I squeaked.

He pulled me into him tighter and I relaxed. A tiny bit.

"No, it's good," he said. "You're not like other girls I've been with...I mean...I know..."

I looked up at him, which was difficult considering his head was resting on mine.

"Do they pretend to like coffee?"

He laughed. "Yes. They do."

I shook my head, immediately hating them all. And when he said he'd "been with" them, what did he mean? Well, I knew what he meant. I silently cursed my virginity and struggled with what to say next.

"They're lying to themselves and so are you."

"Poppy. I like coffee. I'm not lying to myself."

"I bet you didn't like it the first time you tried it."

He thought about it. "No. I don't suppose I did."

I turned over to look at him directly. "So why did you continue to drink it?"

"I dunno."

I poked him in the chest. "It's BECAUSE you liked what being a coffee-drinker implied. The 'image' it gives out. You forced yourself to like it because you wanted to look like a proper grown-up person. When *really* all you wanted was banana milk." I held out the glass again. "Now drink up."

With amusement in his eyes, he leaned forward and took a long sip. He swallowed.

"So?"

"Yeah, it's good."

I punched the air triumphantly. "I told you."

He grabbed my arm mid-punch and again pulled me into him. I settled back against his lean body, proud of myself for winning the argument.

"You are just the teeniest bit crazy, aren't you?" he whispered in my ear, making every inch of my body erupt in goosebumps.

"Every girl is a teeny bit crazy. Some of them are just better at hiding it than others."

"I suppose you're right. I like that you don't try to hide it."

I laughed. "I do try and hide it! I'm just not very good at it. I'm incapable of keeping my mouth shut."

"I like you very much, Poppy Lawson."

I let the words sink in and a smile stretched across my face.

"Yeah...well...you'll do," I replied. And then I squealed again as he tickled the side of my stomach in protest.

Time passed at record speed as we sat there, getting to know each other better. We became one of those incredibly annoying couples who laugh at each other hysterically.

When Noah came back from the till holding two glasses of banana milk, I burst out laughing and got a few dirty looks from customers. We talked about everything and nothing. Hours passed but neither of us brought up anything serious. There were huge questions hanging over us, questions we'd come here to supposedly work out. What was Noah going to do about Portia? What was this weird thing between us? Were we going to get together? If so, what would that mean? I was dying to ask about his past and the rumours I'd heard. I was sure he was intrigued to know more about me too, like why I'd hidden him in a bush so he wouldn't have to meet my mother, or what the deal was with my panic attacks.

But it was so much easier to talk about nothing. We talked favourite movies, favourite bands, books, and all the usual stuff, but I didn't take much in. To be honest, while he was talking, I couldn't concentrate much. I would nod convincingly when really I was examining his gorgeous cheekbones, staring into those black eyes, or fighting the urge to run my fingers through his hair. I think he felt the same because sometimes, like when I was explaining why I told everyone my favourite band was The Beatles when really I didn't have a clue who my favourite band was and I was just copying my parents, he would suddenly cup my face with his hand. It was a surprise to both of us when we looked out the window and saw it'd grown dark. I had one last slurp of my drink and took Noah's outstretched hand.

We dawdled home, wanting to draw out the journey for as long as possible. As we walked past identical manicured lawns, I learned that Noah obsessively read newspapers.

"Really? But they're so depressing."

"You shouldn't hide from what's going on in the world just because it's depressing."

"Now you really do sound like an anti-capitalist rock star."

"Shut up."

"So how many do you read?"

"All of them, including both the locals."

I was stunned. Well, he didn't go to college, and he hadn't mentioned a job. I guessed that gave him time to read all the papers.

"Isn't that an expensive habit?"

He shrugged. "My parents pay."

Silence. We hadn't discussed his parents either. I wondered whether Lizzie's gossip was true. Did he really live alone? At seventeen? I supposed there was time to find out.

"So what's happening in the world then?" I asked.

"Loads. In fact, lots has been happening in Middletown recently."

I stopped in the road. "Yeah right," I said sarcastically.

He nodded. "It's true. Do your parents not get the local papers? There was a story last week from the local weather association. They say there've been all these weird temperature fluctuations. Haven't you noticed we've had random hot days come out of nowhere?"

"Surely that's just global warming?"

"Nope. The weather patterns have been totally out of whack."

I wasn't convinced. Who belonged to a weather association anyway? Boring! "What else has happened?"

"Weird electrical shortages. Totally unexplained. There was this story in the *Middletown Observer* about people who've randomly had stuff blow up in their homes. And remember that first gig I did at Band Night?"

I turned red again at the memory of that evening. The first time I'd met him. "What about it?"

"Well, the amp blew up out of nowhere, didn't it?"

"Hmm. I suppose."

We carried on walking.

"So you didn't know any of this happened?" Noah asked.

I shook my head. "Nope."

"So you don't read the papers?"

"Not at the moment. I've got so much stuff to read for my A levels." I groaned as I remembered my unfinished Psychology coursework.

"What stuff is that?"

"Well, we've just finished *Romeo and Juliet* in English. Ergh. Thank God for that!"

Noah stopped us again and turned to me. "You don't like *Romeo and Juliet*?"

"No. Why does everyone think that's weird?"

"Because you're a girl. Girls are supposed to adore all that forbidden love stuff."

"Not me."

"So you're not a *Twilight* fan obsessed with that glittery guy?"

I grimaced. "God, no."

"You don't cry over Nicholas Sparks novels?"

"Amanda made me watch *The Notebook* once but I fell asleep."

He smiled.

"I just don't believe in all that stuff."

"What stuff?"

"You know. True love. Soulmates. Yadda yadda yadda."

Noah was quiet for a moment. "That's strange."

I supposed it was. Although I wondered how my love cynicism fitted into my feelings for him.

It was like he was reading my mind. "So how do you explain your feelings for me then?" he asked, almost nervously.

"What makes you think I have feelings for you?"

"I know you do."

"You're so full of it."

"Poppy, please? Let's not go there again."

I thought about his question and sighed. "Okay. I *might* like you just a little bit."

"Thank you."

"But I don't think we're *meant* to be together or anything. That's just greeting cards, crappy romcom novels and flower industry induced. It's not real life."

Noah looked almost sick. "That is the saddest thing I've heard anyone say."

I raised an eyebrow. "Oh no, *Shakespeare*. Don't tell me you're an old romantic?"

"I never used to be."

We were at my house now and I didn't want the day to end. The moon had hoisted itself high in the sky, casting white light onto my home, making it look small. The kitchen light was still on, so I steered Noah into the hedge.

"I'm going to change your mind," Noah said, taking my hand.

"Change my mind about what?"

"About love."

I rolled my eyes.

"Seriously."

"And how exactly do you plan to do that? Don't tell me you're going to appear below my window with a rose between your teeth singing 'I Don't Want to Miss a Thing' – because I will ring the police… What are you doing?"

Noah pulled his face towards mine and stared deep into my eyes. And I was lost. My heart began its frantic pounding; I stopped breathing. Keeping his hand under my chin, he brought his face closer until his lips were less than an inch from mine. I could feel his breath on my face and my knees almost buckled. Every atom in my body longed for his lips to touch mine. I waited. I could smell him. He smelled of apples, almost too sweet. Without realizing, I'd slipped my arms around his waist, trying to pull his body as close as possible. Noah brought his face closer – his lips so close now. I closed my eyes and waited for that first luxurious contact…

But, out of nowhere, I felt him draw his head back. My eyes snapped open and he was looking at me with that playful grin again, his head cocked to one side.

"I'll change your mind, just you wait."

And then he turned and walked into the darkness, leaving me quaking.

13

That night I found it impossible not to smile. Like, really smile. One that begins in your core and seeps through every fibre of your body. I pulled my duvet over me and lay on my back, knowing sleep wasn't going to come any time soon. I was glad for that. It gave me more time to think about Noah.

I was struggling to keep hold of all the things I believed in. I already felt like I was falling in love, or lust – whatever word best described it. It was like my cynicism was the outer shell of a sherbet lemon and I'd sucked on the bitterness for so long, eventually I had to hit a sweet centre. I turned on my front and hugged my pillow underneath me. I was proud of how I'd acted. I had been me, and Noah liked that. I'd also managed to control my misbehaving body for the entire day, which was something of a miracle. Right now, a panic attack seemed a highly unlikely event.

Sleep eventually found me, as usual, when I stopped thinking about it. I dreamed only of Noah: his face, his smile, his touch.

When I woke up I was still smiling.

* * *

Of course reality had to hit sometime, and my mother was talented at bringing up unsavoury subjects over breakfast.

As I sat in front of my steaming bowl of porridge, she broke my dopamine-induced haze.

"Have you done your Psychology coursework?"

I choked on my mouthful. *Coursework!* My good mood instantly evaporated.

"I thought you were doing it yesterday."

I nodded. "I was. But I got caught up in stuff." I drained my orange juice to combat the choking.

"Nothing's more important than your education."

"I know, I know."

"And don't forget you have another appointment with Dr. Ashley tomorrow."

Any leftover good mood was officially murdered.

"I do?"

"Yes. I booked you another emergency appointment. I heard you crying in your room on Friday."

I felt awful. No doubt she would think it was something *she* had done. And, like clockwork, she sat next to me and took my hand.

"I haven't dared ask but is everything okay, Poppy? Is it something I've done?" If I hadn't felt so heart-plummetingly guilty, I would've been annoyed at having to relive this situation again.

"Mum," I insisted through gritted teeth, "I'm fine."

"Well, you're quite obviously not. Have I done anything wrong?"

I decided to tell her the truth. Okay, so it would throw up more problems for her to obsess over, but that was better than her constantly blaming herself.

"If you really have to know, I've been upset over a boy."

She wasn't expecting that. *Boy trouble.* She pulled herself back in her chair and actually looked relieved – in fact, she almost looked happy.

"A boy?"

I nodded. Cringed.

"But I thought all boys in Middletown were disgusting?"

"Yeah, well, all but one of them are." I examined my empty juice glass like it was the most interesting thing I'd ever seen.

Mum was quiet for a moment. "So why has this boy been making you cry?"

She *was* happy. She could handle this. It was in the normal repertoire of having a teenage daughter. Unlike scraping your child off the floor when she randomly loses consciousness while buying Tampax.

I tried to think of an answer. "I didn't think he liked me, so I got upset. But now I think he does like me…maybe." I saw an opportunity. "So you can cancel my appointment with Dr. Ashley tomorrow. Now you know I'm not getting madder and everything."

She looked at me sternly. "Nice try, but boy or no boy, you're going."

"What? But I told you what was wrong!"

"You still need to see him. Anyway, you can't cancel last-minute. They still charge."

My stomach sank. So *this* was where telling the truth got you.

Mum leaned forward in her chair, excited. "So tell me about the boy."

"No."

"What? Why not?"

"Because you're my mum and it's embarrassing."

"Am I not cool enough, is that it? Am I not *hip* enough to do *guy talk*?" And then, to my horror, she started waving her hands around in the air, trying to do a gangster movement.

"Mum, I'm leaving the kitchen now."

"Oh, come on. I was only joking."

"Bye." I took my empty porridge bowl to the sink and quickly left the room.

"Well, you still need to do your Psychology coursework before you go off canoodling," she called after me.

"No one uses the word 'canoodling' any more, Mum."

"I don't care, you still have to do your coursework before you canoodle."

"Yeah yeah," I grumbled.

Trying to do any sort of academic activity is apparently impossible if you're thinking about a boy. I sat staring at my textbook for what seemed like for ever, willing my brain to understand the mumbo jumbo. But my brain was only interested in one thing: Noah. At one point I even closed my eyes and pictured Noah reading to me from the textbook and – to my horror – it helped me concentrate. I managed to write a page or so before it occurred to me he hadn't called yet. I looked at the clock on my mobile phone. It was 2 p.m. Why hadn't he called? Had he lost interest already? I shook my head. No. I was not one of those girls. I would NOT obsess over why a boy hadn't called. I turned my phone off and felt a bit better.

Eventually, I managed to finish my rough draft. I read it back and was surprised to find it wasn't utter rubbish. Brilliant. I could take it to college tomorrow and shock my Psychology teacher. I looked at my turned-off phone. It was on my desk, taunting me, willing me to turn it on and check my messages. I left it off and walked downstairs with it.

"Cup of tea?" I yelled out.

"Please, love." My dad's voice came from the living room.

"Mum?" I yelled, in no particular direction.

"She's gone to Pilates."

I turned on the kettle, took out two mugs and dropped a tea bag into each. I tapped my fingers on the worktop as I waited for the water to boil, glancing at my phone every other second. But still, I left it off. After what seemed about a lifetime, the water began bubbling and I made the tea and took both mugs into the living room.

Dad emerged from behind his newspaper. "Cheers, poppet," he said, relieving me of one mug.

I settled on the couch and took a small sip of my drink. "So what's going on in the world?"

He shook back his paper. "It's all kicking off in Middletown actually."

"Ha ha, very funny."

"It's true."

"Don't tell me. A local vicar has run away with a lonely housewife?"

"Honestly, Poppy – we don't live in *Desperate Housewives*."

"It feels like we do."

"Well, if you must know there's been more freak weather. In fact, there was an electrical storm last night. Lightning actually struck some poor lady's house. It's ruined her roof."

I was confused. "I was up most of last night because I couldn't sleep. There was no storm. I would've heard it."

"It was over the top part of town."

"Really? I didn't hear any thunder."

Dad took a sip of his drink. "Mmm, good tea. It says in the paper there was no thunder, or rain. That's what's so weird about it. There was just a random lightning strike that hit this lady's house."

I wasn't convinced. Insurance scam, I reckoned. Didn't storm damage count as acts of God though? "Hmm."

"The *Observer* is saying there's been a lot of weird weather going on lately."

"Yeah, Noah said."

Dad lowered the page. "Who's Noah?"

Oops.

"No one. Just some guy."

"Some guy?"

"Come on, Dad. Leave it. Having Mum interrogate me is bad enough."

"She told me there was a guy. She almost fainted with excitement. I didn't know he was called Noah though."

I fidgeted uncomfortably.

"I'll leave it, pet. Don't worry. As long as he treats you well, that's all I care about."

"Yeah, yeah."

"Seriously."

I drank the rest of my tea as fast as I could, burning my mouth. When my mug was empty enough, I stood up.

"Right, I'm off upstairs."

Dad didn't answer. He was too engrossed in the paper.

I'd left it long enough. Proved I didn't care just enough. I turned on my phone the minute I was out of the living room and impatiently waited for it to load up.

"Come on, come on," I muttered.

It beeped in my hand. I felt a little sick. One new answerphone message. I punched in 4444 and pushed the phone to my ear.

"You have one new message," an electronic voice told me.

Yes, yes, I know that already.

"To listen to the message press one…to save the message press two…to delete the message…"

I jabbed the *1* on my mobile and took a breath.

Lizzie's excited voice echoed tinnily down my ear. "Oi, Poppy – why have you got your phone off? Anyway, I don't have much credit but I just have to say RING ME. I have gossip. Also I need to know if you've done your coursework. You have, haven't you, you swot? You always hand it in on time. Can I read what you've written? Call me or die." *Beep*.

The electronic voice started asking me more questions but I hung up.

Why hadn't he called? I keyed in Lizzie's number. She answered on the second ring.

"Hello, you."

"Hello. What's up?"

"This coursework is sooo boring. Why do I need to know all this stuff? How is this going to help me become the next Hunter S. Thompson?"

"The next who?"

"God, you're hopeless."

"Hey!"

"You've finished it already, haven't you?"

I prepared myself for the verbal assault. "Just my first draft," I admitted.

"I knew it. I just knew it."

"Lizzie, it's not a crime to give coursework in on time."

"Yes it is."

"I can help you."

She was quiet for a moment. "Okay. You're forgiven. Can I read yours tomorrow after second period?"

"Of course."

"I love you very much – you know that, right?"

"Yeah yeah." I paused. "So what's this gossip then?"

"Ooo yes. You didn't come out after the gig, did you?"

I shook my head. "Nope."

"It was fun. I thought I quite fancied that drummer Jack, but then he told me he reads tabloids. Yuck. So I can't fancy him any more. Anyway Noah and Portia were there. Actually, it was lucky you weren't there. That Portia girl is sooo the kind of person you hate and judge immediately. She kept droning on about her designer handbag collection and how Daddy is buying her a flat in London after she graduates. What a cow. She was such an idiot. I mean how rude is it going on and on about how rich you are?"

I felt soothed by Lizzie's account of her.

"Anyway…you know how Noah and Portia were, like, totally all over each other at the gig?"

My stomach felt queasy at the memory. I nodded.

Lizzie must have taken my silent nod as an affirmative. "Well, it was so weird, because the moment we left Band Night, Noah completely lost interest. He dropped her hand and wouldn't really talk to her. It would've been rude, and I would have been mad at him, if Portia wasn't such an utter a-hole. But it got quite funny. She's obviously not used to being ignored and she didn't like it. She got PROPER clingy and kept trying to kiss him full on the mouth when he was in the middle of telling us a story. And he just batted her off like she was a moth or something. And, because *that* didn't work, she then – in full public, I might add – started rubbing his knee and running her hand up between his legs. And, ohmygod, Poppy, we were all staring, but she seemed to get off on it."

I was picturing it in my head and frothing with jealousy.

"But Noah, AGAIN, wasn't having any of it. He smacked her hand like she was a naughty toddler and she turned luminous red. Can you get the colour, luminous red? Oh well. She was completely blushing. And then, to save face, she pretended the whole sordid thing hadn't happened and launched into this insane monologue about how she was scouted by a modelling agency when she wasn't even wearing any make-up."

I let Lizzie catch her breath. She was in such a state of excitement, she almost needed smelling salts.

"So was that the gossip then?" I asked, not sure I wanted to hear any more.

I heard her gasp for air. "No. There. Is. More," she panted.

I sighed. "Go on then."

"Well, Ruth rang earlier this afternoon and told me. She'd gone to band practice with Will this morning. Apparently Portia turned up, dressed like she was going clubbing even though it was a Sunday morning. That's what Ruth said, but I bet Ruth was wearing something equally inappropriate. Ruth said when Noah arrived he looked totally shocked to see Portia there and told her, in front of everyone, that he didn't remember inviting her. Then – and this is where it gets really good – he took Portia off into the corner and spoke quietly with her. After that, apparently she went bloody mental and started screaming. She picked up one of Jack's drums and kicked it across the room – she made a massive hole in it. She called Noah a bastard and ran off shrieking."

I couldn't believe it.

"...So then Ruth followed Portia. Not because she cared too much about her but she pretended to so she could get the gossip. Good move actually, I've trained her well. And Portia told Ruth that Noah dumped her and said he was really sorry but he was in LOVE with somebody else."

I let the words, and their meaning, sink in slowly.

"Can you believe it?"

"No."

"Isn't that the best gossip ever? I wonder who this new girl is? She's going to be hated by every girl in the whole of Middletown."

I gulped. I tried to keep my voice casual. "Good gossip, Lizzie. You've done very well."

"Aren't you intrigued to find out who this mystery woman is?"

"Not really. Why do you care so much anyway?" My words came out harsh but I couldn't help it. I didn't want to be caught up in some sort of pathetic episode of *EastEnders*.

"It's just interesting, that's all." She paused. "Do you think I can still fancy someone if they read tabloid newspapers?"

Glad for the change of topic, I said, "Well, he reads books too though, doesn't he?"

"Oh yes. You're right. Maybe he's okay after all."

We talked for a few more minutes. After I hung up, I climbed onto my window sill so I could digest the new information.

Well, that explained why he hadn't called. There were scarier things now though. I didn't want some rich bitch to hate me. And he had said he *loved* someone else. Did that mean he *loved* me? It was silly. We didn't even know each other. I sat and watched the afternoon turn into evening, deep in thought.

14

The next morning I was grumpy.

No phone call. Not even one piddling text message. I swung myself out of bed, without doing my breathing exercises, and took my bad mood out on everything. I kicked my bedroom door shut, brushed my teeth ferociously and poured my orange juice as aggressively as one can pour orange juice.

I dressed for anger. Despite it being, again, unseasonably warm outside, I pulled out my black Motörhead T-shirt and teamed it with my frayed miniskirt. I smudged as much eyeliner round my eyes as college rules allowed and backcombed my hair. Looking at my reflection, I was surprised to find I actually looked quite good. But donning black had not eradicated my anger and I was still seething with anti-Noah venom as I stormed down my driveway.

"I hate men," I told myself. "You're so stupid, Poppy. Did you honestly think you were different?"

But then my angry musings were replaced with, "But he

told Portia he loves someone else. *Loves*. That could mean
you…"

It was like having an angel on one shoulder and a devil
on the other. And I was so ensconced in arguing with my
two imaginary selves, I didn't notice Noah appear from
behind a tree.

"Hey, Poppy."

He looked almost illegally good. Black shirt – oh gosh,
we were matching already. Dark jeans. Sunglasses pushed
casually on top of that gorgeous head of his.

"I knew you'd start stalking me if I told you where I
lived." It was supposed to be a joke but the anger I'd been
harnessing all morning seeped through into my tone.

Noah didn't look surprised. "Sorry I didn't call you
yesterday."

I kept quiet.

"I had…stuff…to sort out."

I shrugged. "S'alright. I didn't notice anyway. I had stuff
to do as well."

He took my hand and I felt myself melt, annoyingly.

"I'm really sorry I didn't call," he said again, trying to make
me look him in the eyes. "I know you've decided I'm one of
those guys who don't call and wind girls up, but I'm not."

How did he know me so well already? I shrugged again.
It's actually a very effective communication device when
your heart is pounding ten thousand times a second.

Noah stuck his lip out and I knew I'd forgiven him. This
time, at least.

"Am I forgiven?" he asked, making his voice babyish to match his face.

I winced. "You're forgiven if you promise never to talk or look like that ever again."

Noah laughed and put his arm around me. We started walking.

"So why are you here anyway?"

"Is it a crime to want to walk my gorgeous girlfriend to college?"

Wow. I tried to remain upright when, inside, some sort of happy atomic bomb was exploding.

I'm gorgeous? I'm his girlfriend?

"So I'm your girlfriend now?" I asked, proud at my ability to remain nonchalant.

Undeterred, Noah kept walking. "Yep. Sorry, but you have no choice in the matter."

"Well, that hardly seems very fair."

"Do you want to be my girlfriend?" He didn't look concerned when he asked the question. Cocky bastard.

"What about Portia? Isn't *she* your girlfriend?"

He stiffened and I began to enjoy myself.

"Do we have to go there?"

"Why?" I said, all innocently. "What happened?"

"It's sorted. Don't worry about it."

"How's Jack's drum?"

"How the hell do you know about that?" Noah laughed.

"My best friend is the Sherlock Holmes of Middletown."

"Lizzie," he said, shaking his head.

"Was it bad?" We'd reached the alleyways and the sound of traffic was more distant than before.

Noah looked distressed. "It wasn't great. I felt like a right arsehole."

He'd acted like one. I kept walking, still with his arm around me, and looked at the trees growing overhead. The gaps in the branches cast puddles of light onto us. "I want to reassure you, but what you did *was* a little bit arseholey."

"I know."

There was a slightly uncomfortable silence. I hated how things were either wonderful or tense between us. I felt we were on the verge of getting involved in something we couldn't undo, and couldn't decide if that was a good or bad thing. But when I looked up at Noah, the light falling onto his chiselled face, my stomach flip-flopped and I decided it was good. For now, anyway.

The awkwardness passed and I enjoyed having his body so close. The walk flew by and soon we were only five minutes from college and my English lesson.

Noah carefully extracted his arm from round me. "Sorry," he said. "It's been a bit more of a sombre walk than I'd hoped."

I tried to smile.

"It's just, well, I feel guilty about this Portia thing. I can't believe I *used* someone like that. I was just so desperate for you to realize your feelings."

I thought about what Lizzie had said. "Well, if it's any help, it's not like you urinated on Mother Teresa or something. From what I heard, she isn't the nicest person."

165

Noah nodded but then shook his head. "It still wasn't right."

"But she broke the drum. Doesn't that make you even?"

He laughed. "Yes, she did bloody break the drum. That was crazy."

I laughed too as I pictured it.

"Are you free after college?"

My heart sank. Dr. Ashley. I shook my head. "No. Not right after college anyway. I've got a thing."

"That sounds ominous."

I didn't look at him. "It's hard to explain."

I dug out my mobile phone to check the time. I was going to be late. Again. Noah saw me pull a face.

"You gotta go to class?"

"Unfortunately."

"Well, what are you doing after this *thing* of yours?"

"Nothing. Why?"

Noah picked a small piece of lint off my T-shirt and brushed it away. "I was wondering if you wanted to come over to my place and, you know, hang out?"

I remembered his reputation and gulped. What exactly did he mean by "hang out"? What was wanted? Expected?

I nodded my head slowly, trying to calm my quickened breath.

I needed advice. Oh no. I was going to have to tell Lizzie. But she would be so unbearable.

"Is that a yes?" He was looking at me curiously.

I nodded again.

"Alright. Well, I'll come round yours at six-ish and pick you up." He took my hand and squeezed it. Then, before I knew what was happening, he'd turned and left.

I wobbled my way to English, trembling at the thought of that evening. Part of me longed for it to be Saturday morning again. Then, I'd banished Noah from my mind and was getting on with living my uneventful, but ultimately unstressful life. Now, in just one weekend, I'd broken up a couple, acquired a boyfriend and begun panicking about whether I was expected to sleep with him already.

I staggered past desks and slumped into my seat without even acknowledging Frank's hello. I put my head in my arms and concentrated on keeping my breathing regular. But it was coming out in fast rapid pants.

"Poppy, are you alright?" Frank asked.

But I couldn't answer. I couldn't breathe.

Not another one. Not here.

Get a grip, I told myself. Squeezing my eyes shut, I began reasoning to calm myself down: *You don't have to sleep with him. You only just got together. If he expects it, just say no. Kill him if he makes it a problem.*

It worked a little. I felt my breathing ease. I began to hear Ms. Gretching teaching at the front of the class. Her voice got louder and less tinny.

You don't need to sleep with him yet, I repeated in my head.

And, slowly, I felt strong enough to raise my head and meet Frank's worried eyes.

"Poppy?"

"Hi, Frank. What's up?"

"Are you okay? You were having a bit of a special moment just then."

I laughed in what I hoped was a realistic way. "Sorry about that. Didn't sleep well last night and just needed to mentally prepare myself for the next hour of joyous English."

Frank didn't look convinced but let it go. "You're such a weirdo."

"Takes one to know one."

I let Ms. Gretching's boring blaring become background noise again and returned to the problem. I needed advice. Lizzie.

She was easy enough to find at lunch, huddled over that bloody notepad.

I plopped down next to her, mentally preparing myself for the oncoming squeals. "Where are Ruth and Amanda?"

Lizzie looked up from her scribblings. "Ruth's stressing about her Travel and Tourism coursework and has dragged Amanda to the library for moral support."

I looked round. The canteen wasn't as busy as it usually was. Coursework fear must have kicked in and the library was now the social epicentre of campus.

I grimaced. "Poor Amanda."

"Never mind poor Amanda. Poor me! I need your Psychology coursework NOW."

I sighed, dug in my bag and handed it over. Lizzie grabbed it enthusiastically, looking a bit like Gollum from *Lord of the Rings*. I sat back as I let her go through it.

"I can't believe you've finished already."

"It's just a first draft, Lizzie. Why haven't you done it, anyway?"

She turned over a page. "I've been teaching myself shorthand in my spare time."

"Of course you have…"

She started taking notes and I noticed her copying huge chunks of my work word for word. It was time to ask her advice – if only to stop her blatant plagiarizing.

"Lizzie?" I asked.

"Yes?"

"Can I tell you a secret?"

The Psychology coursework was forgotten. She leaped forward in her chair, her eyes gleaming.

"What is it?" she demanded.

Maybe this was a bad idea.

"Hang on. First of all I need you to absolutely PROMISE you won't tell anyone."

Her face fell and I could see her battling with herself.

"Am I going to have to say the words 'off the record'?"

Lizzie laughed. "No. Okay. I promise. What is it?"

I looked around the half-empty canteen to check no one

was listening. Of course they weren't. Lizzie and I weren't of much importance to anyone.

"Well, I'm telling you this because I need your advice. Seriously. I'm proper freaking out."

Lizzie nodded solemnly. "I can do advice."

"Well, the thing is, I'm kinda seeing Noah Roberts."

I wasn't expecting her to scream. The whole building turned to look as Lizzie let out a high-pitched whoop, before her eyes bulged and she stuffed her hand into her mouth.

"Thank you for your discretion," I said wryly.

"Oh. My. God. Are you being serious?"

I nodded.

"Jesus Christ, this is good gossip."

I slapped her hand. "Oi! Off the record, remember?"

"Ahh, man."

"Lizzie. You promised!"

"Okay okay okay." A thought had obviously occurred, as her face lit up. "You're the girl Portia wants to kill!" She looked annoyingly pleased at this discovery. I shushed her the best I could and eventually, when I was just at the point of killing her using my bag and her head, she pulled herself together.

"Okay. I'll be good," she said, her hair messed up from my attack. "So tell me everything. How did this all happen?"

I explained everything. The first night at the gig, what he'd said to me at the Lock and Key, how I'd felt when I saw him with Portia. Then I filled her in on what had happened since we met at the top of the common. Lizzie was a rather entertaining listener. She was incapable of controlling her bodily responses and at all the juicer bits, like when Noah held his mouth close to mine, she sighed and ooooed like she was watching a firework display.

When I'd finally finished, I laid out my predicament.

"So I'm supposed to be going to his later. But what if he's expecting me to sleep with him? Lizzie, I'm terrified."

She thought about it, her packet of Quavers paused in mid-air. "Hmm."

I was annoyed. "Hmm?" I asked. "I tell you my biggest secret in the world and all you can give me is 'Hmm'?"

She dropped the bag of Quavers. "Well, what were you expecting me to come up with? I'm not exactly Miss Experienced."

"But what do you think he's thinking?"

"I…don't know."

I slumped my head on the table and made myself breathe. Lizzie eventually kicked into action.

"Sorry," she said. "But you've surprised me so I haven't had time to prepare a good friend response." She paused and thought about it again. "I think he's obviously into you, judging from what you've said. And you're not going to sleep with him, are you?"

I shook my head. "No way. Not yet."

"Well, he's just going to have to accept that and, if he's really into you, it won't be a big deal."

She was right. But I was still terrified.

"I don't know, Lizzie. I feel like this whole thing is

destined for failure. There's so much about him that sets off alarm bells. Like, I don't know why he lives alone, apparently he has depression, he's a man-whore, and he's also in a band with girls like Portia chucking themselves at him all the time."

She nodded. "Yeah, but it sounds like he really likes you."

"You think?"

"Yeah." She looked me up and down. "God knows why though."

"Don't make me sit on your head again."

We had another mini play-fight, much to the delight of some of the boys in the canteen, who yelled "MUD WRESTLING!" at us. Finally we gave up and collapsed back onto our chairs, laughing.

"I hate saying it…" Lizzie said. "Well, actually I love saying it, but…I told you so." She picked up my coursework again and started copying more of my introduction.

"What do you mean?"

"Well, I predicted this perfect union. I told you you'd fancy the fit guitarist because it's against all your principles. I set the wheels in motion."

With horror, I realized she was right.

"Oh no," I said. "I'm a…a…" I couldn't say it.

"That's right," said Lizzie. "You're a big fat cliché."

Apparently time doesn't behave itself if you're nervously anticipating something. Much as I needed the day to pull myself together, time slid away from me like water. In a blur lunch was over, Photography whizzed past, and – blink – hey, where did Psychology go? Before I knew it, I was sitting in front of Dr. Ashley with the ever-present tissue box between us.

"So what have you been up to this week?" he asked, his notebook poised on his knee, ready for urgent scribbles.

Noah Noah Noah Noah Noah Noah Noah.

"Not much."

I wondered why time had suddenly slowed down again. Now it was dragging. The minute hand of the personality-free clock on the wall was practically moving backwards.

"You must have got up to something."

I needed something to fill the silence. I'd used up Mum-and-our-relationship-issues last time, there wasn't much to say about Dad, and I didn't think I'm-worried-about-my-A-level-coursework merited an appointment at a private health clinic.

"I went to another gig," I volunteered.

"I see. And how was it this time?"

I nodded. "Good. I didn't have another panic attack."

The frantic note-taking began and I wondered if I would ever be allowed to read them.

"That's good, that's good," Dr. Ashley muttered, almost to himself. "And did you do your breathing exercises this time?"

"I did them at the first gig as well."

"I see. Well, did they help?"

"I suppose."

"That's good. That's good."

I interrupted his next surge of note-taking.

"Will I ever be allowed to read those?" I asked, pointing towards his book.

Dr. Ashley looked up and clutched his papers to him protectively. "What do you mean?"

"Well, whenever I say anything, even if it's really boring, you write about it. But I don't know why you're writing."

He put the notebook face down on his knee. "They're just notes, Poppy."

"Yeah, I know. But can I read them?"

"Why would you want to read them?"

I shrugged. "I dunno. Curiosity, I suppose. You could be doodling and not listening, for all I know. Or playing hangman against yourself or something."

I wasn't really sure why I was bringing this all up. But it meant we weren't talking about Noah. That was good.

"I promise I'm not playing hangman, Poppy. Now…shall we get back to things?" He picked up the notebook again. "Has anything else happened this week? Have you—"

I interrupted him. "Dr. Ashley, do you go to therapy?"

That got him. He visibly jerked and took a good couple of seconds to compose himself.

"It's not your job to ask the questions, Poppy."

"I was just interested."

"Well, it's not relevant, is it?"

"You always tell me it's nothing to be ashamed of."

This was fun. I pushed my guilt about Mum's cheque to one side and enjoyed myself.

"It *isn't* anything to be ashamed of."

"Does that mean you go?"

"I didn't say that."

"Yeah, but you didn't say no. Isn't it weird? Like, don't you judge how good they are? Like when a hairdresser has to get their hair cut by another hairdresser?"

"I think we're getting off the point here."

"Is it what made you want to be a therapist? What happened to you? Did it inspire you? It's alright, Dr. Ashley. You can tell me. It's a safe environment here."

I knew I was being a total bitch. Again. But it was too good. His face turned slightly red. But the fun came to an abrupt end with:

"I find it interesting you haven't told me about Noah."

Shock.

Complete shock.

I opened my mouth but he answered my question before I asked it.

"Your mum told me."

He looked pleased with himself. The git. The blood was leaving his face and, in turn, mine was filling up.

"I don't want to talk about it," I said petulantly.

"If this boy is upsetting you then it might be best to talk about it," he said. "Wasn't it the first night you met him? That gig? When you had the panic attack?"

My mouth fell open. How did he know that? I didn't

think Mum or Dad even knew. I must've told them and forgotten.

I definitely wasn't having fun any more.

I refused to answer any questions and sat mute in rebellion until the nondescript clock finally marked the end of the hour.

Dr. Ashley sat smiling, writing notes in his pad. He was obviously quite content with the silence.

15

I was officially a nervous wreck by the time Noah picked me up. Still wound up by my altercation with Dr. Ashley, I'd changed outfit at least eight million times, reapplied lip gloss every thirty seconds and was quivering with fear. When I'd finally decided on an appropriate outfit (funnily enough it was the first one I'd tried on – a casual off-the-shoulder stripy dress), I kept a vigil by my bedroom window, anxiously anticipating the evening.

After what seemed like hours, I saw him walk to my house. I'd allowed him up to the front door as Mum and Dad were still working in their respective offices. They were both civil servants – whatever the heck that is – but it meant they left and returned home like clockwork. Of course, he looked amazing. He was wearing a red checked shirt and jeans, and was whistling. I ran to the door to greet him, smoothing out imaginary creases in my clothes. As I did, I could feel the outline of my matching lingerie set underneath. It wasn't anything too fancy, just an oddly inappropriate Christmas present from my aunt. Pink lacy bra with matching lacy knicker-type things. I'd never really worn it, and I didn't plan to reveal it to Noah just yet, but, you know, a girl has to be prepared.

I could see his shadow through the windowpane of our front door. I opened it, borderline terrified.

His greeting smile made my knees jellify.

"Hello, gorgeous. Ready to see my humble abode?"

I could only nod.

He offered me his arm and we headed down my driveway. It was a beautiful evening. Not one cloud in the sky and the air was balmy – odd, again, for this time of year. Touching him still felt electric and breathing still required intense concentration. We walked down my road, not talking, and headed up another. Less than five minutes later, we arrived at a small block of flats. They were pretty posh, very modern-looking from the outside.

"Home sweet home," he said.

I couldn't help but wonder where the hell his parents were.

He fiddled with his keys, then unlocked the door and took me inside. There was plush red carpet and the walls were a cream colour. We went into the lift and he pushed the button for the top floor. My heart was pounding. I realized we were alone. Like, really alone. I was freaked and thrilled at the same time. As we rode the lift we still didn't really talk and I wondered again what he expected from me.

The lift opened and there were only two doors to choose

from. Noah steered me right and pushed his key into the lock.

"Come on in," he said as he stepped through the door.

I took a deep breath and followed him inside.

His place was stunning, incredible even. The huge open-plan living room was painted the faintest blue colour, with stripped wooden floors and dominated by a large leather couch. The room reeked of Noah. His touch was everywhere, from the piles of dog-eared books scattered haphazardly to the stacks of yellowing newspapers. His guitar took pride of place and his favourite LPs were tacked to the wall like posters. I noticed a distinct lack of any family photographs amongst the "arty" framed shots of his band and was puzzled again about how and why he lived alone.

Noah gave me a quick tour and I tried not to reveal my astonishment. The kitchen was a serious chef's dream, all aluminium fridges and slate countertops. The bathroom was larger than my bedroom, with a giant hot-tub bath and an infinity shower. He quickly opened the door to his bedroom and I caught a glimpse of a giant double bed. I tried not to think about how many girls had already been in there. I failed miserably.

Noah led me back to the living room and offered me a drink.

"Water," I squeaked nervously, feeling like we were strangers.

He fetched me a glass from his perfect kitchen, adding ice cubes from his massive fridge. He handed it to me, then

soulmates

sank into the leather sofa, sprawling across it. I tried not to
think about how many girls must've been on that couch
before. I failed miserably.

I was standing with my arms crossed. I clutched at my
water glass, trying to work out just how out of my depth I
was.

Apparently unaware of my inner turmoil, Noah smiled
and said, "Well, I bet you're wondering why I've brought
you here?"

To seduce me? To take advantage of me? To scare the
hell out of me with your crazy-perfect apartment?

I took a sip of water to soothe my desperately dry mouth.
"I am curious, yes."

Was I supposed to be taking off my clothes now? I wanted
to run away.

Noah took my hand and sat me down on the couch. He
pulled my chin up so I was looking at him. All I could do
was try not to pass out.

"Poppy," he said.

I gulped.

"I had a great time with you the other day, but we didn't
really do what we were supposed to, did we?"

Were we supposed to have sex in the coffee shop?
I shook my head. The lace of my knickers itched the top of
my leg.

"I brought you here so we could...talk – about all that
serious stuff we successfully dodged the other day."

My mouth fell open. "Talk?" I repeated dumbly.

Noah looked surprised. "Yes. Why else would I bring you here?"

The fear and the awkwardness disappeared. God, I was stupid. Talk! Of course. Talking. Like people do. Why did I get so wound up?

With all the tension vanished, I curled up under Noah's arm and looked up at him. "I dunno. Of course. Yeah. What do you wanna talk about?"

He seemed confused by my complete change of mood but went with it.

"Well, there's a lot I feel I need to tell you…about myself," he stammered. "I feel you should…well…know some stuff about me before you get all involved."

Touched by his new nervousness, I cuddled closer to him, loving the feeling of his arms enveloping me.

"Is this about you being the man-whore of Babylon?"

More confusion. "What?"

"It's okay. I've already tortured myself about all the girls you must've brought back here." I wasn't sure why I was saying all this. "So go on – torture me some more about what a stud you are."

Noah wasn't impressed. "You think I brought girls back here?"

"Noah, this place is like a babe-magnet. I'm surprised you haven't installed a revolving door."

I was suddenly un-scooped from his embrace. He stood up, his eyes hurt and face angry.

"I've never brought anyone to my place before, Poppy,"

he said, looking me straight in the eye.

The eye contact made my heart race again and I could feel adrenalin coursing through my body. I'd somehow managed to get things incredibly wrong.

"You...you...haven't?"

"No. This is the only place I can...be...I dunno. You're the first girl I've ever brought here. I stupidly thought it would be special. But now you're just implying I'm some player messing you around."

I thought about it. "That isn't strictly true," I replied quietly. "But come on, Noah. I've heard the rumours about you and your...umm...promiscuous ways." He smiled slightly and relief began replacing the angsty ball in my stomach. "You've not even denied them. So I've got all that to deal with and then you bring me here, and there's a leather couch, for God's sake. What am I supposed to think? I don't necessarily believe you're playing me...well, I really hope not, because my instinct tells me you're not—"

"I'm not, Poppy," he interrupted. "I'm really not."

He sat back down and we stared at each other. Again, something passed between us, electricity, if that were possible. When it got too tense, I crossed my eyes and pulled a face.

Noah laughed. "I suppose I can clear everything up if I explain it to you."

"I'm sure you can."

He looked away. "But I'm scared..."

I was surprised. Noah didn't appear to be a person who

was scared of anything. "Scared of what?" I lightly touched his forearm.

"Scared you'll go off me."

I almost laughed at the stupidity of what he'd said. The fact someone like him could think someone like me was capable of "going off him" was insane.

"Don't be stupid."

He just smiled sadly. "There's a reason for all the rumours."

"I'm all ears."

"I just think you should know before, you know, you fall in love with me or something."

The words spilled out of my mouth before I consciously realized what I was saying, it was such a stock response: "I don't believe in love."

And though I hadn't meant it to, the atmosphere broke, and Noah finally laughed again and pushed me over on the sofa.

"God, sorry. I forgot, Mrs. Strong-Independent-Woman."

I struggled to get myself right again, my hair all over my face. "That's MS. Strong-Independent-Woman to you."

He pushed me over again and I screamed and retaliated, trying to push him over using my feet. Instead he grabbed my foot and began tickling it.

"Stop, stop!" I screamed, trying to wiggle away. I managed to kick my foot out of his hands and flipped my body up, using my arms now to topple his balance. Annoyingly, he caught them too and wrestled me backwards.

I fought with every bit of strength but he soon had me pinned on my back.

Noah lay, practically on top of me, casually restricting my arms behind my head with one hand. My heart had another fit as I adjusted to having his body weight on top of mine. There was no space between us, and I could smell his scent. It was intoxicating. Noah stared at my face, his black eyes scanning every part of it. I stared back, willing him to kiss me. Using his other hand, he brushed a strand of messed-up hair behind my ear.

"This isn't talking," he whispered. His hot breath on my face made me shudder with deliciousness.

I strained towards him a little. Not obviously. But enough for our mouths to be closer. Lust had taken over my body like a parasite, intent on the destruction of any sane part of my brain. "So talk then," I whispered back.

His eyes searched my face and I felt I would never feel this good ever again. As good as it felt right then with Noah looking at me like that.

"Just give me a moment."

I stretched forward but he didn't kiss me. Instead, he righted himself until he was sitting normally.

"Come on, Poppy. It's serious time."

I frowned, irritated, and sat up too. "Alright. Spill then. What's your big bad secret?"

Noah opened his mouth to speak, and then stopped himself. He ran a hand through his thick hair and looked down.

"You okay?"

He looked at me again. And I felt my stomach go gooey. Again.

Noah shook his head. "Can we get a drink first?"

I sighed.

"Go on then."

16

A few minutes later we sat back on the sofa, nursing two cold bottles of beer from his fridge. I curled my legs under myself and watched Noah struggle. It was amusing seeing him so wound up, a nice power reversal. I took a cautious sip and waited for him to start speaking.

He was staring into his beer intently, watching the bubbles foam. Then he tilted his head back, poured half of it down his throat, put the bottle down and turned to me.

"You ready for the monologue then?" His eyebrows rose.

"Nobody actually talks in monologues in real life," I replied. "Movies completely underestimate a human's need to interrupt and ask questions."

Another gorgeous smile. Making Noah smile was quickly becoming my new favourite pastime.

"Okay, I won't monologue."

"Good."

"I'm nervous."

I pushed him, playfully. "Just get on with it."

So he took a deep breath and he did.

"I guess you're wondering where my family is." He took another deep gulp of beer.

"I would be lying if I said I wasn't."

"Well, they don't live with me."

"Why?"

Noah spoke for a long time then. He told me they'd moved to Middletown two years ago. His dad owned a successful software business which had made millions – multi-millions. His mother was a housewife. Both of them were very English, stiff-upper-lip types, very repressed.

Noah was their only child. Their everything.

"It's why I'm so full of it," he said, smiling wryly. "I was told I was amazing every day. It kind of rubs off after a while."

So Mr. Rich, Mrs. Rich and their prodigal son moved to Suburban Hell (i.e. Middletown) so Noah's dad could set up a new office. But within a couple of days, Noah got sick.

"I can't explain it very well. But I woke up one day and I couldn't get out of bed. Every emotion disappeared. I felt empty. Hollow. I wasn't even capable of feeling scared of what was happening to me. Mum came into my bedroom to wake me for school but I wouldn't move. I didn't talk to her. I couldn't."

I took his hand.

"They were good at first. They let me have a few days off and took me to the doctors. They paid for the very best and I got rushed through the system. I think they thought it was a minor blip, something they could fix swiftly, like a software hiccup. So when I didn't get better, they, um, didn't handle it very well."

I watched him relive the memory, his lip curled in disapproval. "It was depression, wasn't it?" I asked softly.

He turned to me. "How on earth do you know that?"

"Everyone knows."

He looked freaked out. "What? Everyone?"

I tried to calm him, stroking his hand. "Well, not *everyone*, but my journalist friend told me."

"Jesus, that girl knows everything."

"I don't think you should worry. It's not done your reputation any harm. In fact, it's just made you even more irresistible. Now you're, like, a project. Damaged, vulnerable, yadda yadda – girls love it. Excellent pulling method. I assumed you'd spread it around yourself to get more female attention."

Thankfully he smiled. I wasn't sure I was saying the right thing, but I hoped I was doing okay. I got the sense I was being let in somewhere other girls hadn't been before.

"Yeah – well, maybe I did tell a few girls to get attention."

I raised my eyebrows.

"It's wrong though. It's not anything to boast about. It takes over your life."

I squeezed his hand in encouragement. "What happened next?"

He started talking again and I began to feel sick. His parents hadn't been able to handle his moods, told him to pull himself together and to stop letting the family down.

"It's such a broken record really," Noah said. "The falling of the prodigal son. It was fine when I was on a high. I was charming, lively, the boy they loved again. But I got these huge bouts of depression and they couldn't cope with those at all.

"Eventually they decided they weren't going to 'indulge' me any more. That's actually the word they used. They bought me this flat, moved to London, and told me I needed to grow up and learn how to be on my own."

My thoughts went to my own mother. Her concerned face, her constant need for "chats" in the kitchen, and those cheques she couldn't quite afford made out to Dr. Ashley. I realized silently just how lucky I was.

"Is that legal?" I asked, not sure what else to say.

Noah shrugged. "I dunno. I'm over sixteen, so I guess so."

"Then what happened?" I asked, although I sensed what was coming next.

"Well, I went a little crazy. What else do you expect? I dropped out of college, had loads of parties and became the 'man-whore of Babylon', as you put it."

"Sorry."

"It's okay. It's true. I was…well…it was shameful. It's not an excuse but my confidence was screwed. I'd gone from being adored my whole life to being shut up in a top-floor flat, left alone. Girls had always liked me…"

I made a face.

"Come on! They had. And I'd never really exploited that before. But, when my parents left, I had so much spare time…just all to myself. And I started going out…and it's really pathetic-sounding, but I needed the attention. I wanted to feel good about myself again and I stupidly thought sleeping around was the way to do it. Then I would feel gross with myself afterwards and never call the girl again – and start looking for someone else."

I got that twinge again. The one that had been burdening me all day. Insecurity. Mixed with a little jealousy. And anger on behalf of girlkind. I brushed it aside, for now anyway. I would no doubt torture myself later when I was trying to sleep.

"But things got better," Noah continued. "I got the band together and that's made things easier. They were the first friends I made here, and being part of a group again helped. I see them most days, they take the piss out of me, we joke around. It's nice. It's normal. Music helps unbelievably. I've always played, my dad taught me how. But, with nothing else left, music became my life and something to construct my day around. I got some of my confidence – okay, my cockiness – back." He fixed me with an intense stare. "And then of course I met you…"

The sun was setting through the large bay windows and it cast Noah in a golden light. His head was lit from behind and it looked almost as if he had a halo. I willed myself to stare back at him.

"Seriously, Poppy, when I met you it was crazy. I saw you in the crowd and it was like everyone else went out of focus. I didn't know that happened in, like, you know, real life."

I remembered that first explosive eye contact.

"I didn't care that the gig was ruined. I barely noticed that my amp had blown up. I was just thinking, 'Oh my God, I have to meet that girl.'"

I rolled my eyes. "Yeah right."

"I promise." He ran his fingers through his hair again and looked exasperated. "Honestly, I cannot tell you how brilliant it was when Ruth came up and I realized you were friends."

I remembered how awful I'd felt when I'd seen them together. It was wonderful to see it from his point of view. Like the expectation of how life should be was, for once, matching reality.

"Oh please no," I groaned. "I don't want to relive what happened next."

Noah gave me a wry grin. "You yelled at me."

I covered my eyes with my hands. "Do we have to go into this? I was so, so embarrassed afterwards."

"Why? For what you said? You were right to say it. Listening to you yell at me was the best thing I'd ever heard. I suddenly saw myself through someone else's eyes and saw what a prick I was. I mean, it was horrendous. You completely destroyed me and continue to do so. But your character assassination is what I needed to hear. And now I know, with or without you, I'm never going to be that person again. I'm never going to use my slightly shitty upbringing as an excuse for being a jerk. So thank you, Poppy. I owe you a lot."

The sun was almost gone and the room glowed red like the dying embers of a fire. I sat, not talking, and felt the hand holding Noah's grow warmer as he stroked the inside of my thumb.

"Why did you tell me all this?" I asked.

"I just needed to let you know everything." He looked nervous. "So you could, you know, get out if you wanted."

I gently stroked the side of Noah's face, surprised at how naturally it came to be intimate with him. His eyes searched mine for an answer.

"I don't want out," I said.

He broke into another heart-palpitation-inducing grin and squeezed both my hands tight.

"I was hoping you were going to say that."

We sat and watched the sunset reflecting on the cool blue of his living room walls. My head was nestling just above Noah's armpit and my legs were sprawled over his lap. He asked about my life and my panic attacks and I didn't feel ashamed telling him about them. In fact, for the first time, I felt I'd found someone who properly understood what it was like to lose control of your mind like that. He asked about college, what A levels I was doing, all the usual stuff.

There wasn't our usual piss-taking that evening. I think both of us were aware we were on the brink of something unusual happening. Something for keeps, rather than another "short-shelf-life" relationship. I felt overwhelmed by everything. My feelings for him, how my body responded to him. I kept feeling the words "I think I love you" bubble in my throat and it terrified me. These were words I'd scorned only minutes before, and now, so quickly, I felt them in me. And with them came the crippling fear that I was about to take a leap of faith, put my heart on a line with a high stamping-on risk. Rejection. Hurt. Humiliation. They all potentially came with those words. Part of me wanted to run home, bury myself under my duvet, and spend time alone analysing everything, finding something I could be cynical about. But the urge to stay with Noah was overpowering. Every part of me wanted to be touching him. Always. So when we saw it was dark and time I went home, I felt crappy.

I waited for him to lock his door, marvelling again at just how, well, fit he was. We left the flat and started walking to my house, occasionally bathed by the artificial glow of street lights along the way. I soon noticed the intervals between street lights were increasing. The pavement was getting rougher, and we were walking into almost complete darkness.

Finally I realized this wasn't the way home. I'd been so distracted by the way his hand felt in mine, how good it was, that I hadn't noticed we were on a bit of a detour.

"Where are we going?" I asked, barely able to make Noah out in the dark.

He squeezed my hand tight. "Shh. We're almost there."

"Almost where? I thought you were taking me home?"

I wasn't scared exactly, but apprehensive and disorientated.

The pavement under my feet was replaced by a narrow muddy path lined with brambles. The darkness delayed it a bit but I slowly got my bearings.

"Are we…?"

"Haven't you been on top of Middletown Common at night before?" he asked, guessing I'd figured it out.

I shook my head. "Isn't it full of flashers and drunks at night?"

He laughed. "Poppy, this is Middletown. Crime rates are zero. It's always empty here at night. I don't know why though, the view is amazing. Hang on."

An eerie glow appeared at the top of the path and we walked towards it. I stumbled and Noah's hand pulled me up without effort.

"Look. We're here."

And the view was so beautiful it made me drop his hand.

I'd never been here in the dark before. Lord knows how many times I had sat up here and looked at the view. But now it was like looking at a completely different place. The moonlight on the grass made it look silver, and beyond that a multitude of yellow spots stretched on for ever into the night. It was where I lived: Middletown. But I'd never seen it like this before. It was a sea of light, all different colours. I could see the yellow lights from people's windows, the white glow of office lights left on by careless nine-to-fivers, the blips of red car lights driving away to more exciting places.

I felt my way to my favourite bench and lea

"It's beautiful," I said, as Noah came and sat n

"I know. I always come up here at night when I f

when I feel like being all deep and meaningful."

"You are such a stereotypical band member."

"Guilty as charged."

"You're going to tell me your favourite book is *A Clockwork Orange* next."

"Nope. It's *The Wasp Factory*."

I groaned. "Even worse."

Noah's face looked pale in the moonlight. He casually swung an arm round my back as we sat looking. I could almost taste the energy coming from his body. I wanted him to touch me so much that I ached. He tilted his head and fixed me with another special look.

"So," he said, "do you still not believe in love?"

I sighed, not wanting to admit I felt I could fall for him; that I'd already fallen for him, like a stupid lovesick puppy with no self-control.

"Is that why you brought me here, to the romantic lights of suburbia?" I said, my voice sarcastic to cover my emotion. "To make a convert out of me?"

Noah cupped my face in his hands as he leaned into me. My body went into sensory overload and I almost drowned in how good it felt.

"Actually," he murmured. "I brought you here to do this."

He dipped his face towards mine and our lips finally met. He kissed me slowly, tentatively. I closed my eyes, ran my fingers through his soft hair, and kissed him back. He tasted how he smelled, like apples. The world dissolved. It was just us. Our mouths. Our bodies. His hands moved down my back and I shivered. He gently pulled me closer to him. Every atom of my body was tingling.

After what seemed like no time at all – but at the same time must have been ages – we broke apart.

My eyes fluttered open, my head still spinning, and to my surprise I was greeted by complete darkness.

"Noah. I've gone blind," I said, opening and shutting my eyes to see if there was any difference. A different type of chill ran down my spine and my euphoric high was replaced with dread. I looked around me but there was only black. The landscape of lights beneath us had disappeared. My heart started thumping.

Noah broke the tension by laughing. "You're not blind, you drama queen. There's obviously been some kind of power cut. Look, I'm waving. You must be able to see me in the moonlight."

I looked towards the direction of his voice, and yes, I could see a vague outline of his head. Relief found me.

"Hang on," Noah's voice said. His form started getting clearer as my eyes adjusted to the dark. "I'll get my phone out and we can use that for light."

I heard him shuffling in his pockets and kept blinking. "I should eat more carrots," I muttered absent-mindedly.

"What's that?"

"Nothing."

"Hang on, I've got my phone here."

Noah's stunning face appeared like a ghost's in the dark, his sharp features deepened by the eerie blue light of his mobile. "Hello you," he said, smiling.

I smiled coyly back. "Hello yourself."

He shone the light on the ground to give me my bearings, then put a protective arm over my shoulder. I snuggled into him appreciatively. My fear was replaced by loved-up smugness.

"Come on," he said. "Let's get you home."

It appears walking home in the pitch-black is easier said than done. I kept stumbling, only to be hoisted up confidently by Noah. And it was eerie walking in complete darkness. Noah didn't help the situation by grasping me round the waist and whispering "Oh my God – what the hell was that?" before tickling me as I screamed in half-fear, half-excitement. We somehow managed to navigate through the trees and made it safely to tarmac. The blackout had hit everywhere. Most houses were completely dark, although we could see the flicker of candles through some windows. We diligently followed the neon blue beam of mobile-phone-light like it was the yellow brick road, and, eventually, came to the top of my street.

Noah stopped and pulled me so I was facing him.

"This is weird," I said. "Seeing my road all dark like this. It's like I know it, but I don't. You know what I mean?"

He raised his eyebrow in a sarky way. "You getting all deep and meaningful on me, Poppy?"

I went to push him but he caught my hands, then wouldn't let go as I tried to free them. "Shut up, you."

"Gladly." And he brought his face down again and carefully brushed his lips against mine.

The street lights flickered.

I stopped him mid-kiss. "Did you see that?"

Noah turned to look at the nearest bulb, which was spluttering between light and dark. "Looks like they're trying to fix it. To be honest I'm not really interested in the blackout right now."

And we kissed again. Melting into each other, losing track of time. Whenever I murmured that I needed to go home, he nodded, then mischievously bent down to kiss me once more. I saw the street lamps flicker through my eyelids. Then it went dark and I knew they'd died again.

In time, we managed to extricate ourselves from one another.

"I really have to go," I said, dragging him in the direction of my house.

"Okay, okay, I'm coming."

When we got to my front garden, Noah pulled me to him one last time to steal another kiss.

"I really do have to go," I said, laughing.

"I know, I know." But he kissed me still, more firmly this time. I felt the tip of his tongue stray ever-so-slightly into my mouth, teasing me, before he pulled away.

"Go on then. It's past your bedtime."

I was dazed, high on the kiss. But my legs managed to summon the strength to walk to my door. I turned to wave goodbye but he had already gone.

I rummaged for my key and unlocked the door.

I could hardly see in the kitchen and walked with my arms out to stop myself bumping into the table.

"Hello?" I called cautiously.

"We're in the living room," Dad called back. I rounded the corner carefully and saw the flickering of candlelight.

I was greeted by both parents. Dad was in his usual spot, reading the newspaper. Mum, for the first time in ages, was actually curled up with a book on the sofa instead of charging around the house finding things to fret about. There should be power cuts more often. It forces people to slow down. Neither of them asked where I'd been.

"You get home okay?" Mum asked. "It's so dark outside I don't think even bats could see."

"Yeah, a friend walked me home. We found our way using the light from our mobile phone screens."

Dad rustled a page of his paper. "How very modern," he said.

I pointed to his page. "So what's going on in the world then?"

He smiled. "Oh you know, the usual misery."

"Glad to hear it." I yawned and stretched. "I'm knackered. I'm going to bed. I've got Photography at nine. A boring theory lecture."

"Make sure you take a candle with you," Mum said.

"Oh right. Yeah. I forgot."

I bent down to collect a candle that had been stuck in the top of an old wine bottle. Half of it had burned down, leaving ripples of red wax dribbled down the sides. Covering the flame with my hand, I took it upstairs and got myself ready for bed.

When I was all make-up-removed and teeth-brushed, I sat at my dressing table and stared at my reflection in candlelight. Did I look different? I felt different. I felt amazing. I turned my face from left to right. Maybe I wasn't so unattractive after all. From the left I could definitely be considered an attractive person. Although candlelight *is* supposed to be flattering. I blew out the flame and my reflection disappeared.

I fell asleep quickly. Smiling.

Anita and Rain watched the screens in silence.

The lab was empty again. All the day's mayhem, with important people running in and out for important meetings, had calmed. A clock ticked angrily, counting down the moments until the place would fill up again.

Code floated on both monitors in front of them, drifting down the screens aimlessly.

The pair sat close together, almost touching on the bench. Rain's hand was a little bit too near to Anita's. She pretended not to notice but had secretly never been so aware of her hand before. It twitched involuntarily, defying her brain and reaching out to Rain on its own accord. She imagined what would happen if her hand did take his. Would he take it back? Then what would happen? Her heart fluttered as she entertained the thought, then she shook her head. It was impossible. She'd never be with anyone ever again. How could she, knowing what she knew? It was just the lack of sleep getting to her.

She returned her attention to the screen, unaware that Rain had been watching her out of the corner of his eye.

What a strange woman, *Rain thought. He'd never hated someone but also liked them so much at the same time. It had been a weird couple of weeks. He'd spent more time with Anita than he had with his family and friends. Most of the time, she was an emotionally-retentive bitch. She'd been in her element this week with all the drama, barking orders, firing everyone at least twice and making unreasonable demands. But then there was the time he'd made a silly joke after being awake for twenty-one hours and she'd giggled into her hair. Or when she'd flinched as their fingers met while he was handing her a cup of coffee, and she'd given him this look over the top of her mug. And then there was just now, when he'd been certain she was about to take his hand.*

Every few moments or so, a green flicker would light the screen. When Rain had first seen it, weeks ago now, he'd jumped out of his skin with fear. He didn't fear it as much now – not now they apparently had it under control.

Another flicker.

"I should have brought popcorn," *Anita said sourly, breaking the silence.*

Rain laughed. "Yeah – it's turning into a bit of a chick flick this one, isn't it?"

Anita's eyes stayed on the screen. "Definitely a chick flick. Let's sell the script to Drew Barrymore and make our millions."

She leaned forward and jabbed at the keyboard, taking another measurement, then straightened in her seat again.

Rain felt his throat go dry before he asked his question.

"So we've found them…now what? I suppose it's time for the separation?"

To his surprise, Dr. Beaumont slowly shook her head.

"No, not yet."

Rain was flustered. "What? But people are in danger."

She spun to face him, glaring. "Are you even considering telling me what I should or shouldn't do?"

"No, of course not," he spluttered. "But I thought…well… this match is a pretty big deal; I thought we would've sent out the collection team by now."

She was still glaring at him. He couldn't believe he'd been so sentimental about this bitch just a moment ago. Must have been sleep deprivation.

Anita managed to compose herself and turned back to the code. "This pair have managed to build a…tolerance towards each other. I've never seen it before but for the moment I think we're safe." She sighed and ran her fingers through her hair. "It's just as well really, otherwise we'd probably all be dead."

Rain didn't know what to say. He was quite sure this wasn't allowed.

"But isn't it better for them? If we break them up now? I mean, if we are going to have to do it anyway. It's going to be bad enough as it is. Why wait longer?"

Anita batted his concerns away with her hand. "Oh, it's fine. Let them have their moment. It's not going to last long, is it? And – it's more fun this way."

The traces of a smile were on her lips. Rain realized she was actually enjoying this, revelling in it.

"More coffee?" He needed an excuse to get away from her.

She nodded eagerly. "Yes please."

He picked up the empty mugs and walked away. When he reached the door, he turned back and looked at her once more. In his absence she had leaned much closer to the screen, her eyes watching it greedily.

She was going to be trouble. He just knew it.

17

My alarm clock didn't wake me – instead my anxious mother shook me into consciousness.

"Poppy, get up. Your alarm failed because of the power cut. You're late for college."

I jumped up and looked at the clock on my wall. It was bad. I grabbed a towel and dashed into the bathroom for a turbo shower.

Despite the pumping, urgent sensation you get when you're running late, I couldn't help feeling heavy with, well, happiness really. My stomach felt like it had a lead ball in it, like a python happily digesting a huge meal while basking in the sun. It wasn't like anything I'd ever experienced. What made it odder was, at the same time, I was a ball of skittish energy, my mind flitting to Noah at any given moment. Was this love? Was it supposed to feel like good sick?

I turned the hot shower tap up and let the water wash away any last traces of sleep. As I shampooed, I thought of Noah. As I conditioned, I thought of Noah. As I shaved my legs and absent-mindedly cut myself with the razor and turned the bottom of the shower red with blood…I thought of Noah. I was only roused from my obsession when an even-more-anxious mother started banging on the door, telling me I was now horrifically late.

It was going to be a wet-hair-to-college day. I yanked on jeans and a T-shirt, madly dabbed mascara on my lashes and was out of the door within five minutes – a muesli bar clutched in my hand and my hair hanging around my face in clumps. I ran down my driveway and smacked right into Lizzie, who emerged from a bush like a spy.

"*Douff!*" I said, winded. "Lizzie? What the hell are you doing outside my house?"

She didn't bother explaining. "Poppy! I've been waiting out here ages. You look like crap by the way. Why didn't you dry your hair? So…? What the hell happened? Did you sleep with him? Was it amazing? Was it awful? Did it hurt? Did you cry? Are you seeing him again?"

I cradled my throbbing arm, which had taken the impact of our collision. "Lizzie. Ouch. Could you not have waited until college?"

She shook her head passionately. "Absolutely not." She linked arms with me and frogmarched me down the street. "So what happened?"

I blushed and struggled to form a sentence. "Errr. Well. It was…good?"

Lizzie reached round with her spare arm and slapped my hand like a naughty child.

"Ouch!"

"Not good enough. I need DETAILS."

I broke our link and used both hands to nurse my, now two, Lizzie-induced injuries. "Seriously, Lizzie, you can't use physical violence to coax information out of people."

"Yes I can."

"Well, if you stop attacking me I might actually tell you something."

Lizzie put up both of her hands, as if surrendering a weapon. "Okay. No more violence, I promise. I think I'm a little bit overexcited."

"You think?"

"Sorry. Anyway. What happened then? Did you sleep with him?"

I cringed a little when I remembered yesterday's freak-out. "No. I didn't sleep with him."

"You didn't?"

I shook my head. A twinge of relief passed over Lizzie's face, almost unnoticeable. I saw it and understood. She liked the fact that we were still on the same sexual experience page. I would've felt the same.

"So why did he want you to go round?"

"He wanted to talk."

"Talk? Really? Is that it?"

I nodded. "Yeah. It got a bit deep and meaningful." I paused. "But we did kiss."

Lizzie whacked me again.

"Ouch? Why are you hitting me again?!"

"Sorry, it was involuntary. I'm just so excited." She put

her hands behind her back. "Look. Out of harm's way now. So start from the beginning…"

I filled her in on the details as we walked. Lizzie seemed to be more excited by the whole affair than I was.

When I finished telling her everything she went quiet for a moment, her eyes wide.

"It sounds like it's getting a bit, hmm…serious…a little quickly," she said, almost to herself.

I couldn't disagree. She was right. "I suppose."

College beckoned to us from the end of the road. A figure, standing against the sunlight, was leaning casually against the gates. My heart started thumping. It was him.

Lizzie clocked him too. "Speaking of which," she said.

Noah shielded his eyes and spotted us both. He waved and made his way over. I was suddenly shy, aware of my half-dry hair hanging limply and my crappy clothes. I also couldn't help but perve a little as he walked towards us. It didn't seem real that I'd been kissing that beautiful face less than twelve hours ago.

He caught up to us. "Alright, you?" he asked. He seemed uncharacteristically unsure of himself, which made me feel more at ease. He nodded towards Lizzie. "And hello, Miss I-Know-Everything. I've heard you've been delving into all kinds of secrets."

Lizzie puffed her chest out. "The press always have a bad reputation."

Noah showed off his amazing grin. "That's because they're always poking into other people's business."

"What sort of business do you mean, Noah? Why? Has anything *exciting* happened in the past twenty-four hours... oww!"

She clutched her ankle where I'd kicked it, hard. I smiled sweetly at both of them.

Noah burst into laughter. "I take it last night is no longer between just us then?"

I started shaking my head but it turned into a nod. "Sorry," I said. "But she used physical violence."

Noah crouched down. Lizzie was still nursing her ankle and evilling us both.

"Are you okay?" he asked.

"No. Your girlfriend is a psychopath."

It felt weird to be referred to as Noah's girlfriend by a third person. It also felt wonderful.

"Lizzie. I know it's your favourite thing in the world to tell everybody everything," he said. "But do you mind keeping this one quiet..." He saw her about to interrupt. "Just for a while...until things die down with Portia. I don't want to hurt her feelings."

Lizzie opened her mouth. "But Portia's a cow! And she broke the drum."

I giggled and saw Noah was trying to stifle a laugh too.

"That may be, but still. Please try to keep it to yourself for now. Do you really want your best friend to be thought of as a boyfriend-stealer?"

I hadn't thought about that. Noah was right. I was suddenly very scared of Portia.

Lizzie was scowling but nodded.

"Okay," she said, giving her ankle a final rub and righting herself. "But only for Poppy's sake. If she'd asked me not to tell anyone, I wouldn't have."

"I'm glad that's sorted. Now can I have a quick chat with Poppy, please?"

I gave Lizzie a silent *Is that alright?* look. She nodded and limped off to the college entrance to wait for me.

Noah wrapped his arms around my waist. He looked gorgeous, of course. He was wearing a faded white shirt that showed off his olive skin. Just the feeling of having his arms on me made me go a little weak.

"Hey, gorgeous," he whispered, leaning in to kiss me.

I kissed him back briefly, aware that Lizzie was staring at us intently while pretending to be on her phone.

"I was just wondering what you were up to tonight?" he asked.

Coursework. Lots and lots of coursework.

"Nothing."

He smiled. "Perfect. Can I meet you after college?"

I was aware of the fact I looked utter crap, and still would when college finished. "Can we make it five and you pick me up at mine?" I asked. "I just have a few things I need to sort out."

"Five it is." He gave me another deep look before walking away. "See you then."

I called after him. "Oi! These things are much easier to organize via a mobile phone, you know? You don't always have to surprise me at college."

He looked me up and down. I felt exposed and shy.

Noah smirked. "Yeah, but that way I don't get to see how beautiful you look."

And, with that, he left.

I tried to compose myself as I walked towards Lizzie and the impending doom of my Photography lesson. She'd been sitting on the gate and jumped down.

"You've got it bad, girl," she said, putting an arm around me. "You look almost sick."

"I know. It's pathetic."

I snuggled into her and she steered me into the college.

Any attempt to distract myself from Noah was somewhat hindered by the intense boringness of my Photography lecture. The room was stuffy with the secreted heat of bodies piled into a small space. There were no windows, no air – just an interactive whiteboard showing one boring slide after another. I hadn't done Photography for the academic side of things. It was the one A level I'd granted myself in which to be creative and have fun. And, to be fair, most of my lessons were spent faffing about in the darkroom. But every so often, in some sort of deluded determination to make the subject "academically stimulating", I was forced to endure a lecture – much like today's – about the origins of photography or some such nonsense.

Grim.

The problem was that whenever I successfully managed to not think about Noah, I would only worry instead. So in my Noah mental breaks, I tortured myself with feeling guilty about Portia, recapping yesterday's awful session with Dr. Ashley and worrying about Ruth's reaction to Noah news. Therefore I was relieved when the bell finally rang, signalling the end of my tedious lesson.

I made my way to the canteen and spotted my friends at our table. Lizzie looked almost purple and I knew it was killing her to keep such great gossip to herself. But I was not at all ready to face the Ruth and Amanda firing squad just yet. They were already playing cards, with Johnno sitting next to them, looking slightly bored. Ruth had done something dramatic to her hair. Again. She'd dyed it a deep vibrant red and cut it short. Nobody but Ruth could have pulled it off, but she looked amazing. Of course. She was wearing a bright red tight vest top that clashed spectacularly with her new do. It strained across her chest and, teamed with a pair of spray-on jeans, meant our table was getting quite a few looks. Ruth was pretending she didn't notice and, to the unassuming eye, was just concentrating on her hand. But I'd known her since primary school and I could see her eyes flickering to each side to survey the reaction. She was also running her tongue along her top teeth – something she always did when she was happy.

I plonked my bag on the table and sat myself in the spare seat.

"Morning, Team," I said. "Loving the hair, Ruth. When did you get that done?"

She smirked at the compliment. "Thanks. Got it done last night. Luckily before the power cut kicked in." She looked at my decidedly lesser-coiffed hair. "Hmm, Poppy. You're having a bit of a special hair day yourself."

Her bluntness stung. I ran my hand through my hair self-consciously. "My alarm didn't go off this morning so it was a bit of a rush-jobby."

"It doesn't look that bad," Amanda said. "It's just not as perfect as it usually is."

"Aww thanks."

"It's alright."

I looked at the game. "So when can you deal me in?"

We played a couple of rounds of Cheat while Ruth gave us a rundown of exactly what she expected Will's sexual reaction to be to her new hair. Lizzie had barely spoken. It was like she was too scared to open her mouth in case my secret came tumbling out.

Ruth laid down two cards and called two sixes.

"Anyway," she said, watching carefully as Lizzie took her turn. "I think I need to give my new hair an outing. Who fancies a drink after college?"

Uh oh.

"I'm in," Amanda said, surprising us. She turned to Johnno. "Fancy a drink? Make the most of this weird summer weather?"

I saw Johnno squeeze her hand under the table. "Sounds

good to me," he said. "I might ask some of the guys along as well."

"How about you, Lizzie? Poppy?" Ruth asked.

I wracked my brains for an excuse. Any excuse. I couldn't use the cherry pie one again. It wasn't exactly effective last time.

"I'll come," Lizzie said. She gave me a small grin. "…But I think Poppy has other plans."

In unison they all swung round to look at me.

"Plans? What plans?" Ruth asked, smelling gossip.

"Umm, coursework?" I ventured, wishing my face wouldn't automatically turn red whenever I lied.

"You're lying."

"I'm not."

"Yes she is," Lizzie added.

I gave her what I hoped was a scary look. "Thanks a bunch," I said.

Amanda looked from me to Lizzie and back again. "What's going on, guys?"

"Nothing," Lizzie and I said at the same time.

"Bollocks," Ruth said. "Poppy. What are you doing tonight that's more important than helping me showcase my new hairdo?"

I groaned and put my head on the table. I couldn't think of one legitimate excuse.

"Lizzie, I hate you," I said, face still down on the table.

"What exactly is going on?" Ruth said, no doubt annoyed the attention had drifted from her new hair.

I waved my hand in surrender. "You tell her."

I could actually hear the smile in Lizzie's voice. "Poppy and Noah are seeing each other," she announced delightedly. I lifted my head cautiously to gauge the reaction. Lizzie looked relieved, like the secret had been choking her and she'd finally dislodged it from her windpipe. Amanda looked confused. Ruth's eyes narrowed.

"You're kidding me," she said.

I shook my head.

"You and Noah?"

I nodded my head.

"Really?"

Another nod.

The card game was forgotten.

"Since when?"

Lizzie answered the question for me. "Since for ever," she said. "Poppy's the one he dumped Portia for."

Great. Thanks for that reminder.

There was a stunned silence while everyone took in the bombshell. Ruth looked as if her centre of gravity had been removed. Amanda was still confused. And Lizzie just looked damned relieved to have let the secret out.

Amanda tentatively broke the quiet.

"Well, that's great, Popps," she said, clutching Johnno's hand, who obviously wasn't delighted to be in the middle of such a girlie conversation. "I didn't know you liked him, but, well, that's cool. I mean you never like anyone, so I'm just surprised really."

"Yeah, Poppy," Ruth said. "What happened to 'no man in Middletown is good enough for me'?"

I hated being the centre of attention. "I guess I changed my mind."

"I think it's sweet," Lizzie said. "You should've seen them together this morning. Poppy could hardly stand upright. She's well smitten."

"I am NOT smitten."

"Yes you are."

"No I'm not."

"Are."

"Not."

Ruth interrupted. "Hang on. What was going on this morning? When did you see Noah?"

Lizzie answered for me again. "He was waiting outside college for her. It was so cute. And he's arranged to see her tonight, which is why she can't join us for the hair-celebration pub visit."

Ruth's eyes narrowed further so they were more slit than eyeball. "Hang on," she said. "You're not going to miss going out with your friends to see some pointless boy instead, are you?"

I gulped. "Er."

"Because you always go on about how friends should come first…"

If I was a braver person, I would've pointed out all the instances in which Ruth called us to cancel last-minute – usually with the sloppy sounds of Will kissing her neck in the background.

I struggled to form an argument. "Well, I did make plans with him first."

"So?"

Then her stupid little face lit up. "I know. Invite him along. It would be great to meet your new *boyfriend* properly."

I curled my arms around my legs and went foetal, hoping this whole conversation would disappear into linguistic oblivion. "Umm."

"It would be nice to meet him properly," Amanda said. The bloody traitor.

"Er."

"That's great," Ruth said, ignoring my obvious discomfort. "Meet you at the Lock and Key at six then?"

I nodded, hating her.

The rest of the day whizzed past in a hating-Ruth blur. I seethed through Psychology, and barely spoke to Frank in English. The problem was that if I'd believed Ruth genuinely wanted to get to know Noah better – without some kind of twisted ulterior motive – I would have been fine. But her reaction to the big revelation had just been, well, nasty really. I reran that first fateful Band Night in my head. I remembered her throwing herself at him, them holding hands, the look on her face as she introduced him. I had never been an "issue" before for Ruth. Our friendship, if you could call it that, had never had to endure us fancying the same guys. Mainly that was because, pre-Noah, there hadn't been one Y-chromosomed culprit in a fifty-mile vicinity that had interested me. But, also, on the odd occasion I had found a man attractive, I'd never bothered to do anything about it. Why? Well, because Ruth was always there first. And my sarcastic-witty-banter flirting could never be a match for her cleavage-thrusting, sleep-with-a-guy-on-a-first-date sex appeal.

After the last bell I made my way home, feeling terrible. I'd been so looking forward to spending another evening with Noah. And now, at the risk of sounding like a huge saddo, I didn't want to share him.

The late batch of sunshine was still burning strong as I let myself in. Mum and Dad were still at work and were almost never home before seven. That was good. It meant no risk of Noah bumping into them and having to answer awkward-parent questions. My air-dried hair lay lank around my shoulders, so I spruced it up with some hairspray and put on a bit of make-up. I then wrestled with my inner-confidence over whether to wear the yellow sundress I owned. It was pretty short and showed off my legs. I would freeze to death the moment the sun set, but thought *sod it*. If I was going to face a raving Ruth, I should look marvellous while doing so. I was just applying some red lip stain when my doorbell rang. My heart started thudding and I went from nought-to-nervous instantly. I grabbed my bag off the banister and went to let Noah in.

He was leaning against the wall when I opened the door,

all James Dean-like. And he'd changed into a gorgeous charcoal-grey shirt.

Noah let out a low wolf-whistle. "Well, look at you," he said. "You look stunning."

I blushed in reply, heart still pounding. I stepped out and locked the door. As I was doing so, I felt Noah's hands snake around my waist from behind. I shuddered with pleasure as he pulled my hair back and gently kissed my neck.

"You're so beautiful," he whispered, his breath hot on my skin.

Another kiss. I almost melted.

"I can't believe I have you to myself all evening."

I turned into his embrace for a long, lingering kiss. Afterwards, my legs like jelly, I stepped back.

"Yeah, about that," I said. "There's been a change of plan."

"Huh?"

"I've been coerced into taking you to the Lock and Key for the evening. Ruth's orders."

Noah's face dropped. "You're kidding."

"I wish."

"Can't you get out of it?"

I shook my head. "Nope. She's rather forceful, as you know. They all want to 'meet you properly'." I made the speech marks with my fingers.

Noah looked a tad pissed off and I cursed Ruth for the millionth time that day.

"So does this mean…?"

soulmates

I nodded. "Yep. My friends know about us. Lizzie, well, she tried..." I broke off lamely.

"That girl needs to be gagged."

"She tried really hard. I think that's the longest she's kept any kind of secret."

In an attempt to pull Noah out of his bad mood, I tried winding my arm around his waist in what I hoped was a seductive manner. He responded, and pulled me into him, but wouldn't look at me.

I attempted to break the pregnant silence that had descended. "Anyway..." I said. "I suppose it's good we're going out. I really don't want to be one of those girls who spends all their time with just their boyfriend."

"Poppy. It's only our third 'date'. I think we're allowed to spend time just us two on our third date."

I hung my head. "Sorry."

"It's okay."

More silence.

Then I felt his hand grab mine. He twisted my arm and, within a second, I was pulled up against his body. I blinked, wondering how he'd managed it so quickly.

"Anyway," he said, his eyes staring into mine, "if I have to share you all evening, I want to make the most of the time I do have alone with you."

And then he kissed me like I'd never been kissed before. He held my face as his mouth explored mine. I closed my eyes and focused on the sensation, as his other hand entwined with my hair. I heard myself gasp but it seemed from far away. My involuntary exclamation seemed to make Noah even more determined. He nibbled my lip gently, then breathed out heavily, and finally his tongue strayed into my mouth. I let out another moan and kissed him back, my fingernails digging into his back. Still kissing me, Noah picked me up and pushed my full weight against the door. If anyone walked past we would probably be arrested, but I didn't care. My brain had gone someplace else. Somewhere where there was only pleasure, only Noah. My hands were now greedily clutching at the back of his neck, pulling his mouth as close to mine as I could. His taste was intoxicating.

And then we were interrupted by a huge rumble of thunder that shook the glass in the door.

I pulled my face away and looked up at the sky. "What the hell was that?"

Noah looked up as well. "Looks like a storm."

The summery sky had all but disappeared in the time that Noah and I had been kissing. Only the smallest patch of blue remained. The rest of the sky was dominated by grey, ominous-looking clouds. The air fizzled with electricity and it had that weird iron-y smell you get just before a really huge downpour. Despite the sun being almost completely blocked, it still felt humid and sticky.

"That's weird," I said, extracting myself from Noah's grasp reluctantly. "I didn't hear there would be a storm today."

"It's probably been caused by all this hot weather."

"I suppose."

"As long as the rain holds off long enough for us to get to the pub." He took my hand, casually, like nothing had just happened.

"So you don't mind?" I asked. "You know, going?"

He shook his head and his dark hair flopped into his eyes. "Nah. It's fine. But promise we don't have to stay the whole night?"

I squeezed his hand. "I promise."

18

When we arrived we found everyone already there.

They were stubbornly sitting in the beer garden even though it was obviously going to piss it down. Ruth and her fiery hairstyle were squished next to Will. He was pawing at her eagerly, trying to pull her into him, but she seemed disinterested. She was facing the pub door, her eyes thin, as if she'd been waiting for our arrival. Amanda and Johnno were nestled comfortably together, talking quietly. This left all Johnno's mates with the task of impressing Lizzie, who didn't look particularly impressed. Johnno's friends were what we called Football Lads. Big on sport, not so big on anything, erm, academically challenging. Not her type at all.

The garden was relatively empty. Most people had probably clocked the sky and moved indoors. We walked outside, each holding a beer.

"Do you remember when we were both here last?" Noah asked, a smile playing on his face.

I thought of that hot sunny day, not so long ago, and shuddered at the memory.

"I was such a bitch." I shook my head.

"You weren't. Well, you were. But I kind of deserved it." Noah swept some hair away from my face. "I'm still embarrassed, you know? When I run through that speech I made about how there was obviously 'something happening between us'. You don't know how much I've tortured myself. I thought, at the time, it sounded really dramatic and cool. But looking back…" It was his turn to shudder. "…Well, it was just dead embarrassing."

I laughed. "We were both stupid. Let's just forget about it and condemn the memories to the cringe cupboards of our brains." I caught Ruth's eye and waved. She gave me a half smile. "Come on then. Let's get this over with."

We said hi to everyone and they chorused it back. Lizzie and Amanda got up to say hello to Noah properly.

"He's so FIT," Amanda whispered in my ear as she gave me a hug.

I waved to Johnno's mates, who I knew vaguely from college, and nodded to Will.

"Alright, mate?" Noah said to him. "You still on for rehearsal tomorrow?"

"Yeah, sure, of course," Will replied, not paying much attention. He was squeezing some body-part of Ruth's under the table, but I couldn't make out which one. Her face didn't give anything away.

"Hi, Noah," she said, ignoring me. "Come sit by me. I've not seen you in ages."

So it was going to be like that then, was it?

"Alright, trouble?" Noah took the seat she'd saved. "Your hair is different."

"I got it done yesterday." She actually batted her lashes. "Do you like it?"

"Yeah sure, s'alright."

I slid in next to Noah, seething. I didn't feel I had the mental strength needed to get through the next hour or so, especially if Ruth was switched onto I-have-to-prove-he-fancies-me mode. I sipped my beer.

"Only alright?" Her voice was all high-pitched, and she playfully slapped Noah on the arm. "Come on. You can do better than that."

I stared into the depths of my bottle and pretended I wasn't there.

"Okay," Noah said. "It's lovely. Very good haircut. Well done."

"That's better."

"I love it. I told you that, didn't I, Ruth?" Will was eager to get involved. "Told you it made you look even more gorgeous, didn't I?"

Ruth ignored him and leaned in further towards Noah. "So you're a one-woman man now, are you?" She looked up at him from beneath her false eyelashes.

Noah took my hand and held it tight. I was so grateful for the reassurance that I could've licked him.

"I am indeed."

"That's a shame."

I gave Lizzie a look over the table. She, like everyone

else, was witnessing this bizarre and entirely inappropriate flirtation. Lizzie raised her eyebrows in an *I don't understand either* way.

I mouthed the word "Help" across to her and she nodded.

"It really is such a shame," Ruth continued. "I heard you had quite the reputation…"

"RIGHT," Lizzie interrupted, in a scarily loud voice. "I'm bored. Let's play a game."

The attention shifted to her.

I mouthed to her again: "Thank you."

She winked.

"What kind of game?" one of Johnno's friends asked.

"Yeah, what kind of game?"

"Umm…er…" Lizzie stumbled. She'd obviously only got as far as "game" in her distraction-planning.

"I know," said Ruth, never missing a beat. "Let's play Never Ever Have I."

A groan escaped my mouth and I tried to turn it into a cough. Never Ever Have I was basically a drinking game where sexually experienced girls could further promote themselves while downing shots and coyly admitting to having al-fresco sex. While people like me, who'd only seen one penis and that was in a Year Nine sex education video, stayed utterly sober and felt awful about themselves.

"Eww, no," Noah said, thankfully. "Anyone have a pack of cards on them? We could play Ring of Fire?"

Amanda, being Amanda, produced a pack of cards from her bag.

"You're so organized," Johnno told her, his eyes full of adoration.

"I...I...I just keep them on me." She handed the cards over to Noah, who shuffled the pack. He put an empty beer glass in the middle of the table and arranged the cards in a circle, face down, around it.

"How do you play?" I asked.

"Be patient. I'll explain everything."

Ring of Fire was apparently a game you played to get righteously drunk. Noah assigned a "rule" to every card. If you broke a rule, you had to drink. And you kept picking up cards until the pack ran out. It was the perfect distraction from Ruth's psychotic behaviour. The rain clouds were still suspended above us, but didn't let loose. We remained outside in the clammy air, having a brilliant time.

I wasn't usually a binge drinker but I was so wound up I found myself on my fourth bottle of beer pretty quickly. In fact, most of us were getting through them fast. Amanda was very pink in the face and kept dropping her head to Johnno's shoulder before shooting upright in shock. Will was getting even letchier with Ruth, which wasn't being appreciated. She was drinking white wine and wasn't as tipsy as everyone else. She sat scowling, watching all of us having fun, and sneering a little. Lizzie had made a rule where everyone had to make an animal noise after they said anything. If you forgot, you had to drink. Crazy but hilarious. Everyone was mooing and baaing and our table was getting many disapproving looks from the few other customers in the garden who just wanted a nice quiet drink.

Noah seemed to be feeling the alcohol as well. He was getting progressively more affectionate. This normally would've bothered me, as we were very much in public. But four beers, it appeared, was enough to make me an exhibitionist. We weren't being disgusting. He just had his hand on my leg. Okay, it might've been moving higher up said leg, but was never allowed above mid-thigh. I wasn't Ruth, after all. My whole body tingled at his touch and the clouds got darker and more foreboding above us.

Another round later and I was undeniably drunk. I could feel my head swimming and was yelling "INK INK, THAT'S THE NOISE A SQUID MAKES", while laughing hysterically at myself. I would be embarrassed later, no doubt, but at that moment, I didn't care. Life was brilliant, perfect, and very, very funny – although maybe only I understood the joke. I'd just plonked my beer bottle onto thin air and it had smashed on the floor, when Noah decided it was time to take me home.

He stood up. "Come on, clumsy," he said, taking my hand. "I think it's best you come with me."

"It's fiiiiiiine," I slurred. "I'll pick it up."

I swung down from the table towards the mass of broken green glass and tried to pick some up. Just as I was about to collect a particularly jagged piece, I found myself being hoisted upwards by Noah.

"I don't think that's the best idea, Poppy."

"It's fiiiiiiiine. I'm a very careful person."

"Leave it to the barman."

He stood me up carefully and I swayed and smiled at everyone – a huge beaming smile. One of Johnno's mates looked a little frightened.

"Right, I'm off," I declared to my drunken friends.

"Reallysh?" Amanda asked, her head on Johnno's shoulder. "So schoon?"

I nodded and it took a moment for my head to recover from the movement. "See you at college tomorrow."

College. With a hangover. The thought pinged into my fuzzy brain but pinged right back out again.

Lizzie struggled to her feet to say goodbye. "Make sure she gets home safely," she told Noah. "Hang on, I'm supposed to make an animal noise. Hee-haw hee-haw! I'm a donkey!"

"Your friends are crazy," Noah whispered.

"I love them very much," I said, still swaying. I tried to say goodbye to Ruth. I was dimly aware that I was likely to say something I regretted, so I blearily picked non-offensive words as best I could.

"Bye, Will, bye, Ruth. Well, we gave your hair a good debut, didn't we?"

She smiled and replied to Noah instead. "Your *girlfriend* seems a little bit worse for wear. She never could handle her drink."

"HELLLLLLOOOOOOOOO?" I yelled. "I am here. I can hear you, Ruth. With my ears. I have ears on my head. And they can hear you."

She ignored me like I was Will. "Well, I only hope she isn't sick on your shoes."

Noah took me by the shoulders and steered me away. I think he could sense my anger.

"She's fine. Come on, Poppy."

He walked me out of the beer garden as I waved backwards at everyone. Just as we left, I heard Amanda let out an almighty "NEIGH", followed by a startled hiccup.

19

It was still incredibly balmy as Noah and I made our way home. Being alone with him sobered me up a little. Only a little. I was trying very hard to walk in a straight line but it was somewhat of a struggle.

"You know what?" I asked, stumbling over my own feet and being corrected by Noah's strong arms.

"What?"

"I like you."

"Hmm. Well that's sort of how these things work, Poppy."

"You don't understand!" I was nestled under his arm, which didn't help the walking-straight process. "It's bad. I'm not supposed to like you. BAD things will happen. I don't let myself like people. Especially not boys like you. You're going to take my stupid little heart and do a poo on it."

Noah laughed. A lot.

"Well, that's a lovely image you've painted for me."

"Oh God. I just said the word *poo*, didn't I?"

"I'm afraid you did."

I hid further in him. "Well, that's done it now. You're

definitely going to poo on my heart now that I've said the word poo. And now I keep saying it. Can I go home now please and DIE?"

Noah dug me out from his armpit and straightened me up.

"I can't take you home just yet. It's only 8 p.m. and I don't think your parents will approve if I bring you home wasted."

We walked more. It was getting mildly more doable, although I still needed Noah's support.

"So where are we going then?"

"Back to mine."

I turned and walked backwards in what I thought was an alluring way. I felt confident. The fact I had just said the word "poo" repeatedly was already forgotten in my beer-infused haze.

"What are you doing?" Noah asked.

We were facing each other now. I took another step backwards and almost lost my balance again. Full of boozy ego, I took his hand and pulled him towards me. "So we're going back to yours then?"

"To sober you up. Yes."

I looked up at him. "You're not going to take advantage of me, are you?" I said softly, my hands now on his chest. "Because I'm very impressionable right now."

Noah broke eye contact. "Come on, Poppy. Stop messing about."

I pouted and then took a (careful) step closer to him. I wrapped my arms around his neck and slowly kissed him there. Noah let out a long breath.

"I'm not messing about," I whispered. "I *want* you to take advantage of me."

Noah very slowly extracted himself from my grasp. "So where did my little feminist girlfriend go?"

I shrugged. There's nothing like binge drinking to change your personality. Those TV warning adverts were right.

Noah took my hand firmly and led me down the street. Although there was a small hidden sober part of me that should have been glad he wasn't taking advantage of my drunken and admittedly forward behaviour, this was obscured by a huge humiliating surge of rejection. We walked (well, I was still stumbling) to Noah's as the sun began to set. The sky looked even heavier and there were far-off rumblings letting us know a storm was approaching.

I followed alongside Noah.

In a mood.

Not talking.

We took a short cut through a field dotted with large oak trees. It was almost dusk and I decided I couldn't be bothered to walk any further. Without any announcement, I let go of Noah's hand and sat down in the long grass.

Noah looked round. I was sitting cross-legged, with my arms crossed over my chest. Pouting.

"What's wrong now, Poppy?"

"Nothing."

"I'm not falling for that one." He sighed and sat next to me.

I looked away – still a bit embarrassed. There were a few houses framing the field, but it was too dark for anyone to see us. I could see an orange glow through the cracks of people's curtains. They were probably all sitting down to eat dinner or something.

I hadn't eaten any dinner. That was a mistake. My mouth tasted sour from the beer.

"Are we just going to sit here in silence?"

"You're the one who finds me repulsive." I sounded like a spoiled child. I didn't particularly care though.

"Poppy. Are you honestly telling me you're in a mood because I won't take advantage of you when you're drunk?"

The sober part of my brain won out for a moment. "Well, when you put it like that…" I smiled to myself.

Noah shuffled closer so our bums were almost touching. He took my hand. "Do you have any idea how hard you are to resist, Poppy Lawson?"

I could feel his breath on my neck. I shivered in the dark. "You seem to be managing well enough."

"I'm trying to be a gentleman. Don't you see?"

"But you're not a gentleman with other girls!"

"Poppy, I don't see you as I saw those other girls. That's why I'm trying to resist your drunken advances. But it's very, very hard. Believe me."

I wanted him to kiss me so much it almost physically hurt. I leaned over and slowly kissed his neck. "Can you resist me when I do that?" I asked. I lowered my head and kissed his neck again.

Noah closed his eyes. "Just about, yes."

"What about if I do this?" I carefully nibbled his earlobe and he let out a small sigh. I showered kisses on his face, his eyes, and teasingly brushed my lips against his. I felt his mouth respond but moved back to his neck.

Noah's mouth hung half-open. "Okay. I'm managing. Sort of…"

"How about if I do this?"

Mustering all my leftover drunken confidence, I kissed him fully on the mouth. I had one hand round his neck, scratching through his hair, and my other slid up his shirt. The moment my hand touched his bare skin, Noah groaned and his resolve evaporated. He flipped me onto my back and lay above me, kissing me furiously. It felt amazing. My skin was quivering and goose pimples erupted over every part of my body. I tugged at his shirt.

"Poppy, I'm trying to do the honourable thing here," he said into my mouth.

"I don't care."

And I didn't. I really didn't.

Every sensible thought in my brain had vanished and been replaced by Noah and the taste of Noah. I didn't notice the sky had turned a deep opaque black above us, or that all the birds had gone silent. My back arched up, pushing me as close to his body as possible. I felt the cool touch of his hand around my waist. His hands strayed up my back and under my dress…

A loud CRACK of thunder interrupted us before things

got more compromising. The shock of it made me scream. We broke apart just in time to see huge forked licks of lightning spasm across the sky.

"What the hell is going on?" I said.

Before Noah had a chance to answer, the clouds gave up their resistance. As if at the click of a finger, the dry air was replaced by heavy curtains of sheeting rain. I was drenched immediately. It soaked through my thin cotton dress, saturated my hair and filled my shoes.

Noah grasped my hand. "Come on, we need to get inside."

We ran, our hands raised pathetically above our heads to try and shield us from the urgent rain. It ricocheted off the pavement and, already, streams had formed and were gushing down the sides of the roads. I kept close to Noah as we ran through the downpour. Sometimes the waterfall was so heavy I couldn't see him. But as flickers of lightning raged furiously above us, his tall dark figure was illuminated in front of me.

"We're almost there," he yelled, his voice muffled by the rain.

The storm showed no sign of abating. I'd never witnessed anything like it. Every crack of thunder was so loud it shook my bones with some sort of apocalyptic dread. I was scared. It was directly above us and I had visions of the lightning touching the wet ground and its fatal force running through the river of a pavement we were now wading through. Another flash revealed we were outside

Noah's flat. Relief flooded through me. Noah managed to get his key in the lock, then he pulled me into the hallway and slammed the door shut behind us.

20

It was much quieter inside. We stood in silence and watched the storm batter Middletown into pieces. A wind was now bending the trees well beyond their normal shapes. Debris was careering down the street and the water levels were rising. Puddles in the road were already almost swamping the pavements. We could hear the gurgle of the drains as they struggled to swallow the vast amounts of rainwater.

Noah took my hand. "Come on. We need to get dry."

He led me into his apartment. I stood in the living room, with my teeth chattering. He went into the bathroom and came out holding two fluffy white towels.

"Here," he said, tossing me one. "Try and dry yourself off as much as you can, but you might need a shower to warm up."

I took the towel thankfully and began vigorously rubbing myself down. My dress was soaked through and, when I twisted the hem, water actually bubbled out onto the floor. "I think I'm going to have to take you up on that shower offer."

Noah raised his eyebrows suggestively but the storm had sobered me up entirely.

"By myself," I added.

He shrugged, grinning. "I didn't say anything."

He led me into his massive bathroom with the giant infinity shower. It had one of those huge showerheads that made it feel like you were being rained on. I'd been rained on enough for one day, but at least this water was hot. Noah demonstrated how to adjust the temperature. Then he left and came back with an oversized shirt.

"I'm going to put your dress in the airing cupboard so it can dry off." He put the shirt in the corner. "You can wear this while it's drying. It should be big enough to cover… er…everything. I'll jump in after you."

"Thank you."

"I'm just going to be in the living room…trying very hard to ignore the fact you're going to be naked only metres away."

I giggled and chucked my towel at him. He caught it, hung it up behind the door, and left me alone.

I made the water as hot as I could stand and then moved under it. It was heavenly. I scrubbed off my make-up, grabbed some of Noah's shampoo and lathered up. I was getting the first initial twinges of a headache – no doubt an early indicator of the hangover to come. I rinsed, then found that, amazingly enough, Noah had conditioner. I smoothed some through my hair before rinsing again. After I dried off, I put on Noah's shirt. It fell to just below my bum and would do for the moment. I looked through his bathroom cabinets and found a hairdryer under the sink. Now that was odd – but useful nonetheless. I plugged it in and blow-dried my hair upside down. I cleaned the steam off the cabinet mirror and looked at myself. Not bad. I didn't have a stitch of make-up on and my hair was a bit fluffy but I looked…reasonable. I took a breath and emerged from the bathroom.

Noah was sitting on the sofa, a towel under him to stop his wet clothes ruining the leather. He was watching the news.

I shyly shuffled over and sat away from him so I didn't get re-wet. Two mugs of steaming tea were on the table in front of us.

I pointed at them. "One of those had better be for me."

"It is. I thought you might need a bit more sobering up." He looked me up and down, and I self-consciously rubbed a hand through my newly-washed hair. "You look alarmingly good."

I picked up the tea and took a grateful sip. "Don't get any ideas," I said. "That drunken predator possessing my body an hour ago has retreated back to the Land of Drunken Mistakes."

Noah laughed. "Well, I would be lying if I said I wasn't a little disappointed. Oi!" he said, as I hurled a cushion at him. "Poppy, I'm joking. I'm sorry I wasn't the gentleman I set out to be. You honestly don't have a clue how…erm… sexy you are. And, well, it's hard not to be a total guy when you're behaving like, well, you know…"

I felt my cheeks burn. I had a flashback of me drunkenly slurring, *I want you to take advantage of me.* I winced.

Sensing my discomfort, Noah edged closer, being careful not to get me wet. He took my hand and I looked down at our entwined fingers.

"Look," he said. "I've not felt this way about anyone before and I don't want to mess this up. I've rushed…things with girls in the past and it's never been special. Ever. I really want it to be special with you."

He started stroking the inside of my thumb. My favourite thing. I didn't know what to say. "Anyway," he continued. "Despite the fact it's remarkably hard not to leap on you, maybe we should cool things off a bit? Get to know each other better? Because I really want to get to know you, Poppy…"

He cupped my face and studied it for an answer. I thought about what he'd said. It soothed me. I'd been so wound up about his sexual expertise that I was becoming someone I didn't quite recognize. And much as the things we did felt amazing, I think I knew in myself it was probably a bit too soon.

"I think that's probably a good idea."

Noah kissed me on the eyebrow. "Good, so we're agreed? Now, if you don't mind –" he stood up – "I'm absolutely desperate for a shower."

He was still soaked through and I remembered the storm. I looked out the huge windows and gasped.

"Oh my God," I said, my hand to my mouth. "It's still really going for it out there."

And it was. The rain was still sheeting down against the pitch-black sky. Yet it seemed far removed from Noah's apartment, like his living room windows were a doorway to a different reality.

"I know." Noah picked up the towel from the sofa. "The local news is going mad. They've put out emergency flood warnings." He saw my face. "It's okay. I've already checked. This part of town is going to be okay. They think. Though it might be worth ringing your parents and letting them know you're safe. I'll walk you home when it stops raining."

Phone. Parents. Mum would be freaking out.

Noah went into the bathroom. I heard the shower start up and walked to the window to get a better look outside. I pressed my face to the glass and my breath frosted around my mouth. The sky was so dark but, in the orange glow of a street light, you could just about catch sight of heavy rain. It was coming down in long lines instead of drops. I wandered back to the sofa and turned the TV volume up. Some poor local news reporter was standing under an umbrella, trying to deliver a report.

"As you can see," she said, her hair whipping around her face, "the conditions out here are very dangerous. Forecasters are telling people not to go outside unless it's completely necessary." A lightning bolt flashed behind her, and a millisecond later it illuminated Noah's living room. She must've been filming not too far from where I was.

They now had a split screen and the newsreaders – safe and snug in the studio – were bombarding the stressed reporter with questions.

"So what's caused this freak weather then, Jennie?" the anchorman asked.

Jennie took a moment to reply because her giant umbrella had blown inside out. She struggled with it, her make-up smearing as the rain hit her. With a tough tug, the umbrella righted itself and Jennie returned her attention to the camera.

"That's a good question, Martin," she replied, professional despite the mascara smear down her cheek. "What's making the situation worse is that not one weather forecaster predicted this storm. It literally blew in out of nowhere. It's got scientists stumped. They think it might have something to do with the unseasonably warm snap we've been having, but at this stage, they're just guessing." She smiled into the camera.

"And how is Middletown holding up?" the anchorman asked, holding his earpiece.

The camera panned down to Jennie's wellington-clad feet, which were ankle deep in water. I gasped as the camera zoomed out to reveal she was standing in Middletown High Street. We'd been drinking there only an hour or so ago. Now most of it was underwater.

"As you can see, there's been some localized flooding," Jennie said, shouting to be heard over the wind. "Businesses are struggling to protect their buildings, as there aren't many sandbags available. Obviously, because this storm was unexpected, there hasn't been any time to bring in supplies. We've not heard of any casualties so far, but residents are being urged to stay inside and sit this one out. If you live near the river and the water levels are rising, take your valuables upstairs. Let's just hope that's an unnecessary precaution…"

I turned on the mute button. I'd heard enough. I flipped open my slightly soggy mobile and, sure enough, I had eight missed calls from my mother and two voicemail messages. I jabbed in my home number.

Mum answered on the first ring.

"Poppy?"

"Yes. It's me."

"Oh, thank goodness. We were getting worried. I've rung about ten million times. Why didn't you pick up? Where are you? Are you safe?"

I sighed and nodded. "Yes, I'm fine. Sorry I didn't pick up, my phone was on silent. I'm okay though, I promise. I'm at a friend's house. I think I'm going to have to stay here until the rain stops."

Mum went quiet on the other end. "Which friend's house?"

I swallowed. "Noah's."

More silence.

"I see."

"We met Lizzie and the others for a drink and then the rain started. We came here because it's closer."

More silence.

"Okay then. Well, try to get home tonight. I suppose if it stays really bad you're going to have to stay over."

That shocked me. The thought hadn't occurred to me.

"Are you sure you're okay with that, Mum?"

"You're seventeen now, Poppy. You're sensible. I trust you. Try and get home, but I promise I won't freak out if you can't get here. But please keep your phone nearby and stay in touch."

"Okay."

"Speak to you soon."

I hung up.

Staying the night with Noah. Ha. Just after we'd decided to slow things down. There was another huge crack as more thunder announced itself. At this rate I was going to have to stay two nights.

The shower was still running, so I decided to ring and check my friends were alright.

I rang Lizzie first, of course.

"The world is ending," she said, without bothering to say hello.

"No it's not. It's just a storm. Did you get home okay?"

"Only just. I think I'm still drunk."

"What happened?"

"Well, Ruth dragged Will off soon after you left, so we stayed for another round with Johnno's mates. Then we looked at the sky and it looked like Armageddon, so we all ran home. I don't really remember much more. That game Noah taught us is lethal! Anyway, are you alright?"

I looked at the TV. Jennie was now standing in water up to the top of her wellies.

"I'm alright. Got pretty wet but I'm at Noah's now. I don't have a clue how I'm going to get home."

Lizzie squealed. "You're going to have to stay the night."

I felt a bit nervous. "Perhaps."

Another squeal. I held the phone away from my ear. "Calm down, Lizzie. The rain might stop."

"Yeah, right. Have you not looked out the window?"

"It might," I insisted.

"Well, make sure you tell me everything."

"Of course."

"I'm going to go watch the news. I bet you college is cancelled tomorrow."

"You reckon?"

"Yeah. It's probably underwater by now."

"It's a bit scary, isn't it?"

"Not for me. I live on top of a hill. Gravity is keeping me safe from harm."

"Well, lucky you."

We spoke for a few more minutes. Lizzie said she'd heard from Amanda and that she was fine. And Amanda had apparently spoken to Ruth and she was fine too.

There was nobody left to call.

I lay back on the sofa, my legs over the armrest. I closed my eyes and listened to the rain hitting the roof. Hard. I was scared. I didn't know if I was ready to sleep next to Noah yet. I didn't quite trust myself. My heart started thumping and I had to squeeze my eyes shut and do my breathing exercises until it calmed down again.

I was interrupted by Noah emerging from the bathroom in a cloud of steam.

"All clean," he announced.

I sat up but almost had to lie down again. He was still wet and wearing only a towel. It was wrapped low around his body, exposing what can only be described as a truly beautiful chest. My heart started thumping faster.

"What?" Noah asked, as I sat there staring. I didn't trust myself to go anywhere near him. He looked too fantastic.

"Umm," I said, blushing. Again. "Let's just say that if you're serious about this 'taking things slowly' thing, then maybe you shouldn't walk out of the shower looking like that." I threw my arm in his direction.

Noah grinned.

"What's so funny?"

He twirled. "Am I that irresistible?"

"Shut up."

He walked towards me, still dripping.

I covered my eyes with my hands. "I can't see you."

Then he jumped on me and pinned me to the sofa.

Having exposure to that much of his skin was like giving an alcoholic a massive beer. Noah, now on top of me, kissed me gently on the mouth and my mouth responded. Without meaning to, I found myself stroking his wet chest. More thunder erupted above us and his towel dropped lower. He stopped kissing me.

"So this taking-it-slow thing…"

"We're not doing very well, are we?"

"Not really."

"Well, I was doing fine until you came out deliberately all wet and naked…" He opened his mouth to protest. "Oh, come on. You did it on purpose."

His open mouth turned into another heart-stopping mischievous grin. "Okay. Maybe."

I sat myself up and tried not to look at his rippling torso. "I didn't take you for the six-pack type. Aren't you supposed to be malnourished-looking when you're in a band?"

Noah shrugged. "I have a lot of spare time."

"It shows."

He grinned again.

"Go and put it away now."

And Noah padded off to the bedroom.

He emerged fully clothed and made more cups of tea. As the kettle was boiling, he switched the heating on and I felt it drift up from the floor.

"You actually have underfloor heating?"

He nodded.

"Your parents really are loaded, aren't they?"

"Yep."

I took a cup of tea from him. We sat drinking for a moment in silent contentment.

"I still can't believe you have underfloor heating."

"I would rather have parents that cared about me. Like yours."

"Sorry. I forgot."

I shifted towards him so I could rest my head on his shoulder. He, in turn, rested his head on my head and we stared at the muted television screen.

"You might have to stay over," he said, watching Jennie wade through Middletown High Street.

"I know. I rang Mum and she said I could."

He looked surprised. "Really?"

I nodded. Noah raised an eyebrow.

"I think she would rather risk me losing my innocence than my life."

"Makes sense."

"There will be no losing of innocence though, will there?"

His smirk faded and he looked serious. "I suppose not. No." He exhaled heavily. "Damn though. It's going to be hard to behave myself if you're lying in bed next to me."

"Maybe I should sleep on the sofa?"

"Ahh, man. Really?" He was stroking my legs, his hand getting a little higher each time.

"Well, if you're not going to behave yourself then I'm going to have to."

Noah pulled my chin towards him and gave me a soft kiss on the lips. "Well, if exerting some self-control is the price I have to pay to ensure I get to wake up next to you tomorrow morning, then I guess I can deal with it."

I kissed him back.

"You mean it?"

"I mean it."

We spent the rest of the evening cuddled up, watching the news updates. I had never felt so relaxed around a guy before. Everything seemed comfortable and natural. Our bodies fitted together like pieces of a jigsaw and conversation flowed without awkwardness. Noah told me a bit about his childhood. About how all he had ever wanted to do was play the guitar. His dad had helped teach him, and they would sit together in the garage for hours, strumming along with each other. Once, his father told him how he'd wanted to be a rock star when he was younger but had given it up when he started his Business Studies degree. Before he knew it, he had a suit, a wife and a mortgage. Noah said it was the only time his father had ever opened up to him. And on that day, he'd promised himself he would never give up something he loved just because life got in the way.

In between talking and munching on some sandwiches Noah whipped up, we would cuddle or kiss. We would take the piss out of each other or play-fight. I hated to admit it to myself, but I'd started to think I'd been wrong about love. That night was everything Hollywood had promised and more. Sometimes when I was talking, or saying something stupid and blushing, I would catch Noah looking at me, his eyes wide and searching. And he would be smiling to himself. And I knew he was enjoying me – me just being me. That was the thing, I couldn't pretend around Noah. My personality just kept tumbling out. But nothing I said or did put him off. In fact, it seemed to enrapture him even more.

And it was the same with me. There were times when he was talking that I would tune out and just look at him. The way his mouth moved, the dimples that formed on his cheeks when he smiled in a particular way. The habit he had of scratching his ear when he was talking about something that made him sad or uncomfortable. I was obsessed with every tiny eccentricity his body had, and everything he said or did just reaffirmed the dawning knowledge that I was completely falling for him. I knew it didn't make sense. I still barely knew him. And I knew I was being a massive hypocrite. Yet I couldn't shake off this sense that we were meant to find each other. That we were each other's matches.

By about 11 p.m., the storm still showed no signs of abating. We could hear the rain attacking the roof as I rang my mum to say I was staying over. She told me to be careful and I cringed a little, hoping she didn't mean what I thought she meant. When I hung up, Noah was standing.

"Right, gorgeous. Bedtime." He offered me a hand to pull me off the sofa.

I made my voice go sulky. "But I'm not tired yet."

"But it's past your bedtime."

"How do you know my bedtime?"

Noah picked me up in one effortless swoop, and carried me to the bedroom. I screamed and giggled.

"Come on. Time for bed."

He flopped me down onto his big double bed and held his body over me. "Hmm," he said, looking at me beneath him. "This is going to be harder than I thought." And he lowered himself down to kiss me. "Much, much harder than I thought."

I used all the physical and mental strength I had to push him off and got to my feet.

"I'm going to brush my teeth. It's past my bedtime, remember?"

I locked myself in the bathroom and got myself ready for bed. I tried to brush my teeth as adequately as I could using my finger. I splashed some water on my face and returned to the bedroom.

Noah was already under the duvet.

"Well, this is weird," I said as I climbed in next to him.

I curled up on my side facing him, one arm supporting my head.

"You sleepy?" he asked.

"Not really."

"Me neither."

I was very aware of how close our bodies were. It felt much more intimate now we were in a bed, lying down.

"Come here," he said, and pulled me to him. He didn't kiss me, just held my body and stared at me, his eyes soft. He was only wearing his boxers, and being able to feel so much of his skin was almost too much. He stroked my hair and then kissed me gently on the cheek.

"You're not backing out of this taking-things-slowly thing, are you?" I whispered.

He stroked my cheek on the spot where he'd just kissed

it and shook his head. "No. It's probably for the best. It's tough though. It's taking all my mental energy not to dry hump you right now."

I giggled. "Wow. And they say romance is dead."

"It's not. And I'm determined to prove it to you."

"Yeah yeah."

Noah turned over and flicked off his bedside light, casting us into darkness.

"I don't think I'm going to be able to sleep a wink with you next to me," he said.

I yawned. Not meaning to. "Well, I've got to get some sleep. I've got stupid college tomorrow."

I felt an electric shock shoot down my leg and I realized Noah had put one hand on my waist under his oversized shirt.

"Are you sure you need to sleep in this?"

"Careful now," I said. "It's not too late for me to exile myself to the sofa."

He didn't let go. "Sorry. I just can't stop touching you. It's like a compulsion."

"That's a new one. Did you make that line up by yourself?"

"It's true…"

My eyes were beginning to adjust to the dark and I could just about make out Noah's features. The whites of his eyes were shining. "I don't mean it just in a…sexual way, Poppy," he said. "Well obviously, yes, I fancy the hell out of you. But it's something more than that."

I lay there silently. My heart began pounding with the

anticipation of what he was going to say next. I was so scared it was going to be "I love you", the words I'd been thinking all evening. Those three daunting words that would change everything, make us even more serious, and make me an utter hypocrite. But I was so much more frightened that he *wasn't* about to say them. That would be worse.

"The thing is…this is going to sound soppy, but it's like my life didn't make sense until I met you. I know we've only just got together, but already my life seems divided into pre-Poppy and post-Poppy. And I just, well, I love every little thing about you. And the truth is…" He stopped for a second and wouldn't meet my eyes. "I love you, Poppy Lawson."

The words sank into my heart, filling my body with a golden glow. I opened my mouth to speak, but Noah interrupted me.

"Sorry. I know it's probably far too soon. And I know you don't believe in all this… You don't have to say it back. There's no pressure. I just wanted to say it anyway. In fact, I've wanted to say it all day…but—"

It was my turn to interrupt. "Noah? Stop babbling."

He stopped.

I took a deep breath and sought out his face in the dark. "I love you too."

The moment the words spilled out of my mouth, I knew I meant them. I was in love. In love with Noah. I had no idea how it had happened or why. But the fact that I loved him was the only thing in my life I was certain about in that moment.

Noah was quiet.

"Do you mean that?"

I nodded. "I really do."

He let out a huge breath. "Really really?"

I smiled. "Yes!"

"I was so scared you weren't going to say it back."

"Well I have."

"But we only just started going out."

"I know."

"And you don't believe in love."

"I didn't. But I do now. I *so* do now."

And we both started laughing. Manically, at the joy and relief of it all. He pulled me right into him and I lay in the nook of his underarm, both of us smiling uncontrollably and bursting into giggles every minute or so.

Old Poppy would've been yelling at the television, chucking popcorn at us on the screen, saying it was ridiculous – ludicrous, even – to say "I love you" so soon. I had changed beyond recognition, become everything I'd ever hated, and yet I was so, so happy I didn't care.

Noah was lying on his back.

"I think it's fair to say I am the happiest guy in the entire world right now."

"Well, that can't be a bad thing."

He turned onto his side, unearthing me so I was on my side too. Our faces were almost touching.

"I love you," he said again.

"And I love you."

"But I really really bloody love you."

"And I really really bloody love you."

And we stayed like that for hours, repeating the words and laughing with joy until sleep eventually found us both. And then we slept soundly together, entwined in each other's arms, while the storm continued to rage outside.

It was taking all of Rain's mental energy for him not to lose his temper. He felt sick, physically sick, and couldn't shake off the sense that this whole thing couldn't be real. It wasn't happening, it couldn't be happening. It shouldn't be allowed to happen.

He read the updated news reports in horror. His hand was permanently glued to his mouse and he unconsciously clicked every five seconds to reload the internet page. It had already gone too far. He assumed someone must've been killed by now, someone always died in floods. If only Dr. Beaumont had just DONE something.

She sat next to him, also attached to her computer, but she didn't seem stressed. In fact, she was almost chilled. She was leaning back, wearing that sick, sadistic smile.

"It's all kicking off now," she said, breaking the uncomfortable silence.

He didn't trust himself to speak so he just nodded and bit his tongue.

"Fascinating, isn't it?" She was oblivious to his mood. "I bet you never dreamed of seeing a connection like this in training.

You can know the theory, hypothesize the consequences, but it's just not the same as seeing it played out in real life."

More silence.

"And this case is just so intriguing. You know, I think their bodies might have adapted to fit each other? Can you believe it? I've never had the chance to monitor something like this, right from the beginning and watch it build. The match is extraordinary. We're going to have to completely rewrite most of the training course. And there's still so much to learn, to see…"

Rain couldn't handle it any more. If he had to listen to her for one more second, he would smash the computer over that smug head of hers.

"Anita, this is WRONG."

Her smile faded. "What did you just say?"

Unable to control himself, everything he'd been feeling these past days came tumbling out of his mouth without a second thought for his career, his future, or his punishment.

"It's just wrong. How can you sit there and do nothing? How can you let this happen? It's actually inhumane – YOU'RE inhumane. What are you doing to these poor people? You don't think it's going to be hard enough when we intervene? You're just letting them fall in love. How? How can you do that? I don't understand." He bashed his mouse down on the desk.

"And what about the other people caught up in all this? If anyone's dead, then that's your fault. You'll have blood on your hands. I don't know why you're doing this, but it has to stop. You have to stop. I'm going to ring the Defence Secretary and—"

"You. Will. Do. No. Such. Thing."

Her words cut through his like a sharp blade through butter. The cold authority in her voice chilled his bones. He dared himself to meet her gaze. Her glare was ice-cold, her face seething with anger. He jutted out his jaw and matched her eye contact.

"I'll do it, Anita. I will."

"No you won't."

"I have to."

"I don't think you understand the situation you're in, Rain."

She was undoubtedly angry but her voice was calm, cool, and that unnerved him. He fidgeted uncomfortably in his chair.

"Do you honestly think the Defence Minister would listen to a nobody like you? Over someone like me? I, personally, think we need to let this match run. There's never been a tolerance built between a couple before. Do you not see the potential here? If we can work out a way for them to be together?" She broke off for a moment, her eyes glinting with something, and Rain's brain jumped to the rumours about her…whispers he'd heard in the corridor about Anita. About her apparently having once had a match of her own. That was why she was considered so important to the company – her "insider" insight was invaluable, they said. But Rain wasn't so sure now. How could someone that… broken be of any use? Wasn't she more of a liability?

"There's no out, Rain, you know that. You knew that when you signed the contract and signed your life away to us. And, as I'm the leading expert in this field, and your only chance of ever getting promoted, I suggest you shut the hell up or you'll be condemned to a lifetime of number-crunching."

Rain didn't know what to say. He'd forgotten about the contract. About how he'd promised to dedicate his whole life to the work done here. He'd been so stupid, so excited about being let in on a big secret that he'd never stopped to think what would happen if he didn't like the big secret.

"Look, Anita…"

She glared at him.

"Sorry…I mean Dr. Beaumont. I understand what you're saying, I really do. But do you not think this is getting a bit out of hand?"

"That is not your decision, Rain, it's mine. Now I suggest you go and make me another cup of coffee before I decide to completely demote you."

What could he do? He walked away to make the drink. This was his bed, he was going to have to lie in it and accept what was happening. As he waited for the coffee to filter, his thoughts drifted to the poor kids causing all this trouble. What he was going through was nothing compared to what they would have to face. Maybe Anita was right. Maybe they should be given their small slice of happiness for now.

Because when it all kicked off, neither of them would ever be happy again.

21

I woke up with the sun shining through my eyelids. I groaned and rubbed my eyes before slowly opening them. Forgetting where I was, I jolted with shock when I found Noah's face in front of mine.

"Morning," he said, a huge grin on his face. He was lying on his side, only about ten inches away.

"Have you been watching me sleep, you weirdo? Because that's not romantic, you know. It's just a tad creepy."

He laughed and covered his eyes with his hands. "I've only been watching for a moment. And it wasn't for creepy purposes, I just knew it would wake you up."

I sat up, hoping my hair wasn't too mad. "An alarm clock is less crazy-stalkerish."

"I know. But it's also less fun."

The sunlight was streaming through Noah's bay windows and specks of dust danced in the glow.

"The rain's stopped then?"

"Apparently so. College is cancelled though. I rang and

checked for you. It's partly flooded. Not too bad, but enough to close."

"Brilliant. That means I miss Psychology."

Noah kissed my cheek, being careful not to breathe on me. "Breakfast?"

I nodded. "Sounds great."

"Cool. I'll make eggs."

He climbed out of bed energetically, while I leaned back and enjoyed the relaxed relief you get when you don't have to get up after all.

Noah stopped at the door. "Poppy?"

"Yeah?"

He looked down at his feet. "What I…we…said last night. Was it just a dramatic thing brought on by the apocalyptic-style circumstances?"

I smiled, enjoying his vulnerability. "It wasn't in my case." I picked up his abandoned pillow and threw it at him. "And it better not have been in your case either."

He dodged the pillow, picked it up and chucked it back. I tried to duck but it hit the side of my head.

"Oooph." I fell backwards on the bed and lay there, a little stunned.

Noah burst out laughing. "I completely, utterly, and totally love you," he said, then bellyflopped onto the bed and gave me another big kiss, before running into the kitchen.

* * *

Twenty minutes later, we were eating scrambled eggs on toast contentedly in Noah's posh kitchen. I was still wearing his oversized shirt and Noah was in boxers. We were sitting on stools pulled up against his beautiful charcoal countertops.

"So you can cook, apparently," I said, shovelling down the eggs.

Noah poured me some orange juice. "It's just one of my many talents."

"Modesty not being one of them, though?"

He took a sip of his own juice. "Ha. You got me there."

My mobile phone gave a muffled beep from Noah's bedroom. I padded barefoot to get it and found a text from Lizzie.

Meeting for coffee and catch-up at 12. Be there.

"Who is it?" Noah called.

"Lizzie."

"What does she want?"

"To meet for coffee later."

I walked back to the kitchen. I was torn. Part of me longed to fill in my friends (minus Ruth) on last night's revelations. But the other part didn't want to leave Noah. It felt like it would physically hurt. I shook my head.

No. I was independent. I had a life other than a boyfriend...

"That's a shame. I was hoping we could hang out today."

"What about band practice?"

"I can cancel. The studio might be flooded anyway."

I shook my head. "Nope. We're not going to be one those THOSE couples."

Noah looked confused. "What couples?"

"You know, the ones that stop having any sort of individual life once they get together. I refuse to." I banged my glass down a bit heavily and some juice sloshed onto the counter. "Oops."

Noah got a dishcloth from the sink and wiped it up. "Have you finished ranting?"

I nodded.

"Good." He took my hand. "I have a life, Poppy." I looked down at my half-eaten eggs, slightly embarrassed by my outburst. "I have managed to live a whole seventeen years without you. And yes, it's been less fun, but I've done just fine. It's just one day, one band practice."

I continued staring at my leftover breakfast. "Sorry."

Noah tilted my head up so I would look at him. "I do get where you're coming from, Poppy. I know you're your own person, which is why I love you. But you don't have to be so scared about becoming a cliché or something..."

I couldn't believe how well he knew me already. It was like he could look straight into my thoughts.

"I do have a little bit of a...thing about clichés," I admitted.

"What is it? You're convinced everyone else is one and you're different?"

"Sort of."

Noah stood up, gently brushed my hair to one side and kissed my neck.

"It's just a relationship, Poppy. They're all clichéd. There's nothing special about us – apart from the fact it's us. You and me. And I'm glad it's you and me, because I feel like what we've found is pretty great. But I think this 'falling in love' stuff is just the same for everyone."

I kissed him on the lips. "I do wish I could spend the whole day with you, you know that, right?"

"What about us having to lead individual and separate lives?"

"That was before you said all that nice stuff."

"God, you're a right little sell-out, aren't you? A few compliments and all your morals go out the window."

I got up and pushed him. "Oi. Take that back."

He caught my hand as I went to push him again, smiling. "Never."

One of Noah's fingers tickled my waist. I batted his hand away but he caught it and wedged my arm under his armpit before tickling me again with his spare hand. I squealed and started hitting him over the head, trying to get him to stop. He laughed and blocked me easily. More tickling. It felt wonderful and terrible at the same time.

"God, is play-fighting our 'thing' now?" I gasped through another tickle onslaught. "This really is a stereotype."

With that, Noah tossed me over his shoulder with ease. I screamed, upside down.

"Right. I've had it with you."

He ran with me to the bedroom, as I continued trying to break free, and tossed me onto the bed. Before I had a chance to recover, Noah was lying above me, his hand on my leg, trailing up beneath my shirt.

"Here's the thing about clichés," he said breathily into my ear. "They might be predictable, but they still feel pretty good."

And then he kissed me and I didn't give a damn about anything for a good ten minutes.

A few hours, and several kisses later, we emerged from Noah's flat to be independent and sociable. My dress had dried adequately overnight and Noah insisted I was pretty enough to meet my friends make-up-free. We were in such a loved-up bubble I'd forgotten the storm. I was crudely reminded the moment we stepped out of Noah's flat.

"Oh my God," I muttered, looking around me.

It looked like a mini disaster zone. Water was gurgling earnestly out of the drain, spilling out onto the road. Broken tree branches lay sprawled across the tarmac; one was sitting comfortably through someone's smashed car windscreen.

"Well, this isn't usual," Noah said, taking hold of my hand.

We walked towards town in awed silence, taking in the unexpected devastation. It got worse the closer we got. A telephone pole had fallen down and smashed into a shopfront. The water got much higher. We managed to dodge most of the flooded bits but there were times Noah gave me a piggyback and waded through knee-deep water. He'd had the foresight to bring some spare clothes and said he would change at the studio.

If the studio wasn't underwater.

When we eventually got to the town centre, despite seeing it on the news, it was still a shock. Sludgy-coloured water lapped at shopfronts, and retailers with saddened faces were sweeping out as much as they could onto the already saturated road. The place where Jennie the reporter had stood was occupied by a small child wearing waders and driving a remote-controlled boat.

"Well, at least someone is having some fun," Noah commented.

"I'm not sure why Lizzie suggested meeting for coffee in town," I said. "Surely the place is going to be closed?"

"Knowing Lizzie, she knows exactly where's been hit, and is already getting quotes from her neighbours to flog to the local rag."

He was probably right.

We continued dodging the worst bits until we arrived at the coffee shop. It was open and I could see Lizzie, Ruth and Amanda through the window.

I turned to Noah. "So I'm off to be a separate entity now."

"Me too."

We stood looking at each other.

"Is it really pathetic to say I'm going to miss you?" I asked, pulling at his T-shirt.

"No," Noah said. "What's really pathetic is that I was just about to say the same thing."

"Oh God, we're officially disgusting."

Noah gave me a quick knee-buckling kiss on the lips.

"Totally disgusting."

The girls already had cups of coffee and so I first went to the counter and ordered my customary banana milk.

Ruth eyeballed it when I sat down next to her. "You're still five then?"

I took a sip. "Yup."

I leaned back on the sticky leather sofa. None of them looked like they'd slept much.

"So what's up?" I asked. "Are everyone's houses okay?"

"Ours is a little flooded actually," Amanda said, wringing her hands and looking upset. "Not badly, just some in the kitchen. But it's wrecked the floor, so Mum is pretty stressed."

"Aww, I'm sorry, hon." I took a sip of milk. "I still don't understand what's caused it. It's so totally weird."

"Well, I think the world is ending," Lizzie declared, looking positively delighted at the universe's untimely death. "I know this girl in my English Language class who's a Christian, and she says right before the world ends all sorts of crap happens. Apparently natural disasters are the warning signs."

"And since when were you religious?" Ruth asked.

"It's just a possibility. And you have to admit this is strange."

I laughed. "Lizzie, you just want things to be strange because it makes a more interesting story."

"Maybe so."

"Well I think it's just a freak thing," Ruth said. "Although it was pretty scary. Will and I got caught out in it and I had to stay at his." She shook back her new scarlet hair. "It was annoying actually. I was planning to break up with him but couldn't because I needed somewhere to crash."

She said it so casually, without emotion. So Will had reached his sell-by date then. To be fair, he'd lasted longer than others, but I still didn't understand how she could be so cold. I'd only been with Noah, well, about a week really, and I already felt quite certain that ending things with him would tear my world apart.

"Woah, bombshell, Ruthie," Lizzie said, springing into supportive-friend action. "Where has this come from? I thought you guys were getting on?"

Ruth shrugged. "We were. I'm bored. You know what I'm like."

I tried to give her a reassuring pat but she recoiled away. "You wanna talk about it?"

"Not really. Not with you. No offence, but I don't fancy discussing my failing relationship when you're Mrs. Loved-Up over there."

It stung. Especially as I had dutifully listened throughout Ruth's numerous loved-up stages with different men.

"Hey come on, that's not fair," Lizzie said. I was surprised. She didn't normally stand up to Ruth. "It's not Poppy's fault she's happy."

"I know, I know," Ruth said, curling her lip. "Anyway, I can't talk about love but I can talk about sex, right? How is he anyway, Poppy? Do Noah's guitar-playing fingers hit all the right spots?"

I looked down into my drink.

Ruth picked up on my awkward silence. "Haven't you slept with him yet?"

Of course I hadn't. She knew this. She knew all the rest of us were virgins.

"Er," I fumbled.

Then it was Amanda's turn to stick up for me. Blimey O'Reilly. It must be a national holiday or something.

"You don't have to tell us," she said reassuringly. "It's not any of our business. I don't talk to you guys about me and Johnno."

"That's only because you haven't even got past the kissing phase," Ruth said, irritated at the sudden lack of patience shown towards her. "And you probably won't until 2090."

Amanda coyly took a sip of her coffee. "I wouldn't be so sure."

Well, that got the attention away from me. We all pounced on her, amazed.

"No way."

"I don't believe you."

"Tell me everything."

"How far have you guys got?"

"Was it any good?" (That last one was, surprisingly enough, from Ruth.)

But Amanda wouldn't unleash any more information. She turned twice as red as me and stared at her coffee cup, mute, until we all shut up.

"Well, this is new," Ruth said. "Amanda's getting some, Poppy probably soon will be, while I'm going to be single."

"Do you really think you're going to sleep with Noah soon, Popps?" Lizzie asked. She sounded anxious. I wasn't sure if it was out of concern for my well-being, or fear that if I did it would separate us somehow. Put us into two different categories.

"We're taking it slow."

"What? He doesn't want to sleep with you?"

Thanks for that, Ruth.

"Of course he wants to sleep with me," I snapped. "But we've only just got together, and, you know, I don't feel ready."

"Well, if I was you, I would seal the deal pretty soon. Men as fit as Noah don't have to wait."

I was about to object but Lizzie came to the rescue once more.

"Come on, Ruth, you saw the way he looked at her yesterday. The boy's totally loved-up." She gave me a smile. "I reckon he would wait a lifetime for you, Poppy."

"Well, let's hope so."

Ruth went to get another coffee and the process seemed to calm her down. She gave me a half-smile, the closest she ever got to apologizing.

"So?" Lizzie asked. "You haven't slept with him yet but has he said 'I love you'?"

I remembered last night's quiet whispers to each other as the rain fell. I turned very red and that answered the question for them.

Amanda and Lizzie screamed in delight.

"Really?" Amanda said.

I nodded.

"Tell. Me. Everything," Lizzie demanded.

I looked towards Ruth. Okay, so she was being a prize twat but she was going through a break-up and having the I-love-you conversation wasn't really fair. She caught my eye though and shrugged.

"Don't mind me," she said, giving me another hint of a smile. "Spill all. Though I don't call dropping The Big L taking it slow. I'm just saying."

More drinks were bought as I described the last couple of days. It felt good to talk to my friends about it, to get their reactions, their opinions. It made it real. This amazing thing happening to me wasn't just a figment of my imagination. They, Ruth included, gasped at all the right moments. When I'd finished describing the previous night's events, they all fell back into their seats, exhausted from the gossip.

We sat savouring it, until Lizzie brought up something I'd almost forgotten.

"So what happened to the whole 'I think I'm allergic to him' phase?"

I thought back to those random panic attacks.

I shook my head. "It's all stopped. It must have been something unrelated."

"Sounded a bit strange anyway. I don't think I've heard of anyone being allergic to anyone else."

Lizzie turned her attention to Amanda. "So?" she said, poking her. "Poppy's spilled. What's going on with you and Johnno. I'm not leaving until I get at least one sordid detail."

The hours passed as we tortured Amanda for information. She stayed tight-lipped though. Even when we stole her handbag and held it to ransom. She told us we would get bored; she was right. After about half an hour, Amanda quite assertively prised the bag from Ruth's hands while she was halfway through telling us about Will's inadequacies in bed. Ruth looked pretty stunned by such daring.

In fact, Amanda standing up for herself was much more shocking than Ruth's revelations. Ruth would always boast about how amazing a guy was in bed when she was going out with them – each conquest would have the biggest willy she had ever seen, be the most adventurous she had ever experienced, etc., etc. But then, mysteriously, after she'd dumped them, she would divulge all these cringy stories instead. I wasn't sure how she expected us to believe anything she said. We weren't goldfish, we had memories, and so we knew she was completely contradicting herself. But she would do it anyway. And we would happily oblige her, playing along. I suppose it was the only real glimpse I got into Ruth's inner insecurity.

Eventually I realized I should be getting home.

"You off?" Lizzie asked, as I stood up.

"Yup. I've not seen my parents since yesterday morning. I should probably drop in to show my thanks for them creating-and-birthing-me and that."

"I'll walk with you."

"Cool."

We said goodbye and walked outside, back towards the flooded part of town. The water had receded quite a bit, which was just as well, as I didn't have Noah to carry me across the puddles. Thinking of him sent my stomach into more convulsions and I realized, to my own annoyance, that I literally couldn't stop smiling.

"So you're in love then?" Lizzie asked, as we carefully manoeuvred ourselves around a giant puddle.

I took a deep breath. "I think so." More stomach convulsions. "I really think I am."

"So how does it feel?"

I looked at my friend. She seemed a little sad. And I felt for her. I would feel a little sad if the situation was reversed. That's the weird thing about growing up. One day you realize that you and your friends can't do everything at the same time. Your lives fragment and different stuff starts happening to each of you.

"You wanna know the truth?"

She nodded.

"Well, in truth, Lizzie, it's a little bit terrifying."

She wasn't expecting that. "Terrifying?"

"Yep."

"How so?"

I thought about my answer, not sure if I could articulate what I meant.

"Well, for one, it's not something you have any control over. And I hate that. It's like I have no authority over my feelings – they won't listen to me. They just make up their own mind and overrule my reasoning. I don't think I particularly wanted to fall for Noah. It's not sensible. And yet it's like I didn't have a choice."

Lizzie laughed. "Trust you to find all the negative aspects of falling in love."

I shook my head. "It's not negative. It's just true. And the other thing that scares me is how crazily dependent I am already."

"No way, Poppy Lawson. I never thought I'd see the day."

"I know. I hate it."

The puddles got shallower as we made our way towards our respective homes.

"Well, can't you make yourself less dependent on him?"

I had to think again to pull together an honest answer.

"I wish I could." I stretched my arms over my head. "But no. I feel, like, bound to him or something. Like if he was taken away, I would never be able to recover. I hate it. I promised myself I would never feel like this over a boy. But

I honestly can't help it. The thought of losing him makes me feel sick…" My voice broke. "Sick? Over losing a guy?" A tear fell down my cheek. "God, Lizzie, what's wrong with me?"

I ground to a halt and Lizzie put her arm around me.

"Poppy, you're supposed to be HAPPY. You know that, right?"

I nodded. Another tear escaped.

"Look," Lizzie said, "I've not been in love so I can't pretend to understand what you're going through. But I know this much. It's supposed to be a happy time. HAPPY?"

"I am happy. That's what scares me."

"What do you mean?"

"Well, I don't want my happiness to depend on a boy. It never did any good to anyone."

"That's just silly. Look at all those trashy romcoms that do so well at the box office. No one in them is happy until they get together with some guy. Or what about those trashy books that Amanda reads? They're all pretty much 'Happily Ever After', aren't they?"

I sniffed. My nose had begun to run. "Yeah, but that's not real love," I said, rubbing my nose with my finger. "Love doesn't work like those films, like it's an equation to be solved. Look at the real love stories. The ones that don't fall into a formulaic, forgettable haze. The love stories they teach in school, the ones that last for ever. In those stories the love destroys the characters. It rips them apart. It makes their lives unlivable. What if it gets like that?"

We started walking again. Lizzie looked like she was trying not to laugh. I suppose I didn't blame her. I was maybe being a tad melodramatic.

"Poppy. Darling. I love you and I'm very happy for you and Noah. But you're not Romeo and Juliet, or Cathy and Heathcliff, or even that couple from *The Notebook* who make everyone cry." Her arm was still around me. "Look, it's the first time you've fallen in love. I think it's overwhelming for everybody. You're just overthinking it…"

I tried to protest but she ignored me.

"…You are. I know you are. It's what you do. But please, can you just try to enjoy it? You've found someone who loves you. You. For exactly who you are. Some people go their whole lives without ever experiencing that and you've managed to achieve it at the tender age of seventeen. So stop worrying and enjoy it. Just don't forget who your friends are."

I knew she was speaking sense. Although I didn't feel relieved, more misunderstood.

But to satisfy her, I nodded and gave her a quick hug. "Of course I won't forget you guys. I'm not Ruth, for God's sake."

Lizzie laughed again. "Ha ha. Aww, poor Will. He's about to get his heart broken, isn't he?"

"I think so."

"Oh well. He should've known better."

As we walked, I felt less freaked out. I was surprised by my outburst really. It hadn't occurred to me I'd been having those thoughts until I just came out with them.

Being with Noah was so captivating that I seemed incapable of producing rational analysis until I was away from him. I suppose that in itself was something to worry about, but I remembered what Lizzie said and silently told myself to enjoy it.

Lizzie and I broke apart at our usual corner.

"Thanks for listening," I said. "Sorry. It must be infuriating listening to me whinge about being in love. I would hate me if I was you."

"Well, I'm trying to be happy for you. Try and be happy for yourself."

"Walk in to college together tomorrow?"

"I'll meet you at the usual time."

22

Dad was in his regular spot when I got in.

"You're alive," he said as I walked into the sitting room, a glass of water in one hand and a Kit Kat in the other.

"Indeed I am."

I sat on the arm of his favourite chair and gave him a quick hug. "Did you guys weather the storm okay? It doesn't look like we got any flooding."

I snapped the Kit Kat in two and gave Dad half.

"We were just fine." He took a mouthful and sprayed a few chocolate crumbs onto his lap. "Mum's upset about what all the rain will do to her herb garden, but apart from that we're unaffected." He took another bite of chocolate. "What about you? Were you safe at Noah's?"

It felt weird that he knew I'd stayed there. I dreaded what his assumptions must be and wanted to tell him about our take-it-slow approach. Too awkward though.

I rested my head on his shoulder. "I was fine. It was pretty scary when we got stuck in it, but once we got inside it was okay." I paused. "It was all a bit weird though, wasn't it?"

Dad nodded. "I suppose they don't call it freak weather for nothing."

We sat companionably for a few minutes, each chomping our chocolate. Dad took out the paper and started reading. I remembered the dig Noah had made about me not reading the news, so I started reading over Dad's shoulder.

The front page of the *Middletown Observer* was dedicated to the storm – they'd somehow put out a special extra edition overnight. The headline was clear, bold and to-the-point: *FREAK STORM BLITZES TOWN*.

"Wow. Has there been much damage?"

Dad turned to the following page. There were pictures of the flooding, with lots of photos of upset-looking people standing forlornly outside their wrecked businesses.

"Quite a bit. They're saying it could take at least a month to get some places back to normal."

"Do they still not know what caused it?"

"They haven't got a clue. They think it's something to do with the North Atlantic Drift, but usually you get more warning if a storm comes from that direction."

We read the news coverage together. I cheered up a little when I saw Lizzie's name in print, crediting her for some quotes she'd gathered from shocked members of the public. The sneaky thing hadn't even told us. But it quickly got too depressing to read any more. I stifled a yawn.

"I'm going to my room."

"Goodnight, poppet."

I went upstairs and got into my pyjamas. It felt good to get out of my rained-on clothes. I gratefully snuggled under my covers and got out my book. I'd only read half a page when my mobile went off.

I looked at the screen and smiled. It was Noah.

"Hello, you," I said, still smiling.

"Alright, gorgeous, how was your day without me?"

"It was delightful." I snuggled further under the duvet.

"Aww. Don't say that. I was about to be ultra soppy and tell you I missed you."

"That *would* be soppy."

"Well, I won't say it then."

Just hearing his voice had made me forget the horrible stories in the newspaper. "Okay," I relented. "I missed you a little bit too."

"Soppy cow."

"Hey!"

"Just playing you at your own game."

I switched my phone to my other ear and rolled onto my side. "So how was band practice?"

I could hear excitement in Noah's voice. "It was good actually. Really good. In fact, we've got a pretty big show lined up."

"That sounds cool. Whereabouts?"

"We got a call today from this guy who helps us get gigs. Do you know Ponyboys?"

I did know Ponyboys. Everyone knew Ponyboys. They'd

been on the radio constantly. They were one of those indie-pop bands that had exploded in popularity after releasing some rocky, catchy love song. Ruth and Amanda were really into them, and I had a few of their songs on my iPod.

"Yeah, of course. Why?"

"Well…" Noah paused for dramatic effect. "…They're playing The Complex in two weeks."

"Yeah. Ruth and Amanda have tickets. So?"

"Apparently they always like to have a local band support them. They found out about us online and listened to our demo. And, Poppy, I can't believe it, but they've asked us to support them."

I sat up in bed. "You're kidding."

"Nope."

"Really?"

"Yup."

"That's amazing, Noah." I couldn't believe it either. The Complex was about a twenty-minute drive from town. It usually hosted quite big names. I'd seen a few bands there in the rare moments I was organized enough to get tickets.

"I think I'm still in shock. We've got so much practising to do. Only two weeks! I hope we don't screw it up."

"You won't screw it up."

"Well, I won't if you're there."

I sighed. "I would love to come, but tickets sold out ages ago." It sucked actually. I would've loved to see Noah on such a big stage. Why hadn't I let Ruth buy me a ticket?

"Poppy. You'll be there. You're with the band. I'll be able to get you in."

It took a while for me to digest. "Say that again."

"I'll be able to get you in."

"No, the first part. Say the first part again."

Noah sounded confused. "You're with the band...?" he ventured.

I sighed happily and slumped back into my pillows. "Do you have any idea how cool that sounds?" I laughed at my own pathetic-ness.

Noah laughed too. "I get it. One of the reasons I got into music was just so I could say the phrase 'I'm in a band' to girls."

"Don't remind me, please."

"Well, you're my groupie now, Poppy. My only groupie. And that means free backstage passes."

I smiled. "Have I ever told you that I love you?"

He laughed again. "If I didn't know any better, I would say you're only interested in me because I'm in a band."

"Well, if I'm your official groupie, doesn't that mean I have to sleep with you?" I said it innocently enough, but Noah went quiet down the phone.

"Noah?" I asked, slightly panicked. "You still there?"

He eventually spoke again. "Honestly, Poppy. You can't just spring that mental image casually into a conversation like that. I can't think of anything else now."

I giggled. "Men are so one-dimensional."

"I'm afraid we are. I'm trying my hardest not to be."

For a brief moment, I entertained the thought of sleeping with Noah and it made me draw breath. I was still terrified, naturally. But when I thought back to the previous night and how it had felt with him in that field, I got judders.

I spoke raspily, surprised by how turned on I'd suddenly made myself. "You sure this taking-things-slow thing is a good idea?"

More silence.

"Honestly, Poppy, are you trying to kill me?"

"Sorry."

"It's okay. I do think it's a good idea. It's just going to be hard logistically that's all." He was quiet again for a moment. "The thing is, Poppy, it's you. You're so special. *We're* so special. And I don't want to rush it. We have a lot of time…" More quiet. "In fact, at the risk of sounding massively soppy, I feel I have all the time in the world with you. I feel like we're for ever."

I really honestly completely and utterly couldn't stop smiling now.

"Do you feel the same?"

There was a nervousness there again. I thought about what he'd just said, and what it meant. For ever. Well, a lifetime anyway. It was daunting to think of being with someone for that long. Yet I knew I would never find someone like Noah again. He was my fit. Outsiders would look at us, sneer, and diminish whatever was going on as "puppy love", but I knew better. I supposed that was why I'd been freaking out. You're not supposed to meet your soulmate at seventeen.

In fact, until last week, I hadn't even believed in them. But I just knew, inherently, that this was right.

I'd kept Noah waiting for an answer and I chose my words carefully.

"I do feel the same."

"Really? 'Cause I don't want to overwhelm you. Honestly? I'm a little bit overwhelmed myself."

"I am a bit freaked out. But, at the risk of sounding like a melodramatic teenager, I feel I could spend the rest of my life with you quite happily."

Noah sighed in relief. "Thank you," he said. "I was getting scared that I was the only one having all these crazy thoughts."

"Nope. Not just you. It must be our raging teenage hormones."

"Well, we might be a little bit young, but look at Romeo and Juliet. They were all true-love and they were only about fourteen. Gross really, when you think about it."

I laughed. "And look how well that turned out."

"Let's try not to kill ourselves, shall we? Just for a while?"

We spoke a bit more about the gig. About Ruth. I told him she was planning to break up with Will and he got a bit annoyed. I found myself trying to defend her, then realized I didn't have much of an argument.

After a while it was time to ring off.

"Anyway," Noah said. "I've been good and not seen you all day, so can I walk you to college tomorrow?"

"Sorry. I'm walking in with Lizzie."

"Well, can I see you after college then? We'll go and do something fun. A surprise. Something away from my flat so we're not tempted to...you know..."

I was aware of all the coursework I had to do, and tried to find a compromise.

"I've got coursework..."

"Oh yes. Of course. Sorry. I don't wanna screw up your A levels."

I went through tomorrow's timetable in my head and found a solution. "I've got two free periods tomorrow. If I go to the library and actually behave myself and work instead of gossiping with the girls, then I should be able to get most of it done."

"You sure?"

"Yep."

"Brilliant. Well, I'll see you tomorrow then."

"See you tomorrow."

"Oh. And Poppy?"

"Yes?"

"I love you."

"I love you too."

23

I met Lizzie the next morning. The weather, in line with its continuing indecisive behaviour, had decided it was winter again, so it was bloody freezing. I wrapped up in my huge parka, a scarf, gloves and hat, and pondered how I'd been sitting outside in a beer garden just two days ago.

Lizzie was hopping from one foot to the other when I met her.

"Dear Baby Jesus, it's cold," she said, her breath frosting in the air. "What the hell is going on? Does the weather have PMS or something?"

She was equally dressed for the chill, wearing her long woollen coat with a trilby hat. Lizzie could do hats.

"I don't know." I stuffed my hands further into my pockets. "But I wish it would make up its mind. It should either be a proper full-blown Indian Summer, or just get on with it and freeze our arses off constantly until May."

We walked quickly to stay warm.

"Oh, I forgot," I said, when we neared college. "Noah's band has been asked to support Ponyboys at their next gig."

Lizzie stopped walking. "You're kidding."

"Nope. He rang and told me last night."

"That's incredible news."

"I know."

"Did Ponyboys actually find them and ask for them?"

"Yeah, apparently."

"Have you told the local paper?"

"Yes, Lizzie," I deadpanned. "That's the first thing I thought to do."

We started walking again. It was too cold to stand still.

"It's a good local news story," she whined.

"Yeah, I suppose."

The college gates didn't have the normal crowd of students dawdling around them as we stomped through. It was too cold.

"Wow. Your boyfriend is going to be famous."

"Hmm, maybe."

It made me a little nervous, to be honest. There would be thousands of people at this gig. Thousands of girls looking at Noah, wishing they were me. And probably thinking he could do better. I pushed the thought from my mind.

"You wanna meet for lunch?" Lizzie asked. We were at the corridor where I went to English and she went to Government and Politics.

"I can't. I've got to do some work in the library. Noah is apparently taking me 'somewhere fun' tonight so I need to rid myself of coursework guilt first."

Lizzie raised her eyebrows. "Somewhere fun, eh?"

"Apparently so."

"That sounds intriguing."

"Yeah. He's picking me up from college."

"Well, tell him to ring the paper."

"Ha ha. I will."

"And hopefully I'll see you briefly at lunch?"

"Hopefully."

"See ya laters."

"Bye."

I walked towards English, wondering what Noah had planned for that evening. Hopefully it was something indoors, considering the cold. I wondered what he'd look like all wrapped up in a scarf, big coat and beanie hat. Something told me he would look very good indeed. I smiled as I pictured it and was so busy mentally-perving that I didn't see Frank walking towards me. I banged straight into him.

"Bloody hell, Poppy. Walk much?"

Frank was half-smiling at me, and half looking pissed off. He was all dressed for the cold too, wearing a big rugby jumper with a stripy scarf tied in some sort of fashionable bow. He looked okay actually.

"Sorry," I said, flustered. "My brain was elsewhere."

"Obviously." He was walking away from our English classroom.

"Where you off to?"

Frank beckoned for me to follow. "Our class has been moved. The room got flooded. Come on, I'll show you."

He took my hand and we started walking. I wasn't sure why he'd taken my hand, and I stared at our entwined fingers with detached curiosity. Frank saw me looking and let go like I was a cold turkey.

There was an awkward silence.

"So what did you get up to on the surprise day off then?" I stammered, desperate to erode the tension surrounding us.

"Er," he struggled. "Just chilled with the guys. Played some video games."

More painful silence.

I knew I needed to break it. Frank and I didn't do awkward.

"Frank, why did you just hold my hand?"

He burst out laughing. "I have no idea. I didn't mean to. And then I was like, oops, she's taken my hand now, I have to just continue with this. But, yeah, that was weird."

"Very weird."

"You have sweaty palms by the way."

I whacked him. "Oi! You're the one who wanted to hold my hand." I made a kissy face.

"I don't know what happened. I must've thought you were some different girl. Fitter, and less mad."

I whacked him again.

"Okay. I deserved that."

The awkwardness dissipated as we made our way to the temporary classroom. It resembled some sort of makeshift dilapidated shack and no doubt Ms. Gretching wasn't going to be happy with the move.

Sure enough, she fixed both me and Frank with evil glares the moment we walked in.

"Poppy Lawson," she said. "Nice to see you're late as usual."

"Sorry, miss." I slunk past her into an available chair. "We didn't know the room had been changed."

Frank sat next to me and we listened to her whinge about the room change for a bit.

Eventually she moaned herself out and perked up while talking about World War I and the trenches. She handed out copies of *Birdsong* and told us to start reading.

"I'm just going to head back to the classroom for a bit," she said. "To check nothing's ruined. Please behave in my absence."

I picked up my copy of *Birdsong* and started reading the blurb.

"Jeez Louise," I said, flicking through the pages. "This doesn't look like the most uplifting of reads."

"It's about the trenches, Poppy. They weren't exactly fun and games."

"I know that. I just wish someone would write a book with a happy ending for once."

Frank started reading the first chapter. "There's loads of books with happy endings," he said, eyes down. "What about those chick lit things you always go off on a moral rant about?"

"How would you know unless you'd read one, Frank?"

"Shut up. I just tried reading one of my sister's once

when I couldn't find my copy of *PHWOAR* magazine."

"You don't actually read *PHWOAR*, do you?"

"Every Tuesday."

"Why are we friends again?"

"We're friends?"

We read. I was a bit confused about what the first chapter had to do with the war. There was just some bloke called Stephen who'd moved to a strange French house and developed a bit of a crush on the landlord's wife. I sighed. Forbidden Love. There it was again. Literature was obsessed with it. I continued reading and could tell it was well written, descriptive and all the usual malarkey. But, as with most books we studied in English, none of the hidden meanings became apparent to me until a teacher or study guide pointed them out.

As I skipped onto chapter two, I sighed again.

"What's up, whinger?" Frank asked, looking up at me.

"The thing is – " I jabbed at the front cover – "I know this is going to be a good book. There'll be similes and metaphors and building of tension and multi-dimensional characters, blah blah blah."

"So, what's the problem?"

"Well, it's going to be depressing, isn't it? I'm not in the mood to be depressed. Life is going well. I don't wanna be brought down by this book."

The room was pretty quiet, despite the lack of a teaching authority presence. Only the cookie-cutter girls that Frank and I loved to hate weren't concentrating. They were passing around a copy of *Cosmo* instead. And there was one student, the token beret-wearing, roll-up-smoking individual-type that plagued all colleges, who was deliberately reading the final third of the book to show off how he'd already read it. He was crying silently while simultaneously looking around to check that people were noticing.

"So you said life was going well," Frank said. "Is this because of your new fella?"

I felt my cheeks go pink. "How do you know about that?"

"People in college are saying you're going out with the cocky dude from that band."

I put my book down. "What people?"

Frank shrugged. "Just people people."

I put my head down on top of my book. "Why does anyone care?"

"I don't care."

I laughed. "Then why did you ask?"

"Making polite conversation?"

"Well, even though you don't care, it's going pretty well actually."

Frank raised an eyebrow. "Really?"

I nodded. "Really."

"Wow. Poppy Lawson, loved up. Who would have thought?"

I giggled and picked up my book.

"Poppy? Seriously? Did you just giggle?"

He was right. My hand flung itself over my mouth in disgust. "Oh my God. I *did* just giggle."

Frank looked over his shoulders. "I think I'm going to have to move places."

"It was only the one slip-up!"

"Giggling though, Poppy? Really? Things *must* be going well."

I fought to suppress another giggle. My skin turned from pink to red.

"So how's his band going anyway?"

"Pretty good. They're supporting Ponyboys in two weeks."

Frank's attention on the book was immediately deflected. "No way! Really? Even I've heard of them."

"Yep, really."

"Wow, that's amazing."

"I know."

"So does this make you a groupie then?"

I chucked my copy of *Birdsong* at Frank's head and he ducked. Unfortunately, the book went flying through the air and hit Ms. Gretching just as she walked back in.

Two hours, a Psychology lesson, and a right telling-off from Ms. Gretching later, I was shut up in the library, desperately trying to get through my workload. I constructed a wall of textbooks around myself to ensure I wasn't distracted. The thought that I wouldn't see Noah tonight unless I got my work done really inspired me to get my head down. I raced through my Psychology case studies and made relevant notes. I started storyboarding my next Photography film.

We'd been given yet another uninspired title, *Together*, and I was trying to think of what photos to take. In the end, I decided to go for the easy option and take photos of my mates. Then I could harp on about the importance of human beings coming together to socialize or some such nonsense. I knew Ruth would be up for more posing anyway. Done and done. Finally, I read a few more chapters of *Birdsong*, thinking it was probably smart to get Ms. Gretching back on side. It still didn't have anything to do with the war yet. But the Stephen guy got it on with the wife. It was a pretty saucy sex scene actually and I couldn't help thinking about Noah and maybe doing it with him. I got all flushed and was therefore quite grateful when my mobile buzzed on silent.

A text from Lizzie.

Alright, geek? Fancy a quick break for lunch? In usual spot.

I realized I'd done more than enough work to warrant seeing Noah, so dismantled my textbook wall, collected my stuff up and made my way to the canteen.

The girls were midway through a game of Cheat when I arrived. Lizzie was obviously losing, judging by the massive number of cards in her hands.

"Howdy, hard-worker-person." She put down five cards. "Four aces?" she added hopefully.

Ruth just pushed the cards back.

"I'm not stupid," she said. "Cheat."

I sat next to Amanda and got out my sandwich. "Who's winning?"

"Me, of course," Ruth said.

Amanda nodded hello, before putting down two cards and mumbling, "Two queens."

"Cheat!" Ruth declared happily, flipping over Amanda's cards. "Take those cards back."

"Well, someone's happy today." I took a bite of my sandwich and nicked a swig of Amanda's Coke to wash it down. "You've certainly cheered up."

Lizzie pulled a face. "You haven't heard Ruth's news yet, have you, Poppy?" she said, trying to rearrange her huge clutch of cards.

"What news?" I looked at Ruth, who was smiling coyly behind her substantially smaller card collection.

"Me and Will are back on."

"What? But yesterday you were all set to break up with him."

"Well, he came round last night and I realized I really do care about him."

I thought about it.

"Hang on… Did Will tell you about the band's gig with Ponyboys?"

She wouldn't meet my eye. "Oh yeah. He did mention something about that."

She was unbelievable.

"That's a nice coincidence."

"What does that mean?"

Fortunately, before I said anything else, Lizzie foresaw the potential argument and intervened.

"Isn't it great, guys?" she said. "Amanda and I can both

use you to get backstage passes. It's going to be such a laugh,
isn't it?"

Ruth and I were still eyeballing each other. I sighed and
let it go.

"Sure. Sounds great."

Ruth stretched her arms out. "I can't believe my boyfriend
is supporting Ponyboys."

I swallowed.

"And they're going to be in the paper…"

I turned to Lizzie. "What?"

She shifted in her seat and looked a bit sheepish. "Well,"
she began but Ruth interrupted.

"Isn't it hysterical?" she said. "We rang the local paper
and they're letting Lizzie interview the band and do a story
on it."

I struggled to digest. "And this has just been decided in
the past few hours?"

Ruth nodded. "Didn't Noah tell you?"

He hadn't.

"Our boyfriends are famous." Ruth tried to high-five me.
I half-heartedly hit her hand while trying to work out why
I was so annoyed.

"I suppose they are."

24

That afternoon the clock moved like sludge trickling through a drain. At one point I was convinced it was broken, even though it was one of those posh satellite clocks. My body started to ache for Noah. My heartbeat picked up, as if it could sense him walking to college and getting closer. As the clock hand inched towards the end of the day, I tried to get myself ready inconspicuously. Luckily my Photography teacher was the "arty" type. She was too busy flouncing around in a shawl, trying to get students to photograph homeless people, to notice me painting my nails under the table. Or applying lip stain. Or the quick brushing of hair and lashings of mascara.

When the bell went I looked, well, nice, hopefully. But my hard work was undone the moment I stepped outside into the cold. My nose started dripping, my hair blew all over the place, and the wind turned my cheeks bright red. I wanted to run to the college gates but forced myself to walk normally.

My breath caught as I spotted him leaning against the college fence. Girls were double-taking and giggling as they walked by, flicking their hair and fluttering their eyelids at him. He looked uber-fit, all wrapped up in his winter clothes. He was wearing jeans, a green jumper, a leather jacket, and a beanie hat covered most of his dark hair. A grey scarf set off his beautiful cheekbones perfectly and my heart beat faster as I approached. He was also carrying a massive bag over his shoulder.

He kissed me softly on the lips, making my knees tremble.

"Hello, gorgeous," he said, giving me another kiss. "I take it you were good and got all your work done?"

I nodded, dumbfounded. "What's in the bag?"

He tapped his nose. "All will be revealed."

"But it's massive! Have you killed someone? I don't want this surprise date to be digging a grave for a rival guitar player or something."

Noah laughed. "As I said, all will be revealed." He took my hand and we started walking.

"So how was your day?" I asked, still curious about the bag.

"It was an odd one actually. The band's going to be in the local paper."

I smiled. "I know that already. I think Lizzie may be somewhat responsible."

"I knew it." He squeezed my hand. "Yeah, well, I suppose it's good publicity. Even though that paper's mainly only read by old middle-class people."

"Lizzie reads it."

"She doesn't really count."

"Ha. I suppose you're right."

Noah started swinging my hand between us. "So," he said. "You looking forward to this fun treat I have planned for you?"

"Of course. I'm intrigued to know what it is."

"Well, let's get you home first so you can get ready."

"Get ready?"

"Yes."

"For what?"

"That would be telling."

"But I am ready." I started to feel insecure. I had redone my make-up, my hair surely didn't look that bad, despite the wind, and my clothes were fine. "Do I not look ready?"

He kissed my head. "You look lovely, as always. But where I'm taking you isn't a jeans place."

"Now I'm really intrigued."

"You're just going to have to be patient."

We walked back to mine, holding hands the whole way. It made me think about what had happened with Frank earlier. It had been him who'd taken my hand... My belief that he wasn't into me was waning a little. I compartmentalized the uncomfortable thought for the time being though, and focused on how Noah's hand felt in mine. The wind was still bitingly cold and I thought I might have to apply an emergency layer of red-reducing foundation on the sly. Noah told me about the photo shoot they were doing for the newspaper.

"It sounds a bit cringe to be honest. They want to photograph us under the railway bridge. I'm concerned they're going to want lots of 'edgy' shots of us smouldering against exposed brickwork."

"Noah. Your band is called Growing Pains. You're practically begging to be shot in black-and-white against exposed brickwork."

"Always with the band-name criticism."

"It's a stupid name."

"Well, I bet everyone thought 'The Beatles' sounded pretty dumb when they first started."

"Did you just compare your band to The Beatles?"

He held up his hands. "God, no. Calm down. Don't worry."

We arrived at my house and I scrabbled around for a door key. As I let myself in, I called out but there was no answer. We were alone.

"Come on," I said, leading him upstairs. "My room's up here."

"I get to see your room?"

"Don't get any ideas."

"It will just be interesting to see where you sleep, that's all."

"That sounds creepy. What is it with you and sleep?"

I opened my door, trying to remember what state I'd left my room in that morning. It actually wasn't that messy. I quickly smoothed out the duvet and kicked a stray pair of knickers under the bed before Noah sat on it and looked around him.

"So this is where Poppy lives?" He took in my framed photos, my old teddy bear (damn it, I forgot to hide that!), and my pretentious poster of James Dean.

"It's not usually this messy," I lied.

Noah reached out for my hand and pulled me down so I was sitting next to him. He brushed his lips against mine.

"It's perfect. I love it. It screams *you*."

He kissed me again, harder this time, and my body went haywire. I hungrily licked his lips and wrapped my arms around his back. He groaned and before I knew it I was kissing him furiously, sitting on top of him. It was the best kind of wonderful.

We came up for air and Noah grinned up at me.

"We're not doing very well," he said, stroking my face. "I seem incapable of behaving myself around you."

I caught a glimpse of myself in my dressing table mirror. Just five minutes of kissing had somehow moulded my hair into an atrocity. I tried to manipulate it back into normality with my fingers.

"Yes, well, I seem equally incapable of resisting nympho-like urges. Anyway, let's distract ourselves. Why are we here again?"

"Oh yes, I almost forgot."

Noah jumped up and began rummaging through his huge bag. Curious, I watched as he pulled out another, smaller pricey-looking bag. He held it up triumphantly.

"What's that?"

"It's for you."

I tucked a strand of hair behind my ear. "What is it?"

"Open it and find out."

He placed the bag on my bed. It was from a posh shop in town – an expensive posh shop.

"You didn't have to buy me anything," I said, turning the bag over in my hands.

"Don't be silly. You're my girlfriend. Plus this is a practical gift."

I reached inside. Something felt soft and I pulled it out slowly. It was red, made with silky material. I pinched it with my fingers and let the fabric unravel to reveal the most gorgeous dress I'd ever seen.

"It's a dress."

I stood there, stunned. It was the colour red that I knew suited me but was never brave enough to actually wear. It had a high-ish neckline and long sleeves. It skimmed down from the waist, ending high above the knee.

"It's beautiful," I said, still staring.

Noah held the fabric up against my body.

"It looks like it's a perfect fit," he said, grinning. "I should definitely get some sort of prize for that."

I couldn't really speak. All I could do was stare at the dress.

"You like it?"

I nodded, then shook my head.

"It's gorgeous, Noah. But, seriously, I can't accept it. I know that shop, and you're too generous."

He shrugged, not bothered. "I've got millionaire parents

with severe guilt issues, remember? Don't worry about the money, just try it on."

"But I have nowhere to wear it to."

"Well, that's where this evening's entertainment comes in." He had an even broader smile on his face now. He rummaged again in his bag, located a white envelope and handed it to me.

I was nervous as I slit it open and pulled out two stiff tickets.

I gasped.

"Tickets to the ballet?" I could hardly believe it.

"Yep. Good tickets as well. My dad has a box. He uses it to schmooze potential clients and it's not being used tonight. I thought you could wear your new dress."

I screeched and hugged him. "Do you have any idea how much I love the ballet?"

He hugged me back. "Nope. It was a lucky guess. But I know how much girls love getting dressed up for things."

"I love love love LOVE the ballet." I got up and did a little pirouette around my room. "I used to dance as a kid, you know? I was actually pretty good. Mum would take me to the ballet each Christmas. I looked forward to it all year."

Noah stood up and I theatrically jumped into his arms. He caught me and spun me around.

"So what happened, Margot Fonteyn?" he asked. "Why don't you still go?"

I sighed. "You know, the usual stuff. I became a teenager

and decided I wanted to go shopping on Saturdays instead of to ballet classes. I regret it, of course."

"Well, I'm glad I picked the right thing to do."

"You *so* did."

"Are you going to try the dress on?"

"Only if you promise not to look."

He held his hands over his eyes. "No peeking. I promise."

I quickly peeled off all my layers and pulled the dress on. I let the fabric swish down and I examined my reflection in the mirror.

Wow. It was a good dress. I looked at least five years older and the shade of red changed my complexion completely. It made my skin look milky and the brown in my hair looked deep and shiny.

"Are you done yet?" Noah asked, eyes still covered. "The suspense is killing me."

"I'm done." I swept my hair to one side.

Noah opened his fingers and peered through. He paused. Then he took his hands away and just stared. I felt myself go as red as the dress.

"What is it? Does it look awful?" I tugged nervously at the fabric.

He still didn't speak.

"What? You're making me feel anxious now."

He grabbed my face and pulled me into a deep kiss. When he pulled away I was left even more flustered.

"What was that for?"

Noah started kissing my shoulders and my arms. "You.

Look. So. Unbelievably. Gorgeous," he said between kisses. "That. I. Can't. Stop. Kissing. You."

I giggled. "You like it?"

"I more than like it." He kissed me full on the mouth again. "Let's not go to the ballet. Can't we just stay here with you wearing that dress?"

"No! I'm all excited now."

"But look at you."

"When do we need to leave?"

Noah looked at his watch.

"In about an hour."

"Well, I need to do my hair and make-up. I can't go wearing a dress like this but with my face looking like crap."

"Trust me. You couldn't look less like crap if you tried."

"I guess that's good to know."

Noah gave me one final kiss.

"I need to leave you alone. I'm like a sex pest. You get ready and I'll go to the bathroom and get changed."

"Don't tell me you're wearing a pretty dress too?"

He nodded. "Yup. And heels. And this DIVINE handbag I found in Coast."

"How do you know about Coast?"

"Girls talk about it a lot."

"Fair enough."

Noah scooted out of my bedroom with yet another mysterious bag. I quickly rang my mum to fill her in. She got a bit too excited and delayed my getting-ready process by at least ten minutes. Then I sat myself at my dressing table and got to work beautifying myself, smiling non-stop throughout. I decided to play up to the red of the dress, so kept my eye make-up minimal and worked on creating what I hoped would be a set of red luscious lips, which *Cosmo* had told me were easy to do in five steps. With juicy lips accomplished, I turned my attention to my hair and decided I just about had enough time to curl it. I switched on my tongs and painstakingly created soft ringlets. I was just spritzing on some of the posh perfume I got for my birthday when Noah re-emerged.

It was my turn to be shocked.

He looked...fantastic.

He'd changed into an impeccably cut black suit with a crisp white shirt and skinny black tie. He'd changed his hair. It wasn't all floppy and messy like usual but moulded and sculpted to show off his jawline perfectly. All his stubble had gone, leaving his face clean and his black eyes startling. As expected, my belly flip-flopped like I was standing on top of a massive cliff and my heart's tempo stepped up a notch.

I was just about to tell him how amazing he looked but he beat me to it.

"Poppy Lawson. You are, without a doubt, the most beautiful girl in the whole of Middletown."

It took a lot of willpower not to act entirely on lust. "You're not looking so bad yourself."

"If I didn't know better I would say that was a compliment."

He kissed me, which caused my body to spasm in delight. He then stooped so his head was resting on my shoulder and he looked at our reflection in the mirror.

"We're not a bad-looking couple, you know?"

I looked at the mirror image in front of me. Noah was right. We did look pretty good together. I almost didn't recognize myself. I was this adult-looking, rather pretty girl, who seemed to radiate happiness. I hadn't realized before how Noah made me smile compulsively; how being with him made me feel so relaxed, so…okay, it sounded daft, but so completed.

Noah looked at his watch again. "Balls. We're going to miss the train if we don't leave now."

And we left the house in a flurry of me tossing things randomly into bags, screaming that I couldn't find my shoes, and having to ring my mobile phone using Noah's because it had disappeared.

25

A very, very cold train and Tube journey to London later, we emerged onto the streets of the West End. It was freezing. People were bustling past, trying to get out of the cold as quickly as possible.

"The theatre is just around this corner," Noah said, helping me through the throngs of people.

I wasn't accustomed to London walking, so kept being elbowed and apologizing to everybody. When we reached the theatre, there were lots of people queuing to get in. Everyone around us was also dressed for the occasion. All the men were wearing suits and I caught glimpses of beautiful fabric peeking out from the women's heavy winter coats.

Noah walked straight past the queue to the front.

"Hang on," I whispered. "Don't we need to line up with everyone else?"

He grinned. "Nope."

I followed Noah with my arms crossed in embarrassment. I'd never been one for queue-jumping and didn't understand why Noah was so confident that he could blag his way out of waiting. But when we reached the ticket office, Noah quietly gave the attendant his name, and the employee's face perked up in recognition.

"Of course, Mr. Roberts, your box is ready."

The attendant gave a subtle signal and another eager employee dashed over. We were ushered through the crowd and bubbling glasses of champagne appeared in our hands.

"Are you the son of the prime minister or something?" I whispered to Noah as we followed the man up a deep red staircase. I took a small sip of champagne, delighted that they thought I was eighteen. The bubbles tickled my nose.

"We're just box holders," Noah said, not too bothered or affected by our VIP treatment. "They have to treat box holders like this. It's part of what you pay for."

We continued up the stairs, another flight, then another flight. Other ballet-goers disappeared through giant wooden doors and the crowd began to thin out.

"Not much further, sir," our helpful attendant said. He was slightly podgy and there was sweat on his forehead from the exertion of climbing so many stairs. We continued upwards until we were close to the beautifully decorated gilt ceiling, adorned with golden cherubs and cloudy skies. Our attendant showed us to a small door covered with red velvet curtains.

"Sir, madam, your box." He gestured with his hand and gave a small bow, which I found a bit over the top.

Then Noah surprised me by taking out a twenty-pound note and discreetly passing it to him. It was an odd thing to watch my teenage boyfriend do – it seemed far too adult. I realized how far removed from my usual Middletown life this evening was.

Noah touched the small of my back and guided me past the red curtains. I was just about to wind him up by asking him if his dad was in the Mafia, when I noticed my surroundings. We'd emerged into a small but luxurious private box on the right-hand side of the theatre. It hovered high above the gathering audience like a reigning monarch. The view was just breathtaking. A sea of elegance stretched out beneath us. Men in perfectly-fitting designer suits led women sparkling with diamonds to their red velvet seats. The twinkling of jewels and sequins on women's dresses played in the light, casting rainbows across the ornate walls. The stage was empty, expectant, awaiting the arrival of finely toned dancers in bobbing tutus.

I took a deep breath and sighed, leaning over the railing to take it all in. Noah pressed his body gently into my back, his arms sneaking around my waist.

"What do you think?" He pulled a strand of my hair back so I could feel the tickle of his hot breath in my ear.

I was still looking out at the spectacle below me.

"It's amazing," I admitted. "We're so high up. I can't believe this is real, that I'm in a real ballet box. I feel like Julia Roberts in *Pretty Woman*."

Noah frowned. "Isn't that film about prostitutes?"

"Yeah. But good prostitutes. There's this bit where Richard Gere buys her a dress – it's red too actually, like this one – and he takes her to the opera. It's so so soooo romantic."

"Hmm. I'm not too keen that you've just compared me to Richard Gere and compared yourself to a prostitute."

I leaned over as far as I dared.

"Wow. There's a box directly below us. Shall we write them a message and dangle it on a bit of string for them to read?" The moment it came out of my mouth I realized I was genuinely excited by the idea.

Noah just laughed and kissed my neck. "You do realize you're the most beautiful person in here, don't you?" he said.

His kiss made me shiver and my body lost any rational ability to behave itself. I pushed myself back onto his lips.

"That's very sweet, but it's not true."

He kissed my neck again, sending wonderful chills up my spine.

"Not only are you beautiful, you're not all vain about it. I love that."

Another kiss.

I was about to answer with something funny and/or clever when Noah pulled me round to kiss me full on the lips, but we were interrupted by the strings of the orchestra starting up. I quickly jumped away from him.

"I forgot we were in public," I said, my heart still thudding.

"Yeah. Suddenly the ballet isn't sounding so great. Can't we just go back to mine?"

I pulled a face. "No chance. Look, I think it's starting soon."

I settled into my large plush seat. There were little binoculars on a stand in front of me and I picked them up and started spying on the orchestra.

"Wow," I said. "That violinist has got an impressive beard." I handed the binoculars over to Noah. "See."

He gave me an odd look but took them and looked in the direction of the pit.

"You're right. That is an impressive beard."

Then he turned that weird look back on me.

"What?"

"I just don't think it's possible for anyone in the world to love anyone as much as I love you right now."

His eyes were intense, burning almost. I obviously needed to point out intriguing facial hair more often.

"I love you too." I took his hand. "Thank you for bringing me here. I think it's possibly the most romantic thing that will ever happen to me."

He smiled. "And the ballet hasn't even started yet." He stretched his arms up and his shirt rose up a little, giving me the tiniest glimpse of his stomach.

I promptly forgot all about the ballet again.

"Do you want a drink?"

"Huh?" I said, still transfixed by the small amount of skin on show.

"A drink?" He gestured to my empty champagne glass. "Do you want another one?"

I shook my head to clear my lust-induced haze. "Er, yeah, sure. That would be great."

Noah leaned over a small table I hadn't noticed and picked up a telephone that I also hadn't noticed.

"We have a phone?"

He held up a finger to shush me and started talking to whoever was on the other line. He hadn't dialled so I assumed the phone went straight through.

"Hi there. Yes, I'm calling from the top box. A bottle of champagne on ice, please? Thank you."

He hung up as my mouth hung open.

"A bottle of champagne? Seriously?"

He gave another non-committal shrug. "It's complimentary."

"Well, in that case…"

I continued my people-watching until the champagne arrived with a glistening pile of complimentary strawberries. It was presented to us in a huge ice bucket by a different man wearing a suit. He nodded quickly, put the bottle down, and left us in private once again.

"Shall we?" Noah asked, grabbing the champagne out of the bucket.

"Why not?"

I got two champagne flutes ready as he wrestled with the cork. With a small pop, the pale golden liquid streamed out of the bottle and I caught it expertly with the glasses. I handed a full glass to Noah and he took it before holding it out to toast me.

"To falling in love, being in love, and staying in love for ever." He chinked my glass and took a hefty sip.

Touched by what he'd said, I chinked back and took a deep sip myself.

"When's the ballet going to start then?" I asked just as the lights dimmed.

I took another sip of champagne. I had just decided that I was, without a doubt, the luckiest girl in the entire universe, when the curtain came up and fifteen tutu-ed dancers leaped onto the stage.

An hour later, when the lights came up, I could think of only two things:

1) The ballet was bloody AWESOME, and

2) Champagne, apparently, goes right to your head.

The swell of people below us began to move from their crowded seats. Men stood against their chairs allowing women to pass so they could spend the entire interval queuing to go the toilet; fidgety children in their smartest outfits clutched overpriced ice cream and whinged to their mothers that they were bored; and an orderly queue began at the souvenir stand so ten pounds could be wasted on a glossy A4 programme.

I, however, had my feet up on the box railing and was draining my champagne glass.

Noah was smiling at me in an adoring way. "You having fun?"

I nodded energetically. "This is amazing. Did you see them dance, Noah? They dance so well, don't they? Why did

I quit ballet? I could have been a prima ballerina, you know. I just LOVE the ballet, don't you? Do you reckon you could jump that high?"

I hiccupped and Noah burst out laughing.

"Poppy Lawson, are you drunk? How? You've only had two glasses!"

I recoiled in my chair with indignation and puffed out my chest. "Drunk? Of course I'm not drunk." I waved my glass energetically, to emphasize just how not drunk I was and the small amount of champagne left flew through the air, and over the balcony.

"Whoops."

I lowered myself to my knees so I couldn't be seen and peeked over the edge of the box. Below us were a group of confused-looking old people. One woman with a damp stain on her vibrant blue dress was holding her hands upwards, as if testing to see if it was raining indoors. A man, who I assumed was her husband, was looking around to try and work out where the sudden liquid attack had come from. Then, as if they knew I was watching, both of their heads turned in my direction.

"Crap," I whispered, and ducked my head back down.

Noah was instantly beside me, crouching down and struggling not to laugh.

"You didn't see that, did you?"

"I can't believe you," he said, between gasps of laughter. "I honestly can't take you anywhere."

"It was an accident!"

"Yeah well, can you try not to drown the audience in the second half, please?"

"Of course I won't."

I decided all of a sudden that I needed the toilet. Quite desperately. I stood up, to find the room spinning ever-so-slightly.

"Oh no," I wailed, with dawning realization. "I think I'm drunk."

Noah did another belly laugh and got up to steady me. "You think?"

"I'm drunk, at the ballet! I've never had champagne before."

"It's just the bubbles have gone to your head, you'll be fine in a few minutes. Although you do realize this is the second time you've got wasted this week? I'm starting to think you've got a problem."

"It's your fault," I muttered, walking to the door. "You make me nervous."

"Where are you off to, waster?"

"I need the loo."

I stumbled slightly into the posh hallway and followed the toilet signs, hoping there wouldn't be a queue. I was lucky. No one else seemed to be using them. Maybe they were only for box occupants.

I did what I needed to do and then examined myself in the mirror while I washed my hands. I found looking at my reflection was a good way of sobering up, so spent five minutes getting myself together. I still wasn't convinced the person in the mirror was me. She looked too happy. She had the expression you saw on the faces of a couple holding hands as they walked through the park on a Sunday morning or on a girl sitting opposite you on the train after her phone beeped and she read a text message from a mysterious person. It's the look of love. And I had it. And I prayed to Whoever that I would always have it.

I got back to the box just as the five-minute bell rang to signal it was nearly the end of the interval.

Noah was sitting with a big two-litre bottle of water in front of him. He handed me a glass. "Drink up, you."

I downed the water and handed it back. He refilled and passed it back. I sipped coyly on the second glass.

"Why is my head spinning? I honestly didn't drink that much."

"I told you. It's because you've not had champagne before. The bubbles are deadly if you're not used to it."

"And I suppose you're used to it?"

"Of course."

I stuck my lip out. "I've ruined the ballet."

"You haven't ruined the ballet." He gestured for me to sit on his lap. "Come here."

I perched myself on top of him as daintily as I could and he pulled me closer. I leaned my head on his collarbone and inhaled the clean smell of his starched shirt.

"I love you very much, Noah," I said, playing with his cufflinks. "Thank you for bringing me to the ballet." My hand moved up his arm and I started stroking his chest.

"You know," I whispered, "I don't think anyone can see us up here…"

Noah didn't say anything but his grip stiffened around my back.

I moved my face closer and kissed him. "We could do… anything…and nobody could see us."

Noah kissed me back tentatively. "Poppy. You *are* drunk."

"I'm not any more!" I protested, curling my arms around his neck. "I was, but only for about five minutes. Then I looked at my reflection, that always helps, but it didn't look like me."

"What on earth are you talking about?"

I couldn't wait any longer. I just wanted to be kissing him, right now, at the ballet.

So I silenced him with my lips and whenever he tried to stop or complain I kissed him harder. Soon his hands were twirled up in my hair and he was eagerly returning my kisses, both of us oblivious to the show we were putting on for the audience below. The lights dimmed and the orchestra began to play. I pushed Noah away mid-kiss and turned my attention to the stage.

"Oi," he said.

"Shh – it's starting."

I pulled my chair closer to his so our legs were touching. Then I gripped the railing and leaned over so I could get the best view of the dancers. They swirled their athletic bodies around the stage in a series of fluid, gravity-defying movements. I was transfixed by the beauty of it, by the costumes, by the way the men seemed able to pick up the women and throw them through the air effortlessly. However, the spell was broken and replaced by a much stronger one when I felt Noah's hand on my knee.

"Hello, you," I whispered, looking down at my leg. His hand had already crept an inch higher.

"Shh," he said, his face still intently studying the stage. "I'm watching the ballet."

My leg had started to burn with his touch as heat radiated out of his hand. Determined not to lose face, I returned my attention to the show, but was scarcely able to concentrate.

Noah's hand moved up another inch, so it was just underneath the hem of my red dress. I readjusted myself in my chair. This was a mistake – it made Noah's hand travel even further up my leg. His wrist was only resting on the middle of my thigh but it was enough to put me into sensory overdrive. Just the slightest flutter of his fingers left me feeling like my body was plugged into a high-power socket. All I could do was try and get some sort of revenge, so I reached out and put my hand as high up his leg as I dared. Noah gasped. I smiled and drummed my fingers as I kept my head facing forward.

I honestly couldn't tell you what happened in the second half of the ballet. All I could say was that it was the most insanely erotic forty-five minutes of my life. I felt as though we were one surging current. Noah, to be fair, was a complete gentleman and his hand never went any higher, but it was still intimate enough to incite a massive reaction in me. Every hair was on end, my breathing ragged. And he, in turn, seemed to be just as railroaded by my touch. His leg was quivering. And at one point it was shaking so badly the rest of his body was practically convulsing.

Is this normal? I began thinking to myself, but with a patter of Noah's fingers the thought was forgotten before it had fully formed.

It was the staccato sound of applause that broke whatever trance we were in.

Noah's hand left my leg as he stood up to clap. I shook my head dazedly and stood up to join him. The tutu-clad ballet dancers were curtsying and beaming at the audience. Surely it couldn't be the end of the ballet already? But the curtains were drawn and the mass exodus began. The crowd jostled to slip out of the narrow exits, bags clutched to their sides, programmes tucked neatly under their arms.

"Shall we stay here a few minutes?" Noah said. "Wait for the crowd to thin out?"

I nodded, still dazed, as he took my hand.

"I don't know about you," he said, raising a cheeky eyebrow, "but I don't think I could tell you one thing that happened in that final act." He bent down and gave me a brief kiss on the lips. "You have a very odd effect on me, Poppy. I think I'm addicted to you."

All I could do was squeeze his hand as my body struggled to return to normality.

I gingerly gathered up my coat and bag, and finished the last of the water off. Noah was right. I couldn't feel the effect of the champagne any more. Maybe it was just the bubbles after all. He held my coat so I could climb into it.

"You alright?"

I nodded. "I'm fine…just…"

"A little overwhelmed?"

I nodded again.

Most of the audience had left. I checked around to make sure I had everything and, with Noah's hand in mine, I left the box and stumbled back into real life.

"Ergh. It's going to be cold outside, isn't it?" Noah said, as we wound down the stairwell.

"I think so."

As we got to the bottom, we saw a crowd had built up near the theatre entrance.

"What's going on?" I asked. "Why aren't people leaving the building?"

We inched our way through the massed bulk of people. The cold air from outside hit my face.

I looked through the windows.

"Uh-oh."

Somehow, in the space of one ballet performance, an aggressive blizzard had hit London and there was a good couple of inches of snow everywhere. Elegantly dressed women were stepping outside and slipping over immediately in their heels.

"How the hell has it snowed so much?" I asked Noah.

He stood on his tiptoes and looked over the heads of people in front.

"I don't know," he replied, looking concerned. "But getting home might be an issue."

Oh God. The trains. England had this annoying habit of grinding to a stroppy halt the moment any unforeseen weather occurred.

"Are we going to be able to get home?"

Noah pulled a face. "I don't know."

We started to barge through the crowd. The hold-up was being caused by people simply refusing to exit the theatre, as if the snow would magically melt just by them being angry at it. After a few strategic elbow jabs, we were out in the cold, with fat heavy snowflakes falling softly onto our heads.

"Let's head to the Tube," Noah said, his hand gripping me tightly to stop me sliding around in my heels. "Hopefully there will still be trains going to Middletown."

I was slightly panicked. I didn't really know anyone in London so there was nowhere to crash if we got stuck. I was also still quite confused. I'd only just woken up from my Noah-induced coma and the heavy unexpected snow was just too random an occurrence to process easily.

We thumped down the steps of the Tube station, hurried onto a carriage and waited impatiently for it to slither towards Victoria Station. Noah held my hand all the way, but not in an affectionate way – more as if he was treating it like a stress ball. After fifteen minutes or so we jogged up the escalators and re-emerged onto the snow-filled streets, slipping every step or so. We ran to the information board at the station and stood in front of it, both shivering.

"Look," I said, pointing. "There's a train to Middletown…
oh…it's cancelled."

In fact, as I looked up at the giant screen, I realized every
departure had a blinking red light next to it announcing its
cancellation.

"Uh-oh."

"Uh-oh indeed."

"What are we going to do?"

"I'm not sure."

My phone went off in my bag multiple times, its vibrating
urgency matching our situation. I retrieved it and saw Mum
had tried to call twice while I didn't have any signal on the
Underground.

"Oh God. Mum's worried. I'll ring my parents and see if
it's snowing at home," I said.

"Okay. I'll check the National Rail app and find out
what's going on." Noah flipped open his phone with a scowl
on his face.

I stomped my feet to try and keep them warm and
dialled home.

Mum answered after only two rings.

"Poppy?"

"Yes, it's me."

"Oh dear. Where are you? It's snowing like crazy here.
Please say you got home from London before it hit?" Her
voice was slightly panicked but I could tell she was trying to
cover it up.

"We're stuck at the train station. The ballet only finished

twenty minutes ago. We didn't even know it'd been snowing."

"Well they're saying on the news that this snow was completely unpredicted, just like the storm. I don't like it. It was only a few days ago I was out in the garden wearing short sleeves. Poppy, what are you going to do? How are you going to get home?"

"I'm not sure."

"There must be some trains running?"

"Yes. Of course there will be."

Just as I finished saying that I heard Noah a few feet away from me, badgering a rail worker.

"So you're telling me there are absolutely no trains running for at least another four hours?" he said, a growl in his voice.

"Oh no."

"What is it?" Mum asked.

"I think the trains are a no-go."

More people had filtered into the train station, lots of them dressed for a night out too. They stood next to us, and I could see the panic form on their faces as they clocked the departures board. Noah was on the phone. I turned my attention back to Mum, who I could hear flapping.

"Oh my, Poppy. How are you going to get home?"

"I'm not sure." My stomach started knotting. More people streamed into the station as other shows finished and they began to pick on the railway workers in bright reflective jackets, demanding more information.

"Maybe I could ring Auntie Suzie? She might be able to

take you in for the night."

I shuddered at the thought. My mum's sister was one of the most awkward people I'd ever come across. She was a very devout Catholic and lived alone in this large spooky town house in the furthest tip of north London.

"Hmm. I'm not sure how she would feel about me bringing Noah along as well."

Despite her worry, Mum laughed down the line.

"Yes. You're right. It might give her an early heart attack."

Noah was now off the phone and making hand gestures to me.

"Hang on, Mum, Noah's trying to say something. I'll call you back."

I flipped my phone closed. "What?"

"All sorted," he said, with an uncomfortable look on his face.

I didn't understand.

"I don't understand," I said.

"I've booked us a hotel room."

I shook my head in disbelief. "You've done what?"

"A hotel room."

"What about getting home?"

"Well, it's not going to happen, is it?"

"But…"

"But what?"

"Well, I don't have any money."

"It's okay. I just rang my parents. They've charged the suite to their company account."

I had to really shake my head this time to ensure my brain was working properly.

"Hang on. When did this hotel room become a suite?"

Noah did his casual shrug, but I could see through it. It was like he was trying to pretend everything was okay for my benefit, but he was obviously just as nervous.

"That's always what I mean whenever I get a hotel room."

"Of course. I forgot."

Noah cupped my face and forced me to stare into his eyes. "Poppy? Are you okay? It's only for the night. I just don't see how we're going to get back so I thought crashing in London was the only answer."

I looked back at him, calmed a little by his gaze. "I'm... fine. It's just, well, a bit of a shock, that's all."

"It's freak weather. Again. You just have to run with it when stuff like this happens."

I knew he was right but still felt a little dazed. And Noah seemed a little...off, too. I think he was trying to be the man – all together – but the situation was bothering him. I could tell. What about it though? I hoped he would tell me. An involuntary full-body shiver reminded me of how cold it was.

"This hotel?" I asked. "Is it nearby?"

Noah smiled, though it was strained.

"Just round the corner. Come on. Let's go."

And he walked me out of the train station, leaving the teeming mass of confused people wondering how they were ever going to get home.

26

The snow was still falling heavily as we weaved our way through the streets of the capital. My shoes were ruined and my feet soaked. Most people we encountered were still in headless-chicken mode, crunching through the wetness in evening finery with their phones clutched to their faces. I allowed myself to feel relief. We didn't have to get home tonight. It was going to be okay. I rang Mum and explained the plan. She seemed shocked but admitted it was the wisest thing to do.

"You say his parents have booked you a suite?"

I turned my face from Noah's and covered my mouth with my hand.

"Yeah. It's charged to the company account."

There was a pause as the neurotic cogs in Mum's brain whirred.

"Does this mean we have to pay them back?"

"I don't think so. I've offered but Noah refused. I don't think booking last-minute hotel suites is such a big deal for them as it is for us."

Sensing he was being talked about, Noah cocked his head and gave me a puzzled look.

"Gotta go, Mum." I hung up before he could overhear anything else.

Noah was right. The hotel was so close that we arrived within minutes. I stopped outside and stared. It wasn't just any old hotel – it had massive marble steps leading up to the glass-fronted entrance and screamed five-star.

"Couldn't we have just stayed in a hostel?" I asked, eyeing the pretentious potted mini-trees lining the staircase. "This place seems a little...pricey."

Noah took my hand and led me up the steps. "When are you going to realize that money isn't really an issue for me? We may as well make the most of it."

A little man wearing a bowler hat came and held the door open. I thanked him, feeling guilty he had to come out into the cold, but Noah strode past him, slipping a note into his hand without looking.

It was odd seeing Noah like that. Okay, I knew he came from money. He had told me. But seeing him in this place, so accustomed to a way of life you're only comfortable with if you can afford to be, was like seeing a different person. I wasn't sure if I liked it. Or him. And the fact he had barely spoken since we left the train station wasn't helping.

Just the reception area of the hotel blew my mind. After the ballet, it was almost affluence overkill, and I was very aware that I didn't know the behaviour protocol. I tried to act nonchalant as I took in the lush red carpet, marble statues and high ceilings. But my mouth kept dropping open. And as Noah checked us in at the giant gold reception desk, I found myself saying "Thank you" at least a million times.

Noah was still…weird. He wouldn't say thank you to anyone and seemed distracted. I tried to hold his hand as we walked to the lift, but he just squeezed it then let it drop.

The lift was gold as well and I gawped as we shot up several floors. With a ping, the doors slid open onto a floor with only one door.

More gawping. "We get a whole floor?"

Noah shrugged. "It's a suite."

Okay. Something was definitely up.

"Of course."

Noah slid a black credit-card thing into the lock and the doors sprung open to reveal the plushest hotel room I'd ever seen in real life, or even in a magazine. It was more a luxury apartment than a hotel room. There was a living room with a cinema-size TV screen and a remote-controlled fire, and a bathroom with a bath you could swim laps in.

I let out a yelp and ran inside to examine everything more carefully.

"Noah, there are dressing gowns!" I yelled at him. "Actual dressing gowns, like in the movies."

No answer, but I was too excited to care.

I ran into the living room and flopped onto the sofa.

"You could actually fit twelve people on this sofa," I yelled again in his direction. "How did they fit it through the door? Ooo, look, chocolates!"

I ripped open the black box and delved into the layers. I picked a caramel and stuffed it into my mouth. Still a tad overexcited, I ran to the giant windows and ripped back the curtains.

I hadn't realized how high up we were. You could see the whole of London. Blobby snowflakes obscured my view slightly, but I could still see the city stretching out for miles. It looked much prettier than usual. All the grime and grey were on hold, replaced by a white-carpeted winter wonderland.

Although I was very excited, much of my enthusiasm was covering for Noah's sudden bad mood. I wasn't sure when it had come on, but he'd gone from perfect to weird somewhere between here and the train station. I was shivering, so thought the best thing was to leave him to stew and get myself warm.

"I'm having a bath."

Again, no answer. So I locked myself in the bathroom.

As the water gushed out of the fat gold taps, I experimented with all the free beauty goodies on display. I poured generous amounts of Molton Brown bubble bath in and opened up all the other bottles to smell them. When the bath was ready, I shrugged off my beautiful silk dress and gratefully sank into the hot bubbly water.

It was gorgeous. I hadn't realized how cold I'd got until I was submerged in the blissfully warm water. To my delight, pressing a button on the tap transformed the bath into a supersized jacuzzi. The pressure from the jets erased any stress I'd felt about the snow, getting home, and what was up with Noah. I even started singing "Kiss" by Prince at the top of my voice, trying to recreate the bath scene from *Pretty Woman*.

I floated about until the water turned cold, and emerged transformed. I climbed into an oversized dressing gown and walked into the bedroom with my half-damp hair swirling around my shoulders.

The bedroom's widescreen television was on and Noah was sitting on the bed watching it. Bad vibes still emanated from him and he barely registered the fact I was in the room. That was enough to make me worry, but then I saw something even worse.

Noah had constructed some elaborate barrier down the middle of the king-sized bed. He had collected all the decorative cushions off the sofa and combined them with spare pillows to create a big speed bump covered with a sheet. He was sitting on his side, intently watching the TV. It would have been less obvious if he'd drawn a line down the middle with paint.

A number of emotions ran through me. Panic. Upset. Hurt. Confusion. But anger won out. And before I had time to run through what I was going to say, I found myself running over, grabbing the remote, switching off the television and then hurling the remote at him.

"What the hell is going on?" I demanded.

Noah held up his hands to protect himself from further missiles.

"Ouch! I don't know what you mean."

He still wouldn't look at me. The anger intensified.

"Noah, I am not one of those girls who will just put up with your crap and sit here smiling sweetly when you're behaving like an arse. Of course you know what I mean."

I pointed to the makeshift barrier.

His eyes followed my finger.

"Oh. That," he deadpanned.

"Of course that." My arms were flailing in the air with rage. "What the hell is it? Do I have some hideous disease or something? You've barely spoken to me since leaving the ballet, you've completely ignored me since we arrived at this hotel, and now I find you've created some kind of physical manifestation of an anti-Poppy force field down the bed. What's wrong? What have I done?"

Anger gave way to sadness and my voice cracked. I realized I was dog-tired; too much had happened today. It seemed like years ago that Lizzie and I had walked to college. And now, here I was, less than twenty-four hours later, trapped in a posh hotel suite with the world outside resembling *The Day After Tomorrow* and my boyfriend behaving like a jerk. To my embarrassment, a single tear slid out of my left eye.

"Am I so repulsive that you have to create an actual barrier to keep away from me?"

Another tear fell.

Immediately Noah was at my side, his arm around me, gently shushing me. I tried to shrug him off, humiliated, but he held on strong and stroked my hair.

"Shh, Poppy. I'm sorry. It's horrible seeing you cry."

"Well don't make me then." I wiped my eyes to capture more tears.

"Do you really think I've made that barrier because I don't like you?"

"I don't know. But it's weird. And mean. And how I am supposed to know why you do anything if you don't talk to me?"

I sat down on the bed, too upset to notice how soft and sumptuous it was. Noah sat next to me.

"Hey," I said. "This is my side."

He laughed.

"It's not funny."

He tried to get me to look him in the eyes. "I know it's not funny. I've been a prick. Let me explain."

I looked up into his beautiful face. I knew I looked a mess. I had a tendency to look absolutely awful whenever I cried, but he'd seen it now. There wasn't much I could do.

"Okay…Poppy…God, this is hard to explain."

"Try."

"Right. Of course…well…I've just kind of flipped out, that's all."

"Flipped out? Over what?"

"This is where it gets hard to explain… About us."

A crushing sense of dread raced through me and I struggled to breathe for a moment. The tears that had been retreating quickly changed direction and began to flow freely again.

"Are you having second thoughts?" My voice quivered.

"Are you kidding? Of course not."

Relief flooded through me and more tears drained out of my eyes. Startled by my reaction, Noah hugged me tight and whispered into my ear.

"Poppy. I'm so sorry. I didn't mean to upset you. It's the opposite of what you think. The truth is, well, tonight has been amazing. But it's been *too* amazing. Do you understand?"

I was too emotional to talk, so just shook my head.

"The thing is, I've told you before, I've never felt this way about a girl. I've never been that interested in what they were thinking or feeling, and it's just been, you know, physical. And with you it's different. You mean so much to me that I'm terrified I'm going to screw things up."

"I don't understand."

"Well, much as I love you, I also massively fancy you. And I wouldn't normally hold off taking things further. But we talked about it and, you know, decided to slow things down, and, well, I agree, I really do, and I don't want to rush you."

My crying had subsided enough for me to enjoy how he was struggling for the words.

"So what happened tonight then? Why have you constructed this massive barrier on the bed?"

Noah did a half-smile. "That's the thing. By me trying not to ruin things, I've gone and done exactly that. Poppy, do you have any idea what you did to me at the ballet?"

I remembered the touching, the fizzle of electricity between us. "Things did get a little heated…"

"A little? Poppy. You have no idea how close I was to jumping you, right there, where everyone could see us."

I giggled.

"Seriously. I've never had an urge that strong. It is possibly the most overwhelming feeling I've ever had. It was like a force bigger than myself. I realized I could lose self-control and possibly just lunge at you and scare you off for ever."

I smiled and sniffed.

"Poppy, I'm serious. I managed to get a hold of myself. I figured if I could get you home everything would be okay. But then there was the bloody snow. And the thought of having to spend the night sleeping next to you, but not being able to do anything…well…I didn't trust myself… so I…"

"…turned into an introverted tosser and made an anti-Poppy device without explaining any of this to me?" I finished for him.

Noah laughed and held my face. "Basically yes. I'm sorry."

I exhaled in relief.

"Are you mad at me?" He looked genuinely worried.

I nodded and then shook my head. "Yes. No. Not hugely. But don't you ever do that to me again. The not-talking. It's horrible and I won't stand for it."

"I know. I'm sorry. Never again."

I thought again of the ballet. Those feelings were

instantly recalled – and we were alone now. There was nothing and nobody here to stop us acting on our hormonal impulses.

I stretched up and kissed Noah gently on the lips. He made a small grunt and kissed me back. Then, one of us, I can't remember who, turned the gentle kiss into a frenzied passion. I lost sense of everything. Before I knew it, Noah was on his back and I was sitting astride him. My eyes were closed in blissful delirium, my arms around his neck, and his hands moving down my side, stroking my body. I moaned into his mouth.

But then Noah pulled away, leaving my mouth empty and hanging open.

"Now can you see why I made the barrier?"

We were both breathing heavily.

"Yeah, I suppose it makes sense," I said, still incredibly turned on.

I got off Noah and he flipped his body over the makeshift barrier.

"I think I need to stay over here a few moments."

I pouted out my bottom lip. "Do you have to?"

"Yes, Poppy. I do."

"But what if I change my mind about this whole taking-it-slow thing?"

Noah covered his ears with his hands. "La la la. I'm not listening."

I reached over and removed them. Just touching him again sent electric volts screeching through every limb.

"Seriously? Am I not allowed to change my mind?"

I wanted him so much. And it would be perfect here – a five-star hotel suite, after the ballet, with snow falling outside. Not many girls could boast that as their losing-their-virginity story. I was terrified, naturally, but I also wanted it more than I'd ever wanted anything. Not so much the physical part, which was the scary bit for me, but the closeness it would bring us. How making love would evolve us as a couple.

I stroked Noah's face, looking up through my eyelashes in what I hoped was a seductive manner.

But all he did was yelp and sit up.

"No no no no no no, MAN, this is HARD!"

I laughed, a little hurt, but amused by his reaction. "So I'm *not* allowed to change my mind then?"

"No."

"That hardly seems fair. Am I not allowed to know myself and what I want?"

"It's not like that, Poppy. You know yourself better than anyone I've ever met. You don't do things you don't want to do. But we are still just getting to know each other. I really don't want to rush. Even though every impulse in my body is telling me to."

I was officially defeated, and knew he was right. We had only just begun seeing each other. It didn't make sense to rush. Especially as I felt this was just the beginning. We had a long time to explore that side of things.

I held up my hands. "Okay. Seduction over. Look, I'm not

even going to touch you. But please! I need a distraction. Put the telly back on."

Noah picked up the remote. "Gladly."

We'd almost forgotten the snow but the 24-hour news channel happily filled us in on the havoc it was wreaking. Noah and I held hands over the bed barrier as we watched a chirpy news reporter excitedly divulge all the grotty details.

"As I mentioned before," she said, a smarmy grin across her overly made-up face, "there was no warning of this snowy weather. The Met Office is just as baffled as the rest of us. But, predicted or not, the capital has effectively shut down as snowfall continues to cause widespread disruption."

The screen changed to shots of snow-induced pandemonium. Cars skidded into lorries, cold dogs shivered, and panicked commuters stared wildly at departure boards in train stations.

"Look." I pointed at the TV. "That's where we just were."

Another equally smarmy reporter was interviewing distressed people in Victoria Station. A timid woman, blonde, with a cold-looking infant propped on her hip, was being interviewed.

"How about you?" Mr. Reporter asked. "How is the snow affecting your evening?"

The blonde talked to the reporter rather than the camera.

"I'm not sure what to do," she said, her voice a silvery whisper. "I only popped up to London this afternoon to meet a friend, and now I don't know how to get home. I think I'm going to have to find a hotel to crash in, but I haven't brought enough stuff for my baby." She shifted her child from one hip to the other. "To be honest, I'm pretty peeved. I don't understand how the weather people didn't know it was going to snow. It's supposed to be the twenty-first century…"

"Christ," Noah said. "We so made the right decision coming here."

The lady continued to whinge, but we saw the reporter put a hand to his earpiece and his expression changed.

"Can I just stop you there?" he said, still pressing his finger to his ear. "We've got some breaking news coming in…hang on…thank you very much and back to the studio." The reporter turned to the camera and waved goodbye, as the blonde woman blinked like an agitated fish.

In the studio, the anchorwoman flashed back onto the screen, her face grim.

"Apologies for the interruption," she said, "but we've just received breaking news that there's been a major accident on the M25 caused by the adverse weather conditions. It's estimated at least twelve vehicles are involved, and there are possible fatalities."

"That doesn't sound good," Noah said.

That twisted feeling came into my stomach – the one you get when there's a catastrophe that doesn't involve you. There is a mixture of relief and empathy, but overall an inexplicable curiosity to know every minute detail.

The screen flicked to a shaky helicopter shot of the scene.

"There are already miles of tailbacks on both sides of the motorway, but the biggest concern is that emergency services are struggling to get to the accident through the snow. We're just waiting for a report from someone on the scene."

I leaned in towards the television but it suddenly became muted. I looked at Noah and he was holding the remote control, his eyes furrowed.

"Sorry. You don't mind, do you? I just don't think I can watch any more. It's too awful."

I shrugged. "You're probably right." I leaned over, kissed him gently on the cheek and took the remote. "Does this hotel have a movie channel?"

"You wanna watch a movie?"

"Not particularly. But I don't really fancy lying here in silence with a huge barrier between us until I'm sleepy."

"We can take the barrier down."

"Wow. Really? Lucky me," I said drily.

Noah began to dismantle the pile of pillows. "Don't get excited though," he said. "I'm putting it back up at bedtime. I still haven't recovered from the ballet."

I laughed and helped him push the rest of the cushions off. "Fair enough. Let's find the most unsexy film ever to watch then."

I flicked through the channels while Noah rang down to reception and asked for some pyjamas. They were brought to us within five minutes and we both changed. They were posh flannel ones, gorgeously warm, but unattractive – enough to help calm our urges. We laughed extensively at ourselves, then snuggled under the covers, leaving a small gap in the curtains so we could watch the snow continue to fall outside.

"So what film have you picked?" Noah asked, shuffling nearer. I snuggled into the space under his armpit.

"Well, it's between a cheesy action film or a cheesy romantic film."

"Ergh. Both sound brilliantly dreadful. What's the romantic film?"

I pulled a face. "*Twilight*."

"Ha ha. Seriously?"

"For a five-star hotel, there really isn't a lot of choice."

"Have you seen it?"

"Nope. Not really my thing. But the girls are OBSESSED with it. Amanda's got them all on DVD and won't pick up her phone while she's watching them."

Noah ran a hand through his hair and smiled. "Well, it will be interesting to see what all the fuss is about."

"I suppose. That actor in it isn't too bad-looking either."

"Hey!"

"What?" I protested. "It's just an observation."

"Well. I'm not going to watch it if you're going to be drooling over Robert What'shisname."

"I won't drool."

"Let's do it then."

*   *   *

Surprisingly, the film didn't suck as much as I thought it would. I was expecting to hate it, but found it mildly bearable.

Noah, however, wasn't so convinced.

He paused it again.

"I don't understand," he said.

"What's there to understand? He's a vampire. She's not."

He shook his head. "No. I get that. I don't understand why girls love this so much."

I turned towards the frozen screen. The two lead characters were staring intently at each other, a habit that had taken up a reasonable percentage of the entire film.

"Well, I suppose it's quite romantic."

"How? How is it romantic?"

"I dunno…because their love is strong enough to get through the barriers life chucks at them…the usual stuff… he wants to eat her…she doesn't want to get eaten…"

"That's what I don't get." Noah looked genuinely confused, and a little childlike in his oversized pyjamas. "You. Girls. What is this obsession with love having to be hard? That it's only true romance if you've struggled incessantly through turmoil? Why can't girls aspire to just meet someone nice without any trouble?"

I felt myself smiling. Oh dear. Boys were just so different to girls.

"I don't think that would make for such an interesting book or movie," I teased.

"I still don't get it."

"Well, you're not a girl."

"Thank God. No offence. But seriously, you girls have it hard."

"I know."

Noah flipped onto his stomach and looked up at me. "Falling in love with you, Poppy, is the easiest thing I've ever done. I didn't even have to think about it. It just happened."

"So? What's your point?"

"Well, does that mean our love isn't worth as much? We've not had to earn it? Are we not a great love story because it wasn't a struggle? We're just...you know... boyfriend and girlfriend..."

He looked so cute, and anxious, that I couldn't help but ruffle his hair.

"Is this really bothering you?"

"Not a lot. I just don't want you to watch this film and wish we had more drama."

I readjusted my weight on the bed. "I'm sure there will be drama. I think it's the falling in love that's the easy part. It's the staying together part that causes all the drama."

Noah gave me one of his deep, searching looks. "I can't imagine ever not wanting to stay together with you," he half-whispered.

"Me neither."

"Even though I'm not a vampire? Or a werewolf? Or that being with me won't cause some sort of insane blockbuster destruction?"

I shook my head. "Plain sailing sounds just fine."

We snuggled further into each other and turned the film back on. Within minutes we had both fallen asleep, our bodies entwined together in the middle of the overly posh bed.

We didn't put the barrier back up.

Dead.

Rain couldn't believe it.

People were dead, actually dead.

He was still in the computer lab, his new home apparently. In fact, he'd forgotten what the interior of his apartment looked like, it'd been so long since he'd slept there. Sleep was a luxury he couldn't afford at this time. He wouldn't have been able to sleep anyway, not now.

When he'd first heard about the fatalities he'd calmly excused himself and headed to the bathroom. He'd then hunched over the toilet bowl and violently vomited until he was dry-heaving. Once the nausea had passed, he'd washed his hands in the basin and examined his reflection in the mirror. He was ashamed to admit he didn't recognize the person staring back at him. The youthful eager face that girls had always liked had disappeared. He had visibly aged at least five years in the past few weeks. His skin was sallow, black bags spread out under his sunken eyes and he'd spotted a few flecks of grey in his hair the other morning. Grey hair? In his early twenties?

None of it mattered – his appearance, his vanity, his pride. He didn't deserve any of it. People were dead and he was responsible. That was something he would never come to terms with.

Dr. Beaumont was still at his side, his partner in crime. Oddly, the last week's events had had an opposite effect on her appearance. She was almost glowing. Her lips were redder, her cheeks more flushed, her eyes a bright dewy white despite her lack of sleep. But any attraction he had for her had vanished. She now repulsed him. She had called the deaths "their little secret", in an almost flirtatious way. It was horrifying.

Rain had no idea what to do or how to handle the situation. He wished he'd told someone sooner, someone higher up than Anita. But this whole screwed organization was so secretive that he had no idea who her superior was. Plus, would they really take his word over hers? After everything she'd done for the company? Without her, they were nothing – and she knew that.

"It's not murder, you know that, right?" she'd told him the night before, while they watched the news. "We're not directly responsible for those deaths."

Rain was still staring in horror at the events unfolding on their global television link.

"But we're not innocent either," he muttered. "These people would still be alive if we'd acted sooner..."

"You don't know that for certain."

"Sure I do!"

He stood up and began pacing. "Anita – sorry, I mean, Dr. Beaumont – if we'd done something sooner, if we'd sent in the collection team sooner, there wouldn't have been adverse weather. There wouldn't have been ice on the road, that first car wouldn't have skidded, and therefore there wouldn't be dozens of people trapped and dying in their cars. Don't you see? Our lack of action has created all these other actions. It's like the butterfly effect. The chaos theory. It's what I learned about in training camp. It's why I took this job. To stop these things happening. To do good. To save lives, not end them."

He sat back down and put his head on the desk. He didn't care if she was going to fire him, although he knew so much they would probably just "dispose" of him instead. He was choking back tears.

Anita, always calm, waited for him to compose himself.

"That," she said, "is one way of seeing things."

"It's the only way."

"You're wrong."

"Really?" He looked up. "How? Please tell me what explanation you have to argue away your guilt?"

She drummed her pen against the table, the only slight signal she might be feeling remorse. "Rain, you know why I'm head of this operation, don't you? I'm sure you've heard the rumours."

He looked away from her. He had heard them, yes. He still hadn't worked out if they were true or not. He'd assumed they were just water-cooler gossip. Anita was hugely respected in the company, yet she was also pretty much despised. Her mood swings weren't saved especially for Rain – she yelled abuse at everyone and they just had to take it.

"Anyway," she continued, "because of my…circumstances, I am, without a doubt, the most important person to this company. You know it, I know it, even that annoying intern who polishes the floor knows it." She smiled wryly. "So, that considered, I will disregard the fact that you've basically just accused me of murder, but only this one time…"

"What's your point?"

"What I'm trying to say is, I know what I'm doing, Rain. You need to trust me."

He looked into her cold steely eyes and summoned all his courage to speak. "If the rumours are true, Dr. Beaumont, then actually I think it would be unwise to trust you."

She jerked back like she'd been slapped. "And what the hell is that supposed to mean?"

He shrugged. Angry, exhausted. "It means how can I be sure you're acting in the universe's best interests? That's why we're here, isn't it? To stop matches coming together. To stop people dying, and the world collapsing in on its axis, right? But you've said so yourself, this couple have a tolerance… And what if you're thinking, they're building a tolerance…maybe I could build a tolerance…with my soulmate?"

He stood up. "And I'm sorry, but your screwed-up little science project means people are dead. It's your fault, Anita! You're out of control – admit it!"

She was teetering on the brink of losing her temper. She put her face close to his, and her words were more like a growl than anything.

"How dare you? You have no right. No right at all. I know

what I'm doing, Rain. We didn't let those people die. It was an accident."

"An accident we could have prevented."

"You don't know that for sure."

"No one forecasted a blizzard."

"Forget the blizzard! Don't you see, Rain? We need to let this match run. You've seen the data, it's like nothing we've ever seen before. This couple are building an immunity – immunity! Do you not think it's worth staying with this? Think about what could happen if we tapped into this? How many more lives could be saved if we were able to 'cure' couples of being soulmates? The readings are unprecedented and they follow no pattern. It's like what we know has evolved, it's got bigger, scarier, even less predictable. Any data we can accumulate before the inevitable separation is like gold dust. It could potentially save hundreds of thousands more lives. What if a match like this happens again? We won't know what to expect unless we run with these two. It's for the greater good, Rain. How can you not see that?"

Rain's eyes remained on the screen. "So these people who died? Are you trying to tell me they're just...collateral damage?"

Anita smiled at him, a wild unnerving smile. She'd lost it. She'd completely lost it. But what could he do?

"Now you get it," she beamed.

That was the moment Rain excused himself to the bathroom and retched until his insides were empty and raw.

27

I opened my eyes to find myself in the poshest bed in the world with Noah lying next to me. The television was still on and had been replaying the film all night. The *Twilight* couple were clutching at each other's faces, the female lead blubbering as they went in for one last kiss. I smiled. Nobody looks that pretty when they cry. And if you kissed midway through a bawl-fest there would be a lot more snot.

I turned it off, then edged my way out of bed, being careful not to wake Noah, before padding over to the window.

I sat on the oversized sill, looking out at the sprawling city below. The snow had gone, as it very quickly does in London. The beautiful white blanket had turned to brown sludge, piled at the side of traffic-clogged roads. I closed my eyes, listened to the city noises and did my breathing exercises. I had another overpriced appointment with Dr. Ashley coming up and wanted to give a better impression than usual.

The world went hazy as I concentrated only on my breath, my ribcage, and my body in the present moment – until I felt the presence of Noah.

I opened my eyes to find him peering curiously at me.

"And what, may I ask, are you doing?"

I looked up at him innocently. "My exercises."

"I see. And what exercises might those be?"

"It's sort of like meditation. I'm supposed to do it every morning."

"Fair enough." Noah looked outside. "The snow's gone."

"Yup."

"Pity. It would've been quite romantic to stay snowed-in for another day."

I leaned my head back and he ruffled my hair.

"Don't torture me. What time do we need to check out?"

"Eleven."

"What time is it now?"

"Half nine."

"Does that mean we have time to get room service?"

Noah smiled. "And that, Poppy, is another reason why I love you."

Twenty minutes later and our hotel suite resembled some kind of massive teddy bears' picnic – minus the teddy bears, of course. To say I got overexcited by the idea of room service was an understatement. Plus, when Noah told me that all room service was charged to the company expenses account – therefore I could order whatever I wanted – I might have got a tad carried away.

"Oh my God, you have to try these eggs Benedict," I said, lying tummy down on the carpet while simultaneously stuffing my face. "They taste like World Peace. World Peace in egg form."

Noah raised an eyebrow from the other side of our makeshift picnic. The stack of pancakes in front of him was so tall they almost obscured his face.

"World Peace eggs? Is that possible?"

"If everyone had these eggs for breakfast there would definitely never be any more wars." I took another big bite. "I didn't know what eggs Benedict was until now, but I think I definitely like it."

Noah laughed and poured himself some freshly squeezed orange juice. "If you think those eggs are good, just wait until you try these pancakes."

"The blueberry ones?"

"Yup."

"Watch out. I'm coming over."

I ran to Noah's side. He pierced a chunk of pancake with his fork and held it out. I closed my eyes and let him slip it into my mouth.

I groaned. "Oh my God. World Peace pancakes! Those are so good! Noah, are the chefs here not cooking for the UN?"

He laughed again.

I grabbed Noah's fork and dived into the fruit salad, spearing juicy pieces of ripe red melon hungrily.

"I don't even LIKE melon!" I said as I shovelled more into my gob.

Noah was just watching me with that special thin smile he used when I was amusing him.

"I've never seen anyone get so excited by breakfast before."

"Are you serious? It's the most important meal of the day. Sometimes, at bedtime, I plan what I'm going to make for breakfast and then get so excited that I can't sleep."

"Very normal."

"I don't care if it's not normal."

Once we (and by that I mean I) had finished guzzling, we checked out of the hotel and got an uncancelled train back to Middletown and reality.

Far sooner than I wanted, Noah was walking me to my door.

"Thank you again for such an amazing evening," I said, planting a kiss near his eye. "I don't think I'll ever forget it."

"I had a brilliant time too." He entwined his fingers with mine before leaning in for a sneaky kiss on the lips – a brief one, in case Mum was looking out the window.

I shivered. There was still a lot of snow in Middletown compared with the melted streets of the capital.

Noah pulled a face. "I've got a bit of bad news, I'm afraid."

"What's that?"

"Don't worry too much. It's just I don't think we're going to be able to see as much of each other as I would like in the next few weeks."

My mood level immediately dropped.

I shook my head. *Strong. Independent. Woman.* I repeated to myself.

"Oh," I said. "How come?"

"Band practice. There's so much to do before this gig. I can't believe it's only two weeks away. We're still such a mess."

"You're not a mess. You guys are brilliant."

"Thanks but we definitely need a LOT of rehearsals if we're going to look semi-professional next to Ponyboys."

I looked down at the snow-covered path beneath my feet, disappointed.

Noah stroked my face.

"You do realize it's going to be unbelievably bad not being able to see so much of you," he said. "I'm not sure how I'm going to cope. Does that make me sound like a soppy idiot? I bet you're looking forward to having a little break from me…"

I smiled to wind him up. "Yeah, I could do with a bit of a break from you actually."

"Hey!"

I laughed and gave him a full kiss on the lips.

"Of COURSE I'm going to miss you, you massive doofus," I said, flinging my arms around him. "Loads and loads."

Noah hugged me back. "Good."

And then we kissed once more, not caring that Mum could be lurking behind the curtains.

Mum and Dad met me in the hallway.

"You made it back – brilliant," Mum said, a plate in one hand and a tea towel clutched in the other. Trust her to do chores on a snow day off work. "How was the snow in London?"

I gave her and Dad a quick kiss. "All melted, but it's like Narnia here still. I'm so not suitably dressed."

They looked at my ballet attire.

"I don't believe I've seen that dress before." Dad was slightly feminine in the way he noticed all my and my sister's wardrobe additions.

I blushed and did a semi-twirl. "Noah got it for me."

"He bought you a dress? A teenage boy bought you a dress?" He pushed his glasses up his nose. "My my my…"

"And he took her to a ballet, and they stayed in a five-star hotel last night," Mum reminded him.

"Hmm, is he rich, this boyfriend of yours?"

"Yeah, I think so. Well, I know so. Yes."

"He must be," Mum put in.

"But you like him? He treats you well? Not just well in terms of buying you things and taking you to fancy places, but he makes you feel good about yourself?"

Where was this third degree coming from? Was Dad actually being overprotective?

"Yes. He treats me very well. You can meet him if you want to."

"Well, that would be nice."

"Can I go upstairs and change now? I'm freezing."

Dad smiled. "Of course."

I went to have a shower. Just before I turned the taps on, I overheard snippets of my parents' conversation floating up the stairs.

"Where did she find this...millionaire?"

"He's in a band."

"Of course he is."

"She's been much more cheerful recently. There haven't been any panic attacks and no more of that terrifying crying."

"I know. That's all brilliant, but I want that to be because she's happy with herself, not just because some boy likes her."

"You don't need to worry. Poppy's always had a strong sense of self – you taught her that. She's allowed to have a boyfriend. It's definitely the age. And he seems to really like her. At least he's not messing her around, messing her up..."

"Yes, you're right. God, it's weird seeing your daughter fall in love though, isn't it?"

I smiled at this as I peeled off my tights and stepped into the shower.

"Very weird. But I don't think it's anything to worry about."

I turned the tap on and the sound of their conversation was drowned out. I felt an overwhelming love for them both. They probably did need to meet Noah. I knew once Dad met him he would realize he wasn't just this jumped-up flashy rich boy. Although it was terribly soon for the whole meeting-the-parents thing. Or was it? Everything about Noah was on super-speed anyway. And it all felt so right. So very, very right.

My phone rang just as I was getting dressed. Lizzie. I prepared myself for the interrogation.

I flipped it open but didn't even get a chance to say hello.

"So what happened then?"

"Hello to you too."

"Screw niceties. What happened?"

"Why are you so interested?"

I tried to pull a jumper on and keep my phone against my cheek at the same time.

"Because last night I was so bored and stuck inside because of the snow, I seriously considered practising snogging on my cat."

I giggled. "Things that bad, eh?"

"I'll live. The news is still my only love."

"Of course."

"So stop stalling. Where did he take you?"

I paused for dramatic effect. "He took me to the ballet."

A gasp. "Seriously?"

"Yup."

"Wow."

"And that's not all of it."

"It's not?"

"No. He bought me a dress to wear. And then we got stuck in the snow and ended up staying in a five-star hotel."

Silence.

"Lizzie?"

More silence.

"Lizzie?"

Even more silence.

"LIZZIE?"

"I'm here…" She was breathing heavily. "Sorry. I fell off my chair in excitement and it took me a while to find the receiver again."

I laughed.

"Seriously though, Poppy, is he a robot? Or has he read some kind of special 'how to be a perfect boyfriend' self-help book? And if so, can we buy multiple copies and plant them all around Middletown for other boys to read?"

That made me laugh again. "It's almost vom-inducing, isn't it?"

"Yes. It's disgusting. I hate you. I also want to hear everything."

"Well…" I started.

"Not over the phone. I want every last detail. Face to face. We're going sledging. You, me, Ruth, Amanda, maybe some of Johnno's mates. Come. And tell me everything then."

"Sledging?"

"Yes."

"Seriously?"

"Uh huh."

"We've never sledged before."

"Well, I figured, as it's quite clear the world is ending, it's something we should tick off the list before the Apocalypse."

"You really think it's the end of the world?"

"Yes. The weather always knows."

I opened my wardrobe drawer, trying to find something suitable for sledging. "It was just a storm, and then some snow."

"And the power cut."

"That wasn't anything to do with the weather."

"They still don't know what caused it."

"Hmm."

"And we've had an Indian summer."

"It's called global warming."

"It's called the Apocalypse. I read about it on the internet. It's something to do with giants and monks, and the calendar ending."

I looked at my reflection in the mirror, and practised raising an eyebrow.

"Well," I said, "if it IS indeed the end of the world, that's such a shame, because it means you'll never have the chance to grow up and be a proper journalist."

Lizzie went quiet.

"Well, maybe it's just the beginning of the end of the world. I'm sure we've still got a few years…decades…on our side."

"Of course."

"Meet us at top of the common at two-ish."

"Will do."

And then we hung up.

It was gorgeous walking up to the common in the snow. It had been transformed into the proverbial winter wonderland, each tree branch laden with a heavy layer of crisp ice. I'd never thought the common could be improved upon but, with snow – wow. It was mind-blowing. It had snowed before in Middletown, but never this much, and I'd never gone up the common in it. Much as I whinged about living in boring suburbia, I did feel lucky right then. In London the snow had all gone by early morning, and everyone still had to go to work and college, but here we still had huge areas left unspoiled by footprints or cars.

Everyone was already at the top when I got there.

"Hello all," I yelled, waving at them.

They waved back. Everyone, like me, was wearing multiple layers and looked puffy and childlike. Even Ruth was wearing a bobble hat, her crimson hair peeking out. All their cheeks were pink, their mouths smiling, as if snow had a way of extracting happiness from even the most determined of mardy bums.

"Don't mention the hat," Ruth said when I got over to them. "I'm praying Johnno and his mates don't come, otherwise I'm going to have to take it off and get frostbite of the head."

Lizzie was wearing a parka I'd never seen before and had the fuzzy hood up.

"Isn't this great?" she asked, her breath coming out as frozen steam. "Look at our sledges."

I saw two tea trays and a rubber ring. "Those are not sledges."

"They'll do."

"You can go first then," Amanda said. She looked the most like a child in her numerous layers, her little face poking out from an array of scarves. "But first," she said. "I want to hear all about this ballet and hotel." She winked at me.

I turned to Lizzie.

"You told them!"

She shrugged her shoulders. "Of course I told them. Why are you even surprised?"

"Isn't it too cold for chatting?"

"Nope," Ruth said. She didn't appear bothered by the prospect of a Noah conversation. Maybe the snow really did wash away grumpiness. "Any reason to delay Lizzie pushing me over a cliff on that bloody tray."

"Alright then."

We stood shivering as I filled them in on the dress, the ballet, the snow, the hotel – although I didn't mention the bed barrier or the fight. They gasped and squealed and, of course, demanded to come round and see The Dress.

"Wow," Amanda said. "I swear you are living in a movie, Poppy. I mean, this stuff doesn't happen in real life."

I knew it was true but I couldn't agree, as that would be big-headed, so I shrugged. "I just got lucky."

Ruth was a bit quiet.

"How are things going with you and Will?" I ventured, hoping she hadn't changed her mind and dumped him since I last saw her.

She smiled. "Yeah, great. You should see the outfit I've got for the gig. It's amazing!"

"It's still two weeks away and you've got an outfit already?"

She gave me a withering look, like I was a child still trying to work out how the world worked. "Poppy, it's a big gig. We have to come across as professional groupies."

I stuck my tongue out. "Ergh. I don't want to be a groupie. Can't I just be the girlfriend of the guitarist? They're lucky to have *us*, right?"

Ruth gave me the face again. "Fair enough. But if you don't sleep with Noah, trust me, there will be hundreds of girls willing to take your place."

"I'm willing to take that chance." My voice broke a little, showing my false confidence.

"I'm just saying."

I tried not to let her words bother me, but they did. They were probably supposed to.

"Come on," Lizzie said, breaking the tension as always. "Let's try out these sledges."

We all groaned but shuffled into position.

"How does this work?" I asked, straddling a tea tray.

Lizzie scratched her head with her mitten. "Erm, I'm not too sure. I think you just sit on it and push off with your feet."

I gingerly lowered my bottom onto it and put my feet up. Nothing happened.

"Nothing's happening."

"Erm…maybe you need a push?"

"Okay. Be careful."

Lizzie gave me a tap. I still didn't move.

"Lizzie, that was pathetic. Push me harder."

"You sure?"

"Yeah. Let's see what these things can do."

And before I knew it I was careering down the hill, screaming, with my hair flying behind me and snow flying over the tea tray into my face.

"Wheeeeeeeeeeeeeeeeeeeeeeeeeeeeeeeeeeeeeeeeeeeeeee!"

I bumped over fox holes, swerved to avoid families walking their dogs, and arrived at the bottom of the hill far too quickly.

I got off, turned, and waved at my friends, who looked tiny at the top of the hill.

"ARE YOU ALIVE?!" Amanda called.

"YOU HAVE TO TRY THAT!" I called back.

The next few hours were spent running up and down the hill, taking it in turns to push each other. Johnno and his friends turned up and Ruth's hat magically vanished into her coat pocket. We turned sledging into a tournament and began racing the two trays. At one point we tried putting two people on one tray to see if the gravitational force (Johnno does physics) made us go faster. Unfortunately we tried this experiment using Amanda and one of Johnno's mates and she was too shy to hold onto him properly. This meant that halfway down the hill, she came flying off the tray and sailed through the air with an astonished look on her face, before face-planting into a massive snowdrift. As you can imagine, this led to A LOT of laughing, and soon the competition had evolved into seeing how many people you could fit on one tea tray.

As the fun continued, the upset from my stunted conversation with Ruth faded, although she'd reawoken that familiar paranoia I felt about Noah. The fact I wasn't going to be seeing much of him for a while certainly wouldn't help either. I tried to push it from my mind though.

Much too soon, the sky got darker and people began to go home. Lizzie and I walked back together.

"The snow's melting already," she whinged, kicking it up with her wellington boot. "Does that mean the end of the Middletown Winter Olympics?"

She was right. It was definitely turning into mush.

"At least it snowed enough for them to cancel college," I said. "It would've been rubbish if we were stuck inside all day."

"Ergh. College. I'm so behind in my coursework it's not even funny."

"Me too."

"Yeah right. You always say that but you always have it done."

"Not this time. I dunno. There just doesn't seem to be enough time to do anything at the moment."

Lizzie fluttered her eyelashes at me. "Is it because you're in luuuuurrrve?!"

I pushed her into a snowdrift. She squealed and struggled to get up, before emerging looking like a yeti.

"Ouch!"

"You look like the Snowman."

"Yeah, well you look like my five-year-old cousin when we dress her up for the Christmas Day walk."

We walked for a bit longer. My feet were beginning to go numb.

"Don't worry about what Ruth said," Lizzie offered, still looking ahead. "I don't think you have to worry about Noah running off with some fan."

This is what I loved about Lizzie. Sometimes, out of the blue, she could just read your mind and say exactly what you needed to hear.

"Thank you."

"I still can't believe he bought you a dress."

I laughed. "Me neither."

"Poppy?"

"Yes?"

"You're very lucky, you know that, right?"

I thought of Noah and how it felt this morning to wake up next to him.

"I know."

It took about ten million years to de-layer when I got home. I stood on the welcome mat, shedding clothes like a snake.

Mum eyeballed the pile of sodden garments next to the mat.

"I'm not washing all those. You've dirtied your entire wardrobe."

I shook one leg to try and get my foot out of my wellington. "I know. I'll do my own laundry. It's cold outside!"

"Hmm."

She walked away unimpressed, probably because she knew she wouldn't be able to help herself and would end up doing my laundry anyway. She couldn't stand to watch me use the washing machine. Apparently I was "too rough" with the buttons.

Once I'd finally removed all my snow clothes, I went to find Dad in the living room.

He was grumbling from behind a giant stack of newspapers.

"Dad, are you in there somewhere?"

His face popped over the top, frowning. He folded up a magazine.

"Your mother is making me do the recycling, rather than enjoy my day off work."

"That doesn't sound fun."

"It isn't. But she's scary when she's in project mode."

"Do you want some help?"

He grinned. "Go on then."

I sat on the carpet and helped him sort out the massive pile of newspapers he'd accumulated.

"Jesus, Dad, why do you keep them all?"

"I might need them one day."

"What? For an exposé on the council's recycling plant?"

"Maybe."

I was about to put another issue on the "toss" pile, when a headline caught my eye. "Hang on," I said. "This is today's."

The front page been blacked out, with all the usual adverts for local taxi companies removed.

TWENTY CONFIRMED DEAD IN SNOW HORROR SMASH

There was a photo of cars crunched up like discarded revision notes, the steel corrugated into ghastly angles.

I had a flicker of a memory from the night before – the TV news.

"Dad?" I asked, pulling the paper further towards me. "Was this on the M25?"

Dad nodded. "Right near our junction."

"I saw it on the news last night. I didn't realize it was so close to home."

I opened the paper. On pages two and three, sandwiched

between text, were a few grainy photos of the people who'd lost their lives. Their eyes looked out at me from the cheap newsprint almost accusingly, like they knew I'd been watching a film with my boyfriend, having a fantastic time, just as their entire existence was being wiped out like solved equations on a school whiteboard.

I shuddered.

"Anyone we know?" I looked at the photos, and didn't recognize anyone.

Dad shook his head. "A few of the bodies have yet to be identified," he said, his voice rising slightly. "But I'm sure if it was people we knew we would have found out by now."

I put the paper down on the coffee table. "Dad? What's going on?"

"I'm not sure, Poppy. Global warming? It's usually something to do with global warming."

I read the paper over his shoulder for the next minute or so, before standing up and stretching.

"You off to bed?"

"Yeah, probably. I should try and get some work done first."

"You seeing any more of Noah this weekend?" His voice was casual, but he was giving me a look from under his half-moon spectacles.

I shook my head. "Nope. Don't think so. He's really busy rehearsing for this important gig."

Dad smirked. "My daughter. Girlfriend of a rock star... I never thought I would see the day."

"I don't like to think about it that way." I smiled back. "I think of it as, 'my boyfriend, going out with an intelligent wonderful girl who he's lucky to have'."

Dad always had this thing about self-worth. Maybe that was where his sudden odd angst about Noah had come from. Maybe he was scared I would lose myself once I started to share myself.

His smirk stretched into a real smile. "That's my girl."

28

I sat before the box of tissues and waited for Dr. Ashley to break the silence.

There was a new framed picture on the wall – another generic watercolour framed behind shatterproof glass.

The session hadn't started well. I'd apologized. It was something I'd always had an issue doing. But the deeply ingrained socializing force of manners prevailed, and I found myself muttering at the beginning of the session.

"What's that, Poppy? I don't think I caught that."

I looked at the ground, like a toddler being forced to apologize to someone in the sandpit. "I said I'm sorry if I was a bit rude last time I saw you."

He rubbed his hands together. In delight? No. Just my imagination.

"That's perfectly okay, Poppy. We all get upset from time to time."

He didn't say sorry back and I couldn't remember if he needed to. But I thought that was the rules of saying sorry – the standard response is "I'm sorry too", even if you haven't done anything to warrant an apology. It's just how people do it.

That had been five minutes ago and I was still waiting for him to talk. The thing was, I knew he wouldn't. Why would he? He would get paid whether I talked or not.

"So if I didn't talk right now, would we just sit in silence for the whole hour?"

Dr. Ashley twined and untwined his fingers. "You don't have to talk if you don't want to, Poppy."

"But you would get paid anyway, wouldn't you?"

Annoyance passed across his face but he did his best to smooth it away with a thin-lipped smile. "I suppose I would."

"It's easy money then, isn't it?"

Another flicker of annoyance. I realized I was being rude.

"Sorry. I'm being rude again, aren't I?"

"How has your week been?"

Classic trick. Distraction.

I shrugged. "Okay."

"Any panic attacks? Unhelpful thoughts?"

I loved his term "unhelpful thoughts". It conjured images of my thoughts as little elves running around in my head doing chores. When had a thought ever been useful? Apart from the major useful thoughts that famous people had, like when Edison thought about light bulbs, or Newton thought about apples. Most of my thoughts were unhelpful. How does the thought *Does my hair look okay today?* serve any purpose? But Dr. Ashley didn't explain them like this.

He said they were thoughts that would only have a negative outcome.

I shook my head. "I've been much better actually. Nothing. Not a sausage."

"And why do you think that might be?"

Another shrug. If I had a pound for every time I'd shrugged in that office…

"Your mother mentioned you've met someone…"

I blushed. I was going to kill her.

"We touched on this last time. I can see from your face you're not too eager to discuss it but this…boyfriend? Can I call him that?"

I nodded, red from head to toe.

"This boyfriend, do you think he's helped? Or is it just coincidence?"

I thought about the fainting spells I'd had when I first met Noah. I'd been convinced it was something to do with him back then. I couldn't help but smile to myself. I'd honestly believed I was ALLERGIC to him at one point. So silly. But it'd turned out to have nothing to do with him. I saw him loads and my body was back to normal. Yes, there were those times when I felt out of breath and my heart felt like it was going to jump out of my chest, but that was just normal love, wasn't it? That was where all the clichés came from. Love just kick-starts adrenalin. And I had learned all about adrenalin from Dr. Ashley. About the fight-or-flight defence mechanisms that my body sometimes decided to employ without my permission.

"You seem deep in thought, Poppy."

"Huh?"

"Anything you would like to share with the class?" He smiled at his own joke. I hate it when people do that.

"Er…"

Could I? I supposed I might as well. Mum and Dad were paying enough.

"Is that possible? Can getting a boyfriend really help? Things do seem to have calmed down since we got together."

He nodded, his fingers pressed together in front of his face. "I see."

"It might just be coincidence. Maybe it's just all my breathing exercises finally paying off."

"Perhaps, but it might not be a coincidence."

"Do *you* think it's a coincidence?" I challenged him.

He picked up his gold pen. I thought he was going to make more notes I wasn't allowed to see, but he didn't. Instead, he rolled the pen between his fingers.

"Hmm. That's a toughie."

I stayed quiet.

"In the brain, things are rarely a coincidence. The links, even the supposedly 'faulty' ones, are actually very logical."

He thought about it a moment more.

"So it's interesting that your…symptoms, for want of a better word, have…diminished since you found a male companion."

I smiled at his description. It sounded like Noah was

someone who escorted me to balls at the local village hall or something.

"So it may be that some of your issues stem from an inherent need to be wanted."

Hang on. This bit didn't sound right.

"...And now you've finally found someone who wants you...you feel *validated*."

My fists clenched. "It's not like that at all," I blurted out.

Dr. Ashley looked concerned. He shuffled up in his chair, making himself look professional again. "Don't worry, Poppy. It's quite normal."

Normal? Wasn't that word banned from therapy? Wasn't that word banned from modern society? You couldn't say the word "normal" any more. It was like the "I'm sorry, I'm sorry too" rule. You'd say the word "normal" and automatically everyone said "Yeah, but what *is* normal?" thinking they were really, really clever.

I could feel my temper bubbling far quicker than it normally does.

I made my voice sarcastic. "Oh, so it's *normal*, is it?" I sneered, scrunching up my nose. "It's normal for all women's problems to stem from needing the validation of men?"

He stayed calm, as usual, even though it was obvious I was about to get remarkably un-calm.

"I didn't say that, Poppy."

"You implied it."

"No I didn't."

"Yes you did."

He put his pen down and sighed. "I'm not going to argue with you, Poppy."

"Do you really think that?" I realized my voice was breaking. "That I'm happy now, that I'm…mentally healthy now, just because I've got a boyfriend?"

He picked up the all-too-familiar box of tissues, pulled one out, and passed it to me.

I hadn't realized I'd started crying. Bloody hell. Almost every session.

I tried to regain control over my emotions, but the word "validated" kept bubbling up in my thoughts like a kettle of poison.

"Are you feeling better, Poppy?"

I nodded. "Yes thank you."

"Do you think you could try an exercise with me?"

Another nod.

His voice was soft now, soothing, like he was reading a bedtime story. "This boyfriend of yours…?"

"Noah."

"Noah? Alright. Now I want you to sit comfortably, relax, and close your eyes."

I did what he said.

"I just want you to slowly let yourself imagine that Noah is, for some reason, not able to be in your life…that you are never to see him again. That he has disappeared without warning…"

I leaned back into my chair and allowed myself to

entertain the thought. Almost immediately my chest began to tighten, my breathing got shallow.

"Imagine waking up every morning knowing you will never see him again…"

I felt my eyes bulge in my sockets. I imagined it. I imagined waking up in my bed, the sun streaming through the window, to nothing. I imagined never being able to smell him again, never being able to see his smile. My throat caught. I imagined walking past his apartment knowing he was no longer in it. I imagined sitting at the top of Middletown Common remembering our first kiss, but it was now empty and we would never sit there again. I gasped for air.

"Careful, Poppy. Breathe. BREATHE."

But his voice seemed far away. My chest heaved, panic began to rise in my throat. I gulped for air but none came. I was choking. But all I could think of was Noah. And the pain. The pain of him not being with me for ever. There was darkness and I stumbled blindly into it. Falling…and falling… And far away I could vaguely make out someone shouting my name.

Sadness. There was unbelievable sadness. My stomach ached from it. My heart felt like someone had literally snapped it in half. I could hear screaming but I couldn't see anything. There was only darkness.

And then I came to.

"Poppy? Poppy? Can you hear me?"

Ouch.

Someone was lightly tapping my face. The darkness was replaced by confusion. Where the hell was I?

"Poppy? I think she's awake."

I became slowly aware that I had a body. I could feel my limbs again. They hurt. Wherever I was, it wasn't comfortable. I couldn't be in bed. Usually bed was comfier than this.

I wanted to open my eyes but the effort needed to do so was overwhelming. I kept them closed.

"Poppy? If you can hear me, wiggle your finger."

Wiggle? I could do that. I instructed my brain to wiggle my little finger and my brain obeyed. I felt it wiggle.

"You're back. Okay. Poppy, when you're ready, try and open your eyes. Take it slowly."

I opened my right eye first but the light hurt. I closed it again, took a breath, and tried one more time. It stung but I kept it open and carefully opened my other eye. I couldn't see anything at first. Just a blur. But the blur became a face. A face I hadn't seen before. It was a tough-looking woman's face. If I was going to be honest about it, a butch woman's face.

"Who are you, please?"

She just laughed. "Your patient is back with us, Dr. Ashley."

Dr. Ashley? Was he here as well?

I turned my head. Ouch. It hurt. Then Dr. Ashley came

into focus. He was squatting on the floor. That was odd. I shuffled to get comfortable but couldn't move my body. I was being pinned down by something. Hey! It was the butch lady. She was holding me down.

"Careful now," butch lady said. "Don't try to move just yet."

"Poppy?" Dr. Ashley's voice was even softer than his bedtime-story one. "Do you know where you are?"

"I'm not comfortable."

"Sorry about that. Do you know where you are?"

I turned my head – it hurt again – and surveyed the room. Dim recognition dawned and got stronger. I recognized the nondescript paintings, the big chairs and the box of tissues.

"We're in your office," I told him, pretty proud of myself.

"Yes we are. Do you know what happened?"

I shook my head.

"You fainted, Poppy. I think you had a panic attack and it caused you to lose consciousness. You're fine but you might've bumped your head when you fell off the chair. I didn't get to you in time and I'm sorry about that."

Fainted?

And with that extra piece of information, all the memories came back to me. Of the appointment, of Dr. Ashley, of thinking about Noah, and he was gone...gone...

"Noah?" I asked, worried.

"It's fine, Poppy. It was just an exercise, remember?"

Relief flooded through me. Of course! The exercise. It

wasn't real. Noah was still here. He was still mine. I felt warmth creep through my veins, making me feel strong.

"Mary, get her up, would you? I think she's feeling better."

The butch lady held me under my armpits to pull me up and set me down on the chair.

"Thank you, Mary. I think I can take it from here."

"Make sure she drinks that sugar water," Mary said.

I looked at the table. There was a glass next to the tissues. I picked it up and took a few sips. It tasted good, much nicer than usual water.

Mary left and we sat in silence. I sipped at the water, confused. "What happened?"

"I told you. You fainted."

I knew that much. "But why?"

"You tell me, Poppy."

The cool leather of the chair felt good against my skin. I slumped into it. I thought back to the idea of Noah leaving – just reminding myself made my heart start thumping again.

"Noah. You asked me to imagine Noah not being in my life."

"I did."

"…And I passed out."

"You did."

I pressed my hand to my face – it was wet. I'd been crying. I hadn't even noticed.

"Well, that's not normal, is it?"

"I don't like the word 'normal' in this room, Poppy."

"Hang on. You used it just a moment ago! Hypocrite."

Dr. Ashley smiled. "And I see you're feeling better already."

"You did say it." He had. I distinctly remembered him saying it.

"Perhaps I did."

"You definitely did."

I smiled to myself, but the enormity of what had just happened made the smile disappear.

"What does it mean, Dr. Ashley?" I felt ashamed and in disbelief. Had my feelings for Noah really become so out of control so quickly? Was he really responsible for my panic attacks stopping? Because I now felt *validated*?

I felt sick.

"It means I want to up our sessions to twice a week."

29

The week before the big gig, my English class had to go on a trip to London. As part of our World War I module, Ms. Gretching made us plod round the Imperial War Museum rather than actually teach us stuff for the exam. Typical. And Frank and I were therefore forced to spend the entire day together.

On the train up, things got weird.

I was looking out of the window while Frank pretended to read a broadsheet newspaper.

"You're not fooling anyone," I muttered, watching sheep and fields streak by.

Frank looked up and I could see his confused face reflected in the glass. "Huh?"

"Your newspaper. You trying to come across all caring-about-the-world. I know for a fact you've only read the sports page and have been trying to understand that double page about the economy for twenty minutes. Stop posing."

Frank folded the paper up. "I wasn't posing."

"Yes you were."

"Okay…maybe I was a bit."

"Told you."

"I'm bored. I can't believe I'm missing rugby practice to go to a stupid museum."

I rolled my eyes. "Poor thing! How will you cope?"

"Shut up."

"I mean screw the trenches – they were nothing. Missing rugby practice is far more upsetting."

"You've made your point."

"I always do."

Frank leaned back in his chair and exhaled slowly. "It's going to be a long day."

The train sped along. I read a bit of Frank's paper. We tried to share his iPod but couldn't agree on what to listen to. I ate a chewy bar and gave him half.

It appeared we weren't so comfortable with each other away from the classroom. Things felt a bit stilted, which wasn't usual for us.

Frank broke the slightly awkward silence. "So, do you know what you want to study at uni yet?"

University. Scary. I had tried not to think about it.

"We don't have to decide until next year, do we?"

"I know that, but you must have a vague idea. UCAS time will come up before you know it."

I'd had a few university prospectuses land through my letter box but I'd only skim-read them. I couldn't concentrate for long. I got too freaked out and chucked them under my desk.

"Well…" I said. "I did always want to do English but Ms. Gretching is kinda putting me off."

"I'm thinking of doing English too."

I was surprised. Yeah, Frank always got good grades but I didn't know he enjoyed it.

"Really? Not Sport Science?"

"Are you kidding? Do you have any idea how many girls do English?"

I elbowed him.

"Oww."

"You're really going to choose a university course based on its pulling potential?"

Frank rubbed his arm. "Not completely, but it's something worth considering. I don't want to spend three years surrounded entirely by men."

"So what female-friendly unis have you looked at so far?"

He ticked them off on his fingers. "Leeds, Edinburgh, Exeter, oh and Sheffield…"

I perked up in my seat. "Sheffield? I'm looking at there!"

"Really?"

"Uh-huh."

"Maybe we'll end up at the same uni."

"On the same course…"

"Maybe so."

We silently contemplated our futures.

"I don't think we would be friends though," I said.

Frank's face fell – for a second – or maybe I imagined it. "Why not?"

"Well, you would be in all the sports teams, wouldn't you? Rugby, football, cricket. Male chauvinism 101? You'd gallivant around the city en masse, boasting about having chlamydia and playing 'hilarious' drinking games with dares. I'd have to pretend I didn't know you."

Frank bristled. "Oh yeah? Well, you'd probably spend all your time watching obscure bands playing gross venues, hanging out in coffee chains arguing about communism, and organizing student protests. And I'd have to pretend I didn't know you either."

"See. I told you we wouldn't be friends at uni."

"Are we even friends now?"

"God, I hope not."

"Me too."

And we both laughed.

Frank began colouring in the squares of the newspaper crossword with a smeary biro. "What about your fella? What will Mr. Rock Star be doing while you further your mind?"

Noah.

Uni.

It was something that had briefly crossed my mind but I'd shoved it out of my brain violently and immediately. The thought was just too painful.

"We'll work something out." I couldn't meet Frank's eye.

His voice was sarcastic. "Yeah, because so many couples stay together when one of them starts uni."

His words stung like ice picks. Remembering what had

happened in Dr. Ashley's office, I tried not to let the panic rise up in my throat.

"Well, it's not for some time yet," I replied, breathing deeply.

"It's only a year away. Think how fast a year goes."

I swung to face him. "Seriously, Frank, quit it! What's wrong with you? You jealous? Is that it? Or do you just hate seeing people happy? Well, shut up. I don't care. And I don't want to talk about uni, okay?"

Frank's face went through a number of emotions pretty quickly. He opened his mouth but didn't say anything. His cheeks went red and he looked down at his paper.

An agonizingly long silence passed while I thought it through. Had this awkwardness with Frank begun when Noah and I began? *Was* he jealous?

I shook my head.

No. That was impossible.

The train pulled into the station. Passengers began to stand up, fellow students included, and started pulling their bags down from overhead.

"Is it over then?" I asked.

"Is what over?"

"Your male equivalent of PMS."

"Me? PMS? You're the one that yelled at me."

"Yeah, well, you were being a dickhead."

"Maybe I was."

"No apology."

He sashayed his hand out like I was the queen. "I'm very

sorry, Poppy Lawson," he said. "I'm sure you and Mr. Emo are soulmates and will be together for ever."

His words hit something in me and I got a sudden horrid feeling in my stomach that something was wrong.

"Does your silence mean my apology has been rejected?" Frank was giving me a quizzical look.

I shook my head. "Umm...no...it's fine. I forgive you."

"Poppy, are you okay?"

No. Something terrible is going to happen.

"I'm fine." I grabbed my bag and prepared to get off the train. "You coming?"

Frank stood up and stretched. His rugby shirt rose slightly, showing just the lowest part of his midriff. He caught me looking, and rather than joke about me perving, he just blushed and pulled his shirt down.

"Yeah," he sighed. "I'm coming."

"He fancies you," Noah announced, swinging his hand in mine as he walked.

"It's not like that. I'm not his type."

"Poppy." He steered me left. "You're most guys' type. Beautiful, smart, funny. What's not to like?"

I blushed. "You don't understand. We're just friends."

"For you, maybe."

"I don't agree."

"Well, I think he fancies you."

"Well, I don't think you're being very supportive of my problem."

"How can I be? You're basically telling me another guy fancies you."

"HE DOESN'T FANCY ME!"

A passing jogger looked at us in shock and Noah burst out laughing.

"Okay. Calm down, gorgeous."

"How can I be calm? You won't take my side AND you're making me go bowling."

Something peculiar had happened after the ballet and it was beginning to piss me off. When Noah and I did manage to see each other between rehearsals, he kept picking the unsexiest dates you could think of. They were always in the daytime. We were never alone. First there was the pancake house, then we went shopping, then for coffee, and now we were frickin' bowling.

"Seriously, Noah, no one bowls any more," I told him, as we walked up to Middletown's bowling alley.

"Then why are there bowling alleys?"

"To personally torture me with."

Noah stuck out his tongue. "It might be fun."

"Nothing involving shoes that ugly can be considered fun."

He grabbed my arm, pulled me inside and paid for two games.

We handed over our shoes to the grumpiest woman in the history of the world, who swapped my red ballet pumps for sweaty clown shoes.

"Isn't one game enough torture?" I hissed to him, slipping my foot in. "Eww! These are still warm."

Noah only laughed. "You look sexy in them."

"Shut up."

But, putting the ugly shoes to one side, I cheered up considerably the moment I bowled a strike on my first go.

"Woohoo!" I screeched, jumping up in the air in celebration. "Did you see that? I'm officially amazing."

Noah nodded in appreciation. "Lucky shot."

"Not lucky. Skilful."

After picking his ball, Noah stood for a while, practising his swing, before taking a run-up and releasing it down the aisle. It took an unpromising angle, before veering off and thumping into the gutter.

I was gleeful.

"You suck!" I covered my mouth with my hands to make a loudspeaker. "Gutter ball."

"I'm just lulling you into a false sense of security."

"Yeah, right."

He picked up another ball, practised again, swung and released. This time the ball careered down the aisle quite aggressively but deviated from course, knocking down only one measly pin.

"Hmmm," I said. "I believe you. Millions wouldn't."

This time Noah didn't smile. He only grimaced.

"I actually quite like bowling," I said, a smug grin on my face. I gave Noah a quick kiss on the lips and got a bowling ball. I lined up and rolled it down. It knocked over nine pins and I let out a little whoop. "I *really* like bowling. Isn't this fun?"

Noah grimaced harder.

One game later (I won, of course) and Noah and I were ready to abandon the traditional approach to bowling.

"I can't believe you got told off by the shoe lady for heckling me so badly."

I giggled. "I can't believe she threatened to chuck us out."

"You were getting quite abusive."

"I got excited by winning. I didn't mean to offend that random man. He must've thought I was heckling him as well."

"Well, do you think you can control yourself enough to play another game?"

We sat together, my head on his shoulder. The place was pretty grimy. There were unexplained stains all over the carpet, groups of tweenagers wearing belly-tops were either flirting or fighting with each other, and Justin Bieber had played on the overhead TV at least three times since we'd arrived. But, despite all that, it still felt like the most romantic place in the world. Whenever I was with Noah it was like someone had rubbed a massive dollop of Vaseline over my peripheral vision, creating this hazy, perfect world.

"I think I can contain myself," I said, thinking it through. "I've got an idea though, on how to revamp the game."

Noah stopped stroking my hair. "I'm excited."

"Did you ever read horoscopes when you were younger?"

"Funnily enough, no, I didn't. I'm a bloke, remember?"

"You don't even know what star sign you are?"

"Oh. I know that. Virgo."

I turned to face him, our noses touching. "Well, how do you feel about Cosmic Bowling?"

His gorgeous grin appeared. "Tell me more."

"Well, I'm obviously too easily excited to bowl the usual way and have to behave, otherwise Moodypants is going to kill us. But how about we switch the meaning behind our scores?"

"I'm not sure I follow."

"Well, we'll ask the bowling ball questions about our lives. Cosmic questions, like a Magic 8 Ball. And when we bowl, depending on what score we get, it will reveal our future."

Noah stood up. "I like it."

"You're up first."

"Okay."

He picked up his favourite blue ball. "What question should I ask it?"

"Whatever you want."

"Hmm. How about, is my band going to end up bigger than Ponyboys?"

"Good one."

He was about to bowl but I stopped him. "Wait!"

He turned around, his ball in mid-swing. "What is it?"

"You have to give conditions to the bowling ball first, so it knows which cosmic path to take you on."

Noah smiled again. "Of course."

"So," I continued, "if you bowl a strike, it means your band is going to destroy Ponyboys. Your first album will go multi-platinum, you'll win every NME award going and end up selling out Wembley stadium."

"I like the sound of that."

"Yeah. But if you only get a half-strike, you'll only do okay. You'll get a record deal and earn enough to be a musician for a living, yet you'll remain obscure and spend your life touring student unions."

Noah nodded. "That still sounds pretty good. What if I don't get any kind of strike?"

I shrugged.

"Well, besides being a terrible bowler, your band will never make it. You'll end up still trying to 'break in' in your thirties, playing gigs in bad venues with empty dance floors. You'll end up doing an office job so awful that you spend half your time crying in the toilet cubicles over how you're wasting your talent."

Noah spun the bowling ball in his hands. "I'm feeling the pressure now," he said. "I'm scared of Cosmic Bowling."

"Aww, you wimp. Just bowl."

Noah really concentrated on his swing this time. He flung his arm back, bent forward, and released the ball. It smashed its way down the aisle, obliterating the pins.

He jumped into the air. "Woohoo! Wembley, here I come!"

He picked me up, swung me round, and planted a dizzying kiss on my mouth.

"You happy?"

"Happy? I'm playing Wembley! The bowling ball said so!"

"Well done. I'm glad for you."

"Right. Now your turn."

We found out quite a lot about our future in the following half-hour. I was going to pass all my A levels, but still only end up at my second-choice university. Noah discovered he would end up obese (gutter ball). I was going to beat Ruth in our who-ends-up-with-the-better-life competition. And Cosmic Bowling also revealed I would have two children, a boy and a girl.

Noah took my hand and squeezed it tight. "Imagine how gorgeous our kids will be," he said.

And I almost passed out, delirious with the promise that thought held.

"Wow," I said. "Our lives are pretty much decided. I don't think there's going to be any surprises now."

Noah pointed to the scoreboard. "Well, it's even-stevens. And you're the last one to bowl, so make it a good one."

"Okay." I picked up a ball. "This last one's about us. If I get a strike, we run off into the sunset and live happily ever after like in a fairy tale."

"You'd better get a strike."

"Oh, I will, don't worry. But, in any case, if I get a half-strike we still end up together but it takes work. We both have a wobble in middle age but eventually we get through it with a lot of marriage counselling."

"Hmm. Not perfect. But I like that we get to stay together. What if you don't knock any pins down?"

I sighed and thought of my appointment with Dr. Ashley.

"Well, that means we don't make it. We end up just being each other's 'first loves', downgraded to conversation fodder at drunken dinner parties. We move on, meet other people, lead separate lives."

The words caught in my throat. Noah, too, looked deeply uncomfortable.

"Well then," he said, trying to make light of it. "You'd better get bowling and decide this future of ours."

I'd never cared about a competitive sport before in my whole life. But right then, I wanted a strike more than anything. I squinted at the set of pins and they seemed further away. I took a breath and lined the shot up in my head. I lifted the ball and ran towards the aisle…but just as I was about to let go, I slipped on something. I wobbled for a second, trying to regain my centre of gravity, but couldn't. I plummeted to the floor. The bowling ball flew out of my hand and backwards into the air, almost hitting the family playing next to us. I landed on my bottom with a massive "Oooph".

There was laughter. Most of it was coming from Noah, some from the near-miss family.

He stood behind me, applauding. "That. Was. Classic," he said, through hiccups of laughter. "If only you could've seen the look on your face! Though I dread to think what that means for our future together. I don't think we made a rule in Cosmic Bowling for hurtling the ball backwards."

I began to laugh too, yet stopped abruptly when I realized that grumpy bowling-shoe lady had stormed over.

Her face was red, her piggy eyes bulging.

"I thought I told you," she said, panting with rage, "not to cause any more disruption."

I looked down at my clown shoes and saw my shoelace had come undone. That was what must've caused my fall.

"It was only an accident," I said. "These aisles are slippery."

"I don't care. I want you both to leave."

I opened my mouth to protest but Noah, sensing trouble, steered me away.

"But it was an ACCIDENT," I said loudly as we swapped our shoes back.

"Shh. Come on. I'll buy us something to eat."

Grumpy lady followed us through the bowling alley, making sure we were leaving.

It was cold outside.

"Did that just happen?" I asked.

Noah put his arm around me. "Yes."

"Seriously? Did I just get chucked out of a...bowling alley?"

"You sure did."

And then we laughed. A lot. Until Noah pulled me further into him.

"I love you so much, Poppy Lawson," he said, kissing the top of my head. "You make me sublimely happy."

I wanted to smile, but also knew I needed to speak up.

"If I make you so happy, then how come you won't see me alone?"

Noah turned me to him. "What do you mean?"

"It's nothing."

"Poppy?"

I looked back down at my feet. "Well, it's just...I'm not stupid, you know. I've not been to your flat for ages. In fact, we've not been alone together since London, and it's like you've planned this huge itinerary of non-sexy activities for us. And I know why."

Noah scratched his ear and looked uncomfortable. "What do you mean 'I know why'?"

"Sex. You've been trying to avoid us being alone."

Noah sighed. "I just thought it would be easier if we kept away from anywhere private. Anywhere with a bed."

"So we've come to bowling alleys and pancake houses?"

Noah pointed at me. "Hey. You can't deny it's been fun."

"Yes. But still...Noah, I don't think it's fair that I don't get a say in all this."

"In all what?"

I gestured to the gap between us. "This. Us. Sex. I don't like the fact you're in charge of deciding when we're ready."

He shook his head. "I didn't mean it like that."

"It's my choice too, you know? I'm not some emotionally

deficient minor you're taking advantage of. I'm your girlfriend."

"I just don't want to rush you."

"You're not."

"But I'm scared I would if we were alone."

I smiled. "Do you not think when and when *not* to control our impulses should be a shared decision?"

And he smiled too. "I suppose you're right."

"If I can beat you that easily at bowling, I'm sure I can handle myself in the bedroom."

"You're right."

"How many times do I have to say it, Noah? I'm *always* right."

And then he squeezed me tight and we went to get some food.

Rain had just about perfected the art of concentrating and sleeping simultaneously. In fact, if there'd been an Olympic sport called concensleeping, he would have won the gold medal. He couldn't remember the last time he'd slept in the ordinary sense of the word. Sleep conjured images of bed, pyjamas, eight hours, alarm clocks. Whereas he hadn't seen his bed in weeks. Clothes and food were delivered to the lab, showers were in the high-tech toilet facilities and socializing was, of course, off the cards until the situation was dealt with. Not that he had any friends left anyway. Most of them had drifted away during his intense training. It turned out that people didn't have a lot of patience when it came to you frequently missing events but being unable to tell them why. The truth was, they wouldn't have been able to handle the truth. It destroyed everything. Everyone. He wished he didn't know the truth. They were encouraged to make friends and date within the company, like some kind of scientific ultra-restrictive dating agency. It made sense in some ways. Rain couldn't imagine finding a girlfriend and not being able to tell them. To hear them say they loved him and not be able to say it back. What was the point? It didn't mean anything.

He was barely computing what he saw on the monitor. His eyes had grown so used to it, he could pick up a reading almost subconsciously. It was almost an instinct now. Dr. Beaumont had said that would happen.

As if she could hear his thoughts, she appeared next to him.

"Rain?" she asked, her voice commanding his attention.

He jolted back to full consciousness and straightened his body in shock.

"Dr. Beaumont?"

He began tapping his keys to cover the fact he hadn't been concentrating properly.

But the keyboard was suddenly obscured by a large backpack. It landed in front of him with a thump, shaking off the last of his dreamlike state.

"Get packing."

"Packing?" Had he just been fired?

"There are clothes for you in your locker. You'll probably need at least enough to last you two weeks."

He turned to look at her. She looked a mess. Her hair, normally so immaculate, was all over the place, her glasses tangled up in it. And her face was blotchy, almost like she'd been crying…if she was the sort of person capable of crying.

"I don't understand—" he began, but she cut him off.

"We're going to England. The private plane leaves in half an hour."

Rain looked in confusion from the bag to her face and back to the bag again.

"England?"

"Yes."

"We're actually going?"

"Yes. Now. You need to pack. Fast."

He half-shook his head. "I still don't understand."

A flicker of impatience crossed her face. "What don't you understand, Rain?"

He jabbed towards the monitors with his thumb. "The readings, there've barely been any. It's been really calm."

"Rain, Rain, Rain, have I taught you nothing?" She ran her hands through her hair. "Have you been watching the data?"

"Yes. It's all been fine. That tolerance you keep going on about seems to be holding up."

She looked at his screen and sneered. "You've only been watching the data that comes from when they're together. You've not been reading their energy levels separately?"

He shook his head. "No. Why should I? It's only when they're together that we have to worry."

"You stupid idiot." She leaned over and pulled up the matches' separate data for the past twenty-four hours. Rain immediately saw the massive spike in their individual energy readings, almost at exactly the same time.

He gasped. "What does that mean?"

"It means they've just decided to sleep together."

His heart plummeted and dread crept through his body. "What? How? They're not even in the same place."

"They're soulmates, Rain. They don't have to be in the same room to make those sorts of decisions – they pick up on each other, remember?"

He stood up, urgency suddenly coursing through him. "We have to get to them."

Anita nodded frantically. "I know. Pack. Now!"

He grabbed his bag and dashed away from his desk, but just as he got to the door he stopped and turned round.

"Anita? It's an eight-hour flight. What if we don't reach them in time?"

Any colour left in her face drained out of it. She barely whispered her reply.

"Then I've made a huge mistake."

30

And so soon it was the day of the gig.

"You're going to sleep with him tonight, aren't you?" Lizzie said. She was hogging my dressing table while applying layer after layer of mascara.

"What? Don't be silly. Of course I'm not."

"You blatantly are." Ruth was in the process of hogging my hair straighteners and had spent the best part of an hour flicking her red hair outwards. "Otherwise you wouldn't have painted your toenails."

I looked down at my perfectly pedicured feet that I'd spent all morning polishing. "Can't a girl just want to have nice toenails?"

"You've never cared about your toenails much before," Amanda said. She was hogging my other mirror and applying lip gloss. "You barely even bother painting them in summer when you're wearing flip-flops."

The girls had come round mine to get ready and have a few drinks before the gig. I'd been looking forward to it. Usually getting ready with the girls was the best part of any night but not this time. No. They were interrogating me for all I was worth.

I took a sip of my rosé wine and sat on the bed.

"I really don't think my toenails have anything to do with whether or not I plan to sleep with my boyfriend."

"You may think that," said Lizzie, putting her mascara wand back in the tube and whipping out her eyeliner. "But subconsciously you're considering it. That's why you're so obsessed with your appearance today."

"I'm not obsessed with my appearance. I would just like to get ready in my own house without having all of you – " I gestured towards them – "hogging all my reflective surfaces and belongings."

Ruth turned off the straighteners and put them, still hot, smack down in the middle of my carpet. I winced but didn't say anything.

"Oh chill out, Lawson," she said. "We're going to make you look beautiful. Don't you worry."

I took another sip of wine. "Yeah. About that…" I examined my un-made-up face in the mirror over Amanda's head. "I think I'm fine to do my own hair and make-up."

"Don't be ridiculous," Lizzie said. "Trust us. You're going to look remarkable."

"Remarkable doesn't always mean good. Sometimes you remark on someone's appearance because they look AWFUL."

"Seriously, chill. You'll look gorgeous. Trust us. We were right about the dress, weren't we?"

I looked down at the beautiful green dress they'd convinced me to buy. It looked just as perfect as it had in the shop. In fact it looked so good I had to actively stop myself from checking out my reflection every two seconds.

Lizzie finished smearing kohl around her eyes and plonked everything back into her make-up bag.

"Voilà." She pouted at her reflection. "All done." She turned to me. "Right. Your turn."

Ruth spritzed her hair with about a gallon of hairspray. "I'm done too. I can help."

Oh dear God.

"Don't look so scared." Lizzie walked towards me with an evil glint in her eye, clutching her make-up bag like it was a dangerous weapon. "You're going to look amazing. Noah's going to think he's won the lottery."

I downed the rest of the rosé and closed my eyes.

"Go on then. Do your worst."

I was scared to open my eyes again. Especially after hearing my friends mutter things like "Oops", "Eww, not that colour" and "We should clean that up a bit". So when Lizzie announced I was all done, I kept them shut.

"Thanks, guys. It looks great."

"Poppy. You're not looking at what we've done. Open your bloody eyes."

I nervously opened one eye, then the other and slowly let myself look in the mirror.

I gasped.

The girl looking back didn't look like me at all. She'd been replaced by some stunning sophisticated woman. Yes, woman. They'd done something to my eyes, kind of smokey, with green eyeshadow that perfectly matched the dress. Cheekbones I didn't know existed had been sculpted using some kind of miracle-working blusher. My lips were a neutral colour, but a gloss had been added to them which tingled and gave me a bee-stung pout. And my usually drab hair was pinned back haphazardly, with a few stray ringlets framing my face.

"Do you like it?" Amanda asked, a make-up brush still in her hand. "Are the eyes too much?"

"I love them," I said, unable to tear my gaze away from my own reflection.

"I did the hair," Lizzie said. "Do you like your hair?"

"It's gorgeous," I admitted. "I don't know how you did it but you have magical powers. I've never worked out how to use a kirby grip properly."

"You're definitely going to sleep with him now." Ruth's eyes were gleaming. "When Noah sees you like this he's not going to be able to help himself."

"Wow, Ruth," I said. "Was that an actual compliment?"

She stuck her tongue out. "You know what? I hate to admit it but you're looking good, girl. I just wish I'd let Lizzie do my hair now. I wanted to see what state she made of yours first though."

"And that," I said, "is what you call karma."

I picked up the wine and divided the rest of it between our glasses. We'd only shared one bottle. None of us wanted to get wasted and ruin the evening.

"I propose a toast, girlies. To having a most excellent evening."

"I'll toast to that," Lizzie said.

"Me too," said Amanda.

Ruth put her glass in to chink. "And here's to Poppy finally getting it on."

I turned to her in mock anger. "I. Am. Not. Going. To. Sleep. With. Him. The toenails mean nothing."

Ruth took a sip of her drink.

"Yeah, yeah," she muttered. "Just wait until you see him onstage."

We caught the bus to the arena in a blaze of girly spirits. The wine had made us more giggly and annoying than ever, and OAPs innocently trying to get their groceries home were getting increasingly vexed by our bad behaviour.

It started harmlessly enough with Ruth singing a Ponyboys song. This got us excited and soon we were all joining in. Then, when we'd exhausted all of their playlist, we moved onto Queen, our personal favourite. The problem was, when you're slightly tipsy, you forget that other people aren't tipsy too and our demands to get the bus driver to sing the Galileo bits of "Bohemian Rhapsody" weren't met with a positive response. I don't think it was the wine behind our annoying young-people-these-days-have-no-respect behaviour so much as the nervous excitement. The anticipation of what the evening held pulsed through our blood. The memories lay out before us, waiting to be made, and then called upon in decades' time when we were old and boring.

When the relieved bus driver eventually dropped us off, the sun had set. Only a red streak from the day was left scorched across the sky, making the arena glow in an eerie light. Teenagers had already formed a queue of quivering underdressed bodies at the entrance. Girls stood with their arms pressed against their chests, tossing their hair back and laughing joyfully despite their lips turning blue and their bare tummies erupting in goose pimples. The boys were dressed in standard gig-going male attire – jeans and a band T-shirt. They were also pretending not to be cold, but they did this by puffing out their chests and distracting themselves by competing to see who could drink the most cans of bargain booze.

We stood looking at the crowd.

"There are a lot of people here already," Amanda said, her teeth chattering and her arms crossed over her black dress. "The doors don't even open for another hour."

Ruth shrugged. "Ponyboys are a big band. People want the best view."

Lizzie was jumping from one foot to another like a child needing a wee.

It was freezing. I could feel my skin pimple under the

thin silk of my dress. "I'm just glad we can get inside straight away."

Lizzie nodded. "Me too. Where do we need to go?"

I scanned the walls of the imposing arena. "I'm not sure. The stage door, I think. But I don't know where it is."

"Well, it won't be at the front, will it?" Ruth said. "Let's walk round the side. At least we'll stay warm-ish if we're walking."

We began walking round the massive building. It seemed like the entire country could have fitted snugly inside, with room for houses as well.

"I can't believe my boyfriend is playing a venue this big," I muttered, almost to myself.

"Mine too!" Ruth interjected. "Don't forget about Will."

Lizzie rolled her eyes. "How could we?" she whispered, and I giggled under my breath.

After clopping along for a while in our high heels, an area full of white vans and a gigantic tour bus came into view.

"I think this is it," Ruth said. "Wow. That must be the Ponyboys' tour bus."

"It's huge," said Amanda.

There was a bustle of activity around a pair of doors guarded by two morbidly-obese and scary-looking bouncers. They were wearing *Men In Black*-style suits and sunglasses, despite it being fully dark by now. They nodded as streams of stocky men carrying sound equipment trickled past them.

"I suppose they're the guys who have our passes," I said,

gulping. I hoped Noah had remembered to put them at the door.

We clattered over, our giddy spirits well and truly concealed, knowing that any bad behaviour would end the evening early. The bouncers turned their heads towards us.

"Groupies have to queue like everyone else," the bigger one said in a booming voice. "I don't care which member of the band you've arranged to sleep with later, go back to the front entrance."

Well, that pissed me off.

"We're not fans," I said curtly. "We're close friends of the band—"

The slightly-less-fat one interrupted. "That's what all fans say. Close friends, my arse. Round the front, girls. Come on."

I bristled inside. "You're not listening to me. We're not silly fans. We're here with the support band—"

The fat guy opened his mouth.

"—and before you interrupt me and insult us further, I suggest you actually check the list, where you'll find our names printed."

"Very well…" the thinner one said, looking angry. "What are your names?"

"Poppy Lawson, Elizabeth Heeley, Amanda Price and Ruth Cosmos."

The man shuffled in his suit and pulled out a battered piece of paper.

"If you girls aren't down here I'm not sure I can let you into the gig at all after that cheek."

"Our names are there," I said, crossing my fingers and praying like mad that Noah had remembered.

The bouncer's eyebrows furrowed as he reached the bottom of the list. "Ahh. Here you are."

I had such a strong desire to say "I told you so" but swallowed it down.

"Will you let us in now?" Ruth asked.

"Yeah." He reluctantly stood to one side. "Through here and to the left."

Once we were safely inside, our spirits recharged and we whooped with excitement.

"Bloody hell," Amanda said. "I really didn't think we were going to get in then."

"Where the hell did that assertiveness come from, Poppy?" Lizzie asked. "Normally you're too scared to send cold food back in restaurants, even if there's still ice on it."

I laughed. "I hate bouncers. They're just bullies on a power-trip. They bring out the warrior in me."

We wandered down the corridor, taking in the buzz around us. There were wires everywhere, miles and miles of them, and everyone we passed appeared to be carrying a clipboard. The corridor seemed to go on for ever. I had no sense of my bearings and hoped a left turn would materialize soon – my heels were killing me already.

Then, as if from nowhere, Noah and his band appeared.

He spotted us and smiled – a huge grin beamed directly at me.

"You made it!"

He looked AMAZING. My knees went weak just watching him walk towards me. He was wearing a ripped pair of dark jeans and a simple black T-shirt, but the shirt hugged every ripple of his chest and showcased the bulge of his arms. He was also wearing a necklace, a tribal-looking beaded thing I would normally mock, yet on Noah it looked casual and brilliant. He'd actually bothered to gel his hair into a slightly messy fifties-style sweep. I wanted to run my hands through it. I wanted to touch his face. My heart started thumping madly through the silk of my dress and it took all my self-control not to launch myself at him.

Then his arms were around me, giving me a hug, and I felt the wetness of him kissing my cheek and smelled his incredible scent.

"We almost didn't get in," I said, mid-hug. "The bouncers were horrible."

"They've been a nightmare," he said. "One called Brian's wife a groupie and made her queue outside. She rang him in a right rage, demanding to know if he really had groupies."

I pulled away from the hug. "Brian? As in Brian from Ponyboys? You've been chatting to him?"

Noah nodded. "Yeah. We've been hanging out all afternoon. They're really cool."

"Well, don't you have friends in all the right places?"

He laughed. "I suppose I do."

The others were all joking together behind us. Ruth had already given Will a massive public snog to "calm his nerves" and everyone was getting on well. Lizzie was telling them all about the bouncers and how fat they were and everyone laughed appreciatively.

It was much warmer inside and I shrugged off my coat.

"Is there anywhere I can put this?" I asked Noah. I held up my coat but he was just looking at me, transfixed. "What is it?"

"Poppy, you look incredible," he whispered.

I blushed and coyly turned from side to side. "It's my new dress. Do you like it?"

Noah was practically undressing me with his eyes. "Like it? Seriously. How am I supposed to concentrate with you in the audience looking like *that*?"

I smiled, revelling in the attention. Then I clicked my fingers in front of his eyes mockingly, like I was trying to break the hypnotic lust-spell.

"Coat," I said. "Where can I put it?"

Noah grabbed my arm and steered me away. "Here. I'll show you."

He led me through his dressing room and into a little cupboard where lots of coats, scarves and bags were hanging up.

"Here," he said. "You can collect it after the gig."

"Thanks." I pulled down a hanger and put my coat on it. When I turned round, I was greeted by Noah's mouth. He pushed me backwards into the coats and wrapped his arms around me.

"Noah? What are you doing?"

He replied between repeatedly kissing my neck. "Come on. You look so gorgeous."

"Don't you need to rehearse or something?"

"Shh."

And that was all the resistance I bothered with before I kissed him right back.

31

We emerged from the dressing room dishevelled and, embarrassingly, our friends cheered when we arrived back.

"You guys took a while," Will said. He had his arm around Ruth and his chest puffed out. I think he was enjoying playing the Rock God role for the evening.

"Yeah…umm…we got lost?" Noah said, laughing and putting his arm around me.

"Lost?"

"Yep."

"In each other's mouths?"

Noah laughed again. "Maybe… So, does everyone have the set list memorized?" he asked, clapping his hands together, pretending it was just business as usual.

"Yes, boss," the band echoed.

"And has everyone peed? I know it sounds weird, but you don't want to need an almighty slash mid-set."

"Jesus, Noah," said Ryan. "I think you can trust us to take care of our own urinary secretions."

"I'm just saying. Rock stars shouldn't pee themselves. It's just not cool."

"Well, I'll go before we go on, I promise."

"What about you, Jack? We all know you have trouble holding...after that road trip to Oxford."

Jack went a bit red while the boys high-fived each other.

"Shut up. We were in that traffic jam for hours!"

"Just go pee and I won't tell the girls what happened."

I hadn't realized it before – I'd been far too distracted with the beginner's guide to uncontrollable lust – but Noah was a ball of nervous energy. He was swinging my hand manically as well as tapping on his thigh. And he was also doing his own mini-tap dance on the hard corridor lino. If he wasn't so cute I would've taken the piss. Instead I squeezed his hand and whispered, "You nervous?"

"Am I that obvious?"

I swept back a piece of hair from his face.

"You're going to be great. You know that, right?"

"I just hope I don't freak out and screw it up for everybody. This is our big shot, Poppy."

His eyes were wide open, vulnerable, and I loved him more that second than I ever had. It rushed through my veins, making me feel warm and sick at the same time.

"That won't happen, I swear. But if you *do* start to freak a little, just find my face in the crowd. I'll be there, front row, fighting off your *fans* with a baseball bat..." He smiled. "And then, whatever's happening, you can be secure in the knowledge that someone loves you. Unconditionally. Even if you end up putting your guitar on backwards and crying." He smiled again. "And that's all that matters in life, in the long run."

Noah's eyes burned into mine and for a moment I thought he was going to ravage me again. Instead his eyes got a teeny bit watery and he stroked the soft skin on my cheek.

"I am so very lucky to have you."

"I know."

My words seemed to calm him and we joined in the banter around us. Ryan was boasting about all the girls in the crowd he could bring backstage for a "seeing-to". I think the excitement had gone to his head. This, of course, upset Lizzie, who went into one of her well-rehearsed rants about feminism. Jack had asked Amanda if he could practise his drumbeats on her back, so she was leaning forward a little awkwardly, trying to smile as he repeatedly hit her. And Will kept trying to get Ruth's attention, but she was too busy trying to spot more important people around us.

A flicker of recognition crossed her face and her eyes lit up. She put her hand up to shush us.

"Guys," she said. "It's the band."

Ponyboys were heading straight for us. Brian, the lead singer, was for some reason soaking wet, like he'd just come out of the shower. He was followed by the other three band members. I didn't know their names – it was always about Brian really. An angry-looking short blonde woman was scowling behind them. I guessed it was Brian's wife, still fuming about the groupie fiasco.

"Dudes and dudettes." Brian greeted us in a faux-American accent and high-fived Noah.

Brian from the Ponyboys. High-fiving my boyfriend, like it was a normal thing to happen.

"Alright, Brian?" Noah replied coolly. "You look a little damp. What happened, mate?"

Brian shook his long brown hair and we all flinched as we got sprayed with water.

"I went out for a cigarette, didn't I?" he said. "You know, to calm the nerves and all that? Anyway, out of nowhere there's this big clap of thunder and it starts PROPER pissing it down and I'm soaked through instantly. Weird shit, huh? It reminds me of that time in New Orleans when…"

And then he was off. I noticed, quite quickly, that Brian liked the sound of his own voice. He didn't seem to care that no one was listening. My friends were just staring at him, like they couldn't believe he was real. His bandmates were just waiting patiently for him to finish, rolling their eyes in a here-we-go-again way. Only Noah was politely nodding and agreeing in the right places.

When the story finally finished – the gist was that it rained in New Orleans and Brian got wet – he looked at his watch.

"Bloody hell, is that the time? You guys are going on soon."

"We should probably do a few last-minute checks," Noah said.

"Good luck, guys, not that you need it. I heard you in rehearsal and you're going to rock this joint." Brian high-fived Noah again. "Of course you won't be as amazing as us."

And he walked off in the opposite direction, muttering about getting dry. His band and wife dutifully followed him.

Our group were quiet for a moment.

"Wow," Lizzie said. "I can't believe I just sort of met Brian from Ponyboys."

"He's a nutcase, isn't he?" Ryan said. "We caught him randomly playing the violin earlier."

Noah clapped his hands again. "Okay, listen guys. It's time. I want you all to go to the loo. Especially you, Jack."

"Oh God, here we go. Bladder police out on patrol again."

"I'm serious. Then let's meet back here in five and get ready." He turned to us. "Ladies, you should probably head out front. The security guys will make sure you get a good view."

A bustle of activity followed, with everyone taking off in all directions. I was about to follow the girls towards the stage when my hand was grabbed back.

"Hey," Noah said, spinning me round into him.

I scratched the top of his chest where his bare skin was on show. "Hey, yourself."

"Aren't you going to wish me luck?"

I played with his necklace. "You don't need any luck, but break a leg anyway."

"Do I get a good-luck kiss?"

I brought my lips to his and they gently brushed. I delicately traced the tip of my tongue along the tip of his and then pulled away.

"Go on, Rock God," I said. "It's your time to shine."

He gave me another gorgeous smile. "I love you."

"I love you more. Now go out there and show everyone how brilliant you are."

And I turned and ran after the rest of the girls, not quite believing that my boyfriend was about to hold the stage at a massive arena gig.

True to Noah's word, the backstage workers let us in at the front row.

"Just slip in here," said a blonde lady holding a clipboard. "You get the best view from this side."

We thanked her and nudged our way into the crowd. Our arrival wasn't welcomed by the large number of girls who'd crushed their bare-skinned bodies into the front row. In fact, we got a lot of people yelling "queue jumpers". Luckily we had Ruth with us. She delighted in the negative attention and flung her middle finger at them with a massive beaming smile.

"Just imagine," she said. "These losers have been queuing in the rain for hours and we get to shimmy right to the front. God, I love sleeping with the band."

Lizzie grinned, obviously equally unbothered by our unwelcome reception. "And I haven't even had to sleep with anyone. I get all this just because my mates are sleeping with them."

"You could so get with Jack if you wanted," Ruth said. "He's pretty into you."

Lizzie made a face and I smiled inwardly, remembering her rant a few weeks ago about true love.

"When will the music start?" Amanda asked. She looked a tad squashed but was trying to style it out.

I looked at my phone. "Five minutes."

"This is so exciting."

"I know."

Considering it was only seven, the place was already pretty full. Usually people don't bother sitting through support bands and just rock up five minutes before the headliners start. The support acts are just a boring thing to get through, something to endure to ensure a good view. But, by the look of things, people were here for Growing Pains as well.

We were jostling for personal space with a few other girls, some of whom were intent on pulling a band member. One girl had an *I love Brian* T-shirt and was excitedly telling her friend about the "really romantic time" she'd had sex with him in some club toilets after a gig.

"It was so sweet," she said. "He made it really special. He lay his coat down on the toilet floor so it wasn't too cold on my back."

His poor wife.

Her friend, a tall girl with long brown hair, was eating up the details.

"Brian's nothing," she said, tossing her hair back over her bare shoulder. "Have you seen photos of the support band? That guitarist! I am so going to get myself backstage tonight."

Hang on? Was she talking about Noah?

"I've heard they're really good," toilet-sex girl said. "And I heard that guitarist is a total male slut. Screws anything that moves."

"As long as it's me, I don't care."

I felt worse.

"Psst." Lizzie nudged me in the side, dragging me from my rage and insecurity.

"What?"

"I don't wanna ruin your night but…" She pointed her finger down the front row. "…I thought you should know."

I followed the line of her finger. "Oh no."

"I'm sure she won't cause any trouble."

It was Portia. I'd forgotten all about her. But she obviously hadn't forgotten about Noah. She had secured a spot right in the middle and was eyeing the stage with that determined look in her eye. It didn't help that she looked fabulous. She was wearing a silver bodycon dress that sparkled in the lights. Her long blonde hair slid down her back like an elongated halo and her face was perfectly made-up.

I groaned. "I shouldn't have come."

"What? Why not?"

I gestured towards all the girls around me. They could sense the band were about to begin so the energy was building and the pushing had started. Previously timid-looking girls had suddenly morphed into aggressive monsters, elbowing people and accidently-deliberately stepping on toes to keep their places.

"This," I said, "is doing nothing to boost my self-esteem."

Lizzie put an arm around me. "Don't be silly. Noah's head-over-heels for you."

"But how can I compete with all these girls?"

"Because," Lizzie said, "you are Poppy Lawson and you are brilliant. Tonight is about enjoying ourselves! Poppy, we have backstage tickets to the biggest gig that's ever come to Middletown. Now swallow that anti-ego sweet you're sucking on and have some fun."

I was about to reply when all the lights went off and everyone started screaming.

My heart began to beat, fast. My mind flashed back to that very first gig – the very first time I'd seen Noah. It seemed like a million years ago.

I saw dark figures walk onto the stage and could sense, from the way my body was behaving, that one of them was him.

The screams got louder, the energy more frenzied. The pushing got worse but the barrier in front protected us.

I saw Noah pick up his guitar on the side of the stage nearest to us. He seemed so far away, even though it was only a few feet. I wondered what was going through his head right then and prayed he would be okay.

Ryan's voice boomed around the arena.

"Evening, ladies and gentlemen. We are…Growing Pains."

The lights came up and the band launched straight into one of their best songs. The heaving mass of the crowd went mental and started jumping up and down in a big thronging heap. My feet weren't touching the ground but I was smiling.

Noah had no reason to be nervous. His hands were gliding up and down the neck of his guitar in a blur. Every note was in perfect timing with the frantic drumming. Ryan's voice was the best it had ever sounded. They were good. And less than twenty seconds in, the crowd knew it. The band knew it too. Noah's posture improved and he looked out into the crowd for the first time – trusting his hands to continue playing so he could take in the spectacle. And his eyes found mine. Mine. My face out of the thousands. He shot me his very best smile. And my knees buckled as I realized I would never fancy anyone but him. Ever again.

Two songs in and the crowd were going wild. Drinks were being tossed through the air with abandon and I was glad we were at the side and not in the firing line. To my delight, I spotted Portia wailing after a nearly-full pint of beer flew through the air and drowned her perfect head in amber liquid. Oddly, a few pairs of knickers were sailing through the air at random intervals. Ryan, who you would never believe was shy in real life, was loving it. He was putting them on his head or flicking them back into the audience.

As the band went into some of their more ska-sounding songs, everyone began to dance madly until the entire standing section was like one big organism. The toilet-sex girls had their arms around me like we were best friends and were forcing me to pogo with them. But I was really only focused on one thing: Noah. I couldn't keep my eyes off him. Lust zinged through my blood; the longing in my body was like a thirst. And, although I would never admit it to Ruth, I was glad I'd painted my toenails. I'd never wanted anything as much as I wanted him right then. His arms around my body, his skin on my skin, his taste in my mouth. I was halfway to diving onto the stage and ripping off my dress.

Unfortunately, lots of other girls at the gig seemed to share the same sentiment.

"That guitarist is so FIT," one of the jumping girls screamed in my ear mid-bounce.

I just nodded, thinking our new friendship would be short-lived if I turned round and said arrogantly, "I know. And he's my boyfriend."

The girls were loving it too. Lizzie was getting her groove on, a sight that was always enjoyable, as she danced like a nutter. Amanda was bopping her head while simultaneously keeping a concerned eye out for flying beer cups. Ruth was leaning over the barrier and licking her lips whenever she caught Will's eye – although, for once, the power balance between them had reversed and Will scarcely gave her any attention. He was in love with the crowd. He basked in the adoration, glowing, like he was a plant photosynthesizing.

After four fast songs in a row, the band drew to a stop. The lights went dark and Ryan approached the microphone (he had left it for a while to go stage-diving).

"Hey, everyone," he said, and had to pause to let the whole place cheer. He shook his head, overwhelmed. "We're going to go all acoustic on your ass now. As you are fully aware, I am a very gifted singer…"

The crowd whooped and cheered.

"…But I'm going to give this one to our brilliant guitarist here." He pointed towards Noah and the crowd erupted again. "He wrote this one, so it's only fair he gets to sing it. Ladies and gentlemen, I give you Noah Roberts."

More screams as Noah approached the microphone and whispered in Ryan's ear. They high-fived.

"What's going on?" Lizzie asked. "I didn't know they did acoustic songs."

"Neither did I."

Noah pulled up a stool and sat with an acoustic guitar on his lap.

"Thank you," he said, waiting for the crowd to calm down. "Right, this is a new song I've written about a very special girl…"

Everything got hazy.

"…Her name's Poppy and she's here tonight."

I couldn't believe what was happening. Lizzie was squealing but I didn't hear her.

"…She's the best thing that ever happened to me, and I just want to let you all know how amazing she is."

And then he strummed his guitar, opened his mouth and began to sing.

It was beautiful. I know I'm incredibly biased – I mean

the song was written about me, for God's sake – but it really was beautiful. I'd never heard Noah sing before, but his voice was like chocolate melted in a warm cup of tea. The lyrics almost brought me to tears. Lizzie had to practically hold me up, I became so emotional. Noah stared at me throughout the whole song and it was like we were the only ones in the room – despite there being a sea of people waving iPhones around in appreciation. I couldn't help but think that things like this didn't happen to real people, especially girls like me. Sure, they happened in films and books and cheesy television shows, but when did this sort of thing ever actually happen in real life?

Yes, admittedly, the moment was briefly ruined by my new friends yelling "You lucky cow!" but other than that it was completely and utterly perfect. When the song finished, the crowd were quiet for a few seconds. Noah looked up self-consciously, like he'd only just realized where he was. Then the clapping started, and the cheers and whoops. His entire face lit up.

"I can't believe that just happened," Lizzie yelled into my ear. "You officially have the most perfect boyfriend of all time."

I could only smile as Ryan retrieved the microphone. The band launched into their final song, a massive beat-heavy tune that had everyone dancing again. I jumped up and down on a euphoric high, watching Noah, loving him and wanting him. And then the last chords rang out to signal the end of the set and the hard-core applause began.

The boys, with childlike expressions of utter happiness, took a bow. I screamed as hard as I could until my throat got sore and Lizzie produced an impressive two-fingered whistle. My hands were raw from clapping, sweat was dripping down my forehead, and when the lights came on it was like waking from a dream. Nondescript background music played as people either went to the bar, toilet, or kept their places for the headline act. The girls and I stayed where we were, jumping up and down, hugging and squealing into each other's ears with giddy excitement.

The rain hammered on the windscreen of the jeep. The wipers struggled to scrape off the fury of water beating down on them. It was dark and the air was filled with the electricity of the storm.

Rain looked out the window. He nervously tapped his hands on his knees, going through procedure over and over in his head, praying he wouldn't mess up. His jeep was first in a convoy of six, leading through the narrow country roads where twists and turns appeared suddenly from the blackness of the rain. He was glad he wasn't driving.

Anita sat next to him, computer on her lap, deep in concentration. Her forehead wrinkled as she deciphered the code trickling aggressively down the screen. Someone from the SWAT team sat on Rain's other side. He'd never met him before, an intimidatingly large officer, trussed up with his helmet, gun, baton and bulletproof vest. The other jeeps were full of more officers, also ready to attack. They were privately contracted in of course. They didn't know what the targets had done. All they'd needed to be told was that the targets were dangerous and needed to be neutralized. Preferably without killing either of them, of course, but then you never knew with these sorts of situations. Sometimes you didn't have a choice. Dangerous people were much more potent if they were unaware of their power. It was like putting a three-year-old in charge of a nuclear missile.

Whispering, so Mr. Butch wouldn't hear him, Rain asked, "This weather? Is it being caused by them?"

Anita's eye twitched but she didn't reply immediately. She shot a sideways glance at the officer and only responded when she saw he was staring aimlessly out of the window.

"I'm guessing so," she whispered back. "The readings certainly suggest so. I think tonight is definitely the night."

Rain shivered, vividly aware of his own mortality and how fragile his unimportant life was.

It could all end tonight, if anything went wrong.

"Have we left it too late?" he asked, voicing his fear. "Will we get there in time?"

"Let's hope so."

That was no comfort at all.

The jeep took a sharp left-hand turn and skidded on a giant puddle. Rain's body jerked and he bashed into Anita, squashing her against the jeep door.

"Sorry."

"It's okay."

"Anita?"

The road seemed to have straightened now, judging from the view afforded by the full-beam headlights piercing into the darkness of the storm.

"I'm a little scared."

He wasn't sure why he was admitting it, especially to her. But it was true. He was terrified and there was nobody else to tell. His family and few remaining friends were thousands of miles away, blissfully unaware of his peril and, if he were to fail, ultimately their peril as well. He needed reassurance.

Anita reached over and took his hand. To his surprise, she gently squeezed it.

"Don't worry. We'll get there in time. They have no idea what's coming to them."

32

A backstage worker beckoned to us and we leaned over the barrier to hear her better.

"The band said you can join them backstage and watch the Ponyboys from there if you'd like?"

"Of course we would," Lizzie said, her eyes almost bulging out of their sockets with excitement.

We slipped backstage, ignoring the evil looks from everyone.

Lizzie was holding my waist and Amanda grabbed hers and Ruth took Amanda's, so we ended up practically conga-lining. Not regulation cool-people behaviour, but we were too overexcited to care.

The band was in the corridor, looking a mixture of elated and utterly knackered. They were all doing that jumping on each other's backs thing that only boys do when they're excited, until Noah caught my eye and shoved Jack off him, beaming. I broke free from the conga line, ran and threw my arms around his neck, squealed and hugged him tight. I could feel his sweat smoosh into my body. He smelled heavenly.

"You were so, so good," I garbled into his ear. "That song for me. Oh my God, Noah. And did you see the crowd? I think there are about two thousand girls in love with you now."

Noah hugged me back. His hair flicked sweat onto my face but I didn't care.

"It went well, didn't it?" Noah was incapable of not grinning. "And you really liked the song? I've been working on it the past few weeks but I was worried you might think it was pathetic."

I planted a kiss on his lips.

"It was pathetic. Horribly so. And if it wasn't written about me I would've been making sarky comments. But it was about me, therefore it was the best moment of my life."

Another earth-shattering grin.

"The rest of the band were amazing as well." I turned to congratulate them. Ruth had pushed Will up against the wall and was attacking his mouth for all she was worth. And Lizzie had got Ryan and Jack involved in the conga. They were snaking up and down the corridor, singing "We rock, we rock, we rock". I laughed and turned back to Noah.

He stared back. His eyes were suddenly intense, like he was seeing right into my heart. I blushed, wondering if he could tell what I wanted to happen that night.

"Why have you gone red?" he asked, cupping my face gently.

I leaned my cheek into his hand. "Have I?"

"Yep. You've gone beetroot. It looks cute."

I flushed further.

"Now you're a beetroot with blusher on."

"Hey!"

"What's making you blush?"

I thought about saying the words – wondered if I could pull it off. Was I sexy enough to talk about sex without it being totally cringe? I wanted him so badly.

"It's just," I said, snaking my arms around Noah's neck, "…I really want tonight to be the night we…you know?"

Noah held me at arm's length and my already-flushed face got even hotter. But his face was plastered with a mischievous grin. His eyebrows were cocked, his eyes sparkling.

"Poppy? Are you sure?" He kissed my neck. The touch on my sensitive skin was enough to make me whimper.

"I've never been surer about anything," I sighed. "Ever."

And with that Noah's lips were on mine fiercely, his tongue plunging into my mouth, tasting me, me tasting him. His arms were grabbing at my dress with urgency and I was stroking his back furiously. The inside of my legs began to burn with a feeling I'd never felt before, like my inner thighs had their own patience threshold that had just been breached.

Then there was a cough.

"Jesus Christ, you two are worse than Ruth and Will. You're missing out on all the conga action."

Jolted back to reality, I turned to see everyone staring at us. Even Will and Ruth had sprung apart to watch the show.

"Sorry," I muttered.

Noah laughed and put his arm around me. "Yeah, sorry. Poppy was just thanking me for writing that song."

"That is all fair and well," said Lizzie. "But there is a victory conga going on here and we demand you join in."

I rolled my eyes then grabbed Noah's hand and took him to the back of the line. Lizzie began the conga again and we snaked up the corridor yelling "We rock, we rock, we rock".

I think it's fair to say we'd forgotten, if only for a moment, that we were at a cool rock concert. The power of the celebratory conga took over and Lizzie's demanding chants were infectious. Everyone was laughing. You could almost feel the relief dripping off the band as they basked in the afterglow.

Of course it all came to an abrupt juddering halt when we conga-lined straight into Brian and the other Ponyboys. They were dressed in varying degrees of cool. There were lots of skinny ties and hair gel going on.

Brian took in our makeshift line and asked the only obvious question.

"Er. Are you guys doing the conga?"

"It's a victory conga," Lizzie explained matter-of-factly. "We're celebrating how well the set went."

Brian spent a moment thinking, then he grinned. "Victory conga. I love it! We should do that too, guys."

The band didn't look quite so excited by the idea.

"By the way, you guys utterly rocked." Brian started individually high-fiving them. "That's the best support we've had in ages. I might have to talk to our manager about getting you along for the rest of the tour."

Noah looked at the others and gave them his half-smile, which I knew was really his I'm-so-excited-I-could-die-but-I-have-to-look-cool smile. "That would be excellent."

"Great. I'll talk to Howie after the show. Speaking of which…" Brian looked down the corridor. "…I suppose we'd better get out there. You guys watching from backstage?"

We nodded.

"Excellent." He swung his guitar over his head. "Let's get this over with."

And the band dodged our conga line and made their way onstage while the echo of applause slammed down the corridor.

We ran after them so we didn't miss any of the set, grabbing a spot at the side of the stage. Ponyboys didn't do onstage theatrics. They just walked out without saying hello and launched into their first song, a ska-type cover of "Walkin' On Broken Glass". It was their biggest hit and the crowd went insane. It was odd watching from backstage. You basically got an incredible band's-eye view. The audience seemed to go on to infinity. I could see why Noah was so keyed up. I was getting high on the energy emanating from the fans and I was tucked away.

Despite the amazing atmosphere, my mind was only on one thing. Noah.

He was standing behind me, his arms around my waist

and his chin resting on my shoulder. An innocent enough position, but it was still setting off fireworks in every inch of my skin. I longed for his hands to move lower, his grip to get tighter. I could feel his hot breath blow through my hair. It sent shudders ricocheting through me.

I tried to focus on the music. Everyone else seemed able to. Lizzie and Amanda were holding hands and bopping. Ryan and Jack were doing that weird boy head-nodding thing, and even Ruth and Will seemed able to listen intently. But to me, the songs were like background music on the radio. All I could concentrate on was Noah. It was almost killing me – raw lust, like nothing I'd ever experienced before.

I was sure he was just as caught up in the music as everyone else, and felt a little ashamed for being so distracted. Then, just when I'd given up hope, he pushed back my hair and gently whispered, "Fancy getting out of here?"

Just the sound of his voice sent another 10,000 electric bolts racing through me.

"What about the gig? Don't you want to stay? Need to stay?"

Noah shook his head. "The roadies are delivering our instruments back to the rehearsal studios tomorrow morning."

He stroked my neck delicately with his little finger. "And I definitely *want* to go. There are so many things I want to do right now, and…" He lowered his voice. "…Most of them involve us being alone."

He took my hand and pulled me away. My friends, lost in the live music, didn't notice either of us leaving.

The corridor was empty as we dashed towards the exit. We stopped briefly in the dressing room to pick up our coats. Giggling, we re-enacted what we'd got up to last time. In fact, my lips seemed incapable of being without Noah's company. We kept stopping for kissing breaks, half passionate, half giggly, before resuming our hasty exit. Just as we were about to leave, Noah pulled me in for one more kiss. He pushed me against the wall, all his body weight pinned against mine, and his hands explored my body while his tongue explored my mouth. When we came up for air, I saw the fat bouncer standing over us, glaring.

"Knew it," he said, his fat face shaking. "I knew you were a bloody fan."

All we could do was laugh as we pushed past him outside.

I'd forgotten it was supposed to be raining. And raining it was. A lot. Within five seconds of leaving the arena we were both drenched.

I held my coat above my head in a pathetic attempt to protect my dress.

"Why does this always happen to us?" I said to Noah, struggling to be heard over the howling wind.

"I'm not sure," he yelled back, raindrops dripping down his face. "But it's getting boring."

The wind was so strong it took a lot of physical effort to

walk to the taxi rank. Some of the crowd barriers had blown down and we trod over them carefully, stepping into unavoidable puddles and soaking our shoes. Nobody else was mad enough to leave halfway through the headline act so we were able to stumble into a taxi straight away.

Noah held out his hand to help me into the cab. I took it. More electricity. I sat as close to him as my seat belt would allow.

"This rain is ludicrous," the taxi driver grumbled, either deliberately ignoring or not noticing Noah's hand move up my leg. "I've not seen anything like this before. And we just had the snow..."

His words washed over me. In fact, I barely noticed the storm hammering at the car's windows. It was like I'd had a lust lobotomy. All that mattered was Noah's hand on my leg and how good it felt.

The journey seemed to take for ever and I ached to finally be alone with him. My mind was rewinding back to him onstage. Ruth had been right, it was the biggest aphrodisiac ever. Finally, the cab stopped and Noah chucked some money at the driver before practically dragging me out of the car. We ran through the rain into Noah's building, and straight into the lift.

The moment we were actually alone, the atmosphere skyrocketed.

There was no small talk. No nerves. In fact, the part of my brain that usually analysed everything appeared to be in total shutdown. Noah pushed me against the lift door and the kissing resumed. Before I knew it, my dress was hiked up around my waist. The bell kept ringing, signalling we'd arrived at his floor, but we stayed where we were, the doors opening and closing, not caring who might see us.

Then, without any warning, he backed away.

"Noah," I asked, panicked. "What's up?"

He leaned in to kiss me briefly and then straightened himself again.

"Not like this, Poppy."

"What are you on about?" My lips began to wobble. "Don't you want to any more?"

And then Noah laughed. "OF COURSE I want to." He leaned in for another kiss but I didn't respond.

"It's our first time, Poppy," he said, running his hands through his wet hair. "I know this isn't a very macho thing to say, but I want it to be special. Not some hormone-driven quickie." He stared me right in the eyes. "I want to make love to you, Poppy."

"I want to make love to you too. I don't understand—"

I was interrupted by the lift bell ringing again and the doors re-sliding open. Noah laughed again.

"Look, can we at least get into the flat? And give me the chance to make the place nice? To calm myself down, so I'm not humping you like a dog on heat?"

I relaxed, finally beginning to understand his reasoning. "Okay."

He looked concerned. "You understand?"

I nodded and he took my hand and led me to his front door.

"Yeah, I get it." I looked down at my sodden feet. "Plus, I've still got my shoes on."

"Exactly my point. Let's not rush this."

He unlocked the door and went in first. I followed after him and stared bemusedly as he darted around the flat, looking agitated.

"What are you doing?"

He looked a bit sheepish. "Just lighting some candles." He pulled out a lighter and began lighting some on his coffee table. I looked around – there were candles everywhere.

"You've set up candles, eh?" I said, smiling. "That was a bit presumptuous, wasn't it? How did you know I would sleep with you tonight?"

Another sheepish look. "I dunno…I didn't… It would've been nice anyway, even if we didn't…or don't. I just had a feeling… Why are you laughing?"

I took off my shoes and pointed my feet at him.

"What are you doing?"

"My toenails. I painted them this afternoon."

He looked confused.

"And…well…I don't normally bother. But I wanted to look my best tonight…I think I had a feeling too."

We looked at each other in wonder for a moment, and then Noah was by my side. This time, instead of a passionate kiss, he held me tight in a fierce embrace. And I suppose it felt nicer. Less frantic, less teenagery.

"Are you still sure you want to do this?" he whispered. "Because I'm willing to wait as long as you need."

I hugged him, letting his apple scent calm me.

"I am so sure."

Anita's computer started frantically beeping.

Reflex-quick, she began tapping violently on the keyboard and muttering maths equations under her breath.

Not wanting to disrupt her, Rain leaned over in the car and squinted at the screen. He tried to read the code but it was impossible from his angle. He left her to it.

The butch officer barely registered the computer's actions and continued to stare vacantly out of the window. His body was spilling over into Rain's seat and it was irritating him. He didn't like to be touched by strangers.

"Shit," Anita said. She'd never sworn before, not in front of him anyway.

"What's wrong?"

He wasn't sure if he wanted to know the answer. His heart was thudding against his ribcage, adrenalin was surging through his body and his breathing had sped up. He ignored these symptoms though. He'd been taught about them in training. It was fight-or-flight – the body's extraordinary ability to cope with fear. The brain's danger mechanism triggered an entire crack unit of biological devices to help ensure your safety. His body was pumping him with adrenalin to give him more strength to kick ass or run from danger. His breathing had sped up, widening his lung capacity so he could run for faster and longer. Even the fact he'd inexplicably started needing a piss was triggered by his brain's defence chemistry. If he emptied his bladder, he would be lighter and could run even faster. Rain would never be able to fully comprehend the powerful impact the brain had on the body. There was so much about it they still didn't know – especially about the potential of the brain and the body when they were combined. Anita always said they were just at the beginning. And, if they didn't all die tonight, maybe they could get a little bit closer to really understanding.

She didn't answer him at first. Her bottom lip was wobbling.

"What's wrong?" he asked again, trying to keep the fear out of his voice.

"We need to get there fast," she said. "I'm not sure we have enough time."

She swung the laptop round for Rain to see. He saw the green code charge down the screen and quickly did the maths.

"Oh dear," was all he could think of to say.

Anita leaned forward and spoke authoritatively to the driver. "You need to drive faster, and you need to drive faster now."

The driver shrugged his shoulders. "Lady. I understand that you're in a hurry but look out the window. I'm driving through a storm here. I'm going as fast as I safely can."

"If you don't hurry up we won't get there in time and you'll die anyway." Anita spoke calmly without any hint of emotion.

An ache of terror spread through Rain's chest. She was right. Could this be the end? All this, and they just didn't get there in time?

The driver laughed. "Ha ha. Very funny."

"I'm not joking. Now drive faster."

The driver looked around and the look on Rain's face was enough for him to change his attitude. He put his foot on the accelerator and the speedometer went over 90 mph.

Blackness sped past the window, raindrops exploding on the glass as Rain looked out. Then, through the darkness, he saw a simple white sign. It was lit up by two lamps and surrounded by a well-tended flower bed.

"Welcome to Middletown."

Rain gulped.

"We're here."

33

Noah's flat was quickly transformed. Flickering tea-light candles emitted a golden glow from every available surface.

I began to feel a little nervous.

Noah pulled me in close, wrapping his arms around my back and began to dance with me slowly, to no music.

"It's beautiful," I whispered, my feet in time with his.

"Not too much?"

"It's perfect."

I thought about it as we spun slowly. "Although for a supposedly heterosexual man, you have a hell of a lot of candles."

He laughed. "I like candles."

"Yeah. But what boy has about ten million?" I looked down at the glass coffee table. "Hang on... Are some of these scented?"

He spun me around. "Don't be silly."

I stretched my neck over his shoulder to see them better.

"They are scented," I said triumphantly. "Vanilla?"

Noah went a little red. "What's wrong with vanilla?"

"Nothing. It's great that you're so comfortable with your sexuality that you can…hey!"

Noah had jabbed me playfully in the ribs.

I jabbed him back, tickling him, and we dissolved onto the sofa in between shrieks of laughter. Noah, of course, was stronger than me, so successfully managed to pin my arms above my head and tickle me mercilessly. I yelped at him to stop, but when he did, I would just whisper "Vanilla" and would be subjected to another attack.

Then, just as my mouth was open, mid-laugh, Noah put his lips to mine and the mood changed instantly. I stretched up to meet his mouth properly and we shared a lingering, delicious kiss. I heard thunder erupt overhead but barely registered it. Noah pulled back and stared directly into my eyes. He looked beautiful. His eyes were so black, his cheeks flushed, his still-damp hair flicked across his forehead. There was a vulnerability there, an open expression only I got to see. Intimacy in its most simple form.

"I love you," he said. "I love you so much it doesn't seem physically possible."

I reached out and gently caressed his lips. "I love you too. Incredible amounts."

And then it was time to stop talking and we fell back onto the sofa.

I didn't hear the cars pull up outside.

*   *   *

The thunder shook the windows of the car. Shuddering, Rain felt primal fear coursing through his veins.

"We're too late," he whispered. "This is it."

Anita's face was pale but her determined, emotionless expression stayed the same.

"If it was too late we would both be dead already."

The jeep and its following convoy screeched down a residential road lined with manicured hedges.

"This is the one," Anita said, her voice full of urgency. "Pull up there on the right. Quickly!"

The jeep jolted to a halt outside a block of expensive-looking flats.

"Right. It's on the top floor. Get in there. Now. Go, go, go, go!"

The officers jumped out of the cars and ran at the door, their weapons already in their hands.

Rain took one look, possibly his last, at Anita.

"Here we go," she said, half-smiling.

They jumped out into the pouring rain and followed them.

Noah's mouth had moved past my neck to my chest. Our bodies were practically fused, bound together, by lips kissing flesh, lips kissing lips, flesh touching flesh. He expertly wound his hand around my back and undid my bra. He began kissing my collarbone. It felt incredible. I sighed and rolled my head back. Then, I felt a tremble and he stopped kissing me.

"What was that?"

There was another tremble, stronger this time. The walls of the apartment shook, the lights of the candles flickered.

"Is it an earthquake?"

The room was still again.

Noah shook his head. "Middletown's hardly near a fault line. I think it was just a big lorry driving past." His mouth returned to my neck and his hand ran up the inside of my thigh. "Now," he said. "Where were we?"

Just as they got to the stairwell, the ground began to shake. Not violently at first, but then a second shock rippled through the building. Many of the officers stumbled and fell on the stairs. Their eyes were wide with confusion and fear. They stayed on the floor, watching almost with admiration as the world began to jerk around them.

Anita, hugging the walls for support, screamed instructions. "Get up there. Get up there now. Get up, get up, GET UP!"

The tremor subsided and Rain tripped over his own feet as he ran behind the SWAT team.

"We're too late. We're too late. We're too late."

He said a quick prayer. For his family, for his friends, and for himself.

* * *

I tugged at Noah's T-shirt. It glided over his head and floated to the floor. His chest was perfect and I explored it with my mouth. His fingers were tracing the outline of my knickers. I almost couldn't bear the pleasure his touch was bringing. I let out a low groan and strained my body towards his hands. He continued kissing my neck as I felt him tug at my pants, pulling them down to above my knees. And then he was up, fiddling with his belt buckle, moulting his jeans. The moment had almost come. Just for a second, apprehension consumed me. Noah looked deep into my eyes and pushed me gently onto my back. I waited for it. The connection, the feeling of us fusing. Becoming what we were always supposed to become – one single entity. Two imperfect people combined to make a perfect match.

Then came a loud, terrifying battering on the door.

They reached the top of the stairs and pelted down the corridor. The officers thumped loudly at the door. Rain and Anita ran past them and joined the leading officer from their jeep at the threshold.

There wasn't an answer.

Anita reached out and knocked again. Her delicate hand produced a surprisingly efficient bang.

She shouted through the door. "It's the FBI. Open up or we'll have this door down."

Still no answer.

She stepped aside and gave the officers instructions. "Try not to kill them. But if they even try to stay touching each other, then neutralize them immediately."

The lead officer nodded to his men. Then, with a bash, the door was down and they all rushed inside.

"What the hell is that?"

We sprang apart, staring at the door like it was a rigged bomb.

"I have no idea," Noah said.

"Is it a joke?" I gasped, pulling up my dress straps to cover myself.

There was another loud banging. This time we sprang together, holding each other with fear.

A voice rang out. It was shrill and sent shivers of dread up my spine.

"The FBI?" Noah muttered. "It *must* be some kind of joke."

My heart was thudding madly as we both stared at the door.

And then there was no door. A mass of soldiers ran at us, guns at their sides. I started screaming and glued myself to Noah.

It's not real. It's not real. It's not real.

Things seemed to slow down. A burly man was heading straight for us and I realized he was trying to grab Noah away. I screamed harder, praying the neighbours would ring the police. I had to stay with Noah. I grabbed hold of his hand and refused to let go, still yelling. "You can't take him! You can't take him!"

Then I felt something pinch my stomach. I looked at my waist and a tiny staple was sticking out of it.

"No," I heard Noah yell, but it was like he was underwater. My head was cloudy and I wanted to sleep all of a sudden. Even with all this madness around me, I felt calm.

You're just dreaming, I told myself.

Noah's facial expressions, the fear in his eyes, his perfect mouth opened up into a wide O, looked like they were made of plasticine. He was being restrained by the strange men in his flat.

I smiled.

And then sleep came and I succumbed to the darkness.

At first Rain thought the place was on fire. There were flames everywhere and it was burning hot. Then he realized it was candles. They were everywhere, on every table. The room stank.

Wow. This is pretty romantic stuff for teenagers, *he thought.*

The couple, understandably, looked somewhere between shell-shocked and petrified. The girl wouldn't stop screaming. When the officers tried to tear them apart, she launched herself at her boyfriend and screamed harder.

"You can't take him! You can't take him!"

We can. We will. We have to.

Rain felt sorry for her.

She wouldn't calm down so they fired a pacifier at her. Within seconds, she was unconscious, her body flopped to one side.

Her boyfriend started screaming and attacking the officers, but he was far too scrawny to make any impact.

The soldiers shot a pacifier into him too and calm descended.

Anita entered and looked round, taking in the candles and two unconscious teenagers on the sofa.

"Well, isn't this romantic?" she said, before she burst out laughing.

They secured the area. Knocked on a few neighbours' doors, told them a lie about the young boy running a massive underground drugs operation. Bewildered, they nodded, taking it in, excited about telling their friends over cups of coffee the next day.

Rain extinguished the candles one by one. The room began to smell like the moment after a birthday cake's candles have been blown out, with all the wishes floating away in the smoke.

There was one left alight on the coffee table next to the girl. Rain bent down to blow it out but was distracted by her face. She looked peaceful at first glance – there was even a little smile on her face. But, as he leaned in nearer, he saw one tear glistening on her cheek. The initial relief he'd felt that his life was no longer in danger was replaced with another emotion, a nastier one.

Guilt.

He sat on the floor and really looked at her. She was a pretty little thing. Her green dress was crumpled and one of the thin straps had fallen off her shoulder. He gently pulled it back up for her and blew out the last candle.

He sensed Anita standing behind him.

"They make quite the pretty pair, don't they?" she said. "You wouldn't think two people so young could cause quite so much trouble."

Rain didn't answer. The boy's face was also peaceful. He should enjoy the unconsciousness while it lasted – there would only be pain from now on.

"We did good," Anita continued. "A bit too close to the bone, but I take responsibility for that. I was the one who let this thing run."

She kneeled down beside Rain and examined the girl's face herself. If she noticed the tear, she didn't mention it.

"An interesting couple of days are coming up. I can't wait to see what we can get out of them."

Rain felt a bit sick. He was suddenly unsure if he wanted to be involved in the next stage. On paper, it made scientific sense. In practice, wasn't it…well…wrong?

The lead officer came back into the room. The floorboards creaked under his weight. "We're all done," he said, with an air of self-satisfaction. "What do you want us to do with the targets?"

Anita stood up and nodded towards them. "Take them back to the centre. Make sure they're in separate cars."

The officer picked up the boy roughly, tossing him over his shoulder like a limp rag doll. Another bent down and, more *gently, picked up the girl. Her head fell back heavily and Rain saw the tear run backwards up her cheek and fall gracefully onto the wooden floor.*

"Let's get out of here," Anita said.

And they left.

34

The worst bit of a bad dream is that moment when you've woken up and think it's still real. And this nightmare was refusing to shift.

I was lying on an uncomfortable bed attached to the wall. I kept sighing, turning over and trying to wake myself up. I wanted to discover I was actually in my warm bed at home, snuggled under my purple duvet cover, Mum downstairs making brekkie, and a text waiting to be read on my phone from Noah, telling me he loved me.

But the dream wouldn't shatter. Whenever I opened my eyes to force myself awake, it wasn't my bedroom I saw. It was some kind of holding cell. There was a sink and toilet in the corner and a teeny tiny window casting a teeny tiny square of light on the wall. My waist stung. I lifted my unfamiliar top and found a scab forming. Where did I get that? Was there a staple? I vaguely remembered a staple. My head was thudding dully – similar to a red-wine-induced hangover. My mouth felt like the Sahara Desert had moved there. There was a beaker of water on the floor next to me but I didn't dare drink it.

I tried to remember how I'd got here and it hurt my head. There was the gig. And then running off with Noah in the rain. When did that happen? Earlier today? Days ago? I had no idea. I recalled his flat, the candles and the sofa.

Noah… Where was he?

And then I remembered – the door being knocked in, the men, them taking him. Screaming.

And nothing.

Panic bubbled its way through my intestines. Where had they taken Noah? I looked around my odd little room, trying to work out where I was, why I was here. No clues. I didn't even know how long I'd been unconscious. All I had was the physical throbbing in my stomach, signalling that something dreadful had happened.

I closed my eyes and prayed to every God I'd ever learned about in RE GCSE that sleep would come and take this away.

I woke again from whatever miserable unconsciousness my body had allowed me to fall back into. The square of light on the wall had gone, the only indication it was night. I lay on my back and tried not to let my brain free-fall into panic. I breathed in and out, resting my hands on my chest, and tried to work out what to do. Ten million thoughts rushed into my head. Where was I? What had happened? Was I in danger? Would I ever get out? Was I going to be killed?

Would I ever see my parents again? Friends again? Noah again?

Then that familiar feeling of suffocation smacked me. I tried to keep breathing but was only inhaling stale oxygen. I attempted a scream but only a gasp escaped, making me panic further. There was no one here to help, no friends, no doctors. I was going to suffocate to death in this strange room, alone. I inhaled again but still nothing. My throat burned and my vision blurred.

Fight it, I told myself, but my body had taken over. I began to choke. Fire coursed up my throat and I felt tears run down my cheeks, hot and wet.

I tried to scream, hoping someone, anyone, would hear. My body failed me and, once more, the blackness claimed me.

I came to when I felt a squeezing under my armpit, but my vision was too blurred to see anything.

There were voices I didn't recognize.

"Is she okay?"

"I'm not sure. She hit her head pretty hard when she fell off the bed."

"You were supposed to be watching her."

"She was asleep! I only went for a piss. I come back and she's having some kind of fit."

"You're not supposed to leave her. Dr. Beaumont said this could happen. She's in withdrawal."

My throat was burning again.

"Watch out, she's going to blow."

I tipped my head forward, heaved, and vomited onto the concrete floor. Someone was stroking my back but it wasn't Lizzie, and it definitely wasn't Noah. I began to cry. Tears slid down my face, joining the mess I'd made on the floor.

"Hey, kid. Are you okay?"

Too scared to reply, I just continued crying.

"I think she's done. Christ, it stinks."

"Go get something to clean it up. And get Rain while you're at it. He'll know what to do."

Rain? Was it raining?

I felt another tug and was lifted onto the bed. I curled up foetus-style, whimpering, with a foul taste in my mouth.

I could hear the breathing of the person who'd stayed. He didn't try to engage me in conversation yet he did sit on the end of my bed. I curled up further so our bodies weren't touching.

Footsteps.

I heard someone enter the room.

There was a voice. American. "Did she have a withdrawal fit?"

How did they know?

The person sitting on my bed answered. "Is that what it was?"

"You were told to look out for the signs. What was she doing beforehand?" The American voice sounded angry. I didn't know whether to be reassured by this. If he was concerned for my welfare then maybe they weren't going to kill me. But if not that, then why was I here?

"Nothing, I promise. She was asleep one minute, twitching about the next."

"You can go now. I'll deal with this."

The person got off my bed and left. I curled my legs further up under me.

"Poppy?"

The American knew my name. I ducked my head into my arms, trying to hide my face.

"Poppy? Are you okay?"

Of course I wasn't okay. I'd been kidnapped – probably by this random American. Why kidnap someone and then be nice to them? Was he trying to get me to have that Stockholm syndrome thingy?

I felt my bed creak and figured he must've sat on it too.

"Poppy. I know you're frightened. I just want you to know that we're not going to hurt you. You're safe here."

I muttered under my breath.

"What's that?"

I kept my eyes closed but spoke. "That's exactly what you *would* say if you were planning to hurt me. You're just trying to calm me down."

"That's not true."

I didn't believe him.

"Poppy? Do you mind opening your eyes? I'm here to help you."

I didn't want to. But then again, it was the only way to figure out what was going on.

Very slowly, I opened them and let my strange prison come into focus. On the end of my bed was a peculiar-looking person. He was wearing a lab coat over a sloppy pair of jeans and jumper. He had long hair and was wearing one of those wooden beaded necklaces that boys who pretend to surf wear. A bit like the one Noah was wearing. Noah…

"Hello, Poppy."

I death-glared him.

"I'm Rain."

"Where am I? Where are my parents? Do they know I'm here?"

He held out his hands. "Hang on, that's a lot of questions all at once. I bet more than anything you're wondering why you're here?"

I figured he wasn't a threat, yet, and struggled up into a seated position. "Are you going to tell me?"

He ran his hand through his hair and sighed. "Unfortunately no, I can't tell you. But Dr. Beaumont wants to speak to you and she'll explain everything."

"Are you going to kill me?" I thought I might as well ask. Find out sooner rather than later.

Rain looked shocked. "God no. Of course not. Did you honestly think…?"

He broke off. "Look. You're safe. And your boyfriend is here and he's safe as well."

Noah? He was here? My heart started to thud.

"Let me see him," I said, a quiver in my voice.

Another head shake. "I'm afraid that's not possible right now."

Noah was here! Here? I had to see him. What were they doing to him? The raw panic re-emerged. More bile rose in my throat.

"Let me see him!" I yelled. "I have to see him!"

The man looked flustered now. "I told you that isn't possible."

The panic turned into rage.

"YOU HAVE TO LET ME SEE HIM!"

My breath caught and my vision blurred again. Noah. I needed him. He would make this go away. I needed to hold him, to have him hold me. To stroke my hair and cup my face and tell me it was all a dream and soon we'd wake up in his light-drenched bedroom and laugh at my silly nightmare.

Although, it was becoming increasingly obvious this wasn't a nightmare.

"Noah!" I screamed.

"Shh, Poppy. Don't get yourself wound up."

"Noah! Noah? Noah. Noah. Noah."

My heart sped up to full-whack. I felt light-headed.

"Poppy?"

"Noah Noah Noah Noah Noah…"

And I fell once more into nothingness, welcoming it this time.

* * *

I woke up to whisperings.

"This is worse than I ever thought it would be." It was Rain again.

"What do you mean?"

"The connection. It's too strong. We should've intervened weeks ago."

A pregnant silence.

I kept my eyes closed and listened.

"Look at her, she's a mess. One attack after another. She won't stop screaming his name in her sleep. And he is just as bad." Rain was talking about Noah! I tried to control my instinctive reaction, desperate not to alert them to the fact I was awake. "He's completely retreated into himself, barely spoken, only to ask if she was safe and if he could see her. When he was told he couldn't, he curled up on the bed and hasn't moved since. They're both in a state, Anita! How can we expect them to live normal lives when—"

The other voice cut him off. I didn't know this voice. Female. I didn't like it.

"Why do you care?"

"I'm just worried about them."

"You need to stop worrying. Remember the threat your life was under yesterday? Have you forgotten already?"

Silence.

"No."

"Good. Now it's time to wake this star-crossed lover."

They meant me. I pretended I was still unconscious.

I could feel her standing over my bed.

"Right, Poppy, up you get. I know you're not really sleeping."

I kept my eyes closed.

"These theatrics aren't going to help. I need to talk to you. We can either do this the easy way, with you cooperating, or we can do it through force. It's up to you, honey."

Her voice sounded breezy, but I could detect the evil underneath.

Reluctantly I opened my eyes and surveyed my kidnapper.

She was unexpectedly pretty. Tall, thin, designer glasses. Her hair was scraped back laboriously into a tight bun. She wasn't smiling.

"That's better. Are you coming for a little chat?"

I just stared back, half frightened-rabbit, half stark-raving-angry.

"Good. Now, I'm afraid we're going to have to handcuff you."

She registered the shock on my face.

"Just for our own personal safety. It's merely procedure."

Their safety? They were scared I would hurt them? I was the one who'd been kidnapped, sedated and locked up.

I held out my hands, deciding I'd be difficult once I was out of this damned cell.

Rain took a pair of cuffs from his coat pocket and clasped them over my wrists. I stood up.

"Follow me then."

My legs felt weak. Partly from fear, partly because I hadn't used them for who knew how long? My cell opened out onto a small corridor. I looked round frantically for a hint of Noah but couldn't see him anywhere. The lady held up a pass at a security door, it beeped and slid open to reveal another long corridor. I followed them through.

The place was like an international space station. Whatever this operation was, it had money. And technology, judging from the eyeball-scanner that opened the doors. We didn't come across any other people, which was weird. Somehow it didn't seem like a natural lack of people, but rather an artificially enforced closure, like the building had been deliberately cleared for me.

We stopped walking when we reached a small white door.

"We're here," the lady said.

They led me inside, un-handcuffed me and gestured for me to sit. It was a small room. Nothing particularly fancy about it, just a table with three chairs. They sat opposite me. There was a plate of sandwiches on the table and a glass of what looked like banana milk. I examined the plate. Hungry as I was, could I trust it?

"You should eat," the lady said. "It's Marmite sandwiches and banana milk. Your favourite."

I had no idea how they knew this but it made me feel sick.

"And no, it's not poisoned," she said, guessing my thoughts. "As my colleague, Rain, told you earlier, we're not here to hurt you."

My stomach growled, like it could sense the food nearby. I tentatively picked up a sandwich and nibbled on the corner. I swallowed. Nothing happened. I took another small bite. And another. Then I took a sip of banana milk and waited. Still nothing. I took another sip.

Soon the plate was empty. The lady looked pleased.

"Good, good," she murmured.

I stared back at her.

"Why am I here?" I asked. The food had helped me regain my courage.

"Why don't we start with introductions?" she said. "Hi, Poppy. I'm Dr. Anita Beaumont, and this is my assistant, Mr. Rain Hamilton."

I ignored her. "Why am I here?"

She ignored me in return. "Now," she continued, "we've been aware of you for a very long time, although you might not have been aware of us—"

I raised my voice. "WHY AM I HERE?" I kicked my chair back as I stood up. "Do my parents know I'm here? Are they okay? Where's Noah? What have you done with him? What right do you have to imprison me here? You're not the police."

Anita narrowed her eyes. They looked like slits behind her thick lenses.

"Sit down, Poppy."

I didn't.

"Sit," she said more sharply. "And I'll answer your questions."

Like a petulant teenager bored in a Maths lesson, I rolled my eyes and sat back down on my chair reluctantly. "So?"

Anita put both hands on the table and leaned forward. She spoke quickly. "We're allowed to keep you here under terrorism laws. There's been lots of hoo-ha about these recently in your country, but legally I'm allowed to keep you here for twenty-eight days."

My head swam.

"Terrorism?" I shook my head. "There must be some mistake. I'm not a terrorist. Noah and I…honestly…there must have been a mix-up. I would NEVER hurt anyone. I'm not dangerous."

Anita eyed me over her glasses.

"To the contrary, Poppy, at this moment in time, you and your *boyfriend* – " she almost spat the word – "are considered the two most dangerous people on the planet."

I let the meaning of her words sink in, and then I laughed and shook my head. "You're joking."

"I most certainly am not."

I put my hands on the table. I didn't mean to bang them, but I did. "This is insane! I'm not dangerous. I couldn't even punch someone without hurting my hand."

"It's going to take a while for me to explain this to you."

I shook my head. "You need to explain this to me? Aren't I supposed to be the terrorist? Aren't you supposed to be interrogating information out of me? Where's your permission to keep me here anyway? I don't see any warrant for my arrest."

Anita calmly reached into her jacket pocket and took out a piece of paper. She unfolded it and pushed it across the table. It had an official crest on the top. I saw my name and Noah's. There were also the words *Strictly confidential, matter of national security.*

"What's this?"

"It's a warrant for your arrest. As you can see, it's been signed by the Minister of Defence as well as your Prime Minister."

Prime Minister? My head got fuzzy. I put the paper face down on the table.

"Poppy?"

"I want to go home."

"You may be able to. Don't worry about your parents, we've been in contact with them. They know you're safe and they're not worried. But I'm afraid you and I need to have a talk first."

I raised my head and looked at her. "About what?"

"About you and Noah."

At the mention of his name, fresh tears catapulted into my eyes. "I don't understand what's going on or what we've got to do with anything…" My voice choked. "We're not dangerous and we've not done anything wrong."

By now the tears were escaping rapidly. I let them fall, no longer caring. If they were able to keep me here for twenty-eight days then they would have to put up with my crying.

Anita turned to Rain. "Do you mind leaving us alone for a moment?" she asked.

I didn't want him to leave. He seemed nicer than her.

He didn't seem eager to go either but pushed back his chair and exited.

Anita and I were left. Just the two of us.

35

I looked at her and she looked at me.

I felt exhausted already.

She broke the silence.

"Miss Lawson. What I'm about to tell you is a secret, kept so fiercely private that probably less than a hundred people know about it on this entire planet."

"So why are you telling me then?"

"Because it's your right to know. I can promise you, you don't *want* to know it, just like I didn't want to know it. There's no going back. Your life, from now on, is going to be very difficult."

I wasn't sure I had the capability for being surprised any more.

"Well, go on then," I said, not sure how the situation could get any worse.

"Are you in love, Poppy Lawson?"

The question was so direct it actually did surprise me.

I glared at her. "I don't see how that's any of your business."

"Oh, believe me, it's my business. Well, are you or aren't you?"

I thought of Noah and it made trickles of warmth radiate through my body.

"Yes," I answered, head down.

Anita leaned back in her chair, almost casually.

"It's a strange scientific phenomenon, love," she said. "We're still, to this day, trying to get a grip on it. It does all sorts of unpredictable things to the body. Did you know, for example, that when you're in love you're less likely to feel pain?"

I shook my head.

"Intriguing study. They tested a load of loved-up students in America, couples in the first throes of romance, and found their pain thresholds were much higher. Just because they had the comfort of another person loving them – someone to text at bedtime."

I waited for her to continue.

"It makes you more creative as well. Did you know that?"

I shook my head again.

"It's true. The electricity produced in the brain while you're going through what popular culture calls 'The Honeymoon Period' is so strong it actually stimulates creative firings."

She took off her glasses and then, to my astonishment, rested her heeled feet up on the table.

"Of course love actually helps your overall health. You're less likely to get sick. And, my current favourite discovery?"

Her eyes were excited. "They've recently found that love actually has a drug-like effect on the body. Isn't that incredible? Scans show the receptors that light up in the brain when a person is in love are EXACTLY the same receptors that light up when a drug addict jacks up, or snorts a line. This is why humans are so, well, crazy when they fall in love. It's this feeling that produces cheesy love songs, drippy poetry, what causes people to have affairs. That's because someone in the giddy first throes of love is effectively a drug addict. It explains the dopamine-rollercoasters, the irrational insecurity, anxiety and jealousy. The physical withdrawal pangs you get when you can't see your boyfriend for a week."

Despite my anger, fear and upset, I was actually finding this all quite interesting. I leaned forward to hear better, comparing what she said to how I felt about Noah. It seemed to fit.

Anita let out a long sigh. "Of course," she said, "it's all fantasy."

I raised an eyebrow.

"Oh come on, hon, you're a teenager. Aren't you supposed to be a cynic at your age? This initial rush of love isn't anything romantic, it's just biology. The purpose of our species, Miss Lawson, is to reproduce. That's it really. We like to think there's more to it than that. We write fancy literature, build tall buildings and philosophize about the afterlife, all in a desperate attempt to try and leave a piece of ourselves behind. We pretend we're not only here to produce offspring, die and then leave them to it. But that's the meaning of life. Reproduce and die. Depressing, isn't it? No wonder we've constructed this fantasy of love to cover the disappointment."

She put her feet down and leaned over the table conspiratorially. "Do you want to know a secret?"

I figured she was going to tell me anyway but nodded. She was obviously enjoying the dramatic build-up.

"Love is just hormones," she whispered.

"Hormones?"

"Yep. Millions of hormones. Our silly species pretend it's much more than that. That we get to 'pick' who we love, that things are 'destined' and that someone out there is The One. It's ludicrous. Love exists to facilitate the mating process. When one person is drawn to someone of the opposite sex, they are drawn there on one basis only – will sleeping with this person provide me with healthy offspring?"

I stretched my arms out. "I did GCSE Biology," I said. "I know what you're trying to explain. You're talking about pheromones, right? The scent we're supposed to unknowingly secrete that attracts people to us?"

Anita twitched. "Yes. You're right. I'm impressed." She smiled slightly. "Our pheromones are like our own personal brand of perfume. But instead of smelling like vanilla, or roses or Mariah Carey's new commercialized whiff, it's more like a scratch 'n' sniff story of your genetic code. Subconsciously, members of the opposite sex smell you and can tell if your genetics are compatible."

I thought back to all my pre-Noah rants about romance. "I knew all this already."

She ignored me. "But, what I find interesting is humans' refusal to accept it's all as clinical as that. They want to believe in love, they *have* to. When really they're just imagining a deep and meaningful connection to make them feel better. Pathetic really."

I was becoming increasingly aware that I really didn't like this woman. She may have had science on her side, but her views on love and relationships were just…backward.

"Wow," I said. "Someone's obviously single…"

Dr. Beaumont didn't appreciate that comment.

"Oh yes, that's right," she said, shuffling through her papers. "I read that you have attitude. Love to be sarcastic, don't you?" She pulled out a sheet of official-looking A4 with a flourish.

"Here we go." She began reading the page. "Poppy Lawson is an intriguing patient and very strong-minded. She's the only one I've had who actively seeks argument in the therapy room. She has that usual adolescent habit of always thinking she's right and usually dismisses information that suggests otherwise."

I looked at her in shock. "What the hell is that?"

She put the paper down.

"That is a report written for us by your psychiatrist, Dr. Ashley. He's been keeping an eye on you under our instruction."

"You got my therapist to spy on me?"

Anita smiled. "He didn't have much choice. Kept droning on about patient confidentiality but we're not a force to be argued with. Anyway, he provided an interesting insight into your relationship with Noah."

Noah.

His name triggered so many emotions it was hard to keep them under control. I thought back to my previous sessions with Dr. Ashley and it began to make sense. There was that weird one where he'd asked me about Noah and I'd lost my temper. In fact, he'd seemed determined to bring up my boyfriend even when I wasn't mentioning him. The realization fell down around me like giant jigsaw pieces I hadn't yet finished assembling.

Dr. Anita was looking at me, a smug smile on her face. "You've gone quiet."

I gave her my best-ever evil. "Let's just get on with this, shall we?" I said. "You were at the bit where everyone in a relationship is a deluded idiot."

Her smile strained.

"Well, the real point I was making was that for ninety-nine per cent of humans, the reality is they find someone they're genetically compatible with, convince themselves they're 'in love', release some hormones and stay together through shared experiences and bonding attachment. Then they die and their kids continue the chain."

"You should be a romance writer," I said dryly. "I can imagine that version of *Romeo and Juliet* flying off the bookshelves and getting on the *New York Times* bestseller list."

Anita winced slightly. She turned to another page in her file and scanned it. "This brings us onto you and Noah."

I sat up.

She took her glasses off, relaxing almost.

"Tell me, Poppy. Do you believe in soulmates?"

"I'm quite sure *you* don't."

Anita smoothed an invisible strand of hair away from her face.

"Actually," she said. "This is the part where it gets *really* interesting." I couldn't help it. The way she'd whispered the last sentence made me lean across the table.

"As I was saying, real life and real love isn't romantic."

The overhead light flickered.

"Whereas the idea of a soulmate is very romantic. People love it. The idea there's one person out there just for you, your perfect fit, your other half. The thought is so intoxicating humans ignore the fact that, if we were to have a soulmate, we'd probably never meet them. I mean, what are the chances that your soulmate is, conveniently enough, Tony from work, or that girl from the pub?"

I nodded. I could see her point.

She put her glasses back on and lowered her voice.

"The thing is," she said softly, leaning in close, "what people don't know, is that every so often, yes, two people are born on this planet who are essentially the perfect match for each other."

I shivered. "Perfect match how?"

"This takes into consideration a lot of things. But, mostly, genetically they are opposites in a way that makes their attraction astounding. Scientifically they are the perfect couple. There are a few select people born with a missing puzzle piece, shall we say? And when these particular pairings meet, it feels as though they're complete."

I noticed the way her eyes appeared to sparkle as she got into her stride.

"Of course, odds are still against them. The likelihood of ever meeting your perfect match is slim to nil. Usually it's a rich kid from New York paired with a poor farmer in the Philippines. When are they ever going to meet each other? Statistically it's practically impossible for any of these unique pairs to meet. It's a big world. They just pass through life, falling in love hormonally like the rest of us. They may even get married and have children. Although lots with a perfect match choose a life of solitude. Not consciously, but merely because they feel something is missing."

I thought about the file she had on the desk. I thought about her having Dr. Ashley spy on me. Then I thought about how I felt when I met Noah.

I shivered again.

"You've obviously had people spying on me and Noah," I said. Anita nodded. "Am I allowed to ask why?"

She straightened herself in her seat.

"Because, quite simply, if these couples meet each other, it's potentially catastrophic."

"I beg your pardon?"

"It's more dangerous than your small head can even imagine."

I remembered what she'd said earlier. About how Noah and I were the two most dangerous people on the planet.

My voice was tiny when I spoke.

"And Noah and I are...?"

Anita gave me a hideous smile.

"That's right. You and Noah are a match – destined to be a match. I suppose if you were going to be romantic about it, you'd call yourself soulmates."

36

"Soulmates?"

"That's right."

"Me and Noah?"

"Indeed."

The enormity of what she was saying wouldn't register. One side of my brain, the practical, cynical Poppy side, was sneering and saying *Yeah, right*, while the other part, the new romantic Poppy, born and nurtured since meeting Noah, wasn't the faintest bit surprised.

I wanted more answers.

"Why are we dangerous?"

"It involves some complicated science. Some of which we are still researching."

"I'm sure I can keep up."

Dr. Beaumont leaned further over the table. "I warned you earlier," she whispered. "You'll wish I hadn't told you."

I thought of the horrid prison cell I'd slept in, and said: "I don't think you can tell me anything that would make things worse."

She smiled. "Okay." She was pacing back and forth now. "I've already told you about the powerful effect ordinary love has on people – couples who are only together because of basic hormones."

I nodded.

"Well, when we've studied these 'normal' couples compared to 'soulmate' couples, we've found a major difference."

She turned on her heel and looked at me. "Do you know what happens to the body when people fall in love?"

I shook my head. "Nice things?" I said sarcastically.

Anita raised an eyebrow. "Very clever. Love is actually a very chemical process. When you fall for someone, it's like dropping a chemical warhead into your body. And there's not much you can do to control it. Dopamine – our 'happy' hormone – floods the body, as I said earlier, giving you the same high as taking drugs. Then there's norepinephrine." She ticked it off on her fingers. "More commonly known as adrenalin. That's the hormone that explains all the sweating palms and racing heartbeat. Then serotonin gets chucked into the mix – that's another happiness hormone – responsible for making lovesick people act crazy."

"That sounds like quite a cocktail."

"You have no idea." Anita opened her mouth to say more, but stopped herself and shut it again. She pulled out her chair and sat down, staring me straight in the eyes.

"Do you know how much electricity and magnetism a human being produces?"

I shrugged. "A lot?"

She smiled at my answer. "Not very scientific but yes, a lot. More than people realize. In fact, it's electricity that powers the heart and keeps it pumping blood round the body. People don't really know that. We have our very own generators, right here." She briefly touched the top of her left breast.

"…Then, as well as that, we have haemoglobin in our blood cells. It's made of iron and has a strong magnetic force. It's what they use to do MRI scans."

I rolled my eyes. "This is all very interesting but you're still not telling me how this makes Noah and me different. What is it that makes us soulmates?"

She went quiet for a moment. "Well, from what we can gather, 'normal' couples aren't too affected by this chemical cocktail. But with 'soulmate' couples it's very, very different."

"Different how?"

"This is the thing. In a normal pairing, the love hormones don't alter the electrical and magnetic make-up of a body. Yes, you get a bit flustered, anxious and sweaty, but that's it. But the difference with you and Noah is that these love chemicals somehow tap into the electricity and magnetism in your body. As the hormones surge through you, they seem to trigger some kind of reaction… The 'love' you share starts creating a strong electrical and magnetic current."

I was lost. "Huh?"

"That's what we've found from studying other couples

like you. What makes it even more interesting is that these currents are created before you even meet each other and fall in love. Love chemicals blast out of your brain and into your body if you're within two miles of one another. We're still at the beginning of our understanding but it appears the energy released acts like a homing missile, enabling you to seek one another out, like two magnets jumping together from a distance. The electrical and magnetic impulses are so strong they're almost an unstoppable force. It can be very destructive though—"

I broke her off. "Destructive how?"

She stretched out her arms and gave a little yawn, then took a small sip from her glass of water.

"Tell me, Poppy," she said, her voice different, softer, less authoritative, "when did you start getting panic attacks?"

I thought back to that awful day at school in Geography. "Two years ago."

Anita nodded. "Interesting. And tell me, Noah's depression? Do you know when that started?"

My memory fluttered back through time like a flick-book, stopping on the page where Noah had opened his heart to me in his flat; when we'd first started loving each other, trusting each other. It already felt like a lifetime ago.

"I think he said it began when he moved to Middletown."

Another nod. "And how long ago was that?"

"About two years ago…" My mouth dropped open as a million pennies dropped. "Hang on, are you saying our problems are related?"

And for the first time since our meeting, Dr. Beaumont actually looked a little bit sorry for me. "Bingo."

"But how? I don't understand…"

"You got close enough to pick up on each other and the electrical currents sent everything haywire. Having Noah so close to you was like being strapped into an electric chair and turning the switch to full-whack."

My memory flick-book whirred onto another page and I remembered the night of that first gig. That terrible, terrible panic attack. Another whir, and I thought back to all those first meetings. The way my heart would pound like that of a baby bird about to be snatched and eaten, the way my breathing became staccato like an experimental piece of orchestral music.

Noah was causing all that?

"Is that why, when I first met Noah, I had a massive panic attack?"

Anita didn't seem surprised by this revelation. "Yes. And it explains Mr. Roberts's sudden problems when he moved to Middletown and near you. Bodies react in different ways to the currents. For you, the impact was on your body's normal mechanisms, like breathing and heartbeat, whereas Noah's reaction disrupted his brain's electrical firing patterns."

I didn't speak for a while. I was glad to have answers, but at the same time, there were so many more questions. I'd have to remember to tell my poor mother that none of my mental health issues were her fault. She'd be delighted. That was, if I ever got to see her again.

"Go on then," I said. "I'm ready for it. Why are we dangerous? Surely this electricity is only a nuisance to us? I can live with the odd panic attack if it means I get to stay with Noah."

The doctor's eyes went dark and she began to talk in her scary voice again. Whatever sympathy I'd been receiving was finished.

"That simply isn't the case, Poppy. When two people match, these forces don't just affect the couple. Their individual electric currents begin to feed and build off each other, they get supercharged and create their own force field. The brain and the body are very powerful things. And if the simple act of two normal people thinking they're in love can stir creativity and prevent pain, just imagine what can happen with a soulmate couple, whose brains and bodies are programmed to connect perfectly. It's the energy equivalent of a power plant."

I took a sip of my water and noticed my hands were shaking.

"Ultimately this electricity is too much. Your bodies create all this energy but there isn't an outlet for it – so it escapes into the surrounding area. You're probably thinking, how much damage can this sort of thing do? And you'll be surprised. Our planet's existence depends on a perfect yet delicate balance. There's equilibrium everywhere – the North and South Pole, the ever-shifting predictability of the oceanic tides – laws and motions that need to remain ultimately stable. But you and Noah produce an astronomical amount of energy, which upsets this balance. It can cause electrical surges, short circuits; it can upset patterns in the weather and even has an impact on the shifting of tectonic plates."

I couldn't help it, I burst out laughing. "Yeah, right," I said. "Noah and I are hardly causing volcanoes to erupt. We're not Marvel Comics characters."

The laughter didn't go down well. Anita gave me a death glare. "At least twenty people have been killed since you met Noah," she said.

That made me lose my temper. "That's a horrific thing to say. We've not done anything to hurt anyone!"

Her voice was sarcastic now. "Oh, haven't you?" She picked up another file and flicked through it. "Now, let's see…oh yes. You caused a power outage across an entire town not too long ago, although no one was killed that time. And then there was the flooding. Didn't that ruin at least a dozen local businesses? Of course, there was the snowstorm you caused. That created a massive pile-up on the motorway, resulting in many deaths." She turned to another page. "And, I'm not sure if you're aware but your actions last night caused a minor earthquake. Had we not, let's say, interrupted proceedings, we wouldn't be here to have this pleasant chat."

I couldn't stand this disgusting woman sitting in front of me. "How dare you? We had nothing to do with any of that. It's just coincidence. How dare you try and blame those deaths on us?"

"If anyone is to blame, it is I," Anita said, and I was surprised by her sudden change of tone. "You weren't to know what you were doing and we didn't get to you quick enough. But I've not finished explaining, Poppy. What you need to know is that certain...activities – okay, I'll be blunt here – sexual activities, lead to a massive secretion of arousal hormones which jump-start the currents. Yours and Noah's sexual arousal is like chucking ten gallons of lighter fluid on a massive bonfire."

I blushed.

Anita noticed and smiled grimly. "Look back on it, Poppy. When all these things happened, what was going on with you and Noah? Had you kissed? Were you acting on your impulses? You can hardly be blamed. As I said, the sexual attraction between a match like yours is almost unimaginable. And when a matched couple has sex, the energy released is huge and disasters happen."

My tears were hot and I was angry. Noah and I had been about to have sex. If I were to believe her, this odd stranger, if we'd gone through with it, what would've happened?

Disaster? I shuddered.

She was still talking, more soberly now.

"My job, why I'm here...is to find these couples and separate them before they can have sex. Otherwise, quite simply, people will die. And I've not always got there quite quickly enough, Poppy. The last time I failed was two years ago."

She looked down at the table and I caught a glimpse of

the human behind the hard official exterior. A moment of guilt, expressed with anger.

"A typhoon. So many lost. Although if I'd got there two minutes later, we would all be dead."

I shook my head violently. "No no no no no."

"Yes, Poppy. It's true."

"It's not true. It's just coincidence. Accidents happen, bad things happen. That's life. You're lying."

"I can assure you I'm not lying. Why else do you think you are here, Poppy? Why do you think there's a signed authorization from your Prime Minister stating I can hold you in custody for twenty-eight days? You and Noah are dangerous together. It's a scientific fact."

I started to cry. Terrified at where this was leading. "We never meant to hurt anyone," I sobbed.

"I know you didn't, but the fact is, if you stay together, you will," she replied quietly.

The word "if" cut through me like the pain of jumping into ice-cold water. *If* we stayed together. If. Before today I'd assumed Noah would be a part of my life until the day I died. Now it might not be allowed.

"Why doesn't anyone know this?" I asked through guttural sobs. "Why is it all such a secret? It's not fair. People should know!"

Anita lost her temper again. "Are you completely stupid? How do you think the world would react to that information? That there are couples born every year who have the potential, if they meet, to wreak havoc on the world if they have sex? There would be widespread panic. And what about confirming the existence of soulmates? That they're real? It would destroy society as we know it. Families would break down, relationships would fall apart. Everyone would want to know if they had a match, and try to find it! It could cause utter devastation."

She shook her head, trying to shift the apocalyptic images from her head.

"No, it's best this way. The world needs our protection. In the way that we provide it."

"And how long have you known about all this? I mean, whoever you work for? Whatever it is you call it? How long have you known? Years? Centuries?"

"It's been about fifty years since the company was properly established, since we could prove what we knew and the impact it had. But throughout history there's evidence suggesting that people were guessing at the devastation caused by true love. Maybe they weren't aware of the science, but many great thinkers and literary geniuses advanced this notion that true love always self-destructs.

"Think about *Romeo and Juliet*, for example – two star-crossed lovers whose addiction to each other destroys everything. Shakespeare's story of doomed love is responsible for practically every popular love story ever told afterwards – because it makes sense. Think of Cleopatra and her love for Anthony. Their magnetic attraction sparked wars that killed thousands. Or there's Emily Brontë, with her story of Heathcliff and Cathy, driven literally mad by their love for each other. It's not just in literature though. We have renowned historians, geologists and scientists doing top-secret research for us. They're managing to link major natural disasters throughout history to the electrical and magnetic patterns typical of such a match. It's astonishing really."

Again, my head wrestled to digest the enormity of what she was saying. It all seemed so far-fetched on the one hand, but when I looked back on my time with Noah, coincidence didn't cover everything. The way the town had blacked out when we first kissed, the storm that had erupted over our heads as we passionately made out in the field, walking out into a snowstorm after that intense sexual tension at the ballet…

My tears were causing me to choke. I could take no more. I needed to know what was going to happen to me.

"So me and Noah…?" I asked.

Anita looked me straight in the eye. "You can never see each other again," she said, and each word ricocheted through me like a bullet. "We will take one of you away, give you a new life, and the other is allowed to stay. There will be no more contact. Ever again. It's best if you forget the other ever existed."

I zoned out then.

You can never see each other again.

For just a moment I tried to imagine a life without Noah, without ever seeing his smile, or having him tuck a stray piece of hair back behind my ear or tasting his mouth on mine.

Then there was a searing hole of pain in my chest where my heart should have been and I began screaming. The pain was intolerable, like I was being used as a rag in a giant tug of war, slowly being ripped into two pieces.

My heart writhed under my ribcage in agony.

It had broken.

It had been obliterated into thousands of pieces and could never be put back together.

37

I had blacked out again. When I woke up I was back in my cell, the huge gaping hole still in my chest. I willed myself to fall back asleep to escape the pain.

A cough, however, distracted me from this endeavour.

She was there. The doctor, seated patiently in the corner of my cell.

"Hello, Poppy," she said, like she was my mother waking me for school. "You feeling any better?"

I turned my face back to the wall. It was cold. I shivered under my thin blanket.

Anita didn't seem bothered by my ignoring her.

"You're probably feeling a little drowsy," she said to my back. "You gave us no choice but to sedate you."

I wished they would sedate me again. I just wanted to sleep, for ever if possible. I thought of Romeo and Juliet and envied them. If only I had poison to stop this insatiable pain, instead of living a life where a massive hunk of me had been amputated.

"Poppy?"

I didn't reply.

"There is another way, you know."

Still no response.

"You didn't let me finish before. There might be a way you can still see Noah…"

The pain evaporated instantly and I sprang up in bed.

"How?" I asked desperately. "I'll do whatever it takes. I'll never touch him again, I promise. Just please, let us stay together."

She looked ill at my enthusiasm.

"You and Noah have displayed some interesting characteristics. Things we haven't seen before in a match. Your panic attacks and his depression, judging by our last experiments, should've got worse the more you spent time with each other. However…" She paused, searching for the right words. "…It appears somehow the two of you managed to build up a tolerance to each other and can control the electrical impulses coursing through your bodies."

I remembered how sick I used to get around him, the way my heart would pound and my breath quicken. Then it had gone. It had only reoccurred when I imagined life without him.

"So this hasn't happened before?"

She shook her head. "No. Not ever. I admit it was one of the reasons I left it so late before intervening. The readings were so unexpected that I let things roll. Usually we split matches up as soon as we locate them."

"So you let Noah and me fall in love with each other?"

I asked, anger lacing my voice. "You let things get this far just because it was good for your experiment?"

I began shaking with rage, and yet more tears were threatening to spill. I'd always cried when I was angry.

"I'm afraid I did." There was no sign of remorse in Dr. Beaumont's voice. "It was best for the company."

"What about what's best for me and Noah? Two innocent people you've just used and played with like puppets?"

"Come off it, Poppy. Like you wouldn't do it all over again if you could."

I shook my head. "No. Not if you're going to take it all away. Not if I'm going to have to live my whole life without him. It's going to be so much worse knowing…"And then the tears spilled and I snorted and spluttered while she watched me, not amused.

"If you would stop crying and listen, I'm telling you there might be another way."

"Well, what is it then?" I sounded like a spoiled child but I didn't care. Fresh tears kept replacing the spent ones.

"You'll never be able to have a normal relationship together, you know that now. It's too dangerous. But we – the company, I mean – can learn from you both. Your… resistance to each other needs to be studied further. If you agree to stay and live a life with us, you'll be able to see him."

"How?"

She shrugged her shoulders like the answer was simple. "You'll be able to see him during the experiments we conduct."

I snorted. "So we'll be like guinea pigs, poked and prodded in a scientific lab? That will be the extent of our relationship?"

"Well, we may be able to arrange some kind of supervised visits, times you'll have together to talk. There'll always be someone with you, of course, in case your impulses get too strong and you act on them."

I shook my head with disgust. "That's not a relationship."

"At least you'll still get to see him."

I looked at her then, really looked at her. And despite my eyes being fuzzy and full of salty tears, I felt I could finally see her clearly. She was soulless. There was something missing from this woman. Something significant.

"Why are you so horrible?" I whispered.

She bristled. "We're not here to talk about me." She smoothed down her lab coat.

But her reaction spurred me on.

"Seriously, what happened to you to make you like this? How can you be so heartless?"

She stood up. "I said, that's enough." Her voice was sharp now.

I saw a tiny flicker of pain cross her face. That was enough. I got it.

"This happened to you, didn't it?" I said, proud of myself for working it out. "You have a match, don't you? And you've been separated and that's why you're so nasty."

Her lower lip trembled slightly. "Stop being silly, Poppy."

I had hit on something.

"How does it feel?" I asked, refusing to let this go, tears ebbing. "To break up happy lovers for a living? What do you think your match would make of you now? If he knew you now actually *worked* for the people that split you up? Do you think he'd still love you? Or would he be so disgusted that it would destroy whatever electricity you shared? 'Cause that's all love is to you, isn't it? Electricity? Science?"

"I TOLD YOU THAT'S ENOUGH!"

She was standing now, her face red, furious. I smiled triumphantly.

"We are in the process of conditioning your boyfriend." She used the mention of Noah like ammo. "By this afternoon the two of you need to make a decision. There are only two options. Help us or never see each other again. Have fun deciding."

She stormed out of my cell, telling the guards to lock the door behind her.

I was left alone for several hours.

Once the tears and anger had subsided, I began to think about love.

I had never felt it was worth wasting much thought on the subject before Noah. But I'd been the odd one out. I thought about all the romantic novels Amanda devoured or the romcom films Ruth was so obsessed with. Even Lizzie had told me she was waiting for love. Yet, as I'd seen it, it wasn't a concept that ever lived up to the expectation.

We'd been conditioned into believing in happily ever after, but did it really exist? Dr. Beaumont had told me explicitly that, for most people, true love wasn't real. It was just couples kidding themselves, smelling pheromones, trying to live out a Disney-inspired fantasy. Yet those couples supposedly living a lie still weren't that happy. Mum and Dad were practically the only couple on our road that hadn't divorced. It was so common these days – relationships seemed to break up as easily as thin sheets of ice. And here I was, with scientific proof that I'd actually managed to stumble across my one true love, and things were even worse. True love, make-believe love – it was all the same. It ended in misery. And that truth was so universally hard to accept that we'd made up fairy stories and happy endings to cushion the blow.

I thought about what Anita had said. Would I do it all again? Falling in love with Noah had left me with a dependence I'd never thought I could stand. He was now my other half. And we were going to be separated. For ever. I was going to feel incomplete for the rest of my life. I would be missing a part until I died. It was my burden. But if someone could wave a magic wand so I'd never meet him and erase the last few months, I wouldn't let them.

I felt utterly blessed that I'd had that time.

That's maybe why we do all hang onto love. Because matches or not, real or fantasy, those snippets of love are the only moments in life when you're ever truly happy, when all the shit feels worthwhile. It's like the world stops revolving just so it has time to look through your window and note your euphoria.

That's worth the pain. Don't you think?

Musings aside, I was terrified and I had no Noah to make me strong. The pool of light on the floor of my cell moved slowly towards the wall as the sun sank lower in the sky.

Evening was coming.

Decisions needed to be made and I didn't know what the right answers were. I lay on my back and stared at the ceiling. My hands rested on my ribs as I felt my breath move in and out. Tears continued to flow silently and solemnly from the sides of my eyes and dripped down into my hair.

Soon it was dark.

My thoughts were interrupted by my cell door opening. That Rain chap was there. He gave me a little embarrassed half-wave.

I glared back in return.

"You hungry?"

I shook my head.

"You should eat."

I didn't reply.

"Suit yourself."

He came and sat on the chair, man-style, turning it backwards and straddling it. It felt a bit too informal considering the circumstances.

He spoke softly and with much more empathy than his colleague. "I believe Dr. Beaumont ran through your options?"

I snorted. "I would hardly call them options."

Rain gave me a sad smile. "Well, what do you suggest?"

"You let both of us go and trust us not to cause any more trouble?"

Rain shook his head. "You know that's not possible. We've tried it before. The consequences have been…"

"Yes I know, dire, death, terrible. It would be different with Noah and me. We're responsible."

Another sad smile. "That's what others have said in the past. Your attraction is too strong. You can't help it. It's not your fault."

"Then why have you locked me up like a convict?"

Rain looked round the interior of my current bedroom. "Yes, the British facilities are a bit…prisony…I suppose."

"No doubt in America I would have had an en-suite and my own parking space?"

Rain smiled again. "Not quite. But it's a bit nicer."

I looked back at the ceiling, wondering what was going to happen next.

"Why are you here?"

I heard him mumble something.

"What was that?"

He coughed. "I said, Anita's given you your options and we were wondering if you've made a decision?"

I laughed. "Are you kidding? How am I ever supposed to make that decision? It's unmakeable."

"That's what we figured," Rain said. "Anyway, if you agree to help us with our studies we'll need both of you. It needs to be a mutual decision."

"And how do you expect us to work that out? With us cooped up in separate cells?"

"We've decided to let you talk it through with each other."

I leaped up off the bed. "You mean I get to see Noah?"

My eyes were wide, a tidal wave of butterflies raced through my stomach, and a smile spread from ear to ear. I ran towards Rain, about to give him a hug of gratitude.

He raised his hands up. "Calm down, calm down."

"When do I get to see him?"

"Calm down! Look, you're not going to able to get close to each other. You get that?"

I nodded furiously.

"And just because we're allowing you to see him doesn't mean anything has changed."

More nodding.

"And you've got to be careful," he said, a slight quiver of fear in his voice. "Remember what you're capable of, Poppy." His eyes softened. "You don't want to hurt any more people."

I nodded once more in agreement, then waited patiently for him to speak again. When he didn't, my words came flooding out. "So when can I see him? Now?"

Rain smiled, despite himself I think. He nodded.

I raked my hands through my hair and then jumped backwards.

"Oh no! I must look like hell! Do I look okay?" I hadn't seen my reflection in two days. I hadn't even washed.

Rain's smile broadened. I decided he was sort of okay.

"You look lovely," he said, like I was his daughter about

to flounce off to a prom. "And Noah is your match, remember? He's going to think you look fabulous even if you're wearing a sack."

Still, though, I ran over to the little sink and splashed my face with water.

"Okay. All done. Can we go now?" Desperation was raging through my skin so violently I almost wanted to scratch it out.

"Let's go."

38

Rain led me down another confusing maze of corridors and I scuttled beside him, trying to grab glimpses of my reflection in the windows. Finally he stopped outside a door and unlocked it.

"Noah's already inside." My heart leaped just knowing he was near. "You'll be watched through mirrored glass." I opened my mouth to object. "It's okay. We won't be able to hear you but we need to keep an eye on you. Now listen carefully. A glass divide will stop you touching. It's for everybody's own protection. There's a small hole, however, that allows you to hold hands. If either of you do ANYTHING to try and break the glass, you'll be separated immediately and we'll decide your futures for you. Are we clear?"

I gulped.

"Right, in you go."

Rain turned the handle and I burst past him and ran inside. And there – looking crumpled but still beautiful – he was.

"Noah," I yelled, and ran at him.

His face broke into that delicious smile. "Poppy."

I smacked into the glass, unable to get closer. It was so clean you could barely see it but it spread solidly across the room. When I tapped on it with my hand it was thick and strong.

I burst into tears immediately. "I can't get to you," I said, wailing.

"Shh. It's okay. Sit down at the table and we can hold hands."

There was a table that cut through the glass with a small narrow gap at the top.

I sat and stretched my hand through. Noah clasped it. Feeling his touch sent shocks all through my body as I sobbed and sobbed and sobbed.

The lights of the lab flickered.

Noah still had a half-smile on his face. "Careful," he said, looking up at the lights. "You don't want to blow the place up. Then we really would be terrorists."

I couldn't believe he was making a joke. It made me love him even more. I grabbed at his fingers, squeezing each one hard to check they were real.

"Don't cry, Poppy. It's going to be okay."

I cried harder. "How can it possibly be okay?" I shouted. "They're splitting us up. Didn't they tell you? We caused the blackout, and the flooding—"

Noah rolled his eyes. "And the snowstorm and the earthquake, yes I know, I know."

"But not just that, Noah. People have died. Because of us." I sobbed harder and Noah shushed me in a soothing parental way.

"Poppy, that wasn't our fault. We didn't know. We couldn't have helped it."

"It's just so scary. Everything's so messed up."

"I know. I know. Ssh, you're okay." He stroked the inside of my thumb with his and the movement calmed me. I looked deep into his dark beautiful eyes and searched his face for answers.

"Did they tell you our options?" I whispered.

Noah looked angry. "I would hardly call them options."

I squeezed his hand. "We can still be together…if we cooperate with…"

Noah shook his head. "No way, Poppy. I won't do it. I would rather spend my life without you than have our love morph into some wannabe-God's science homework."

I giggled at his description of Dr. Beaumont. She obviously hadn't made a great impression on Noah either.

"How are you so calm? Aren't you scared?"

Noah looked to his left. A mirror dominated the whole wall. I could just picture Dr. Beaumont sitting behind it, licking her lips, wondering if we were going to agree to be her pet guinea pigs or whether she could just delight in splitting us up instead.

"I'm sure we can find a way round it."

His bottom lip jutted out stubbornly. He was serious. He had a plan.

I raised an eyebrow questioningly.

"Trust me." With his left eye he gave me the quickest of winks, so slight that only I would've noticed it.

Noah cleared his throat. His voice was different, louder, a little rehearsed.

"I've been thinking about it and it makes sense for you to move back to Middletown and for me to be relocated."

I wasn't sure if this was part of the plan or not. Either way, his words sliced through me like a hundred blades.

"Noah. Don't be stupid."

"I'm not. It's logical. You've got your family there, your friends, college…"

A fresh wave of tears appeared. "But I don't have you!"

"You'll get used to not having me around."

He sounded cold and it made me cry harder.

"What about your band?" I wailed.

At this, Noah's face softened. He pulled my hands under the gap to his side of the partition and kissed them. The lights flickered overhead and he stopped abruptly.

"I'm sure the world can manage without the musical talents of Growing Pains."

I let out another sob and Noah cocked his head to one side sympathetically.

"Here," he said, beckoning me to the window. "Don't cry, come here." I hiccupped and brought my face up to the hole. Noah reached through and cupped it, wiping away my tears with his thumb. I melted into his hand and closed my eyes, wishing I could stay touching him for ever.

The whisper of his breath tickled my ear. He barely spoke but it was just enough for me to hear. "Follow my lead. Keep crying. I love you."

Then the warmth of his hand was gone and my eyes opened. Noah had righted himself. His face had changed. I realized he was crying too. Not girl crying, all red and blotchy and dramatic, but two tears lay frozen on his cheeks.

They broke my heart.

He stood up.

"Noah, what are you doing?"

He didn't look at me – his face was a mixture of grief and anger. He walked over and banged his fists angrily on the mirror.

"We're done!" he yelled. "We're not going to be your love guinea pigs."

The mirror glass stayed intact. You couldn't tell what was going on behind it.

Noah banged on it again, more aggressively this time.

"I. Said. We're. Done!" he yelled. "Come on. Time to split us up like naughty children!"

I stood up. "Noah, what are you doing? Once they take us away, that's it. Don't you want more time with me?"

He gave me a dirty look, and I hoped, prayed, this was part of the plan, otherwise I might cry for ever.

"What's the point? We may as well get used to it now."

I sat on the floor and began sobbing again as Noah continued to bash the glass. The door flung open and Dr. Beaumont burst in. Rain stood nervously behind her.

"What is going on in here?" Her eyes were wide with anger. "You almost damaged our facility."

"I don't care," Noah said. "We've had our talk. We're not going to help you, you horrible little bitch."

Anita looked like she'd been slapped. She sucked in air, her cheeks puckered, and then slowly blew it out. "If that's what you've agreed, that's what you've agreed."

I let out another sob and she looked at me, disgusted.

"And does Miss Lawson agree with all this?"

I just continued crying. Noah looked beautiful. His eyes were blazing with anger, his face wet with tears that glistened on his face, highlighting those cheekbones. I didn't know what was going to happen, but I figured if this was the last time I ever saw him, I would remember him like this. Strong, fighting, full of life.

"She agrees."

"Have you decided who's going to leave Middletown?"

"Yeah, me. Take me and dump me where you want. I don't care."

"It won't be like that. We'll build a new life for you."

Noah shrugged. "Whatever."

"That's sorted then."

Anita did a quick dainty click of her fingers and two guards sprang up behind her like boomerangs. She pointed to us.

"Take the girl back to the cell for now," she instructed. "We'll sort out her readjustment later. As for the boy, there's a helicopter waiting at the top of the building. Please escort us there."

And then it hit me. This was it. Whatever Noah had planned wouldn't work. There were guards, armed by the look of them, and we were in some high-security labyrinth.

I began to scream. It wasn't voluntary. Screeches poured out of my mouth, ear-piercing and terrible. Everyone winced.

"You can't take him! You can't! You can't!"

One of the guards was unlocking the glass door on Noah's side of the room. I noticed more tears had fallen onto his face. I wanted to touch him so badly. His eyes were locked on mine and I could see desire leaking out of him too. I screamed again.

"No, Noah! I love you. I love you."

He broke into a sob. "I love you too. So much."

The other guard was coming towards me.

"Stay away from me!" The ferocity in my voice was so strong he actually halted. Noah's guard had unlocked the door now and was pulling the handle. Suddenly Noah barged past him, knocked him to the ground and was running straight at me.

"Stop him," I heard Anita yell.

Then everything went into slow motion.

Noah was speeding towards me, his arms outstretched. His guard was on the floor, struggling to get up, and mine was nearing me. I sprang onto my feet, feeling weightless, and ran to Noah. I could feel the electric current surging from my heart to his heart, pushing me towards him.

"Stop them!"

But it was too late. Noah reached me and I fell into his arms. I went to hug him but he stopped me. He jerked my chin up roughly, lowered his face and kissed me urgently.

I heard a distant scream. The scene went hazy.

All I could focus on was the burning in my mouth, the delicious taste of Noah, the electricity fusing our bodies together. I kissed him hungrily, plunging my tongue back into his, trying to swallow him so I could keep him for ever.

There were noises, and heat.

We broke apart and saw the entire glass wall smash into thousands of pieces. It hung, suspended in mid-air for a second, before careering onto the floor. Noah smiled and dipped to kiss me again.

There was another smash.

The glass coverings on the overhead lights cracked and fell around us like dangerous snowflakes. My security guard toppled to the floor, blood running from his chest. My stomach twisted with guilt.

"Noah, he's bleeding."

He shot a look at the guard, who groaned and tried to get up. "He's okay." And he kissed me again – we needed to get out.

Then we watched in wonder as the light bulbs burst into flames and mini explosions ripped through the room, setting random things on fire. Anita was screaming, her hands over her head, protecting herself from the carnage falling from the ceiling. Noah squeezed my hand and I knew it was time to go. A burning light fitting came loose and hit

Anita directly on the head. We ran past as she fell with a thump. Rain was crouched in the doorway, his face a picture of pure terror. He was blocking our exit.

He looked up at us, eyes wide, and I said only one word to him.

"Please."

Rain looked from Noah's face to mine and I could see his inner conflict.

I held my breath.

"Please," Noah repeated.

Then Rain sighed, and rolled to one side, letting us past.

"Be quick," he whispered. "You don't have much time."

And we stepped over him and ran out into the maze of clinical corridors, hand in hand.

39

My palms were sweating as we fled down corridor after corridor, looking for an escape.

"Where are we going?" I asked between pants.

Noah didn't break our pace. "I don't know. We need to get outside."

White sterile walls streaked past us. We ducked left, then right, then right again, trying to find a path through the maze.

I tripped over my feet.

"Hurry up, Poppy. The alarm will go off any moment. Then we're completely screwed."

I ran like I had small wings attached to my ankles. Raw primal fear pumped adrenalin through my veins. The warmth of Noah's hand in mine made me feel invincible.

We turned and ran smack into a heavy locked door.

"Shit." Noah looked up and down. The door was solid metal with no doorknob. It only had a little keypad on the side and a retina scanner.

"What are we going to do?"

I could hear the panic in my own voice. Maybe I didn't feel so invincible after all. Anita could be coming round at any moment, raising the alarm, summoning guards to punish us.

"I don't know. Let me think."

Noah's face was screwed up. I looked back at the corridor behind us, imagining the sight of Dr. Beaumont appearing at the end. I shivered. When I turned back to Noah, he was smiling. He had a plan.

"What is it?"

"I think I know how to open it."

"How?"

"It might set off the alarm."

"Well, then what would we do?"

Noah cupped my face and the lights above fizzled. I looked up at them in dazed wonder before Noah forced me to look at him.

"Listen, Poppy. You've got to do as I say. As long as we're inside this building, I want you to focus on how much you love me, how much you want me. Remember the other night? Remember what was happening before they came? How good it was? I want you to focus on that the whole time we're inside, okay?"

I nodded, not sure what he meant.

"But the *moment* we get out – *if* we manage to get out – stay with me, follow me, but put me out of your mind. Imagine I don't exist. Pretend I'm not there and you're running away alone. Got it?"

I didn't understand and he saw it in my face.

"You've got to trust me, Poppy. I think I've worked out how this, us, works. I'll still be by your side, I promise, but once we're out of here, imagine I'm not. Promise me?"

I got it then. Noah didn't want us to get tracked in the highly unlikely event that we escaped. If I was loving him, I would be emitting some kind of traceable current. I hoped it worked. It was all we had.

"I promise."

Noah smiled, and despite our circumstances, my stomach flip-flopped.

"Right. Let's do this."

Then Noah reached for the keypad with one hand and cupped my face with the other. His face bent and met mine. Fire raged through my lips as he kissed me; electricity pinged through my body. I groaned and grabbed at his face with my hand, pulling him closer.

We were interrupted by the most awful noise.

A shrill bell rang out, piercing my ears like a thousand needles. I opened my eyes. The corridor was steeped in the red flashing light of alarm bulbs.

"Poppy, we did it."

I could hardly hear Noah over the din but followed the direction of his pointed finger. The door had been blown off its hinges. Electrical wires were hanging out of the keypad, emitting a mini firework display of sparks. The blown door led to another corridor but this one had a glass ceiling. I looked up. I could see the sky. It was a deep shade of grey and rain was pelting down, hitting the glass with force.

I pointed upwards. "Did we do that too?"

Noah grinned. "I think so." He grabbed my hand. "Come on, we need to get out of here."

We began to run again. I was out of breath, but the rhythm of the sirens worked as a drumbeat, spurring me on.

"We need to find a window that leads outside," Noah yelled.

My feet thudded heavily beneath me. We were in another maze, skidding from one corridor to another, trying to keep the sky in sight. All the corridors looked the same, one set of blank sterile walls after another, all flashing red. Yet Noah acted like he knew the route. I followed, as I would always follow him, wondering where the guards were, why we hadn't seen them yet.

My feet were getting heavier, my breath more laboured, as we turned another corner. There it was. Our escape. A large glass wall with a small glass door, leading outside, where a storm was raging ferociously. I squeezed Noah's hand and, at that same moment, lightning spasmed across the sky.

"We're almost there," he said.

We broke into a sprint. The glass wall got closer and closer, until I could almost reach out and touch it.

We were going to make it. Only a few more feet...

"FREEZE!"

I spun round and gasped.

The guards had arrived.

Line upon line of them stood and stared at us. They carried batons and all sorts of other weaponry. It was the look in their eyes that terrified me. It was deadened, like emotion had been vacuumed out to ensure whatever disgusting violence was necessary could be used to get the job done.

There were so many of them. The biggest guard, standing in the middle of the front row, grinned to reveal a crooked line of yellowing teeth.

"Stay right where you are," he said. "We don't want anyone to get hurt now."

"Noah?" I whispered.

He replied without moving his lips. "Trust me."

And I felt warm again.

We both instinctively took a step backwards.

"I said don't move!" The guard raised something that looked like a gun. A taser maybe?

Noah held his hands up. "There's no need for that." His voice was steady and calm. "We'll come."

The man laughed, revealing his hideous teeth again. "And I'm supposed to believe you, am I? After what you've done to our guards? Not to mention Dr. Beaumont."

"Put the taser down." Noah's hands were quivering but his voice didn't betray him.

Another laugh. "It's not you in charge, mate. You don't get to make the rules."

Noah cocked his head to one side. "Fair enough. Well, if you don't mind, I'll just kiss my girlfriend goodbye then…"

He grabbed my hand and the guard's face transformed.

"Hang on, not so fast." He looked up nervously at the overhead lights, waiting for them to explode.

"I want all of you to put the taser guns down," Noah said. "We'll come, no trouble, I promise. There's too many of you to outrun. You know that and I know that. But this isn't how I want things to end with Poppy. Not like this, not at gunpoint. Come on."

He sounded so genuine I almost believed him.

I felt strangely powerful. There I was, facing armed guards, and yet *they* were scared of *me*. Noah and I, our love, was that powerful. It gave me comfort.

The guard whispered to a man on his right who nodded.

"Okay. We'll put them down and walk slowly towards you. You are going to let us handcuff you both and take you back to the lab. If there's any funny business, we will use force. We're allowed to hurt you and we will if necessary."

"Agreed."

One by one the guards put their guns on the floor and slowly began walking towards us. My heart began pounding. How were we ever going to escape?

"Remember what I said, Poppy," Noah murmured and he pushed me back against the window with a thump and kissed me for all he was worth.

We'd shared many electrically-charged kisses before but this one was, by far, the most powerful. It was full of urgency, both of us well aware it was probably our last. His lust was overwhelming. I responded instinctively to his body. The taste of Noah was intoxicating. Heat spread from in between my legs up through the whole of my body. Noah's hands were all over me, stroking me under my top. There were yells and shouts from the guards but I didn't acknowledge them. I'd forgotten them really. Clarity consumed me. It was like the world had stopped pivoting. This was how it was supposed to be.

Me and Noah. Noah and me. Always.

Then the earth began to shake violently.

The kiss interrupted, I looked down and watched my feet move from side to side. The spell was broken for a moment. The guards were nearing us but had stopped still, terror gripping them as, they too, looked to see an invisible force shake their bodies from under them.

They began walking slowly backwards.

"Don't stop." Noah began kissing my neck and the clarity returned. I leaned back into the pleasure.

The ground shook harder.

I returned my lips to Noah's, wanting one last kiss before we were caught. There was a sound of shattering as the glass exploded and smashed behind us. I held onto Noah, trying to keep my balance as the universe shuddered around us. I heard an immense cracking noise. I opened my eyes mid-kiss and glanced sideways. The ground had opened up. A huge crack had erupted between us and the guards, too big for anyone to jump over.

"Noah, look!"

He stopped kissing me. "I knew we could do it."

The earthquake stopped and reality snapped back.

"They're coming for us again."

The guards were charging back to their guns.

"Time to go."

Noah pulled me in for one last kiss, which created a roar of thunder overhead. Then we clambered quickly through the shattered glass and escaped into the blackness of the storm.

40

I was soaked in less than a second.

"Remember what you promised," Noah yelled.

And I did.

We ran down a grassy hill, slipping on the drenched ground, skidding in mud. I was half-running, half-falling. I took a breath and banished Noah from my mind. I could hear the rapid pulls of his breath next to me but tuned them out. At the bottom of the hill was a dark barrier of trees – it looked like the beginning of a forest. I urged my aching body to get there faster, pushing my hair out of my face where the rain had plastered it there with such force. I could still hear the sirens echoing from the facility behind me. Fear spurred me on and the woods got closer. I ran and ran and ran, my path lit with occasional lightning. And then the rain wasn't falling as hard. I had made it under the canopy of the trees.

I was still aware of Noah's body close to mine but forced my brain to ignore him. I wasn't sure who was leading who. We were silently communicating directions without acknowledging each other, like two ghosts playing hide and seek. The rain got lighter as we got into thicker forest. At one point a helicopter flew overhead and we split up and spent half an hour hugging the sodden floor. It was borderline impossible to ban Noah from my mind. I was scared my brain would betray me and release some kind of traceable energy field.

We began running through the trees again. The chopper came back periodically but was quieter as the dense overhang of trees protected us. It was surprising, the body's ability to just keep on running. I'd always been picked last in PE at school, destined to spend netball lessons standing around awkwardly and ducking if the ball came anywhere near my head. But somehow my body had found an inner strength. Terror was propelling me forward – desperation forcing my feet to lift and fall repeatedly. We ran for maybe an hour, maybe several – I wasn't sure. Eventually our pace slowed and the rain stopped. The first slivers of dawn cast weak sunlight on random areas of dense undergrowth. Without talking, we came to a stop simultaneously.

I surveyed my surroundings. Who knew where we were? I assumed we were still in England, judging by the accents of the guards in the facility. But whereabouts in England was anyone's guess. Everywhere I looked there was forest. Towns, civilization and, most importantly, help could be hundreds of miles away. I remembered the official signed letter Anita had given me and my stomach ached. What help? Who would help us?

Noah was climbing up a small hill and had apparently spotted something. I pattered behind him, looking for any clue as to where we could be. At the top of the hill we had a slight vantage point, but saw only the ocean of trees surrounding us. My heart sank. Noah pointed to a small collection of rocks. They appeared to be a makeshift entrance to a small cave. It wasn't help, it wasn't food, but it was shelter. My legs felt like I was carting around two logs of lead, my balance was shot and my lungs felt ready to explode. Rest would help. Then we could figure out what to do.

We scrabbled inside and examined the cave. It would do. It went deeper in than we'd first thought and had remained dry during our self-created storm. I fell against the wall, letting exhaustion seep through my body. Everything hurt. Noah collapsed in the same way opposite me. We sat staring at each other for a while, collecting our breath.

"Are we allowed to talk to each other?" I asked him, my eyes half-closed.

He winced. "I don't know. I'm not sure how it works. I'm making this up as I go along."

I smiled at him reassuringly. "Your guessing has got us pretty far."

He looked down at the ground. "Probably not far enough."

I longed to go over and hug him, to feel his arms around me and be comforted by his touch. But I knew I couldn't. Even the thought of it could be dangerous.

Sensing my upset, Noah forced himself to grin. "I can't believe we got away. Did all that just happen?"

I nodded. "I'm still waiting to wake up from whatever nightmare this is."

His smile faded. "I knew what we had was special," he said. "But I never imagined…"

My eyes filled with tears. "Noah? What are we going to do?"

He leaned his head back against the stone and closed his eyes.

"I don't know. I just knew that, whatever happened, I needed more time with you. I couldn't end things like that."

A tear plopped down my cheek. My wet clothes were sticking to my body.

If I closed my eyes, two lives presented themselves to me. There was the life of Noah and me together. On the run, constantly looking over our shoulders, never being able to kiss or even touch, knowing that if we acted on our impulses, lost concentration for even a moment, then people could get hurt. Could our love survive that? Was that a life? What was the point in having a soulmate if you weren't able to live the life that lovers should. A life of lazy lie-ins on Saturday mornings, kisses when you get home from work, the thrill of waiting for them to touch your skin, or just evenings on the sofa watching nothing on television, your bodies entwined, oozing comfort and affection out of every pore.

Then there was the other life. The life I would lead if we separated. The agony of spending every living day knowing I had a soulmate but couldn't be with him, trying to make love happen with someone I wasn't supposed to be with, constantly thinking about Noah, wondering where he was, what he was up to, whether he'd managed to fall into the usual "faux" version of love, always feeling incomplete, always carrying that emptiness.

What choice was that?

It wasn't one. The word choice implied you *wanted* to pick one over the other. I didn't want either. Both would bring pain, perhaps for every day of my life.

I lay my head back against the rough wall of our cave and sighed.

Noah's eyes bored into me, watery and full of exhaustion.

"What are you thinking?" he asked, a twinge of worry in his voice.

My voice spoke without consciousness guiding it.

"We can never be together," I said. And when the words fell out of my mouth, I knew they were the right ones.

But my heart. My heart was breaking.

Noah's face crumpled. "Poppy, don't say that! We've made it this far. We can learn how to be together in a new way, a way that doesn't hurt people."

I shook my head. "I can't. We're worth more than that, Noah. You know we are."

"So you're just going to give up on us?"

His words stung.

"You know that's not what I mean. Think about it. Can we honestly spend the rest of our lives never even holding hands again? Never kissing? Never making love? Could we even get married? We wouldn't even be able to consummate it. We wouldn't be able to have children. It would destroy us, Noah. You know it would. What we have is so special, I don't want it to fall apart. I don't want to watch us fall apart."

I saw a tear slide out of the corner of Noah's eye. It made me cry harder.

"You said it before, that night in the hotel. Love isn't supposed to be forbidden. It's supposed to be easy. I don't want our love to struggle. I want it to always be like this, even if it's only left in my memory."

And then Noah was standing and running over to my side of the cave. He flung his arms around me and buried himself in my shoulder.

He was crying.

"You can't," I said. "They're going to be able to find us if we stay touching like this."

"Then they can find us." His voice was strained. "You're right, Poppy. I hate it, I'm terrified, but you're right. I can't be with you but not be with you. I want to remember us always like this. As perfect as we are. Young, and so in love we can hardly see straight."

I laughed through my tears. "And of course a massive danger to the whole of civilization?"

He laughed too. "But of course! They should make a movie about us."

"Or write a book. Amanda would love it. She loves all that crap."

"Well at least Amanda would be happy."

"And Lizzie would want to sell our story to the national press."

"Of course."

"The modern day Romeo and Juliet?"

Noah stopped laughing and clasped his hands in mine, a desperate look in his eye.

"Promise me, Poppy, that we won't become like them?"

"Like who?"

"Like Romeo and bloody Juliet. Don't ruin your life or end it, just because we're apart. Live it. We can't be together, but live it for me. Make the most of it. And I'll live mine for you. And I'll try and be happy for you and you've got to try and be happy for me. That way, somehow, we'll always be together. We'll be living for each other in the only way we can."

I nodded through another sob. "I promise."

Noah went to kiss me but I stopped him.

"We can't. What if we hurt people?"

"There's no one around for miles, I'm sure of it. Please, let us just be together one last time. Let's make a memory we can hold on to when we're old and grey. A feeling we can access at any time to remember what it is to be loved, to be really truly loved and to be really truly together."

There were no more words, only feelings.

As Noah and I kissed, the heavens didn't open and rain hell on us, the earth didn't shake, a blizzard didn't blow in. Instead, the sun shone a little brighter into our cave, making us warm again. The sky went the bluest I'd ever seen it. We kissed for for ever, or maybe minutes, I can't remember. But I do remember smiling. The sort of smile that hurts your stomach, it's born from so much happiness. The smile your face can only produce if you're really, truly in love.

We curled up together on the cave floor. Noah was behind me, pressing every part of his body against my back, stroking my hair. The sun shone in through the gaps in the stones, making the world glow like we were stuck in an angel's halo.

We closed our eyes and slept together.

And when we heard the helicopter we kept our eyes shut. Noah squeezed my hand and I knew it was his way of saying "I love you".

I squeezed it back and we lay still.

When they came for us, we were both still smiling.

The End

It started just like any other day, with the sun rising.

It streamed through the curtains and my halls-of-residence room was transformed into a deep egg-yolk-yellow colour. I closed my eyes, feeling the sun burn my eyelids. I wasn't going to go back to sleep. I could tell.

I watched the glow of light move slowly up the wall as time passed. It was incredible really. How the world can just keep on truckin', doing what it always does, without giving you personal acknowledgement that today wasn't just like any other day. That today was going to be hard. I threw off my duvet and the cold air hit me. It was almost Christmas.

It was exactly two years ago today that they took him.

I'd already texted my course friends and Frank to tell them I was missing first lecture. With the grades I'd been getting, I reckoned I could get away with it. Frank and I'd ended up at the same uni after all, and did, on occasion, find the time to go to a "grungy" gig (much to Frank's bemusement) or struggle through essays in the library together. I had Lizzie visiting that weekend and I'd cleared the weekend of essay work so we could properly celebrate her making editor of her student newspaper. She was arriving tomorrow, and I couldn't wait to see her. Lizzie was still the thread that kept us all connected, and I was sure I'd hear all of the gossip about Amanda, Ruth (and Ruth's new boyfriend, no doubt).

I skipped breakfast and stuffed my completed – and hopefully first-class – essay into my shoulder bag. Wrapping my knitted scarf around my head multiple times, I braced myself for the cold walk into campus.

They're a weird thing, anniversaries. Marks in time against particular dates – small squares in the calendar that you count down to with either dread or excitement. Most of the time, life is all "What's next?" "Who's next?" "Where the HELL am I going, please?" But on anniversaries, you take the time to stop and look back and it's like watching a play of your past dance across your memory.

At this exact time two years ago, Noah and I must've been handing over our letters. The letters they'd somehow found the heart to let us write. So we can always be there with each other, in a small way, as calendar squares are marked off, one by one, in the galloping blur towards whatever comes next.

Nobody was really sitting outside in the union garden; it was far too cold. I was glad for the solitude. One, because I needed to do this alone, and "alone" wasn't a concept easily achieved at university. And, two, because banana milk becomes an even more uncool beverage to drink when you become a university student.

I took a seat on a cold picnic bench and turned my face to the weak winter sun. I picked up my glass and held it to the sky.

"Here's to you, Noah," I whispered to the heavens. "And here's to us."

I closed my eyes, wishing, waiting...

And, just as I'd begun to worry I'd only imagined it last year, on that horrible first anniversary, it happened again. A breeze picked up out of nowhere, rattling the trees, lifting my hair and giving me goosepimples. The air smelled like apples. I felt him all around me.

"I love you," I said, and the sun suddenly burned brighter, illuminating every bare tree branch, giving my surroundings a yellowy silver lining. It was us doing this, together. I knew it. Because, wherever he was, at this precise moment, I knew he was looking at the same sun and thinking the same thing.

Here's what I've learned since that awful day. What *should* happen isn't always what *does* happen, especially where love is concerned. Happy endings are reserved strictly for the fiction shelves of bookstores. In reality, people don't chase their lovers through airports to stop them getting on aeroplanes. The most popular guy in school doesn't fall for the class geek. Friends don't suddenly realize their eternal adoration for each other at the countdown to New Year's Eve, on the top of the Empire State Building, in the rain.

Noah and I could never run into the sunset.

Real love doesn't mend everything. Real love doesn't conquer all. And, most importantly, real love doesn't require a happily-ever-after – that's not what it's about. But real love does change you. It moulds you. It burns your heart into a charred cinder that relights like a phoenix, stronger and more blazing than ever.

I took another sip of my drink and smiled. I was so proud of myself. For getting here, after that awful time following the separation when I never thought I would breathe again. The true test of life isn't how you cope when everything is going in your favour; it's how you deal with things that could destroy you, if you let them.

I reached into my bag, pulled out my special notepad, and the letter fell out from between the pages. I wanted to cry just seeing his handwriting. I traced the imprint his biro had left on the paper with my fingers and swallowed the lump in my throat.

I unfolded it and read it again, although I knew all the words off by heart.

Poppy,

There is so much to say, so much I will probably leave out by mistake and then I'll hate myself for ever for missing the opportunity.

But, if this is all you'll have left of me, this is all I need to say really. I love you, Poppy. I will never have the chance to say that to you again but every time you read this, know that it is me saying it afresh, wherever I may be.

I will always love you, for ever, with every bit of my soul.

Whenever I feel the sun on my face I will think of you and those last moments we shared together. I am so grateful we were able to make that memory. It will help me every day.

Life is long though, Poppy. Don't break our promise to each other. Don't make your life a sacrifice to us. Be you, be happy. Find happiness in everything you do. I ask only this: every year, on this day, let's look to the sun and raise a drink to each other. Let's both take a moment to remember us as we were. And that way, we'll always be together.

You are perfect and I am yours for ever.

Noah.

That's the thing about love. However you have it, however you've had it – it never goes. Once it's touched you, it's touched you for ever. You'll be permanently scarred by its brilliance. You can walk through the rest of your life with that wonderful knowledge...

Someone once loved me and it was beautiful.

No one can take that from you.

And there are times, sometimes, when you need to remember that. Acknowledge it. Remember how lucky you are that you ever had it at all.

And then there are the times when the only appropriate thing to do is stop crying, let it go, with light and love in your heart, and to continue living your life to the best of your ability.

Acknowledgements

I actually can't believe I'm writing my acknowledgements page for my first novel! You'll have to bear with me a bit here because I've fantasised about doing this since about the day I discovered what books were.

So, firstly, a huge thank you to Maddy, for making this pipe dream real. Thank you for not only being a totally kick-ass agent, but also one of the loveliest people I've ever met. Your support of, and dedication to, *Soulmates* has literally changed my life. There will never be adequate words to express my gratitude for that.

A massive bigs-up to Usborne, the perfect home for Poppy. I don't think there is anything else you guys could've done for this book and I am so happy you took *Soulmates* on board. Thank you for all the tireless hard work you put in to make it so much better.

cue emotional orchestral music

Writing this book has been a bit of a journey, so I just want to thank the people responsible for holding me together throughout the process.

To Mr. Dundas, for helping me believe I could write when I was a disgusting grumpy teenager who thought everything I did sucked. And to Jonathan Foster, whose brilliant-albeit-terrifying teaching made me the writer I am today. It is a beautiful gift to have a teacher in your life who inspires and moulds you. I was fortunate enough to have two.

To Rich, for being there from the beginning, and helping me right through to the end. Even when you didn't have to. Words are silly things, really, when it comes to such a thank you.

To Lisa, my unrelenting cheerleader. Thank you for reading the MESS that was the first draft and championing it from day one. Your support has been unyielding and wonderful, and yet I repay you by blatantly plagiarising bits of your life. Thanks for a) not minding, and b) generally being a frickin' fantastic mate.

I want to thank my colleagues at TheSite.org, for their incredible support throughout this process. Especially to Emma and Nic, for dealing with my emotional rollercoasters eight hours a day, five days a week. I am so proud to work with you guys and to be part of the amazing work you do helping young people.

To my wonderful sisters, for putting up with me. Eryn, I only hope your Poppy has less drama than mine. And to Willow, for being so patient with me constantly trying to hack into your young brain.

To Owen…well for everything. For holding my hand through this process, especially when I'd made some tough decisions that I didn't know were going to turn out okay. Thank you for seeing the light when I couldn't. Thank you for reading a 140,000 word messy manuscript about two lovestricken teenagers, and thank you even more for liking it. I couldn't have done it without you… but no, you're not getting a joint byline.

And, finally, the biggest thank you typing can muster to my beautiful and amazing parents. To Larz and Olivia – thank you for absolutely everything. I am so lucky to have you, you don't even know. Everything I do is to make you proud.

Brilliant, young and British...introducing:

HOLLY BOURNE

Holly graduated with a first-class degree in Journalism Studies and spent two years working as a local news reporter on the *Surrey Mirror*, garnering a nomination for Print Journalist of the Year in 2010. She now works as a journalist for TheSite.org (www.thesite.org), an advice and information website for 16-25 year olds. Holly is twenty-seven and lives in London. *Soulmates* is her first novel.

Q&A with Holly

Where did the idea for *Soulmates* come from?

I've always thought there's this big disconnect between what we want love to be, and what love actually is. That we're spoon-fed happily-ever-afters and dramatic romantic gestures as love, whereas real relationships are a lot more complicated than that.

I started writing *Soulmates* in the midst of the *Twilight* epidemic, where huge sections of bookstores were suddenly dedicated to dark romance stories. I read the *Twilight* books and quickly became utterly obsessed with the "forbidden" love of Edward and Bella. And it was also a bit like, *Why has nothing this romantic ever happened to me?*

It got me thinking about why we always want love to have this huge overarching dramatic narrative. Why do we crave fireworks and drama and forbidden-this-and-that, when it's actually probably not very good for us? So I took the most romantic idea of all – soulmates – and thought, *What would happen if finding your soulmate was actually the worst thing ever?*

What is your favourite part of the writing process, and what was your favourite scene to write?

I have two favourite parts:

1)   The wonderful heady early days when you get A New Idea and all the excitement that comes with that.

2)   When the whole thing is finished and you didn't screw up aforementioned idea and there's a half-decent first draft sitting on your laptop.

All the stuff in between points one and two is generally HORRIBLE and fraught with neurotic obsession, insecurity, and a hermit-like existence.

My favourite scene to write was the last scene. I hadn't planned to finish the book that day – I just thought I'd sit down and write a few words. And then, without warning, it all just kind of poured out of me and hours passed without me realizing. This never happens, and usually I find writing is like pulling out wisdom teeth with a teaspoon. But, with the ending of *Soulmates*, it just wrote itself and when it was done I was a sobbing mess – perched alone on this couch, in an empty flat, feeling massively melodramatic. The last few paragraphs of *Soulmates* haven't been touched throughout the entire editing process.

How did you get into writing?

I trained to be a journalist and was a news reporter for two years on a local paper. In my humble opinion, news journalism is pretty much the best writing training the world will ever give you. Any self-indulgence with word counts, or jarring adjectives, or meandering away from The Story is beaten out of you pretty quickly by your terrifying editors.

Grateful as I am for that training, I found dealing with people's problems on a day-to-day basis, and then having to write about it in an exciting way, almost utterly intolerable. The idea for *Soulmates* was floating about my brain for a while and, on one particularly gruesome news day, I came back from a twelve-hour shift and just started writing. It became my little sanctuary from the horrors of the job, and it built from there.

Who is your favourite character in *Soulmates* and why?

Funnily enough, neither of my protagonists! It's probably Lizzie. I always wrote her with a big grin on my face. I love her brazen ambition, her no-nonsense delivery, her utter inability to keep a secret, and yet she would have Poppy's back always. There is a big soft spot for Frank in my heart too.

How long did it take you to write *Soulmates*?

It took two and a half years of fitful writing bouts, punctuated with leaving my job and deciding on a whim to drive from one side of America to the other which, as you can imagine, took a while.

Did much change in the book from your first draft to the book we're reading now?

You are fortunate enough to be reading the condensed version of this book which has been cut to normal-ish length. The first draft was at least 30,000 words longer, and much thanks to my agent and editors for saying "Umm, no, CUT," and "No, we don't need a 4,000 word chapter where the girls go shopping for Poppy's gig outfit."

The setting of the epilogue is also different, as in my first draft I jumped way waaaay into Poppy's future where she was an adult and quite a few people found that jarring.

Do you have any tips for aspiring writers?

It's so hard to not just regurgitate good advice I've nicked off writers much better than myself – mainly the whole of *On Writing* by Stephen King.

But – simple as it sounds – just sit down on your arse and write something! Stop thinking about doing it and do it. Stop telling people about doing it and do it. Stop worrying it's a monstrosity against literature and do it (and, from my experience, the worse you think it is, the better it may be). Only from writing and writing and writing will you make a first draft, and only from a first draft can you start creating a half-decent book.

Oh, and when you're not writing, read. Read all the time.

We all found ourselves tearing up at the end of *Soulmates*... Which books make you cry?

I am very much one of life's criers. Anything sets me off – reality TV weddings, *that* Adele song, and, on an uber-emotional day, spotting a raggedy pigeon on a train platform which only had one leg.

That said, when it comes to books, I very rarely cry. Even if the author kills off my favourite characters. Without fail though, the end of *To Kill A Mockingbird* makes me cry every single time I reread it – which is at least once a year. It's never a big bawly cry with snotting into a tissue, but a few stray tears leak whenever Scout is standing on Boo Radley's porch and I marvel at just how beautiful words can be.

Can you give us a teaser of what we should expect from your next book, *The Manifesto on How to be Interesting*?

It's about a girl called Bree, a loner and wannabe novelist who decides her life is too boring to be a writer, so she starts identifying what makes a person interesting and dedicates her life to conforming to those ideals, blogging about what happens.

And finally...do you believe in soulmates?

I believe in love. And I believe in souls. Whether souls are connected to love, and your soulmate is someone you're romantically supposed to be with...well...I don't ruddy know, and writing a whole book about them hasn't helped me much.

But if you believe in soulmates, well then, that's a gift, and don't let anyone tell you otherwise.

Six rules on how to be interesting.

Five weeks to the party of the year.

Four queen bees to infiltrate.

Three shades of blonde highlights.

Two boys.

One girl.

No turning back.

THE MANIFESTO ON HOW TO BE INTERESTING

by Holly Bourne

I'm boring. I'm a nobody. I don't live life. I don't embrace life. But that's all about to change. Because I am starting a project. Here. Now. For myself. And if you want to come along for the ride then you're very welcome.

What's my purpose? I'm going to become interesting. I'm going to become somebody you want to read about.

How?

I'm going to do all the things you're too scared to do. And then I'm going to tell you about it. If you're really brave, you can do it with me.

This is the manifesto on how to be interesting. I'm going to pinpoint EXACTLY what it is that makes a person worth caring about and then do it.

I'll let you know how I get on.
It's not going to be easy.
But then interesting things never are, are they?

COMING SEPTEMBER 2014

Check out more spine-tingling,
earth-shattering YA reads at